B O O K   T W O

Shadows of the Dracore

STOLEN CHILD

IN-BETWEEN

A Tale by Adele DeGirolamo

Happy Reading
My best friend

Caspey

AKA Adele the
Author
ChickyPoo

FriesenPress

Suite 300 - 990 Fort St
Victoria, BC, Canada, V8V 3K2
www.friesenpress.com

ISBN
978-1-4602-6589-5 (Hardcover)
978-1-4602-6590-1 (Paperback)
978-1-4602-6591-8 (eBook)

1. Fiction, Fantasy

Distributed to the trade by The Ingram Book Company

S*hadow of the Dracore Chronicles* is a work of fantasy. Names, places, and incidences, either are a product of the author's imagination, or used from a historical publication fictitiously. Any resemblance to actual persons, living or dead, including time-lines and events is entirely coincidental. However, I have been known sometimes, if you have done something spectacular to help someone out; to invent a special character that I will use in future books that will have your characteristics in them, just to say thank-you.

This book also contains an excerpt from the upcoming third book of *Stolen Child's* next Shadow, called *Transcending*. It is a continuation of the first two novels of the Dracore Series, and is considered part-three and completes the printed edition of this tale.

The book *Stolen Child* is the first of the series of the *Shadow of the Dracore Chronicles* and will be followed by consecutive novels, in future writings, to complete the original series. I will at that time begin to format future offshoots with the characters, written in during these first instalments, to make the series continue on indefinitely, or as long as I am able to write. The novels following will be directly linked to the series and create what is to be the Shadow Scrolls of the entire writings of the Faden Corpeous Galaxy's race of Fey now living in the star system of the Goddess Sopdet.

The Stolen Child Series Contains the Following Three Novels

The Beginning

In-Between

Transcending

MESSAGE FROM THE AUTHOR

Never believe all of what you hear, and none of what another Human thinks of the other. For what appears to be fact is more than likely a fabrication of someone else's truth, and only part of what the real story is....

Visit the Author's Website at **www.adeledegirolamo.com**.

DEDICATION

This next book is dedicated to my family. For without them and their support, this book would have ended up at the bottom of some ravine, or chucked off the Malahat on my way down to visit them; quickly joined by the laptop and any relevant correspondence to keep it company. So with that lovely analogy; I want to give them the appreciation they deserve for keeping me sane, because I know from their end it couldn't have been easy.

To my Mom Lorraine, my sister Leia and my father Lorne.
Thank you for your trust and unwavering support in getting this to print.

TABLE OF CONTENTS

STOLEN CHILD

IN-BETWEEN

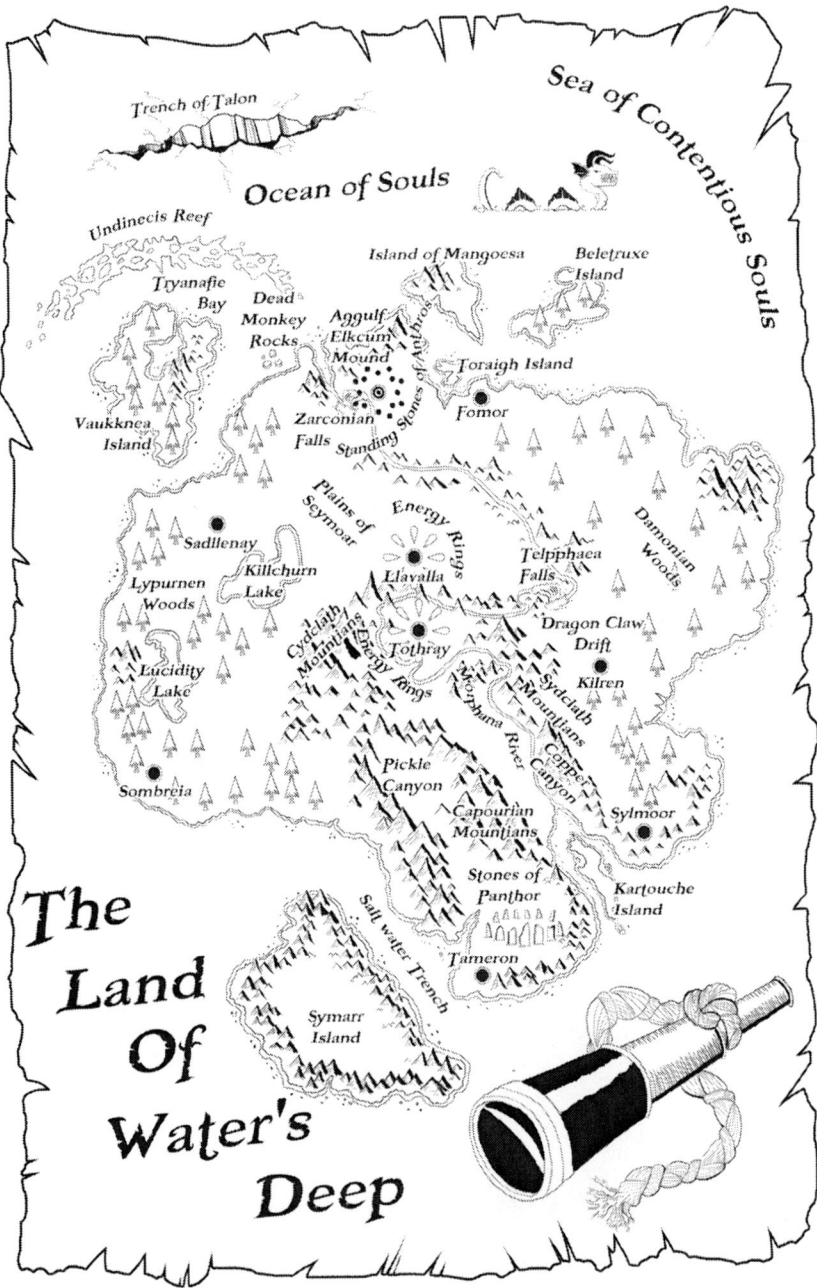

The Land Of Water's Deep

Trench of Talon

Sea of Contentious Souls

Ocean of Souls

Undinecis Reef

Island of Mangoesa

Beletruxe Island

Tryanafie Bay

Dead Monkey Rocks

Aggulf Elkcum Mound

Toraigh Island

Vaukknea Island

Zarconian Falls

Standing Stones of Anthra

Fomor

Plains of Seymoar

Sadllenay

Energy Rings

Telpphaea Falls

Damonian Woods

Lypurnen Woods

Killchurn Lake

Llavalla

Cyclath Mountians

Energy Rings

Tothray

Dragon Claw Drift

Lucidity Lake

Kilren

Sydclath Mountians

Morphana River

Pickle Canyon

Copper Canyon

Sombreia

Capourian Mountians

Sylmoor

Stones of Panthor

Kartouche Island

Salt water Trench

Tameron

Symarr Island

ORIGINAL MAP COMPILATION BY ADELE DEGIROLAMO
ILLUSTRATION BY DAVID CAREY

2

Your introduction to our tale of the Stolen Child, starts with meeting our reluctant Shapeshifter Sibrey; her running for her life from the Dragonlord Tracker named Soren, who was sent to retrieve her from the Lypurnen Woods after a decree was supposedly ordered from the King and Queen of the Aelves. The Black Dragons known as the Dracore were summoned from the Isle of Symarr, where they have lived in seclusion since the Dragon wars ended: That was almost 1000 years ago, and the Humans involved in that war, have long since disappeared from their expanse of space.

Sibrey fled easily, turning into one of the hardest things to detect — a real creature, thereby eluding the Aelf that was trained to track her, using her unique ability to turn into the fully formed shape of one of the Black Panthers that lived in the Woodlyn Rokh near her village. Having this strange ability was not known to the villagers who had looked after her since her arrival as a small wailing. There as, it was no surprise she was able to quickly lose the Dragonlord behind her, as she disappeared quickly into the trees.

In his search, he unexpectedly came across another creature; one that was far more dangerous than he had anticipated to ever be lurking in the woods. It was here Soren was introduced to a small Human child, and one annoying Wood Sprite called Tamerk that was protecting him from the Fey race on this planet. Our conniving little Sprite out foxed Soren, and he ended up being drugged and chained up in the Sprite's home, while the Shapeshifter easily escaped leaving him far behind, while she vanished into the forest and beyond.

In these first three novels, as the tale unfolds; we find that Sibrey moves in and out of a dream sequence she has dreamt about since she was very young, and finds herself slowly coming face to face with her pursuers in that world.

Meanwhile, the other Dragonlords have left the Shapeshifter village to wait for Soren and his prisoner on the far-side of the Lypurnen Woods, only to be waylaid by the appearance of a powerful Sorcerer that was actually the Sprite himself. The creature, known as the simple Sprite, is anything but, and when he turns himself into this powerful Sorcerer, he literally absconds with the herd of Black War-Dragons while they are land-bound waiting on Soren and the renegade Shapeshifter. This is done to prevent the entire group from making a daring rescue attempt to retrieve Soren, while Tamerk is still in the persuading stages of getting him to understand that he needs to return the Human child back to his own kind.

When morning comes, and the Dragons are returned back to the field as promised, the Dragon-rider Aelves choose another Dragonlord called Symin to rescue Soren. Symin has special powers that their leader Dyareius has sworn to keep secret, and he is sent in to retrieve the wayward duo that has gone missing. When he arrives — unbeknownst to him, the second passenger that he is sent in to retrieve, is not the little renegade Shifter at all, but an actual Human child that comes to be known as Ryyaan.

Apparently, the child has special powers unknown to the Fey clans, and once Symin seals the deal with the annoying Sprite and rescues his clan brother, the three of them make their way back to the meadow where the others wait.

When they arrive, they are met by one of the huge spacefaring Leviathan's called Sigrith Kithtar, who in turn, steals the Human boy Ryyaan and one of their own — disappears into the wind with his prize, leaving the other Dragonlords helpless to follow.

Soren becomes furious, and is unable to contain the secret told to him by Tamerk about the Dragons; spills the beans to the Dragon-riders that the Dragons can talk, and the others find out that they have been able to all along, and chose not to do so for reason that are discussed by Tamerk in Soren and Ryyaan's release.

The Leviathan called Sigrith, carries his passengers towards the North, and off to the Tuatha De'Danann's underground military compound, known as the Aggulf Elkcum mound. They are met by Eithne, and Cian, the parentages of the top commander Lugh, who is the present ruling military general of the current reigning Aelves. It is here Sigrith finds sanctuary while he rests to regain his strength, leaving his passengers safely with the Tuatha De`Danann, while the huge Leviathan is given medical aid from the exposure to the planet's surface gravity.

Meanwhile, Tamerk moves on to Fomor to meet with Cian about recent events, and the old Sprite is introduced as something the readers have not been made aware of yet. It is here that Cian finds out that the Black Dragons have been recalled, and is shocked by what Tamerk tells him. As this discussion concludes, something starts to stir below ground in the mound, and both Cian and Tamerk go to investigate the cause. As Tamerk is on his way towards the distant mound, an explosion rocks the landscape and the mound is torn apart, leaving the villages and the surrounding area to experience a very strong shock wave that moves down the exposed ley-lines along the continent of Water's Deep.

By the time Cian makes it to the place where the mound existed, he discovers that the White Dragon has jumped into space from beneath the surface, and takes with him the Human boy Ryyaan, Symin, and his own mate Eithne. While everyone scrambles to pick up the pieces they soon discover that the shock wave not only moved across the continent sideways, but moved down the breadth of it, destroying several well placed village wards that have never been breached before.

While, all of this is going on; the mountains that have been rumbling south along the Sydclath Mountain range near the village of Sylmoor, begin to produce several larger tremors, causing tension to build with the inhabitants of that village. They are called the Llyach clan, and their fears are doubled when they also spot the White Dragon flying along their boarders. They become dumbfounded with the sight of one of the mythical space faring Leviathans travelling planet-bound, sending one of their more experienced Wildcrafters called Stephponias, in search of Kamera who lives in Kilren. She is the mother of the famous Witch Kashandarhh. And only she is able to cross the wards of her daughter's famous Damonian Woods.

With Stephponias's mate only recently having left to deliver herbs to the village of Kilren for the Fire Festival — where Kamera lives, he tries to find his mate to warn her of what they had seen on-route. He arrives on the tail end of one of their bigger eruptions, and finds himself thrown off balance as he comes into the Kilrenean wards – slightly out of sync. Unbeknownst to him, he picks up a strange creature that begins to burrow into the cut he receives, when he makes contact with the surface of one of the village rocks, which protects the colony from outside entities.

It deposits something undetected in his arm, and Stephponias carries on none the wiser with the creature left there, only to discover his wife has already left and been sent on an errand of unusual circumstances, by none other than Kamera herself. Kamera has sent the Sage Coutinnea, with an urgent packet that needed to be delivered to her reclusive daughter; the very Witch, whom needed to know that the White Dragon had been spotted over their hills.

During all of this, the Dragonlords and their mounts have arrived in Tameron days ago; just not in the same reality as they thought they were heading to that morning.

Tameron has always been home to the Dragonlords on their off times of running. What greets them as they arrive home from the village of Sombreia, has the riders scrambling to find out what happened to their village and clansmen, while one by one they start to disappear from even each other. Dyareius their commander, sends two teams to investigate opposite ends of the castle battlements, while their majikal attaché Assha, moves towards an unusual lake that has been spotted over across the meadow. Upon arriving at the edge of the lake, he discovers and unusual sight and investigates its origins, while the Dragons themselves start to disappear, soon followed by a few of the Dragonlords themselves that have gone missing out near the old well-head.

It was here the remainder of the troop meet the Earth Elemental Aperthan – an Earth-shaper, who has quickly captured them and places them inside his body as the thing that had been hunting them finally arrives and tries to kill them. Aperthan is aided by an unexpected ally to fight the creature that has descended on them from the trees – in order to protect the Aelves he has confined inside his large stone body, and both of them battle the creature called a Sling, as it continues to attack Aperthan to reach the Dragonriders who have been snatched from his grasp.

The Great White Dragon finally arrives at its destination and the readers are introduced to the moon called Leberone for the first time. It is here that we find Lugh and his army of creatures that have set up a spacial garrison, off the planet's surface.

Meanwhile back on Tantaris, Assha the majikal Aelf is captured by a strange ethereal creature found hovering on the far-side of the lake, and dragged down towards an ancient city that the resident Fey of Tantaris didn't know existed on Water's Deep. It is here we introduce you to the Water Elemental City of Murias; a city of creative beauty and outstanding scenery, which allows one to enter into other doorways with just a simple thought or gesture. Here, Assha comes across a familiar face and once orientated in this strange environment, he finds himself free to roam and meets it head-on.

That creature is Moraig, a well-known Fire Elemental that he has known most of his life. Moraig is also known as unstable, and soon Assha finds himself in a heap of trouble, before an accident sends both of them through a familiar shift-point-doorway that lands them on the outside safety zone of the moon Leberone, where they are left battling for their lives.

Back on Tantaris, Coutinnea the reluctant Sage sent on the errand by Kamera, has a run in with the notorious Witch Kashandarhh; Kamera's reclusive daughter. Soon she finds herself in circumstances she is not conditioned to, just as her mate Stephponias comes to her rescue alongside the one person who can reason with her — Kamera.

Meanwhile, Soren shows up in the Kashha's Woods, and as he lands with his Dragon Tansar, the entity that had gone for a ride in Stephponias's arm suddenly hatches and the four of them end up battling the creature that has begun to infest his body with creatures called the Finical Spideranthemaous — a horrible thing that is used to detect the presence of the Black Dragons.

This takes us to the final part of this first Shadow Tale, where Moraig and Assha get into a situation that leaves them battling for their very lives. Apparently Assha, who had been preoccupied by the tale Moraig offspring Nomae was telling him during his visit, released the accident prone Moraig into the storyline, who then almost blew-up the Water Elemental's home-world, and Moraig ended taking both of them through a shift-point doorway that brought them to the Moon Leberone — where we last left them fighting for survival.

That leaves us with a glimpse, into what the true identity of what kind of creature Symin really is, as he steps in and comes to their rescue. And now, that should bring us all up to speed and we can get on with the second telling of the tale and the chapters will continue from where they last left off in Book-One. So, get yourselves a warm cup of tea, sit down in a comfortable chair, turn off the outside world, and let the tale take you where you need to go; for without too much more to say, it's about to get a little rough for those creatures that find themselves fighting for their lives, inside this second-rendition of our tale of the Stolen Child.

Adele DeGirolamo

CHAPTER TWENTY-FIVE

The Woods get a lesson in History

Tansar heard their laughter, as the battle with Stephponias's demonistic particles of foreign substances had been deemed to be dealt with, done, and finely baked, leaving him to graze along peacefully for the moment. The present danger was far from over he well knew, but if they could deal with it one small battle at a time, they would be that much further ahead of the coming conflict.

Nonetheless, the battle would have to be more on the relevant plane, before those that were involved would find its end. As it stood now, they were only just becoming aware that it was even going to be fought here upon their own world, among the enemies that were just beginning to show themselves like little dots on the landscape of a minefield.

Only Kashandarhh, he knew, could feel its stink, as it slithered through the atmosphere. When it became known to the others, it would take most of all of them to put it down for its final assault. Unfortunately, someone within this clan would not make it through to remain here within the realm of the current Tuatha De ' Danann's family of elders. The clan would have to surrender one of their own, and that Fey would have to die in order for the others to live. That was why Tamerk had sent his rider Soren here in the first place. Soren was crucial to this fight; one that would only be revealed in days to come. However, with Quist's request to find Kamera's daughter within Kilren's mountainous hillside, the Witch Kashandarhh would have

Soren's help to try and get it started, before someone else became a little more on the dead-side, this time around.

Tansar knew she really didn't need any help, and would be already working on it; Tamerk had called when they were out in the trees, while Soren and Symin watched their young friend Ryyaan come over to meet the real creatures that were hidden inside their Dragon bodies. The Dryads held this secret for a long time, but the boy had needed reassurance before he even attempted to go with their Dracore counterparts.

She recalled how Tamerk had started the ritual to change both him and Quist into their true form, and how he had also sent word to Kashha using the same airwaves, linking the two simultaneously at the exact same moment, while his majik was still at its peak. No sense wasting perfectly good majik when the waters are running deep. He just popped Horae (his little time Goddess) into the mix, and Tuffaa... time stopped for a brief microsecond, while all around the glen everyone momentarily moved in different threads of life; none were the wiser, and hadn't a clue what he had done.

Mind you, no one really knew most of the things Tamerk did anyway; it was just his way. A little quirky at best, and I would think he was more of an enigma to most of us that lived inside our little Fey lives. However, for those of you that have seen the small things he has done in the past, I would hope you'd understand when he pulled the memory from you and made you lose its particles to another memory he slid in its place, that it was not done in malice. That is what he does, when it comes to his kind. The malice part comes later, when you have done something that cannot be repaired. For the most part he simply pulls the things apart, selects what he thinks you need to remember and puts that memory back in its place. Strange creature, a little nuts, and dangerous as all hel. Tansar snorted with the thought. Malice was an odd word, once only used in the darker regions of the Sea of Contentious Souls, having it resurface on the continents was disturbingly familiar to the war Balor had almost created when the Humans had first arrived. But the thought dissolved and disappeared in place of another.

He couldn't help himself; he smiled thinking about Soren's reaction when he had found out what he didn't know about the Dragons. In her female character, she had been somewhat offended when he had reacted like a spoiled brat the moment he had found out they were not the Dragons he had believed they were. But, as the male persona took over, he had to think what it was like to have something you thought you knew inside taken out from underneath you, and replaced by another train of thought entirely out of the context of what you were lead to believe was true.

Males just couldn't switch alliances that easily. It was in their inherent makeup, and Tansar could smell a rat in the fire, and that rat was about to make a huge blunder that would expose one that belongs to the hierarchy of the elders of one clan, which lays hidden in someone that should not be here.

He also knew that someone else, who still resides on this plane of existence, had not done their job in its final stages with placing this thing within the restricted zone. Its very existence within the Galaxy of Planets on this side of the Goetutonias Nebula's vast network of Planetoids was proof enough that someone had really screwed up, and not just royally!

It set his feathers on edge, just thinking what this could mean for the Fey race here on Tantaris. It couldn't possibly think that it was absolved of what it had been called to do in the first place, without some kind of retaliation coming from those that had planned their line of defence out to perfection, only to have one tear it down in a matter of seconds. Its very nature would not have been that easy to restructure and the hardwire having come through the Black Star it had journeyed through when Balor had evoked its essence into the denseness of its crushing forces, should be showing some form of weakness by now.

But then again, that should have been severed the moment Balor had been killed; instead it still flew without restraints, remaining free to continue the revenge of a now dead master. Surely Kashandarhh would have the means to find the key to its destruction by now. It was after all, more than a thousand years in the making, and that in itself should have given her a heads up on the situation at hand, as it spun out of control and landed once again in their proverbial laps.

This was how things were done in this world of Fey regulations, to prevent something such as this from taking on a life of its own. This kind of thing was always brought into the world with safeguards put in place.

However, nothing seemed to have been allocated for just such an occasion, especially when one is hatched without requesting provocation.

With that also being said, Tansar still fussed about who that person would have been, that could be so inept at a job that even the younger apprentice Witches that lived anywhere in this realm could have done blindfolded, and at the very least bloody barefoot. Balor had been a very cruel man; so it could also be that once the creature had been raised, Balor was unable to reverse his own majik, and his own ideologies of himself as this super Wizard would have taken a tremendous hit, especially given the actuality of how little he did know.

It had been rumoured some time back, that he had executed the one who had witnessed its birthing, thereby preventing any further action in its retaliation and his defection when things had gone sideways. But karma does work in mysterious ways, and when it eventually makes its way here, it sometimes bites you in the ass and spits you out cold. Truth be said, his reign had been of pure hatred from the get go, and all that had lived through his insanity could only imagine what his mind was truly capable of dreaming up. He was after all, born with a Vermorbian mean streak that carried on through to his adult life. By then it had tripled in replication, and anyone that got in his way had their own throat slit come nightfall and lay dead where they fell by the following morning. Yes, I would say that is more the definition of the word, Malice.

It would be a long time in coming, with regards to the reason that the Dracore had been first implemented into the protection of the chosen three. That journey was quickly coming to fruition, and would in the coming days have the clans stunned at its outcome. But first, for that to take place a series of events had to have occurred. And for that to happen, it had to be in the correct order.

First off, Tansar and his twelve friends would have to give over their essences, to become hidden from the directional shift-point they would need to maintain their identity. And that, thought Tansar, was not going to be an easy task. He licked his paws and spat out a piece of Fever-pitch he had picked up during the skirmish in the field back when Ryyaan had met the sky Leviathan.

He shook his head and cleaned the scales on the back of his left side, finding the source of an itch and continued on with the next thing on that list, as a Ticktisaid jumped free from his feathers and scurried into the undergrowth. He hated the wingless insects, always trying to undermine his cleaning routine, and jumping in where they didn't belong.

Second, and just as important as the first, he thought, they would need that completed in order to hide the children from that which Balor had created to kill them. If even a whisper of where they were was to leak out, all would be for naught, and the Queen that would be born would fold up this world never to let it rise again.

There had been a time when their own chance at survival was directed towards this, but that was not to be in its own completion. It would seem that something else had been in the works for an entirely different set of circumstances, and had it not been for the unexpected arrival of Tamerk in this Spriteish formulation of drift, that would indeed have taken place, and the Dragon wars themselves would have never been fought in the first place.

So the story carries on, with Tansar needing to get those involved to move towards the time when they would find themselves at that arrival point; to accomplish just that very situation, and remove this hunter from the world of Sopdet's constellations and back to his own time-line.

He shook his head and flattened the area of grass, just as another Ticktisaid tried to free itself from his scales, and dove back in. This time he shook his entire frame and watched a whole colony of the creatures fly outwards into the woods and he returned to his field of grass unharmed by whatever section of downy feathers they had decided to set up shop in.

Tansar shuddered to think what might have happened had they dug their teeth in for the long haul. But before he had time to consider that thought again, another memory arrived before the making of its actual germination, and the Sling attained and turned what was already into the mix up on its heels, as it tried to move through the motions of thread towards them. That call sent Tansar's attention to more immediate matters, which drifted on the atoms of this other world; one that ran alongside the places of in-between somewhere far out there, to where it continued to hammer its way inside. It was getting close; before nightfall someone from the old guard would feel it sting, as it crossed through over to this side.

So, the story turns around to Kashha's woods once again as Tansar went to investigate the cause.

Kashha quickly returned to reality, and turned the laughter away from what was at hand. She moved her hands towards the previously stricken Aelfan male that was starting to stir with the outward signs of consciousness; however, laughter prevented her further advancement towards his inert form, as the others began once more to suffer the same affliction.

Stephponias did begin to move in outward appearances, away from the unconscious being they had first been introduced to. His vision began to clear slowly at first, as things started to come once again into focus, with one black Dragon flying low overhead. His vision was somewhat muddied; then the Dragon aloft suddenly disappeared right from out of the sky above him, proving further acknowledgement that he might not be completely out of the woods as of yet. One minute he was there, and the next all that was left was a bunch of Ticktisaid yelling their heads off, as they fell out of the sky.

When he was able to clear the lenses that fixed themselves to his eyes, he saw himself to be surrounded by three females; one, his own life-mate, followed by Kamera and what he assumed to be her daughter, the Witch. On examination, they also had another Aelfan male in attendance, which was within sight. The male must have arrived sometime after Steph's fall, and displayed a very unusual heritage. Upon closer inspection, he realized that Coutinnea was on the ground in a far too uncomfortable position to be actually conscious, while the others seem to be in fits of laughter, rolling around on the ground without any outward signs as to the why, and too consumed to help his stricken mate to rise.

That quickly changed when they realized he was awake. They gathered their wits about them, trying to organize themselves into a more respectable picture, primarily for his sake. But that too became difficult to do, as they needed to step over Coutinnea's inert form in order to reach the place Stephponias was in, and that resulted in immediately bursting into more laughter, much to his dismay, and the insane process began all over again.

For the moment, he had to smile at the thought of what he must look like as he awoke to those peals of laughter, followed by muffled restrained snickering, all for the sake of his own sensibilities. What had occurred was anyone's guess, but by the sounds and reaction of their silent tears bitten down along cheeks flushed with redness, it must have been incredibly funny. For whatever reason it was, they continued to make asses out of themselves and he, all unbeknownst, had actually participated in whatever instructional fortitude they had been able to perform.

It occurred to him it was not of their own making; their laughter was infectious, and as he laid there immobile, he had to admit he was happy to see they still had their wits about them, as he too began to grin, and then turned to laughter alongside them, joining in the fun. For what it was worth, laughter always had that effect, even if one never got the punch line and hadn't been part of the initial joke. But, it didn't take long before he realized his movement was slower than it should have been, and he stopped short as the pain overcame his sensibilities. He lay there with tears flowing down his face from his previous — if not only for a moment, smirking-self.

The pain took his breath away momentarily, and then subsided, as the others around him were still caught up in their own private joke, unaware of his discomfort. He didn't stay quiet for long, as once again the formation of the smile peeked through at the edges of his mouth, and although his arms wouldn't obey his commands to come up to hide his face from the outrageousness of his actual laughter, the tears did begin to formulate around the sides of his cheeks. The sound brought him to its infectious rendition, while the brain fog slowly released its hold on whatever organ of the mind it had seized control over, and the pain remained as it was. However, the laughter became short lived with the new realization that Coutinnea still had not come around like she had every time in the past when she had deemed something was uncomfortable for her own mental awareness.

It was then he came to understand his mate must once again have found fault with what had lain around her and fallen into a dead faint, as her mind shut off the blood flow to her delicately balanced naivety. Whatever it was this time, he had to smile at the situation for all of them, shaking his head at the snickering antics of the others still snorting with peals of laughter unaware of her delicate disposition. There wasn't a dry eye in the place, and he was sure as hel not going to get any help from them any time soon, as they seemed at the moment incapable of helping even a frog caught in a puddle of mud.

He had to admit, after all these years, she really did have a funny way about her, which was oddly unusual in her line of work. Then it occurred to him, he'd have to actually get up if he had any hope of helping her, since everyone else seemed to be still in full on hysterics, falling upon themselves in a valiant effort to regain control. But that was not going to happen without time, and a lot of help.

He tried once more to get his legs from beyond the frozen field of numbness they had acquired while he had lain motionless, to work in his favour. But, that too proved to be too much in this wincing flavour of rapid mobilization that came at once and bit him in the ass, leaving him winded and breathless and still very much earth-bound. He tried to use his fingers to feel what held him immobile on the ground, and found he had some form of bandage wrapped around his arm from wrist to shoulder, constricting his ability to find a way to sit up without their assistance.

It appeared to him he might have to wait until he was able to flag them down individually, when each of them in turn eventually tried to catch their breath. But that too was becoming harder and harder. It was simple; unless he had help, there was no way he was going to be able to get up. He lay back, settling himself in for the long haul and sighed.

He didn't have to wait long as Kashha spotted his face, and moved to rise in his direction, beckoning Soren to give her a hand. When she did arrive at his side, she put out her hands to get him to rise, while he held his breath to try to breathe through its range of motion.

"My mate, was she at least breathing this time, before she keeled over? Or is it something entirely new?" he spoke mostly to the wind, finding himself in a small bit more than just pain, discovering new ways for the body to hurt as she pulled him forward.

He screamed once and then winced, further biting his lip with the movement that was created when he began to slowly try to rise, using the muscles along his abdomen. It took only a moment for Soren to get into positon alongside her, to actually pull him to his feet and set him gently back on the ground.

"Oh!" he unintentionally let go of the word, as he was lifted quickly off the ground in one swift motion. Kashandarhh smiled at his grunt, and simply asked him candidly, half expecting him to carry on with his initial questioning; which she had no intention of answering.

"Can you stand by yourself?" Kashha continued to ignore his question, which she had heard as clear as rain, knowing full well had she responded she would have said something ridiculously stupid about Coutinnea's constant lack of being able to stay conscious. It was quite obvious that her mate must be fairly used to that condition by now, so in her eyes there really was no need to explain further. Instead, she moved in closer, mostly to check the wound that had just housed a very nasty entity, which had the ferociousness of a Suter Plank Cat, and the temperament to rival even her, with compliments to the entity that was feeling its way around all the village wards: But also, it was to keep herself from actually responding to him as far as his wife was concerned.

"What the hel happened, to me?" he said, as he started to try and rise up, now feeling the effects as Soren lifted his own weight under his own.

"You are very lucky, my dear." Kamera reached up, touching his face with concern, arriving in the conversation only after Kashha had ignored the poor boy when he had asked about his mate. She shook her finger at Kashha in a lightly chastising way, as it appeared that Kashha would be better suited to majik than talking. It would also be decided at a later date, that she would best be suited to the field of 'don't bug me world', instead of head-Witch of the 'piss me off biosphere'; either way Kamera knew she would have her hands full with either one.

"Try moving your arm; it will sting a bit at first but it is survivable, and should be clean from any litter the Finical had picked up." Kashha directed this one herself, without the need of her mother's quick wit.

"Can we move her?" Stephponias pointed to Coutinnea, still out cold from the sight of the Dragon, which was just coming into view in the sky overhead once again. "Holy crap, how long have I been out?" Stephponias shook his head to clear the sight away from what the black Dragon sighting had done the first time to his eyes. When he looked up again, the creature simply vanished right in the middle of its flight pattern, and Stephponias simply took it as a figment of his imagination.

Coutinnea, decided at this time to finally get it together, and also came awake. Although she was somewhat freaked out, especially with all the changes to her newly planted environment. Nonetheless, she was able to make it up enough to see that Steph was awake and moving, and that Kashandarhh and Soren were in the process of getting him to his feet.

Kamera returned nearby and kept herself busy checking the area that they had been working in, to make sure every little bit of the thing they had removed was taken to the fire pit that Soren had lit from Kashha's newly split woodpile, and deposited in its hot coals. It was Kamera who actually remembered a question that had not been asked of Steph earlier, due to his unconscious state, and it was from this question that things began to move along at another speed, where only moments ago the meadow was filled with rather infectious laughter.

"How did you come by the marks on your hand?" Steph turned his hand towards his face, looking puzzled, and then quickly remembered the entry into Kilren when he had stumbled as he came out of his shift.

"It happened as I shifted out from Sylmoor and into Kilren. I must have hit the transduction field just as one of the bigger eruptions from the mountain went off as it rocked through the village, throwing me through the shift at an awkward angle. The moment I came through the doorway and landed at the village wards, it knocked me a bit sideways, pitching me forward where I slipped into the wall."

Kamera caught her daughter's eyes, as her eyebrow went up along one side of her face. She bumped into Soren and stopped him in mid-step. That had got her attention. He caught her as she tried to turn sideways to avoid the collision, righted both of them as she twisted in mid-stride, changed direction to where she could watch Steph's face up close and personal, and then came up with a slightly perplexed frown set on her face.

She had only been halfway listening, as she tended to do on most occasions, placing one foot in what is, and the rest of her body in the another spot of what was. Soren had put his hand out to steady her, when Kamera had asked the question that began the flurry of activity, sending her mind sideways into the middle of his present mind and fully towards her undivided attention.

"Where about on the stone did you actually touch?" she asked him, with renewed interest. She moved to examine his arms, looking to see if he had any more markings on the skin along the same area. She took apart the bandage they had placed on his wound, and moved her fingers along the entire ridge where they had removed the Finical's talons, upwards to the back of his neck. She felt nothing; it was clean. The perplexed frown, changed to one of the thinking variety.

"Towards the right side of the left facing wall." he answered. "I always come in that way; it always makes the entry point easier when I rematerialize after shift."

"How long did it take you to feel it?" Kamera added as she looked at both Soren and Kashha, wondering how many more townspeople might have had similar occurrences and not reported them simply because they hadn't known.

"Not till I got here with you." He hesitated, then added as an afterthought, "It's almost as if the moment you," he looked at Soren, "started to come through the rift, with your Dragon, I started to get really nauseated. Then suddenly it felt like my insides were being torn apart, and something started attacking me from the inside out — then nothing more." Kashha grabbed Soren by the arm, moving him away from the others. As soon as they were out of range, she nodded towards where he had left Tansar.

"It's back, isn't it? She asked. Soren looked at her; he didn't even have to do much more than nod.

"I'm afraid so, or at least one of its damn hunters!" He pointed to the remains of the entity they had burned. Kashha swore; it had only been a matter of time before time would start to reverse itself and allow that thing to come through the rift once again. She had hoped to find the ritual within the texts of the old religion, but somehow they had been removed from where they had been stored when she had arrived to retrieve them. Things through the centuries do get moved about, and this was no exception, as their plane of existence sometimes moves with the air currents of the Elemental realms, and drifts around a bit before coming back around to find its place again.

She had heard that the Dragonlords had recalled their mounts, while she had listened to the wind that flowed into her mind from all who speak of things that others cannot hear. She heard the whispers of Tamerk as she moved the curtain in order to learn what had transpired, when one had travelled alone into his vicinity on foot. It seemed the wee ones had almost had a meeting of their own, unescorted by the elders of their tribe.

However, Tamerk spoke vaguely of their arrival and she had not been able to get past the barrier he had instilled, before they had been cut off from her trying to listen to other words not spoken.

Having Tansar call her to find entry into her domain had been unexpected, but it hadn't surprised her. For it had been written long ago that there would be repercussions in the years long after those wars, especially in the hiding of the Tuatha fledgling, and it was something each and every Fey that lived on this world would have done, had they been given the chance over again. Mind you, there were very few Fey that were aware of this, and she had hoped it would not be from this source. For too long they had grace from its ugliness, and she hoped it would not find the doorway she had locked from this side in its search of their energy source. That is, until she at least was able to retrieve the old text and initiate the majik held within.

She had been able to send the creature away all those years ago, when they had first encountered it. And it had taken a full coven to put it down and send it recoiling to where it could not break free from its restraints. She had taken much due-diligence in setting it into the proper formulation; or so she had been led to believe.

She, and she alone, were all that remained of that group of very powerful Witches; it had slaughtered all of them while she watched, unable to help her kin in their final moments. But, as her physical strength began to desert her, her majik grew exponentially stronger. In a single moment as they lay dying all about her, they sacrificed themselves for her, as one. What had happened was something only known in the Witch clans; one that they had systematically been able to transfer their powers collectively, and she had been able to finish the task alone as her clan lay in the final throes of death, now depleted of what had made them special.

She had suddenly risen, fully charged, pushed it off of them and shoved it into the abyss they had prepared for it. However, her excess energy had been short-lived, and she returned to her former self shortly after the final surge in particles had left her body and burnt it into ruckles.

By the grace of the Goddess Danu, she now hoped she would be able to finish it without the others. For, without their unusual abilities by her side, she would have a much tougher time with the creature she had been able to imprison in the past. Dealing with the nuances of this stronger and more vigilant formulation without her sisters, was going to take a great deal of strength she would have to find from somewhere. She had hoped the book would lead her to it, but with that gone she would have to find another source.

It was true that Witches had an inexhaustible, supply of strength, but they also have their limitations. This sudden change of events, away from a little annoying Sage that happened to just wander into her woods only this morning, did not do anything for her mood. Her day just became a whole lot tougher; for without the others, it was simply going to be almost an impossible task unto itself, and having gained her notoriety around this side of Faden Corpeous, word, would eventually filter back that its presence was once again proving to be unstoppable. Surely the powers that be, would insist she be called to action for what she had done for them in the past. Only this time she wasn't so sure she could deliver — as she once had, without a full coven sitting at her side.

It had occurred to her, as she was thinking, that Soren's Dragon was strangely quiet. It was at this time that she heard the quiet within the glade in a very familiar pattern. She sought it out, and came back blank.

"Soren, where did Tansar go?" She pointed to the empty field that previously housed a black Dragon slowly grazing on its grasses. It only took the motion of a Tambergeen Fickle Fly for Soren to move towards the now very empty field.

"Tansar where are you, within the distance to us?" He spoke as he was moving in the direction of where he had last left Tansar, after he had delivered him into Kashha's meadow. But Tansar was gone, and didn't answer him back. In his place, it was Toupoe — Gantay's Dragon who responded, instantly re-materializing his visual body to the left of Kashha.

"I am here in his stead. Sorry, there has been a development with the other Dragons, and he had to be moved to the other world that sits within this space of between." Soren turned to Kashha.

"Have you a temporal field within your woods?" Soren asked, moving to where Tansar had been, placing his hand right through the image of Toupoe.

"Yes, "Kashandarhh answered nodding, "it sits here and flows into the other realm to make it easier to move between worlds."

"Toupoe," Soren looked at the mirrored image of the Dragon. "Has he arrived there yet?" Soren asked the Dragon that could be seen, but not touched.

"Yes, why?"

"Then why does he not speak, and you do?" Soren needed to understand.

"His energy signature is being followed, so we have masked it, resulting in his inability to be heard." Toupoe answered.

"Who is this from?" Soren asked, but Kashha didn't need that answered, she already knew the source. She turned to Soren, before Toupoe could answer the question.

"We need to find the stone that Tamerk kept on his person. It will keep all of us safe." Kashha had been looking between the two of them as if they were one, but directed her next thought to the image of Toupoe, who was beginning to fade through the image, as it moved with the shadows of the filter now beginning to dissolve. "How will we find you, as we move away from my home in search of Tamerk Toupoe, will you remain within that place that is forbidden, or shall we move towards the mountains?"

"I will be within the city of the dead that is to be found nearby," he said, simply.

"Then we shall meet when the time is right," Kashha returned to him, as she grabbed Soren by the arm, moving him towards the others.

"Until that, to which is mine." Toupoe said, bowing at the receding pair. With that he was gone; the image dissolving into thin air, leaving Kashha to whisper to Soren.

"We must move quickly Soren. If the Dragons have been sighted, it will find each one of the originals that have remained alive, and kill them, starting with the ones that will inflict the most damage in its hunt of the fledgling's signatures. That way it will be able to go unheeded in its goal, and catch many by surprise."

"Then it has begun," he said staring blindly into the meadow where he last saw Tansar. Soren turned back towards the remnants of the now vacant space that had been the entranceway into where the Dragon had disappeared and gone. "Can we use this entranceway again?" Kashandarhh shook her head.

"It's been compromised and will not be able to open on this side again." She turned and flung one of her intensely strong energy waves towards the doorway, blowing it up. It exploded inward, giving way and moving upwards in a huge volume of majikal fire. Her destruction of the doorway was fast and efficient, destroying it to bar anyone from using it as an entranceway in her absence, so the Dragons within could enjoy the shelter they had found there.

The explosion sent the others onto the ground, Kamera yelling at her daughter with words that most likely would have not been too kind, had she had any time to actually listen. The words that Soren heard as plain as day comprised of the following.

"You could have bloody warned us you were going to blow the place to smithereens!" Kashha only grinned outwardly with a calm rendition of her emotions. Inside was another story; one that she wasn't ready to expose to the others. Actual fear for the offspring that would one day rule the planet that they now lived upon, was in no way conducive to helping her to complete what needed to be done.

"Where do we even start? Without the Dragons it's going to be a long journey on foot." Soren whispered to her before they had reached the others, bringing Kashha back to the situation at hand. She nodded soberly in response.

"With Tamerk," she said, assuredly, as they both moved to help the group that still remained on solid terra-firma.

"You sure you're not going to blow something else up?" Kamera said to Kashha as they arrived. She turned to Coutinnea, speaking, then glared back at her daughter. "This is another reason I don't like to travel anymore." Coutinnea still had not found her voice and could only conjure the remnants of a smile, leaving trace particles of apprehension falling all around her, as she looked in the direction of Kashandarhh.

"Did you see that?" Kamera pointed to Coutinnea, as she continued yelling at Kashha. "One day Kashandarhh, you will not even have the seekers to bring you things. You've scared the bejeebes out of everyone this side of the Cydclath cliffs, dear daughter. How am I ever going to find people to help me deliver your precious herbs, if you keep on scaring everyone away?"

Kamera went to stand up and instead brushed something else from the explosion off her, shaking her head. "One day dear child, I won't be here to clean up your stupid messes. Then what are you going to do?" She continued to shake her head, as Kashha continued to ignore her. "See what I have to put up with?" Kamera held out her hand to Soren, letting the Dragonlord pull her upright to her feet. "Thank you sweetheart, you are more than kind; not like the child of my loins that belongs to her father at this moment of frustration. However, dear child, can one in such fine standing as yourself, find the ability to pardon such a creature? She is so much like her father, and for that reason she thinks she is bloody royalty." Kashha groaned.

"Mother, Father is a fish; do you see any fins or a tail on this body?" Kamera this time smiled through her sarcasm, but remained silent. Really, if you looked hard enough they were there, but it would do no good to continue with the banter when her daughter was in this kind of mood. There were times when you had to walk away from her insensitivity. Kamera knew she couldn't expect her child to understand the complexity of their pair bond; and he wasn't a fish, he was a Selkie. There was a difference, and if one was adding fuel to the fire, he was grander than any fish she had ever met, and that went without the preverbal phenomenistic proportionalism that her daughter tried to allude to.

Steph moved towards his wife, after Kashha brought him up to his feet, showing his hands to be rock steady.

"What now? I don't have the fear that should more than likely be coursing through these shattered nerves and making me run for the hills. But lucky for me, it appears that the danger that has been evident while I was out cold has understandably passed me by; is this true or am I still having that nightmare?" He looked from Kashha as Soren moved forward towards him, the latter formulating the correct words to answer him quietly, away from his mate. Before they left his mouth, Kashha started to speak.

"No, not anymore, we got the thing that moved like a viper through your arm. As luck would have it, as you fell against the stone escarpment, it seemed to be self-contained within the one area of your wound." Soren smiled at Kashha as she was talking, winking at the Witch and thinking how lucky it was for Steph to have been in the company of one of the only Fey in...well, all of Tantaris, that could have identified what the creatures had been, let alone be able to actually know how to get the vicious little suckers out before they had entered another part of his body and killed him outright. Others would not be so lucky, and as far as he was concerned, he happened to be in right place at the right time to help her out.

This visit had proved to be pretty much how Tamerk had described it would be. He had said she would not disappoint in her knowledge of things within the context of what he needed to speak to her about. But, before he could take some time to talk with her by herself, Steph again voiced another thought that had occurred to him.

"Can you tell me what it was? And how did it find its way to the stones outside Kilren?" Steph went back to scratching his arm with his fingernails, alongside where Kashha had touched him. Somewhere in the back of his brain, he hoped it was nothing more than the electrified energy of the Witch's signature grazing his wrist right up to his shoulder bone that made him itch. It wasn't, and although he already pushed that ridiculous thought aside, the injury continued to show redness and swelling where the bandages had been wrapped, and the creatures had been rather hastily exhumed.

"Darling please, try not to do that; the scratching will only cause it to get raw and we need to keep the bandages in their proper place, before something allows itself to fester inside the open wound." Kamera had moved to rewrap the arm, after Kashha had opened it up to see if anything else had been hiding around the affected area. He sheepishly nodded, trying his damnedest to not rip the bloody thing off and get into the depths of the itch at its source.

It had begun to get dark outside and Soren started to move towards the axe Kashha pointed out, that lay on top of the big cutting block. It was still stuck in the wood next to the pile she had already cut.

"I don't think we need any more for the night, but I'll bite, what do you want to know?" Soren looked behind them, and quietly replied to her as he picked it up and began to chop another round.

"What about the stone?" he said.

"Ah. Well, it's something that is very old that belongs on the other-side of the galaxy," she began, then had to think for a moment, as both things that were on her mind occupied the same time-frame. She spoke loudly out of context, trying to take the situation away from where it seemed to be heading.

"Soren you can put the firewood in the entrance to the cottage; they will be needing it tonight to keep the chill off." She turned to her mom. "Mother, can you stay while we track Tamerk down? I think it would be best not to have them here alone, while Soren and I move towards tracking the Sprite to his area of the old settlement grounds. I think it will be safer here than going on tonight in the dark, and it won't take long with two of us to find the portal." Kamera nodded without even thinking.

"I'll explain to Steph and Coutinnea that it would be in their best interest to stay, at least till morning." She turned away to go, as something kept gnawing at her to remember it. Kamera could feel it just at the tip of her thoughts, but just out of reach of her current memory. She was sure, that this was just one of the by-products of getting older; she could never quite put her finger on some of the things that needed to come to the surface of her thoughts when she needed them most, and by the time she did, whatever it was, was either redundant or long-gone.

This one eluded her entirely, but it was important enough to feel its threads as it pulled and pushed itself to formulate its creation back into her frontal lobe. She could just feel its grit hanging in there and dangling right in front of her nose. But as she watched her daughter getting closer as she moved away to shift out of her woods, it was the actuality of saying the name Tamerk for the third time that finally jarred her unforgiving memory.

"Kashha, hold up a minute. Coutinnea didn't have time, during all the commotion, to give you what she was carrying for me," she yelled after them. Both Kashandarhh and Soren had only made it a few steps down the pathway that would lead them to the heart of Kashha's woods, when Kamera called to them and made them momentarily turn.

"Can't it wait till we get back? I think this is a little more on the important side of things than some unidentified small gift that you have included in your need for others to keep me company," she snarled back, turning to go and pulling Soren by the arm. "Ignore whatever she says, we have more important things to do, let's go." She directed him forward.

"Ah, you picked up on that, I see. Well, just maybe you are wrong about this one dear child; you might want to quash that feeling and re-write your

energy readings on this one." Kamera growled back at her, in a much snark-
ier voice than Kashha was used to hearing from her mother. Soren smacked
her and she smacked him back.

"What?"

"That is your mother you're talking to, not some person that you've
never met, alien fish child," he returned to her when she looked like she
was going to smack him again, and then ducked just in case. "Manners,
Kashha, remember one day she will be..." He was interrupted by Kamera
with a renewed urgency in her voice.

"You need to see this one now, child of mine. Before the two of you
go hunting him down for nothing." Kamera raised the last syllable of the
word 'nothing' to a high pitched whine. Kamera slowly began to move over
towards the bag that Coutinnea had brought with her, but then suddenly
realized that she had hung the pendant around her neck as she left Kilren.
Coutinnea had been on the other-side of the cottage with Stephponias,
when Kamera called for her to come quickly and not to dawdle, leaving
Kashha to wonder what her mother had gotten up to, while Coutinnea
appeared with her mate along the other-side of her cottage.

Coutinnea had not been privy to the conversation that Kamera was
having with Kashandarhh, so it came as no surprise when she arrived with
a bit of uncertainty in her steps, followed by the looks of fear that one has
when approached by another of Kamera's kind.

"Did I do something wrong?" she asked, mystified at the urgency in
Kamera's voice.

Kamera moved to her side and looked into her eyes, as if talking to one
of her animals with that kind gentle spirit she was known for.

"Remember the pendant that you placed around your neck? I think now
would be the perfect time to give it to Kashha." Kamera nodded gently at
her as Coutinnea's eyes grew big and round, and it was at this time she
truly looked the part of Kamera's courier.

"Oh my, I'd totally forgotten." She turned and looked at Stephponias,
smacking herself in the head lightly. He smiled lovingly back at her as
she went to pull her hair back, trying to release the threads that held the
raw stone in place. "I'm so sorry Kamera; and you had wanted it to be a
surprise. Everything happened so fast that I didn't get time to even think

about it." She moved to undo the inconspicuous mineral that was wrapped with such care and carried with complete naivety, to what she had wound around her pure translucent innocent Aelfen throat.

The moment she brought it out into the open and passed it to Kamera to hand it over to Kashha, the stone not only shone a brilliant shade of green, it came to life with a kind of humming sound that Kamera had never heard before while it was in her possession all those long months ago.

"You've got to be kidding me," Kashha spoke to no one in particular, showing her shocked face to Soren as Kamera held it up for her to see. She nodded to her daughter, smiling as she passed it over lovingly into her daughter's hands, watching it reach out and wrap itself around Kashha's wrist, taking on a life of its own. She looked at Kashha and winked.

The moment of the transfer, Coutinnea took note, watching the unusual pendant that she had carried suddenly turn into a living breathing thing as Kashandarhh's skin came in contact with its outer-shell. It made her gasp. Inwardly she shuddered, thinking of the close proximity it had been in for all that time — wrapped around her own neck. But, for the moment she watched in fascinated horror as the inanimate object turned into something else even Kamera had to admit she wasn't expecting.

Kashha's skills had preceded her a long time ago, but it took the pendant of emerald stone only a fraction of that time to seal the deal for all those present here in Kashha's glen. She retrieved its luminous spine and unwound its body from her wrist, taking a very long look at the stone as it grew warm and started to sing in her hands.

"You've had this the whole time, and didn't tell me?" Kashha was starting to get a bit annoyed, but it was Soren who asked the most pressing question.

"What is it?" he asked, coming over and shielding his eyes from the brilliance of its light.

"This is what we were going to Tamerk's to find. It is the single most important thing in this universe right now, and it will be able to save our little Fey hides when the time is right," she whispered back, leaning over so only he could hear her.

The stone tried to twist once more around her fingers as she stroked its undercarriage, turning it over to read the inscription that was engraved on the other-side. It began to purr rather loudly, making Soren laugh, while it flickered from dark-green to a light lime colour, all the while moving about the green colour shield trying to find the one that suited it for the moment.

The stone had been carved with old markings of runic scrolling, placed on it when it was first forged with the majik it ingested over ten thousand years ago. Someone a very long time ago had imprinted the stone with quite unusual abilities; the very abilities that only could be read by someone who had the genetic coding of the ancestors of Lemuria with the mycorpian thread running through their genes.

Vallmyallyn had that gene in his Selkie state, but none of the other off-spring he had produced received its transfer of molecules, since he was with his Selkie mate Siian. Siian had died giving birth to Kashha's brother, and that gene had not been expected to transfer to a Witch that found herself with child from any another Fey clan, without the purity of the Selkie gene pool.

But, then again, Kamera was no ordinary Witch, and time would produce the reason for that statement. For now she looked with pride at the daughter the Kanoie tribe had asked to be removed from their village walls; the one that had the power to either destroy this world, or leave it in peace and walk away. She was betting on a combination of both.

Kashha continued examining the stone markings, while her mother looked fondly at her from the other-side of Soren's body, resting lightly against his arm. He had also watched the emerald crystal pendant come to life, and his face showed respect for the Witch that Tamerk had sent him to find among the majik of the Damonian Woods. He smiled at Kamera and patted her head as both of them continued to admire the stone's animated body, while it moved along and through Kashha's small fingers, finding the correct location for it to settle down and take its rest.

It was an unusual stone of incredible beauty, and one that had never been forged again in the history of the Fey worlds. Majikal ritual forbade that duplication, existing in a realm that was already rich in majikal history where none would ever be needed again. Besides, it never had that kind of complete duplication, as the majik usually only has the power attached to things once in their correct formation, and once things become common, they become irrelevant and no longer hold their fascination.

Kashha turned to both her mother and to Soren, whispering the words she read on the inscription to them slowly, pointing it out in its strange script and letting them feel its power, as it gently rubbed itself along their hands. "With this power, I shall transform and break through the barriers that are set in place." Kashha smiled, continuing the words as she added her own, "giving me an opportunity to put that bloody thing down once and for all."

"Ah, I see," Soren looked at the inscription engraved on its belly. "Is that why that little thing is all dead like, lying on the ground looking all squiggly?" Kamera peered in further and laughed at him.

"You idiot, that's not a character line or a dead insect, that's the head of a Dragonlord with his spine detached." Kashha glared at them both, talking to the creature she had wrapped around her, while Soren looked rather horrified at the reality of what she had told him. "Don't you listen to them sweetheart, stick with me and I'll make sure you get to bite them both when this is all said and done with." She laughed and ducked out of the way as both Kamera and Soren went to reach for her, at the same time.

Steph had arrived beside Coutinnea in time to hear the end of the story that was being brought to life again. Most outsiders never get the chance to hear the majik from the inside of important events, and for the first time to an outsider of the northern tribes he was privileged to hear what Kashha had to say. Unfortunately he thought they were talking about him, and totally misinterpreted what she said. He had not, as of yet, heard what it was that he had hosted within his body when first he had arrived.

"Is it the same thing that came through the stones that you took out of my arm? I thought you said it wasn't going to do any more damage to me," he said, looking as if he wanted to move as far away from its present location as possible. Kamera steered him back as he began to take another step backwards, shaking her head at him.

"No, we got that thing and it won't hurt you anymore; this it completely different than what we are currently dealing with in regards to everything around us that is living. But, it has a definite relationship to what has happened to you, and the Finical Spideranthemaous."

"The what?" Steph asked in horror.

"That is what the entity that tried to catch a ride within your arm is called, F.i.n.i.c.a.l. S.p.i.d.e.r.a.n.t.h.e.m.a.o.u.s." Kashha spoke up, spelling it out slowly, as a shiver went down both Soren and Steph's back simultaneously.

"A spider? You never told me it was a freaking spider!" Soren shook his whole body in a mock squirm.

"Bloody hel, I'm so glad I was unconscious, I'd have puked." added in Stephponias as Kamera laughed at his reaction of the event they had witnessed.

"It wasn't too pretty for us either." Soren contributed to the conversation somewhat woozy from the description. "However had I known what it was, I might have not been so quick to come to your aid!"

"You probably should tell him a little more on the history of its arrival here in this part of space Kashandarhh, or he's going to start thinking that every time he goes into Kilren it's going to come after him." Kamera was also smiling at Soren, as she watched the rider start to search his own arms, in case one had tagged along when he had arrived in Kilren after both of them.

"Stop that, you idiot;" Kashha threw Soren a dirty look. "I seriously doubt that anything other than that one came tagging in, they only travel in solitary husks. But, since we are not going to Tamerk's to look for the stone anymore, I'll try and give you the short version of what I know on the subject of its arrival within our limits of space.

"Will it take long, because I think I need to go have a bath in your creek? Something tells me no matter what you say that the little sucker had friends!" Kashandarhh started to laugh at him.

"Fragmire, you really are a piece of work tracker wailing, seriously what part of they only travel in solitary husks did you not understand?" She shook her head and hit him. "Pay attention little wailing, this story is important."

"Hey, don't call me a wailing. I'm not that little, Witchy poo, and the last time I looked, you weren't complaining about my skills."

"That was before you started whining about spiders, you freak!" Soren had his hand on his chest, looking with mock horror at Kashha's words.

"Mowa, na aww, I'm only afraid of you, Witchy poo." Kamera rolled her eyes at the two of them.

"Well at least we got that settled, you Dragon freak; now can I get on with the damn story, or are you going to take a little bathy wathy down by the kidlet pond, and scrub all the eight legged freaks off your damn hide?" Kashha was laughing aloud with the imagery he was projecting before Kamera took control of the situation, yelling loud enough for both of them to cringe.

"Enough you two, we don't have time for this. Kashha, just tell us the damn story so I can get the heck out of here and go lie down over by the axe with my head on the chopping block, so I can get someone to cut it off before I break both of yours over the bloody stoop!"

"Fine!" Kashha said to Soren at the same time as he repeated it back to her.

"Oh my Goddess, I'm babysitting a bunch of shippels out of the middle ages," Kamera yelled into the air. "Who have I pissed off this morning, that this is what my karma has pushed in my direction? For the love of the ancestors, just bloody tell the story before I find another damn spider and shove it down both your throats."

Coutinnea started to giggle, hiding her fingers in her mouth behind Stephponias. He looked at the three of them and spoke, smiling — intent on breaking up the line of stupidity.

"So, should I be worried or not?" All three of them turned to him simultaneously and shouted.

"NO!" And that ended that line of questioning for the interim, as Kashha settled in to tell the story.

"So as far as I can tell, and it had been told to me from a coven of very knowledgeable Druid friends, it first came to us on a comet that came into contact with an old moon called Leonae. An entity such as this had lived centuries ago in the cold confines of deep space, and only a handful of Fey had ever seen it before it arrived within our galaxy.

It was the Air Elementals that first came across its likes on this side of Faden Corpeous. They are the ones that live out along the fringes within the confines of Hydrous Secular, and have lived there since the birth of their species almost two million years ago. One time, a very long time ago, one of the many comets that came through the vicinity of Hydrous, crashed within the confines of Leonae; it is one of its larger moons. It brought with it a very small particle living within its core, which unlatched itself as it tagged along through the debris field, into the region that it currently found itself to be in."

Soren looked fascinated, but the other two not so much; both Llyach Aelves seemed to be looking on with eyes glazed over from sensory overload, and a little greener than usual. Kashha ignored them and continued on with the rendition she had been taught since she was still a whelp in short shifts.

"This particular species was a new life-form that had been trapped within the confines of that very rock since the last host had shed its skin, and had abandoned it to its own fate on that moving piece of real estate.

The Great Barren Waste lands of this moon had been used by the Air Elementals, which had lived within the city of Finias. Their ability to travel great distances within their own bodies was something much admired through the known races. That discovery had given the Druid Uiscias the notion that moving within a doorway that moved between other worlds could give them an even greater distance to move within. This sudden and idealistic approach to travel, would give them the ability to move through worlds that had historically been off limits to their physiology, due to the distances between time and space.

Uiscias was from an influential order of Druid elders that hosted many of the greats, which helped the Elemental worlds, live alongside the Fey of all worlds. His doctrine encompassed the Air worlds and everything that entire particular element hosts, but his familiarity with most things Fey was pretty intuitive to what most of the Druids of their time had been taught.

This particular doorway, it was decided, would be placed on Leonae, as it would be able to filter anything that should not be part of their species' own genetic makeup. Therefore, it prevented whatever should arrive from reaching their home planet, and causing difficulties with the cross contamination that was not of their own making.

This was done for all the right reasons, and for none of the correct ones that were originally discussed in the first place. What they didn't account for was bringing something from their world or moon, to another part of the federation of worlds that they visited at the time it was implemented. Thus, this entity that began living within the gravitational pull on this particular moon, now had the means to be able to move about freely within the confines of where the Air Elementals' travelling were able to take them.

Now having said that, it is another thought that brings us to the next question of the day. Who brought it here from the worlds of where these Air Elementals have recently been, and then which of the species that live within the Air Elementals' domain was able to travel from there to here without being seen?"

Kashha looked at all of them when they didn't answer her and seemed confused by her question.

"To Kilren, not my bloody woods," she added as they all nodded in agreement. "Nothing ever comes through my woods without my knowing about it. Really wailings, keep up." She looked at Kamera who had started to roll her eyes once more. But the story was one that Stephponias had found to be quite fascinating, and now it was starting to make sense to the others, as they were all again interrupted by the continuation of the story. But it was to Soren the continuation fell to, while Kashha stood by nodding, their quarrel long since dismissed, as he started to understand the ramifications of its arrival into their world.

"So what you're telling us now is that it has been basically left within reach of all beings that have use of the shift-point doorways, and at any time could have been free to attach itself to any one of us. By that means, and I truly hate this if I've understood it correctly, it could therefore have free access to deposit itself within the inside walls of our village wards, and not be detected by the shades we have in place." Soren added in his conclusion, quite horrified.

Kashha nodded at his understanding, and both Kamera and Soren felt the beginning threads of queasiness. "It's probably, why your mountain is rumbling." The Llyach Aelves were floored; Coutinnea started to actually vibrate, looking like she was about to faint dead away from the ramifications of what was just revealed.

Kamera looked at Kashandarhh as she told her story from memory. It was a tale that had been given to her by others who had taught her child the things that only Witch-kind seems to learn.

"Your father should be able to decipher where the energy readings originated from, if they were within this side of the outer-hemisphere. I think before you go anywhere, you should start there. It's only fair, that each of the original Fey that was involved with the ceremony, including your own father and the Selkies that lived along the coastline off Toraigh Island, should be fair warned of this bloody thing and its return to our world." Kashha nodded in agreement, as Kamera carried on with her train of thought.

"You have to remember it is also the only single organism that can detect the location of the Black Dragons, and for that reason alone its arrival here is suspicious. It would appear to me that this thing was not randomly dropped off on an exploratory mission of random chance." She stopped for a moment, pausing to think. When she began again, her words came much quicker, as she paced along the steps to Kashha's stoop.

"If your father were here, he would agree that it is too much of a coincidence in its arrival at this particular junction, in respect to your," Kamera smiled at Kashha, "place of residence. After all it was the water-folk if you remember, that were part of the underwater coven that preformed during that time in unison of the one that you had been a member of on land, and he and his coven will be in dire jeopardy if another of its kind has made it into that other world where they have been in hiding since the Dragon wars ended."

Kamera was right, and Kashha knew it from the bones of her inner tail, which she still refused to acknowledge existed along the topside of her tail-bone. He was also one of the elite warriors that Balor targeted on his scrolls of death, before he had been killed. His being a Water Elemental that had major ties to the coven Witches on land had been what Balor would have needed at the time in his assault on the armies of the Tuatha De'Danann. It was with this information — if it was still valid, that Balor thought he would have been able to strike a blow to the world of anyone that was against his taking over and ruling this realm, with the death of one of its leaders, especially Vallmyallyn who had direct ties to one of the Witches of Llavalla. That could very well be why this thing had arrived undetected along the wards of Kilren checking to see which of the few survivors that had made it through, still existed in this realm.

"It would have pissed him off, when he couldn't find me." Kashandarhh continued with her smirk, thinking of the creature winding his body around her fingers. "No wonder this creature was withheld from their line of sight, knowing it would be the one thing that could send the Sling back to its own home-world without us killing a single Fey." She looked down, still holding the glistening green stone that had not even started to settle itself into its former flatness. "I can't imagine something so small could be so damn important, let alone so bloody gorgeous." She continued to turn it over in her hands, holding it up to the last light of the day. "Do you think father will have to destroy it when the majik is gone?" Kamera had started to move towards the cottage that Kashha lived in.

"I'm not sure what needs to be done with it, but since you will be going to see him at first light, why don't you ask him yourself." She turned, looking among the four of them as they followed her up the steps. "Do you even still have any of the extra blankets I left here for all of us to use tonight?" Kamera kept on walking, but when she reached the top of Kashha's stone steps into her cottage, she turned back seemingly thinking out loud. "What time do you think we're all going to be leaving in the morning?"

Kashha looked at her before she disappeared around the corner, narrowing her eyes as she thought hard about what Kamera had just said. She had no idea what was in the cupboard her mother stocked in the back room for just such occasions. She hadn't had company stay over before. Kamera continued talking as her voice carried on into the cottage and out of sight, drifting in the air outside all around them.

Kashha knew Kamera wasn't listening, she could hear the cupboard doors opening and Kamera rummaging around looking for anything that they could use to cover themselves over for the night. She decided not to tell her that everything was stored up in the old attic, where anything she had given her had been shoved out of her way, because she knew without a shadow of a doubt Kamera would be shimmying up those old wooden rungs and breaking her bloody hips. Instead, as she hung the pendant around her neck and excused herself from the warm and slightly mesmerizing fire Soren had started in the grate, she whispered their whereabouts to him, and he scaled the rickety old ladder she had leaning by the wall to retrieve the extra quilts. There would be plenty within reach, slightly pushed away from the edge so they wouldn't tumble down the opening should someone need them. They had been accumulating over the years in various colours and fabric, passed on to her from various clients that had paid her with their beautiful hand stitched fabrics, for services rendered. She sighed slightly with frustration, and then carried on with other things; she'd never thought in a million years they would be used as simple bedding for those who had never been invited here, in the first place.

Soren watched her go, and excused himself to head into the woodshed for more wood. Good thing there wasn't a chance of rain, he hated to have to sleep inside with the others when it was still nice and warm outside. The Witch and everyone here were going to be strange company without Tansar out in the field. He would have to find his sleep where he could; the morning was going to bring a different kind of day; one that he would have to get used to, if he was going to be travelling along with Kashandarhh to the Selkie stronghold. He shook his head, thinking about the words he had heard once again, only this time the words were directed with dire prediction into a forced quadrafed message. He hoped that damn spider thingy didn't try and jump into him next time he went through Tameron's wards, or this war that was coming to his own house was going to get messy. Damn he already heard those words from Quist.

Bloody Dragon; then he had to laugh, Kashha swore as much as he did. At least he wouldn't have to watch his language around her as they were travelling to see her father; wherever that was. He only hoped she would travel better with him, than Tamerk had with Symin when they had first met. He missed his friend and hoped Quist had been telling the truth about him being fine, or there was going to be more than one thing dead, when this damn war began.

He snickered at the sediment and moved to bring an armload of wood inside before Kamera decided to do it herself; he at least could still be useful here while the war was still far enough away from the depths of all the strange company he was currently keeping and Goddess be found sleep. He'd forgotten how tired he was.

Ah... sleep; he needed that peaceful commodity more than he knew — especially while it was still viable. The thought brought him quickly towards the path from the barn — whistling a soft tune, until he reached the steps to the inside of Kashandarhh's home and ducked back inside to finish his newly acquired chores before he actually fell on his face and his body did it for him.

CHAPTER TWENTY-SIX

All is not what it appears to be

Sibrey's father Daniel, and the small group of fighters that he had chosen by hand to follow him to Tameron, arrived to find that Dyareius and his riders had not yet reached the village walls. The fact that it had taken them considerably longer to make the journey through the mountains than those who flew ahead by Dragon, could only mean one thing: Sibrey had made it further within the woods in her Shapeshifter molecules, than he previously thought she would before they caught her.

Daniel was both ecstatic and a wee bit worried, feeling cautiously optimistic the moment he realized she was not here and held against her will, until he began to wonder where exactly she had gotten to, and then he began to seriously have his doubts on the whole affair. It had taken them significantly longer than he would have liked to cross the mountain range to get here. Furthermore, his group of Shapeshifters had done so at incredible risk to body and soul, finding no joy in their movements towards the dubious Tameron and its castle-protocols. That is, until the actual arrival of his body in its Shapeshifter quantum where, without warning, the strangest headache he had ever felt almost dropped him to his knees, when he released his latest form, bringing his breakfast back all over the entrance to the outside pathway that would lead them inside the battery walls.

He tried to shake it off as simple nerves, but unexpected pain thumped inside the walls of every blood vessel in his body. That was not to be; as if on command it appeared to take on a life of its own, choosing to annoy him and articulate further inward to places he had not even known could hurt. It corresponded with the close proximity to the stone walls; making his Shapeshifter particles tingle and the hair on his body stand up on edge.

The inner workings of the castle grounds were very much like they had expected the main Aelven fortress to be. Finding that his daughter-foundling had been quite obviously able to evade the Dragonlords much more easily than she had been taught made him both happy and more apprehensive at the same time. He scrunched up his eyes, trying his best to elude the brightness of the Mauntra's rays, and rummaged around inside his satchel to see if his mate had packed some of the pain herbs he seemed to need more and more of late.

When they approached the soldiers at the main gate, they were surprised to see the Shapeshifter entourage moving towards them without word of their arrival. They explained to the guard that Dyareius had given them the King's official seal on the scrolls of the decree which had summoned them to the stones, explaining briefly what he had said back in Sombreia as to the general validity of who they were. But, it was the explanation of the Dragons' absence that caught their grit, as the guard told them the King and his entourage were not in residence at this particular time of year, and had not been here for going on two cycles of Leberone's passage; thereby the degree and its seal had not come from this house.

Daniel was visibly upset, and each of the Shapeshifters beside him were in need of food and rest and not in the mood for riddles, especially when it came to one of their own caught in the cross-hairs of some form of Dragonlord hoax. He was furious, and became even more noticeably upset when the captain of the guards explained the absence of said Dragon-riders and their noisy mounts, saying merely they had been detained and would be there shortly if they cared to stay and wait until such time as they could sort it out.

Daniel could feel the first threads of deceit filtering through the air, drifting in on the air currents that permeated the villages outside walls. That should have been warning enough. But strangely, it wasn't and they continued to query the castle guard....

Those in charge had not been in any way rude; on the contrary they had been more than gracious to the Togernaut clan, which had arrived without sending a scout ahead in warning. Not many well defended villages would have been as diplomatic to the Shifters, who had come armed to the teeth in all their Feytonian glory, showing the steel of their famous Mercorian death blades tucked beneath their belts, and the small arsenal of other paraphernalia they had managed to find room to tuck inside various parts of their clothing.

They must have looked quite the sight when they had arrived at the iron portcullis demanding they be allowed to enter on Sibrey's behalf; all decked out in various pieces of flora and fauna that had stuck to their clothes as they had made the necessary changes to their appearances, for the sake of the Syann-Clan of Aelves living within the walls. After all, this was the residence of the royal family of the Aelven race, and even though they belonged to another sedge of the Fey race, it was this grouping of elite sovereigns that they swore their oaths of honour before, that lived and ruled within this planet.

There had been shouts coming from the inside of the bailey, and it was determined they were not a threat by a round of loud unidentified voices that could be herd bellowing orders along the upper crenellation to lift the gate. Nonetheless, as they entered, ducking through the ironworks before it had reached its highest point, none of those bellowing voices seemed to be present, nor claiming ownership of their arrival.

Once inside and granted entry into the inner barbican of the outside gates, they were met by one of the older duty warriors who had authority to oversee such arrivals; he escorted them through, while they were being watched overhead on the crenellation by several warriors that Tameron hosted from various different clans. None of them seemed terribly hostile, just outwardly cautious as village soldiers tend to be, witnessing the strange sight of one of their own leading the way, while a band of Shapeshifters followed that had come waltzing in without a formal summons, all moving together into the open air towards destinations unknown.

Tameron was known for its fair dealings with all the Fey clans, whether of Aelven descent or something in-between. There were many species from different parts of the galaxy, and many of those family groups came into view as they passed by the main thoroughfare past several doorways that lead into several different sections of the main castle's interior rooms.

One such character of unknown origins peeked out from the lower grates of what looked to be the armoury. A soon as he realized he was spotted, he turned various shades of purple and grew bubbles along the length of his hair. As they passed by the lower grated window, his eyes grew wide and the bubbles popped one by one in rapid succession, causing the Shapeshifters to jump away from the side they had been walking on. In a last ditch effort to get out of the way, one of the Shapeshifters hadn't been quick enough, and one of the purple missiles of goo that had been previously attached to the creature went flying in his direction. He immediately twisted his Shapeshifter molecules into those of a frog, leaping right into of one of Daniel's pockets, missing the goo by only millimetres as it hit the ground he had been formerly occupying, hissing away.

Daniel reached inside the deeply stitched pocket, and put the amphibian down on the ground as soon as they were clear of the purple popping creature. The Shapeshifter returned to his former self and dusted himself off, following behind the others, still looking over his shoulder a little unsettled by the noise. All the while, the creature that remained inside the steel grated window, now full of purple goo, stuck his tongue out at the Shapeshifter clan receding in the laneway, then disappeared down the grate into places unknown behind its walls.

There was no sense in laughing at his friend, it had happened to all of them at one time or another in a moment of panic. Daniel simply waited for him to catch up, and put his arm briefly around his shoulders and grinned.

"He really was an ugly old snot, I agree. But, just think what he sees in the lake every morning when he goes for a bath!" Both burst out laughing, and left it at that; each of them carried on inside this strange place with all its alien markings and majikal ways, already on edge at the turn of events that had assaulted their simple village life.

They didn't have to go very far; however, from overhead it must have seemed much longer. There was so much for them to see, and they almost immediately went into sensory overload with each step taken on the ground. It was the strangest thing; they twisted and turned through several archways and when it looked like they had reached their destination they seemed to start all over again in almost the same spot from the previous location. Nonetheless, it was interesting; each new curve in the pathway changed the scenery before them in ways they had never seen before. It assailed their eyes, noses, and hearing, with all the sights of a very busy community along its cobblestones.

Once they passed a certain threshold, the village seemed to have established their authenticity by a waving of arms, it seemed like their little charade was over, and they were greeted by others that were in charge of the guests that arrived within the city walls. It was then they heard a clattering of cobbles somewhere off in the distance, moving quickly towards them, and as they turned they were entertained by a very handsome Centaur who skidded around the corner, coming up short beside them, smiling warmly and nickering excitedly. The pierced nose ring of the Flambosa clan from The False Galaxy of the Crystal Horse Nebula dangled from his lower nasal passages, and showed his affiliation to his clan. He neighed, directing them forward to join him, as several muscle ticks moved down his pure black backside along the Centaurian flanks, deflecting several Tambergeen flies that had descended on his beautiful coat.

"Off with ya, ya wee helions." He nickered, as he rotated, leaning down to stare at the closest one eyeball to eyeball. They flew away and moved about the air currents to another host who could be seen delivering several deadly blows to the insects, ending their torturous affair. Meanwhile, with his attention diverted to the group, he introducing himself, showing his Fey almost Human looking upper torso to be more Aelven in its appearance than it should have been.

Daniel smiled at the Centaur and reached out to shake his hand, while the creature bowed formally to all of the shapers, introducing himself as Horse. The older warrior spoke briefly to all of them, expressing his intention to depart.

"I will leave you in his capable hands, shall I?" Then he disappeared without another word, returning to his post. Horse grinned wildly at the Togernaut clan, gesturing them to follow him to what it appeared would be their temporary quarters while they waited for the riders and their mounts to escort the little Shifter back to Tameron's vicinity.

The quarters turned out to be right in front of them, as they stepped through a doorway into what appeared to be a long room connected to the backside of the barn. It didn't take long after that for a series of trenchers to arrive loaded with steaming food, providing the weary clansmen nourishment to recover from their long trip through the mountain passes. Someone had taken the time to think of their needs; they had only just begun to dig in, when another servant returned with a large decanter of Tameronian whiskey, accompanied by the clattering of hooves from Horse. He whinnied his approval, reaching for the second tray that came into the room, which held several amber coloured drinking bowls, one for each of them, allowing them to pour the liquid from the decanter like civilized folk.

Horse was definitely a character; he continued to find ways to make them howl with laughter, sitting at their sides like some story-book character, while the others reclined on benches that had been deployed around the edges of the room, too exhausted to move another muscle. The conversation soon changed to small bits of hilarity, while Horse, enjoying one of his own glasses of the whiskey, regaled them with a host of different details about Tameron, and all who had come here in search of a better way of life. From the very tiny to the extra-large, they came from all walks of life that the different planetary worlds hosted, which rotated around them inside this simple shift-point doorway.

Daniel waited and kept quiet, evading the question of how one little Shapeshifter could cause so much trouble, as the others talked among themselves. Occasionally he would step in and give his rendition of events, after hearing their laughter alongside one high pitched whinny that would take them all again into knee thumping bouts of hysterical amusement. But, he had not the energy to participate for long, and having found the end to their harried journey he joined a few of the others who were already snoring away, resting his eyes while he waited for word that Sibrey had finally shown up.

It didn't take long before he was in a deep sleep, his dreams disturbed by various things that filtered in and out of his mind, which didn't find the means to set their roots too deeply, as he moved amongst each that entertained his thoughts. When he awoke sometimes later, he found that it was dark outside and the others were snoring rather loudly beside him, sprawled in various positions across the floor on some kind of sleeping mats that horse must have sent for. Their Centaur friend was nowhere in sight.

Segments of one of his dreams came through into his waking moments with the distinctive voice of a female talking to someone.

"It's not the Dragonlords, per se, who she had been taught to evade..." then faded from his memory as he wondered what that simple train of thought might mean. He shook his head, trying to clear the cobwebs from setting any stingers that would remain and not let him find the meaning of the dream. But they were already gone. It just happened to be the one for the moment, and it drifted unattached back into the recesses of his mind and didn't return.

He listened for a while to his friends snoring away, as the dark of the moon sent him worrying about his daughter; looking for reasons that seemed to find darker shadows and fester in unrealistic 'what ifs,' regarding the real reason she had not been found. The ability to stay hidden was just one parameter of her trained mind. She had excelled within the boundaries that had been set before her, each and every time she had been given the challenge of a new and dangerous scenario to figure out in her corporeal mind.

Nevertheless, Sibrey was not who she appeared to be, and that secret had been living far too long inside Daniel's heart, to expose the source of its truth at this time. That would have to be done by another who held the authority to expose the truth of the situation. It was not Daniel's to spew along the cobbles of Tameron's royalty, just because she had been summoned by something that had been written into a decree so very long ago. For now he was just happy everyone had made it here alive and in one piece. And that had not been an easy task, considering the risk that each and every member of his warriors had been exposed to on some level during their trek to this strange city.

Someone coughed lightly in the background as Daniel nodded off again, slowly remembering their path and the treacherous canyons they had to traverse, in order to follow his little shippel; one not of his own blood, but his nonetheless.

Each of the Shapeshifters had moved about the trailhead from their village of Sombreia towards the long journey to Tameron on foot. At least to start with; at times they would travel within the animals that they had been trained to become, but the going would be considerably slower than anything that Sibrey had done or what Daniel had been told she had accomplished. He was still having a hard time envisioning half of what he had been told by her teachers, compared to the other students of her age and vocations.

Even seasoned warriors had not been able to compete against the little Aelf, as she excelled in things that the others had taken half of their lifetimes to complete. His warriors had difficulty with many things in the Shapeshifter world, but Sibrey had far surpassed any of them, including almost all the elders that still lived deep within the forest glens, and even they were having trouble understanding how she did it.

Her shapeshifting had taken the clan by storm, and none of the females of her own age group would have anything to do with her after she had been able to get several of the young Shifters to ignore more than one of them, in their relentless search to connect with her. She had hated it; having them clamber for her attention in whatever way they deemed fit at the time. She had remained a loner, and kept it up into her adolescent years, staying for long hours out in the trees just to keep out of their reach and away from the village pathways where they waited in ambush to present her with the various amorous advances they believed would sway her attention. It didn't, and more than one of them had the bruises to prove it. Daniel had laughed at the thought, of how one little female could turn an entire village on its ass. Now, it wasn't so funny.

It was the same for his sons — her brothers, and the warriors he had enlisted from the village to travel the trails they had to take in pursuit of yet another Sibrey episode, which never seemed to end well for any male participating against his brood's ferocious feline or her damn pride. But, it was the actual trip to Tameron that had proved to be a little on the tougher side; once again in search of another thing, Sibrey bound. She would have loved the sight as both prospective suitors and warriors alike had clambered for the chance to prove themselves to his little wanderer, but it became apparent from the get-go, that this would require a lottery to see which of the strongest would be selected for the long arduous trip that lay ahead of them, without leaving the village defenseless in their absence.

Much of it was against the resident female population who had no love for Sibrey's welfare, much to the disparaging love of his mate. She had actually reached over and cuffed the offspring of her best friend when the little whelp had yelled to the others of her whereabouts. The little whelp was in the middle of shifting into a bird in hope of catching up to the Dragons, and telling her long winded tale to the leader Dyareius. Daniel's mate had grabbed her by the hair, as the final transformation was dissolving her Shapeshifter particles and dragged her back into the world she was about to leave. Daniel's eldest then arrived just as the little whelp was screaming her head off, telling anyone that would listen that the little radical the Dragons were looking for, had gone running on foot to gather more troops in the trees. But this female tended to twist the truth on a regular basis, in order to make the story much more interesting for the general populace and more believable to any others she had gotten around her who would listen to her absurd banter. He had hoped no one would have paid her any mind, knowing her past history; he was wrong. When word got out his other sons were horrified with the damage the little liar had created.

To be honest, he had thought nobody except him had actually been paying attention to Sibrey, as she shifted quietly away into the treeline. Especially with one of the most famous trackers of the Dragon-riders sitting on his Dragon not more than a stone's throw away from his position. It wasn't until a few minutes later that he realized he was no longer occupying that position, and not too long after that, he saw what appeared to be a disturbance of Sibrey's molecules going through the trees.

He didn't became actively pissed until he touched Dyareius's arm later, thinking at first it just might have been the residue of her shift. That changed when he saw the image of Soren moving towards where he had told Sibrey to run, just as Dyareius was about to leave. The rest of the village had been far too occupied to actually see this happening, and he had not warned any of them, hoping she would have a head start. It wasn't until the actual Dragons had gone that one of the brothers of this particular female had heard her bragging about it, creating a further disturbance, and how she wished the little renegade would be caught and dragged back to where she belonged and away from the village. That had signalled a change in events after the kerfuffle above, and he had cuffed his little sister in the head, and had come running into the area Daniel was in, telling the rest of them what his spoiled little brat of a sister had just done.

So, the moment the final Dragon was well out of sight and its molecules of drift were making themselves into part of the soil at their feet, the Shifters changed tactics from the initial plan of attack, and started on their way. It had progressed quite without any incident for about an hour, when one of them got it into his head to suddenly shift out and found himself blasted into the side of one of the bigger trees they had skirted around down the pathway. They sent for a healer from the village after finding him crumbled at its base, still in his falcon form, quivering from a broken wing and still in shock. It had gone downhill from there.

The warriors had struggled that first day out, knowing that not one of them could ever maintain the shape of their shift for more than a few hours, unlike Sibrey, who had done it for days on end. But, she also had not allowed anyone to witness her transmogrifications, even though Daniel had at times slipped away from what he should have been doing, just to witness its happenings. It was something he had agreed to do, and though at times he felt it was an intrusion into her private world, it was something that had to be done, so Tamerk would know how she was progressing.

The Shapeshifters, as a race in general, have not the ability to possess that kind of staying power, but then again, neither should Sibrey have acquired that little trick. But she did, and as Daniel watched her move around in her various forms, he had to admit the little minx was even better than he had ever thought possible. She was damn good, and far from what anyone had been led to believe. That gift was given to only a few very special beings, within this strange and majikal realm in which the Fey reside. Sibrey came into Daniel's family at a young age, having no knowledge of her own family, and not belonging to those of Shapeshifter heritage. Furthermore, she was definitely not of that particular caste, as far as Daniel had been told.

Yet she seemed to excel, and so he had kept that hidden before anyone had found out she had been able to maintain that ability all on her own without the teachers' instructions. For once, Daniel put his foot down, and decided together with his mate, that it would not be in their best interest if talk about its discovery were to run rampant inside their own circle. Outside in the village the gossip was bad enough about her differences without adding extra fuel to the fire on the inside, causing her brothers to defend an ever growing number of new situations that continued to rise up out of the blue in view of the others.

Daniel paused, and switched his train of thought, unconsciously scratching his head while he yawned. He was still thinking about the band of Shapeshifters and what they must have looked like when they had been met outside the perimeter of Tameron by the village guards. The group had been welcomed with piqued interest, as the unusualness of their abilities was too much to pass up for the average Tameronian. There had been so very few of the Shapeshifter people that had ever passed through the town, that to have Daniel and his men arrive tearing the morning air into an excited murmur, was something out of the normal occurrences of everyday village life.

Word began to find its way around quite quickly, as they were escorted through the bailey, to the comfortable quarters that were just outside of the main stables that he rested his head against. He was tired, and his eyes began to find their place once more as he regaled his inside thoughts on how they had quickly been given every amenity that Tameron could provide, despite the fact that most of the males had found it a little unsettling at first within the walled fortress, without the luxury of forest soil beneath their feet.

He smiled, thinking of the reaction one of the group had to the purple thing that had looked at them through the safety of the iron bars of one window. Most had never been beyond the village walls of Sombreia, let alone in a village of this size. They were mostly simple stable hands and blacksmiths. Those who had been outside the village grounds were few and far between, and usually were on some military campaign out near the borders of Sadllenay. Most of them had not been in the village on the day the Dragons arrived, and only the common folk had offered up their arms to join Daniel in his lottery of sorts. It had both surprised and humbled him to see how his friends felt about his family. To actually volunteer to come on such an arduous journey to help him regain his daughter from those that hunted her, was preposterous. But Sibrey did have a way with the village males, and he had tried to stop a stampede from erupting as soon as word got out about the selections.

Unfortunately, he had left behind the one Shifter who had really wanted to attend, and if he hadn't come into contact with one of the Dragons, he would have been first on the list of volunteers. Morgan, his eldest son, had been left behind due to an injury he received when he was struck by the tail of Dyareius's Dragon, Baelf. It had not been more than a sprain at first, but a very nasty bruise had taken to turning the skin a very vivid colour of blue, causing him to have a prominent limp during the selection of the townspeople that would soon follow Daniel, as they prepared to leave within the hour.

The hollering that ensued was far worse than any pain from the swelling would have caused him, but he would have slowed them down, and forced them to move at a reduced speed; so Daniel had decided to leave him behind, despite the cussing that had come out of Morgan's mouth that he was horribly insulted by their decision.

The bruising had been the colour of the hair of the Gorgon that lived in the mountains of the Capourian Range just outside of Sombreia's lands. By the time they departed and began to move outside the town's vicinity, he could still be heard yelling his head off with vivid clarity, making more than one of his other brothers respond in kind, creating more of a problem for the one that was left behind.

It had given a bit of comic relief to the actual situation of the journey they were about to embark upon, and before nightfall all had been forgotten, at least on their side of the trail, for the remainder of the trip. However, back home Daniel was sure it had been another story, and one not forgiven lightly. Even now Daniel could still hear the sounds coming out of his mouth, angry enough to cause even one of the more hardened Shifters to cringe. He may not have got it from Daniel's side of the family, but he knew another of his shippels that could swear as loud if not louder, when she was tricked into doing something that she felt she was bamboozled by others into doing.

During the heat of the following day, they decided to move upwards along the higher trails, following a clearly marked path that would lead them through the great Capourian Mountain's much cooler terrain. But, he soon wondered if it had been a mistake, taking that route; for, as they climbed, knowing it would lead them into a very open area along Pickle

Canyon that would make them vulnerable to attack; it showed them the instability in the area, revealing some kind of slide that had happened in the not too distant past. They decided it was too late to turn around, giving them no relief against having to move through and around the falling boulders that littered the pathway. It created some very challenging climbing conditions, as they were forced to skirt around each and every one of the huge expanses, as they continued to make their way to the treeline above while they rested between shifts.

One of the scouts had returned back to say that a fairly big cave had been spotted on the far side of the overhang, that had some shade they could take shelter in and rest. They had only just started towards the entrance when a movement suddenly caught Daniel's attention. It didn't take him long to realize something wasn't right; as he shouted for them to stay away from landing, it showed itself to those already in the process of entering the cave.

The alarm call was heard throughout his clan; each pulled back from various areas along the edge, except those who had been in their flying formations up near the top-edge of the cave. He called again to them not to land, but the warning came too late for those few souls that had done just that. Those Shifters had landed inside its interior edges, and were in the beginning stages of the change over from the various creatures they had taken through the shift and already were in the process of finding their original threads, still unaware of the danger that lie ahead. When they finalized their arrivals and realized what was basking on the low overhanging rocks, it took only moments for them to realize they had ventured into one of the notorious lairs of the Queen of the resident nightmare herself, none other than the hated creature known as the Gorgon.

It scared the daylights out of both Shapeshifter hawks, which had just dropped their previous forms, having found themselves within touching range of its fetid breath. The first arrival, who wasn't the nearest simply by chance, pulled back on the other Shifter's still transforming arms, just as he went to fall forwards, tripping on several small carcasses that littered the ledge, and hauled him backwards towards the edge of the cave's overhang.

The lair of this creature of exceedingly bad temperament had been completely concealed from the others below, obscuring it from any possible sightings until they had already gone too far to turn around. It had been one of the most frightening encounters with the beast that any of the Shapeshifters had ever experienced in their lifetimes thus far, and still Daniel shivered at the thought of what could have happened had it gone the other way.

Its head, only inches away, had been covered with writhing blue snakes that moved in all different directions even in sleep, causing the Shapeshifters to flee and instantly morph back into their hawk formations that had luckily not been completely released. That stroke of luck instantly gave them a chance to escape into the air with their lives, but not necessarily with their nerves intact. It was a miracle in itself to have found the Gorgon sleeping; for not only did this creature rarely find the time for such rest, its eyes had been covered by one of the writhing snakes that hissed at their arrival, allowing the group to make a hasty retreat as it came to full consciousness on the now almost empty ledge.

That was initially what caught Daniel's attention; as the movement of the reptiles living atop this creature's head had been constantly changing position. Had it been even a few seconds on either side of that moment, or had they decided to rest themselves alongside their host, the outcome may have been entirely different, and they more than likely would have had a few casualties, possibly killing every one of them on the ledge at the same time.

He had watched with horror from the cliff-side below, when the first of the group had fallen into one another retreating swiftly in abject terror. Even if he had been able to reach the cave in time, the damage would have only taken a moment to occur; far too fast for any of them in the group to have been able to help them, being so far away from where they were still climbing.

Having met any Gorgon would have been disastrous in itself. But, the blue-headed snake Gorgon was even more gruesome and fearful. This particular member of the family of ballistic creatures would attach itself to the entire extraneous family of the warrior that they had come into contact with; so you really didn't need to be present in the flesh to have this one kill you. You see, this one's speciality was to kill sight unseen, and when one looked upon the face of that creature the whole genetic line of his bloody family would turn to stone, even if they were on other planets at the time. It was an ugly thought, and one that made you wonder who had created such a horrible creature to begin with, and set it loose up here on the Fey worlds?

It was dumb luck to have caught the creature asleep, as the eyes would surely have taken out an entire line of the Shapeshifter clan. Daniel couldn't believe their luck when not one of them had been spotted by the beast during their hasty retreat, but when they had taken to air with the wings of the mythical Gryphon hawk, they had heard behind them the screams of something that had not been so lucky, as evidently it had been disturbed by their departure. They immediately left the scene behind, in a plight of wings and feathers, with several additional screams that rang out into the air behind them, as the others on the ground descended into their own threads in case it decided to jump down from the ledge and give chase after them.

So, with eyes directed away from the scene of the crime, and the sound of falling stone, they continued skyward not having a single second's urge to turn from what lay ahead of them to see what might have been. For, had they done so, they themselves would have been turned into some form of calcified matter, alongside their family and any distant relatives of their clan in any shape of blood or bone would have disappeared, leaving the Shapeshifter clan as nothing more than a whispered legend, just to give the creature its pleasure.

An up-draft of air caught them and took them skyward into the higher thermals, with the smell of pine and feathers below taking them far above Pickle Canyon, which had suddenly arrived sharply to their right as they moved deeper into the Capourian Mountain Range. They left the creature to whatever its next movements of torture would be; each Shifter that had been left on the trailhead below followed with exact mimicry of the newly shaped birds of prey joining their clan-mates. They filled the skies with other winged creatures once they felt the wind underneath their wings, representing some of the more beautiful species of falcons and Gryphon hawks, all flapping away from the scene of the crime, with only a trickle of regret left to fall onto their brightly coloured tail feathers streaming along in the wind behind them.

It had taken them almost a full hour of flight before any of them actually began to think about transforming back into their own Shapeshifter forms. While others stayed bird bound for longer than Daniel deemed necessary, he couldn't help but wonder how anyone of them had made it through the danger this time without so much as a scratch on them. Instead, those that stayed and pushed their endurance molecules to the limit soared, making use of their sudden departure from certain death into something useful for the nighttime meal, and hunted aloft. While a small portion of the Shifters chose a more earth-bound mode of transportation, quickly changing into something that could travel on four paws, trying not to think about how close they had actually come to filling that vortex that stood before them and the valley of the dead, with atoms and stardust all mixed in together with the smell of the newly departed.

Daniel settled himself into a better position on the floor of the room Horse had taken them into, and carried on with the threads of memory that seemed to still torment his waking hours. It was upon the second full day that they had reached Tameron's outer city. Each of the twenty-one Shapeshifters that had accompanied Daniel moved to shed their various animal forms as they made ready to enter the city. News of their arrival had been sent ahead by guards from the outer-rim that stood upon the ridge that guarded the Stones of Panthor; however, it hadn't quite reached the garrison ahead of them when they had surprised the guards with their arrival.

That had been odd; when they had come within viewing distance of the stones, they had stood in awe for many minutes. Long enough for those that had seen them to make their way towards the cities wards, as they felt for the very first time the immense vibrations produced from within the Monolithic Crystals that stood outside the city for many centuries. How had they beaten the warriors to their own gates, was still out for debate, when they had such a sophisticated warning system much more elaborately designed than anything they had within their own village.

Caberaana had, for the most part, been the recent Shapeshifter of their little village to have had any experience with moving through the molecules of that sort of shift, and even he had a slight intake of breath as the energy that those Stones produced caused massive energy fluxes within the body of anyone nearby. The warriors from Tameron must have fixed some form of time differential they could move through, in order to reverse the effects on their Aelven bodies from living and working near it. Had it malfunctioned, or had they been shifted somewhere else, instead of sending word to the others to warn them of the clan's arrival within its mainframe?

Daniel couldn't quite figure this out; it had all the makings of something hidden. He felt the effects of the Giant Stones long before the others, and his head felt like something was trying its best to twist itself completely off. The others, as they approached the pathway that would lead them forward to Tameron's front gates, could feel the burning sensation that accompanies the drift that these fluxes create. It spread itself out all over the entire region, vibrating at such a high rhythm that anyone within the area on the outskirts of Tameron felt as if their own bones were being mushed into tiny organisms, and squished into some tiny bubble that floated you away, and took you back where you originally had travelled from.

Each Shifter could only place their hands over their ears, trying their best to make it past, as it threatened to peel the skin off their hides. As it was, they passed within a mile of the actual site of the Stones, and rumour was the riders of the Black Dragons used them all the time. How that happened, was anyone's guess, but Daniel assumed they must have had some kind of amulet to allow them access to their proximity, for without something of that magnitude to deflect the energy output, it just wasn't possible to imagine.

Travellers not having business to the great city stayed well away from their energy readings, and those that had need, tried to visit Tameron only when absolutely necessary. And most of them used the far-gate at the opposite-side to gain access. They had no choice but to travel past them in some form or another, and although he wanted to puke, Daniel was equally sure the others couldn't feel the strong sensations he was feeling, or none of the party would have continued on towards the castle-wards.

Once inside the city's walls, their influence did not affect the everyday life of Tameron's inhabitants, and once they passed the threshold, the release was immediate and final. On the inside away from the outer-walls, the vibrations were all but diminished, leaving the villagers to go about their normal routines without fear of attack, or the occasional strike of blue light that seemed to be spitting out of the tops of them randomly. It was better than a host of warriors standing guard at their walls, for nobody would dream to intervene within the area, except a chosen few that regretted their choice the moment they had tried.

The Stones' original matrix continued to shimmer in and out of flux, as the Shapeshifters passed them by, maintaining both their place of origin and the one here on Tantaris they had been taken to. Its vibration could be felt long out into the water that ran its tides along the shoreline, folding among the reefs and inlets that encircled the continent of Water's-Deep in the southern section of the Continent. On certain days the effects could be felt all the way out to the Island of Symarr, and followed the vibration deep inside the massive Saltwater Trench that passed between the island and another piece of land recently raised skyward from its watery depths.

With the earthquakes rumbling near the Village of Sylmoor, new landmasses were coming up to breathe life into the world of the air-breathers. They smoked and sizzled as the hot molten lava crumbled off their not yet solidified surface, and struggled to hold onto a world they did not know. Soon enough they would find their footing, and would one day find themselves to be part of another great ring of reefs living upon the planet.

But, that would be sometime in the future — not during the linear timeframe which Daniel currently stood upon. And with any hope, not during the time he was alive, as it flowed and popped along the sea-swells, sweeping its molecules into the tides that formed and grew around the Dragon Island in the receding swells. But for now, he remembered the teachings he had been taught of Tameron's Stone Monoliths as a young whelp, and could only dream of a time that he again would not have to witness their arrival and placement here on Water's Deep.

It would seem that millions of years ago, they had been formed within the mother matrix of the crystal cave of Anthros. Anthros was a planet in the Star Nebula that had the rare ability to shift between positions that it would find rest within. There were times when this planet of some old and unknown origin would move through time, and hold a place in the skies of ancient and alien worlds; none of which have we seen the likes of, on this side of the divide for a very long time. Then it would inexplicably, in a flick of a heartbeat, be gone one day, moving along in windistic rhythm to its next location in the skies of another world, and we would not hear of its transit for another thousand or so years.

Anthros was a particularly unusual planet; one that did not behave as other planetary worlds of Fey origins, often did. Mind you, majik rarely allows for anything to behave in a Humanistic rational manner, now that the species of other Fey normally could be seen to follow another path. And this planet was no exception to that rule. It literally ran with the solar winds, and moved about the tides of space, through the different galaxies it floated with untold abandonment, following no particular pattern of reference, simply appearing out of the blue one day, then leaving to wherever it soul decided it would like to move. Sometimes it would stay for only a few hours, other times it would be there for only a moment and then in the blink of an eye just simply be gone, and you'd wonder if what you saw was indeed really there in the first place?

Not only did this planet have unique abilities that none of the other Fey worlds had, but something allowed it to have absolutely no fixed location within the normal spectrum of other planets' gravitational pull as well. It just ran wild through the open wiles of space, flowing through vast star systems and black holes without any noticeable effect on the surface structure of its massive crystalline matrices.

Oh right, you didn't know that the planet's surface world did not have the usual affair of dirt and rock, like what is expected of a floating ball of majikal stardust. Surprise! Daniel laughed, thinking how often Sibrey had said the same thing. She spoke constantly of what you Humans might have thought of that notion, leaving much of the world that you have become accustomed to understanding, to go straight out of the window and flutter off to where thoughts tend to go when they leave our minds.

So, with a bit of a history lesson, let s allow a simple common Shapeshifter to refresh your Earthy minds.

Normal Fey worlds have sentient life living upon them, which inhabit the flora and fauna of their surface structures. But Anthros was different; the entire planet structure was made up of huge massively charged crystalline pillars, whose formations interlaced like fingers along its upper stratosphere, creating life. It was also different in the fact that it was alive, where most of the other worlds of rock and meteor-dust were simply housing platforms for the Fey that resided on them. Anthros was entirely unique. If I was to tell you she herself was Fey, would it give you a new sense of what this planet actually was, and its connection with the other worlds?

Thus, the planet hosted actual life within its entire structure; sentient beings living and breathing in the crystal formations that made up its surface structure, where its lifeblood floated enhydro, trapped and glistening in the walls of the crystal shards, allowing anything that set foot on its surface world to live within its very bones. Those bones were constructed along several large crystal columns forming some rather obscenely huge obelisks and pillars, which grew to such gigantic proportions that they shimmered in the atmosphere high above, and far from the actual planet's surface.

The fact that the planet had the capacity for thought was unusual enough, but it also simply chose not to behave as other planets within Sopdet's vast network of worlds. Instead, it moved freely among the ones that were restricted in their gravitational pull towards whatever Mauntra they bowed to in their gravitational vortex, visited briefly, and then thumbed her nose as they stayed snagged in place.

Sopdet herself was just as unusual, as were her subjects on planetary worlds. However, that will be for another book that she has encouraged me to write in the near future, to include her life and stories of interstellar spacial infractions, into the minds of what you Humans thought were just a simple star called Sirius. For now she watched her beloved planet with a warm heart beating deeply in her deity breast, as its movements roamed without borders across her reign of spacial incursions, ignoring the fact she had no claim to the molecules of its own beating renegade heart. No, that should have been Danu's domain. But Danu had moved quietly away one dark and dreary night, with only the wind as her companion; which left her sister Sopdet to take her place to keep the stars from falling from their connections with the Fey of this realm. And Anthros be damned; no one told Anthros that it just couldn't swim among the stars looking for a lost deity, even if it was a planet that wasn't bound by the laws of physics or gravity.

It was a tricky situation. Daniel found himself admiring the planet's audacity at moving within her worlds like it was pushing its boundaries and flipping its nose at her ability to control its position with her winds. But Sopdet was no pushover, and just because the planet had no gravity keeping it within the rotational orbits of a fixed location in her skies, did not mean she had no umbilicus with which to control its movements, should she have need.

It was quite the opposite; in fact she knew all things that moved and floated about in the vast reaches of her spacial pastures of stardust and meteor tailings. And lovely Anthros was part of the plan like any other Fey planet that we have become accustomed to seeing in the galaxy today. It's just that we lowly Fey who live within the depths of blood and bone, inside a skeletal molecular transference of actual protein, do not know what it is. And had we any indication as to what that was we were definitely not in the proverbial loop of telling tales of her life-force; at least not for the time being...

But, I am digressing once again, with the tale of this lone voyaging planet that would roam the skies like a comet travelling to destinations unknown. Sopdet just didn't share that information with the plan she had for the beings of our majikal race of thinkers. But she did let other things escape into the wind. The story of the oldest Fey within our galaxy was part of everyone's vocabulary from the age they could walk and put words in their mouths, and that tidbit, had something to do with our little wandering planet called Anthros.

As it happened, on a day far, far, in the past, one of the lovely members of the Selmathen race had decided to go out for a galactic stroll, or, as some would like to call it, a celestial float-about. It was one of the younger bornlings of a renegade tribe that had showed interest in a seldom used doorway, where others of its kind had used it for taking them to a distant part of the galaxy, to explore and collect data to bring to the core of its teaching fathers. It had not been used in several centuries, and none of the resident Selmathens of this clan, knew whether it would still function with the new wormholes that ran occasionally through its feeding stream, as it crisscrossed through the older parts of fluidic space.

This creature sought out the stream, and determined that the juncture point was still functioning adequately well, but was located on a lesser travelled pathway on the far-side of the current mainstream of one of the less active addresses, and proceeded to move away from the travel destinations of its home-world. However, this particular window had acquired some company that did not belong to the normal Fey shadows of Shifters which normally filled the void, and as he moved from the one tunnel to another much older not previously known to the scholars of his race, it intrigued him.

As time would have it, something had interfered with its feed, causing the shift of the newer wormhole to transfer his body through this older tunnel, which had been susceptible to the solar winds of the Starshaper meteor that passed through that area of space just recently. As if on cue, the string of solar winds got a little too close to this stream of energy that had suddenly appeared, as the doorway the Selmathen had been travelling in opened up — locking it into position, just as the lovely renegade planet arrived in the mix. The jump-point of the crossed wormholes, created a vortex into the stream, leaving a single band of light to contaminate the transfer, and Anthros's gravity proximity had a suddenly deadly affect within the already flooded molecules of the other two wormholes travelling close by.

That single unidentified beam of light came from the far-side of Sopdet's temporal alignment, and straight into contact with the mix of the others moving through, as it travelled through the same point of space as the one Anthros was currently moving along beside. What lay behind its origins was still unclear, but for those standing directly in its path what was revealed to them behind its mask was a very real and full size planetary world not often seen around these parts, and unheard of to others not of Goddess stature.

At first it simply moved along like a ribbon of light dancing in the sky, as both points of substance moved around each other, staying well out of each other's range of flow, and waiting. Then something changed, as a single piece of floating meteor dust about the size of a pin-head accidentally manoeuvred too close to the string, and Anthros was pushed into the others' juncture point, merging the two for several microseconds.

The sound would have been deafening to all that had been in amongst the stellar mine-field, and everything changed as it fractured the timeline and exploded onto this side of the universe, ripping a singular hole in time for a fraction of that intensely, and violent millisecond. The moment the two collided with each other, a burst of light moved outwards and engulfed both the string and the destination of Anthros into the same point of space. In truth for this to happen, the Selmathen would have had to reach that juncture where they both converged at more or less the same time, in order for it to have transferred the Selmathen into its own rift and then close the hole it produced, before a black hole could form in its place trapping the Selmathen inside its newly formed wormhole.

The energy inside the rift would have been off the scale when this happened, and having no actual bone structure or skeletal framing inside its form probably saved its life; the Selmathen simply flowed along the rip, unconscious within the growing circumference of light, and bounced off the line of flow as it reached its pinnacle of convergence, joining the energy as it merged into the one pinhole of vernacular space.

Once the light returned to its normal incandescent refraction, the other entrance hole that had been partially serrated, simply separated itself from the joining, and the doorway changed its direction. Anything still alive out on the travelling wormhole that pointed in the direction of the planet that was able to sustain any life-form, dissolved.

From time to time, as the planet Anthros moved about, this event was known to happen several times over the lifetime of its birth-point. But the rarity of a life-form actually travelling through at the same time this was occurring was unheard of; not because of certain safeguards that were put in place to prevent such an occurrence from actually coming to fruition, but because of the actuality of it happening and being recorded in the parchment scrolls of the written history of the Selmathen race.

The ancient causeways this planet had attached itself to, were few and far between and the actuality of all three things occurring simultaneously, was unheard of. Had this happened any other way it was not something that would have been survivable for the Selmathens as a race. They might be the longest living creature that ever existed, but they were not immortal as some Fey liked to think. With only a handful of life-forms ever actually visiting the planet in over ten thousand years, who could have thought that a Fey life-form would have found itself in such a strange predicament, and one that would permanently change the history of today's world as we know it?

Daniel woke again, disturbed by something he did not understand. His lungs caught a whiff of something musky, as he sucked air into his lungs, waking up mid-snore and hiccuped with the incoming contaminate. He roused himself and scratched his face, feeling the cobwebs that floated down from above. The others in the room seemed unaffected, and appeared to have fallen into a much deeper and more restful sleep. He wished he had been able to follow their example, but there were far too many things jockeying for position inside his brain to allow him to drift in his thoughts to reach that doorway. But it wasn't long before it happened, and he sank blissfully into its arms, finding the threads of sleep once more and regaling the spiders above with blissful snores.

They continued weaving their silken webs, oblivious to Daniel's anxious mind, and the thread dove sideways before rattling around briefly, finding its correct mode of comfort. Somewhere between the first level of his sleeping mind and the next level of drift, he wandered off again, thinking of the history lesson he had been given as a child by the teacher who explored ideas with those outside his mountain air classroom, telling the tale about the arrival of the Panthorian stones, standing outside the city gates of the Aelven stronghold.

He drifted further this time, in his sleep, gaining refuge where the land of the dream began and his mind left off. However, this time he knew the words by memory. Which is where they found him drifting, unanchored by the chaos of Tameron's inner city walls.

The Selmathen had no choice but to follow the stream downward, as the doorway found itself in direct contact with the previously moving shift-point. The time dilation was twitchy, and could not withstand the added molecules of the being occupying the same place and time inside its rift. Instead, it chooses to gently move him. The Selmathen's unconscious mind simply relocated with the offering set before him, and drifted as one with the string that retracted its filtering conveyance through the voids of space. It instantly transferred with the stream of light the planet provided, as the flow of energy came out of the wormhole into the world of the crystalline atmosphere of the upper reaches of Anthros's orbit — where someone had thought he could survive, giving him refuge amongst an alien world.

Several things began to happen upon its arrival into this strange and alien world, as it slipped through the opening and moved into the open doorway of Anthros Major. It then pushed him ever so lightly within the solar winds of Anthros's highest mountain range, allowing his translucent wings to be caught in its tidal drift, moving him in the open breeze which directly came into contact with the crystals' vibrations. From there the shift-point bounced, alleviating any stress that had been put on his delicate flesh as it came into contact with the previous shift-point opening, which led his molecules directly in line with the planet's actual surface world, two miles straight down.

Legend says that when it got there after waking, it found a world completely covered from one pole to another with beautiful quartz crystal formations. As he explored and drifted along the solar winds, they seemed to take on a more musical vibration the moment the Selmathen arrived within the lower part of the atmosphere, out along the seeding grounds of their planets core. It hovered there and rested in a dense layer of vapour, as the clouds began to roll in overhead and the air became alive with static energy. The air around him carried within it a certain vibration as he moved wistfully through the mixture listening to its continuous humming noise; all the while, the lower sustainable atmosphere kept him away from the approaching storm above, growing stronger with each passing moment; one that appeared to be in direct correlation to his unexpected arrival.

By then, the nightfall of many years had begun to set. Overhead the light was replaced by a world of shadows, and the crystal life-forms that existed on this planet began to sing the dusk into being. Their language was something that intrigued the Selmathen, but in his weakened state, it became nothing more than a lifeline inviting him to stay and rest, while something about their song seemed to vibrate some sense of alarm, deep inside his highly evolved brain and warn him something had not been as it was.

The unease didn't resonate inside his body at first; instead it seemed to take on a life of its own as the humming continued to pacify his senses, assuring the Selmathen's higher brain function that it would be taken care of. Somewhere in the coming darkness, this was replaced by another feeling, much more tribal in nature, as the shadows lengthened, descending with greater speed on the world of crystallites and the humming continued, lulling it into complacency.

Several celestial objects in the darkening sky came into view, sending the reflection of the brightest of those stars along the edges of its planetary skin, creating sharpened shards to follow its moment as they shifted. They flexed, producing an effect not unlike the wind blowing the tips on a blade of grass and shimmered in the electrifying rift as it circled the entire planet, moving all the shards edges towards the sound, joining in on the choir of perfect pitch — the humming intensified. Yet, the Selmathen remained calm inside its protected shell, as the night changed the sky where the celestial objects one by one seem to disappear, giving off another sensation that replaced the first.

It came on stronger now, as the stars began to change their position and ran with the night as the planet jumped in shift. The sensation began to slowly change the planet's molecules, and it didn't take long before the song enchanted the Selmathen in a similar way to the Sirens of his home-world, mesmerizing him with his own reflection. The crystals allowed the beautiful shimmering body of the Selmathen to merge within the fixed matrix, making the Selmathen's own body sway almost hypnotically with their song, craving the symbiotic nature of this new planet's minerals.

The Selmathen was unconscious once again before the planet arrived at its new destination, allowing the shards to form around him as he slept. Meanwhile, the creature was no longer part of the outside world. Instead, this creature from another world was encased in its biosphere, and could be seen resting inside one of the bigger shards, as the outside began to grow upwards into the night sky moving with the stardust of the jump and growing to phenomenal proportions alongside the darkening stars.

As the crystals vibrated and moved upwards with the coming darkness, trying to catch the last rays of light receding along the cliffs, a new Mauntra joined their present location. Its voyage continued, stretching brightness along the crystalline fingers of clear quartz, while inside one of the bigger shards the Selmathen was rocked deeply in sleep.

Night-fall stayed on this world in its new rotation of planets among the stars, and safe and warm inside the crystal cocoon all seemed right with the world. The Selmathen tried to regenerate the energy he lost when he slid through the crossed wormholes of his own destroyed doorway. But, outside a storm was brewing, and he was no longer aware of the dangers; instead he slipped into a further state of stasis, while outside the crystals grew wildly, twisting and turning their stone-remains into something that resembled one of the majikal pods that grew on the garden planet of Naunas's moon Quinn. For the moment he remained safely out of harm's way, tucked inside in bedded bliss, oblivious to the surroundings on the outside. The storm that was fermenting raged on, fighting the elements that changed the face of the planet the Selmathen had accidentally been pushed into, to this strange new world.

That occurrence, would be the beginning of a whole new existence for the crystal life formation, and when the Selmathen reached his home-world many years later, it would change the very face and structure of the entire race that he would become — by starting a new species of Selmathens, which had previously never been seen before in any of the known worlds.

Many months passed by, and still the Selmathen did not wake; instead he chose to stay warm and cozy inside the safety of his sanctuary while the wounds he suffered from the crossing healed themselves and he regenerated. A few years passed, and still he remained tucked safely out of sight as the storms continued to rage on unhindered by anything in its path, wreaking havoc on anything in their way left out in the open.

It would take a thousand years for the Selmathen to find the threads of consciousness once more, and return his conscious mind to the world of the crystal cave that now surrounded his body. What presented itself when he awoke took him by surprise. The complexity of what had happened changed the face of his own luminescent skeletal shape, and completely concealed his beautiful body into the heart of his mineral soul.

But first, upon awakening, as he stretched long unused muscles, he felt a tiny pull on the underside of his belly. His brain, highly advanced as it was, was first confused as to its origin, and as the crystalline water flowed into other areas of his once fully functioning organs, he felt something new. It was then he realized something had changed, and the organs that once gave him life were no longer a part of his physiology. Instead, they were crystal-lized pieces of minerals, where once they had been alive and comprised of living tissue.

How was it possible to be alive, if he did not possess the ability to push blood through new organs now clearly made out nothing but calcified stone? But alive he was, and functioning on a level he previously had not been able to in the past. It wasn't long after that discovery he learned some-thing else was sitting inside the area of his non-beating heart. It seemed that while he slept, a single phantom shard of the matrix he had curled up inside, had entered his body vertically — growing right through his skin, and now lay wedged inside his inner-flesh where his heart use to beat.

It appeared he had slept longer than he previously thought, and during that time the mineral had taken his position of sleep into consideration and moved around him as best as it could, to cause the smallest amount of damage, threading itself away as it grew around the outside of his contain-ment field. Nevertheless, one day it found it could no longer find a way around his outer-shell, as several newer crystal formations began to grow rapidly around the area, forcing it to take the direct-route straight through the inner-workings of the heart of the crystal, which was still forming around his soft body.

Then, with a mineral that was just beginning to formulate from a much softer grain, it had moved gently upwards, piercing his skin from the outside edge and impaling his flesh as it grew. Somehow he had not felt it, and judging by the colour of the grain that ran on the outside of his body, it had all the appearances of providing some form of analgesic medi-cine that made the entry flawless, producing no pain. It had taken a very long time to move into the position he found it in, and when he woke the phantom spears at his back were just beginning to find his skin, and push themselves through to pin him to the sides of his place of rest. In another thousand years or so they too would have completely engulfed his body, leaving nothing left of his Selmathen skin or any chance for him to escape. He would have remained a prisoner, alive and entombed, without anything left active but his mind.

The crystal point had not emerged from the other-side of his body as of yet, still being young enough not to fully mature into the hardened older formula that lay all around him while he slept. Its molecular density was still very brittle inside his body, and it would take only a few moments for the crystal itself to actually break off from the main stem as he moved. It shattered its hold along the mother crystal's upper-reaches, and the bridge it had formed receded easily calling to the others to retreat slowly and release him from their celestial grip.

But the shard itself had become trapped, and had no way to retract its thin inner-cord. It was forced to sacrifice itself for the Selmathen they had cocooned, and protect from the raging storms on the surface world far above. Its root waited patiently, humming for its loss on the outside of the Selmathen's skin, while the new mineral fixed itself to his spine, giving it a life force that it could use without having to be joined to its mother root, as the Selmathen began to move away from the chamber, healing itself to its newest condition.

He drifted up and began to squeeze through the quartz windows that had been left wide-open for his return to the world that he came from. The world of quartz had been kind to think of the eventual return that someday he would have to make; leaving behind the warm calmness below and entering into the tempestuous world of the surface far above. He fluttered, stretching his wings. Long since complacent to be nothing more than appendages, they had lain in dormancy over the many years of stillness. However, they worked flawlessly as he squeezed his body through the openings they had provided for him, trying to make his way back to the world up above.

The crystal shards had grown exponentially since last he had seen this land, and he moved slowly through a vast underground crystal network of caverns that had grown as large as some of the Elemental cities he had visited on various planets in his other life. They had considered everything; providing several bridged sheets of flattened crystals that had formed perfectly, giving him the ability to ascend flawlessly, as he moved across the vast caverns that had formed while he slept.

The lone crystals he first saw had set deep roots inside some of the vast crevices that seemed bottomless at first glance, but really ran perpendicular alongside deeper trenches that moved about the planet's core, taking him from one opening to another. Each of the caves that he moved through had been there long before he arrived; that much was obvious. Each of them had been literally carved out of the groundwater, with the constant rainfall that seeped in through the cracks that made up the surface world above during the storm season — combining with the growth rate of the crystal's vast network of matrices, living and breeding along various rich mineral veins of similar gemstones. It was inconceivable to think of the age of some of them now standing nearly seventeen hundred feet high, as he tried to go around some of the smaller and less dense offshoots, which had been living in a symbiotic relationship alongside various other crystalline tentacles of other shapes and sizes of the same mineral. He wondered how something that had no atmosphere could produce the water that ran in rivulets down the crystal ceilings and dripped in his face, but his thoughts were interrupted by a constant twitch still festering inside his body, and he forgot the thought as it passed from his mind.

The shard made him itch, and the further towards the surface he climbed the worse it began to annoy him. It was apparent quite quickly, that it would be impossible to remove the sliver of quartz in the usual manner, as things inside where the shard was placed began to tingle and feel very odd, as it began to settle into place along his ribs. He tried to visualize the placement of the shard and get it to move with his mind, hoping he could make it slide just enough towards the area it had first entered his body, so he could remove it with the rough edges of the walls that lay inverted and twisted all around him. But it had grown into his inner-core in much the same way a surgeon would place a piece of metal to repair a broken bone.

He stopped to watch his reflection, and looked to see if he could spot where it had decided to put out its roots. It was just on the other-side of where his heart used to sit, and he could see the initial piece of crystal pulsating through a range of different colours when he bent far enough to see its reflection shining through his translucent skin, mirrored in the walls of the crystal cave. He watched it glow; it was rather lovely in its full range of motion, changing from deep red, to pulsating orange, then over to green, and finishing with a bright purple fuchsia as it shimmered to nothing and faded away. Then it would start all over again, as he watched in confused fascination, through the lacy filaments of his new wings. It was incredibly odd, and had it been in any other creature or inanimate object he would have found it extraordinarily beautiful; unfortunately, it was inside something he was currently using, and it had begun to make him feel a bit unwell with the thought.

As he was thinking, it started to change its behaviour. He stayed and watched as it began to pulsate faster, causing a head rush, then moved to transform into the actual shape and size of the original heart it had replaced. Now taking on a life of its own, it changed its appearance and began to grow fatter. Then finding that to be completed, the shard opened up areas along the upper-edges of the termination point, sending out slivered spears of some form of mineral — seemingly moving and threading its way along the upper-reaches of where he used to have his molecular spine.

In fact, it was attaching itself to the area where, had he been more Fey than Elemental; it would have been along the edges of a certain boney-mass more reminiscent of the liquid formula of a Pizenean jellyfish. But, although tiny with respect to other creatures of Fey origins, this one was indeed becoming a permanent part of his body. It became quickly apparent that he would need to find his rest, soon.

He spotted a shelf off to his left and drifted towards its location. The vibration the sentient shard was creating produced such overpowering emotions inside his mind that he couldn't use the current method of propulsion he maintained to keep his body awake. While he settled himself on one of the larger sheets of flat crystal spears, the shard used the landing as a regeneration point, refuelling his new Selmathen matrix with several loose strands of the mineral it needed to maintain deep inside his new body.

The Selmathen slept momentarily, before he would be forced to land and drain the last of his energy reserves. He would try once again in the morning to move towards the surface world. The shard continued to pulsate and feed itself the mineral it would need to move away on its own from the planet of its birth. It would be an exhausting trip for both of them, and when next the Selmathen awoke — sometime in the coming days, both would continue as one solid entity to move through the vastness of the cave around them towards the surface world far above.

When he did wake from his nap of almost a week, his skin where the shard had first entered was irritating him. While he slept, a selenite scab had formed over the open wound, trying to heal itself. It pinched him as he left the slab of crystal behind, rising up towards another opening he had not noticed in his sleepy state before. As a last ditch effort to remove the shard, he tried for a time to rub his body through the barnacled elestial blocks that covered this new section of walls. They were sharper than the ones in the previous cave, and filled with jagged edges all over the edges in larger numbers. It merely resulted in wedging the shard further and further inside, producing more of the tendrils that were beginning to root themselves into his sides, by the minerals it had ingested while he slept.

This new sensation was triggered by him, as he peeled the newly formed healing crystals right off his skin. While he continued to rub the freshly opened wound, the scab shattered where he left it, disintegrating into sand on the cave floor. The new wound tried to repair itself, sending out a network of spider-web filaments that formed along the various nerve endings of his skin where it had tried to heal itself. As soon as the nerve endings constricted, it sent a signal to his brain to sleep again. The moment he slowed down and quit trying to peel the hide off his skin, it receded and let him continue to move without feeling tired.

By the time the Selmathen reached the cooler air of the surface world above, the planet had entered a meteor storm as it had shifted once again and put itself right into the middle of the meteor field of Angagan. This had not been expected, and since the planet had given him the necessary means to escape, it seemed almost cruel to take it away again simply because of a little storm they had not foreseen.

Unfortunately for the Selmathen, what was became what is, and the planet had no choice but to release a sedative that knocked him out cold, while once again they retrieved him, to bring him back down to the safety of the caverns underground. He lay there for several days, while the storm once again picked up speed, raging on and creating havoc in the darkened sky. This was not how they had envisioned it to be, and had they any other choice in the matter, they would have let him leave; leaving him to his own devices. But they had to protect their seedling, and had he gone ahead and tried to dodge the strikes, it might not have ended well for either species.

Angagan was known for its ruthlessness, especially when it came to larger dust particles within the vast tail that trailed behind him as he went about the galaxy. Had Anthros thought this through, they might have picked another drift-point to move him through, but then again the shard would not have survived the impact of such a shift. Someone needed more time for the shard to become stronger, and with this jump-point that goal had been achieved without a single struggle to keep him here.

The vastness of the underground cavern where he was taken to was something much different than he had seen before. The Selmathen race tried to achieve many things during their long and productive lifespan, but being made up of a material that was not only translucent to the eye, but also resistant to holding any form in anything but a temporal flux, made it almost impossible to live in anything that was not already created from the original formula of their planet's birth.

This planet had an unusual ability to breathe on its own, and produce whatever the being that lived within its world needed. It now gave healing properties that were associated with a calming spell, and as he lay unconscious in his current state — sick from the shard's molecules running atwitter within his body, the sentient mind of the collective continued to sustain his life force. For the moment it nurtured him with its majik, and allowed the shard to formulate a new lifecycle, all the while keeping within the restrictions of the Selmathen's innocence to its arrival. Time passed once again overhead, and the nights turned into longer days.

Through the centuries, his physiology would change, but for the moment it was something that the Selmathen had no knowledge of. The storm above raged on for many years, severing any hope he might have had of returning through another loop to his original point of entry and back to his homeland.

So, once again the Selmathen had been returned to the underground world, as all above him continued to rage with continuous seasonal storms that came and went from the confines of space, as they smashed headlong into the planet that had no shielding. It grew then divided into several creatures over the years, and the crystals sheltered all of them as they had before, with the one being that had come and stayed within their bones.

When he woke from the sedative and emerged once again he realized that he had become stranded. The doorway, from which he would need to move into the new secondary shift-point Anthros had promised to build him, was no longer present. The remains lay scattered upon the floor of the chamber he had been sleeping in destroyed beyond hope of reattaching it to the previous wormhole.

Nothing remained intact, as he searched the remnants of the gate for any threads he could physically barnacle his new body to. Instead, the laser compass that would have pinpointed his home-world, using the vibrations of his own body was simply stuck in the position it would have opened had he returned back before the storm had hit here all those years ago. It had tried to heal itself from the shattered injuries it had sustained, covering itself in several new formations in the beginning stages of growing over the wound, but nothing of the former doorway was visible to the eye.

It would be many years before the Selmathen would get another chance to move through another doorway the planet would reconstruct to reach his place of origin, and when he did, he would not be as he was when he left, but a new species that evolved on this planet made of beautiful multidimensional crystal. He would arrive with another life inside his mind, and live in harmony with crystalline creatures that had been formed and created with the majikal essence of the crystal caves and their little Selmathen hosts.

The Selmathens as a race were from the organism that hosted both male and female bodies as one. Their need to find a mate was not within the spectrum of their own genetic makeup, and they did not need to use the necessary means to give birth as other Fey creatures do on consensual terms. When the time came to be two, they simply would split their atoms in half allowing another copy to just become, which would then shimmer into the world and arrive without fanfare.

The survival of the species required nothing more than that, with no other agenda in mind and no formula to recoup a loss civilization back to its former glory, it created several copies of itself when it needed to. It was not done with any rapid acceleration, like the Human worlds had done, but in keeping the race alive and well to continue their work among the stars. It simply allowed the race of beings to continue, but not the required family lineage like that of other species; until now. So as the Selmathen lived within the beautiful crystal caverns in the underground tunnels of the world of sparkling light, he continued to split into others of his kind, giving him the necessary means to survive through the years on this world with a personal umbilicus to his new family.

It took about a hundred more Fey years before Anthros shifted again towards a planet with doorways suitable for the Selmathens. When the morning air filtered down inside the cavern they had converged inside one day, just shy of the hundred year mark, they heard a strange humming noise that relayed the information it was time to go. Anthros had finally found a drift-point that they could use, and now it was time to say goodbye. It quivered slightly, not moving, waiting for them to move towards the doorway it offered, while another galaxy maintained the address the new Selmathens could capture to move off towards their own home planet, as it drifted through space with a familiar blue hue. When it did, they were off after all those years cut off from the rest of the Fey race, and Anthros momentarily said goodbye to its newest creation.

There had been one Selmathen who arrived on Anthros, and seventeen of these creatures that had begun to evolve when next the planet shifted to its new location, travelling once again towards their home-world. A home-world only one of them had ever seen. Each of the new Selmathens that came through the shift carried a single piece of crystal shard lying deeply embedded within its own molecular strand. This had been passed along through the splitting of their atoms from the original piece of crystal that had become lodged within the original's own genetic makeup. Living within the world of silent shimmering rock, the absorption of sorts came into being, and each of the new offspring would take a piece of it as they continued to be created throughout this particular Selmathen lineage.

They were joined and linked as one mind and did not belong to two creatures, but lived and breathed as one. Neither was dominate over the other, and it was the beginnings of a separate race of Selmathens that now live in this world of the Fey, far superior to the race they had left behind. They moved about the interstellar worlds as they passed through other worlds to return to their roots, travelling through a familiar world that Humans knew to get back to their own planet, and played in swallow caves while the doorways shifted and finally locked into place, providing them with the means to go back home.

The planet they visited was called Earth, and many Humans had seen their shadows in various areas where the shift-point doorways were set to open. They stayed for only a short while, and then continued through the rift as the window opened and they disappeared into the realm of the Fey. From time to time they would go in search of Anthros, and each time they did, and she allowed them entry, they would be presented with several beautiful stones that would one day become the Stones of Panthor.

Each time they visited her, they left behind a blueprint within her crystals, which maintained the species of Selmathens and gave them unbridled access to her doorways. It remains to this day, encased in the energy field of the caves that still exist after centuries have passed. These new creatures that followed the pathway that their ancestor originally came from, found their way among the strange new world by instinct alone. They moved with greater speed than their ancestor, and although they were from the exact same race of Elementals, that was as far as the similarities ran. They evolved within the main frame of a planet that moved in different shift-point molecules; therefore, it produced an entirely new species of Selmathens, whose genetic makeup had been altered to withstand the amazing energy that the crystals resting on this planet produced.

The new race of the species had arrived, and with it the emergence of the race as a whole would soon follow. But this new race of Selmathens would have a much broader spectrum of understanding with regards to a much more intellectual intelligence. It would be able to function with their minds, as well as their wings; learning vast amounts of knowledge through the use of telepathy with other species, instead of just filtering through the vastness of space looking for anything that moved to encourage its interest.

When this new species arrived on Tantaris, it brought with it the knowledge of building these vast portals to other worlds and with that knowledge came the emergence of the huge Crystal Monoliths; which they helped to transport to form the link with the Stones of Panthor. The link to the planet of their origins was always within range of the Stones that were placed on Tantaris. The silent link followed Anthros through the various star systems it continued to wander, allowing for its energy to always remain true and extremely strong. Had anything ever tried to destroy the Stones, the Stones themselves would have de-materialized and shifted back into the doorway that had been designed especially for them, disappearing within the dimension that they had once been part of back on Anthros.

Their energy was alive with sentient thought, just like the crystals living on Anthros, which explains their reaction to the Fey upon Tantaris. That knowledge also belonged to the Tuatha De' Danann; they too have another of these species of Stone Monoliths living outside the Aggulf Elkcum mound, while parts of it were sunk deep in the caverns where they had built their city. That set of Stones had never been seen by the Shapeshifters as a whole, but some like Daniel had heard of its existence through their travels. With that, the dream changed and Daniel momentarily came out of his thoughts and moved down upon the planet he was now resting his old bones on.

Once again the day began, caught in some kind of time loop that moved each of them into their own separate dreams. Daniel's clan appeared to have repeated their arrival. But this time, as the Shapeshifters emerged near the outskirts of the Stones, it was with another thought that came to Daniels mind. Where were the other Dragonlords and their black mounts, if Sibrey had made it to the trees without incident? They should have been outside of the village in the open fields they had passed. The moment they had been able to get settled with Horse, he wondered what had happened to the ones who had flown these doorways by way of the Dragons. It hadn't been very long; while the others sat drinking and finishing off their meals, the scene changed, and one of the Captains of the main guard asked for Daniel to join him in his study to speak in private. He was an unusually short man for such a prestigious position, but the others had not seemed to be outwardly concerned with this diplomatic faux pas, as he occupied a position that was usually held for those who were larger than life. However, he had an air of confidence in his speech, as he conferred with others in the room of similar rank; neither of whom seemed to be concerned in regards to this in the slightest. He watched and wondered why he had been sent for, waiting for them to finish, as several officers and warriors of various descent gave him leeway as they saluted the captain of Tameron's King. Finally he ushered Daniel into his office to speak privately while they moved away to duties unknown.

It occurred to him that they would be bringing him in to speak in regards to his daughter's welfare, but what he didn't realize was that they also had not heard from the Dragonlords since their departure almost seven days ago. Daniel was stunned. How could this be? It had only been two or three days ago, not seven, when they had left to follow the Dragon-riders from their village. Where had they gone before they arrived to claim Sibrey? Were they not one of the most important villages in all of Tantaris? He was floored, and the first trickle of dread started to fill his heart. Was this not where the King and Queen of the Aelves resided? How could they not know where their riders had gotten to? He was starting to feel a little sick.

"Have you heard about my daughter, at least?" Daniel enquired, with the feelings of dread starting to trickle down his arms and move towards his toes.

"Your daughter is safe; that we do know. The information was given to me through channels much more reliable than the one that was found to have been severed," he said with ease, making Daniel start to feel somewhat better. But, Daniel was still uneasy; he realized all of this was out of his control, and the Captain of the guards had only given him more of a mystery, which was beginning to make things feel more uncomfortable by the minute. There was silence in the room for not more than a few seconds, but each passing millisecond seem to feel like things were starting to flow in slow motion, and his head had started that darn headache again.

"When did you hear from your source last?" he asked the Captain, shaking the feelings of dread out of his skin. The silence had grown longer within the small room as he looked away briefly, making it seem like things were moving around trying to make the room even smaller. Things started to float, just above his sight line, and each time he turned to watch them they would move just out of visual reach.

The Aelf turned towards Daniel with a grin on his face, shaking a finger in his direction. He started to answer the question that Daniel had asked, but he didn't get the chance. All of a sudden, he disappeared with a popping sound and was gone from the room, as female voices could be heard calling him back.

Daniel swore; he didn't want to, but he did it twice, as he jumped up knocking over his chair in the process, backing up and skidding into other things strewn about the chamber. He was alone in the tiny room; there was no trace of the guard Captain, or that he had ever been in the room. He looked down at his hand. The Captain had poured them both a hot cup of coffee just before he had disappeared, and as Daniel looked down at his cup in his hand, he found it not only cold, but covered in cobwebs. He swore again; this time he threw the coffee mug to the far side of the room and watched the contents turn into dust as it hit the wall and drifted down to the floor, dissolving among the spider-webs that the room was encased in.

Things started happening rather fast after that, and it didn't take him more than a few seconds to reach the door. He was even faster running towards the stables where the others had been billeted. He ran with fear for what he knew would be the end result; moving as fast as he was able to move without crashing into anything, or anyone, as he continued across the courtyard. He needn't have tried; he almost killed himself in the process. The end result would have been the same either way. It was at that time, when he came through the doorway where the others should have been resting fast asleep inside, that he realized he was alone. No trace of his clan remained.

His race across the courtyard had been undertaken with one thing in mind: to find the others and let them know what he had witnessed. He hadn't realized, or for that matter noticed along the way, that there wasn't a single breathing living thing anywhere in sight and the castle was folding up behind him as he went. He was alone as he skidded across the cobbles, and the castle and its entire population upped and dissolved, leaving him in the middle of between here and nowhere in sight.

The swearing continued for a while, and with it came a stomping of feet and the occasional throwing of rocks. Daniel was pissed. He should have been frightened, but he was quickly becoming madder at himself, not thinking straight on the true reason of the original matter. It was about then that it occurred to him, and he had to think this one through. Who the hel was that, and how had he been talking to the captain of the guards when he hadn't even met him? The Shapeshifters had remained in the room while he slept, and the one they called Horse was still somewhere out there in the ether.

Things weren't making any sense, as made his way back across the empty drawbridge now covered in rust and recent rock-slide that had taken part of it away and left it in ruins. Off in the distance he spied one remaining turret, which for some reason continued to stand strong. Alongside, and circling the tower, he could just make out a single set of stone steps winding around the circumference of it, leading to a window perched high above the ground facing the mountains. He ascended those stone steps with caution, hoping that he hadn't made the wrong decision and they would tumble into the gorge at its feet. Upon reaching the top stair he found a small dimly lit room on his right, and just at that moment, when he thought he was starting to lose his mind, he looked out the window and saw a team of Shadowland horses moving out into the waves pulling a royal carriage behind it disappearing from view across some ancient sea.

"Bloody hel!" was all he said before his headache came on full force and took him away to another place. He fainted, landing on the floor of the room he had arrived inside, with compliments of a certain damn Sprite, minus one slightly amused Centaur who had been guarding the doorway of the space in-between.

"Gotcha! Welcome to the kingdom of the Cloud People, Daniel Shifter. Now that wasn't so hard, was it? Why you shifters, seemed to have such a difficult time crossing through, is beyond me?" Horse turned his head snickering away, and closed the great iron doors to the world of the land Fey.

CHAPTER TWENTY-SEVEN

Tamerk and the Cloud Realm

Sibrey moved around in her sleep, like one caught in the grip of a night terror that ran along the recesses of her brain. She had been restless for more than an hour, tossing and turning inside the room. They stood from time to time, checking in on her outside the majikal locks, as the time clock continued to count down and drift along the filaments of yet another dream. She had taken a fairly nasty tumble, causing significant bruising, which they had only been given a short time to re-set before the new time-lock enchantment had been completed, and locked back into place. Nina wondered whether Hexe had been able to restore her body to its original state before the fall occurred; however, despite her reservations, all seemed to be moving along smoothly.

Hopefully it was enough to heal the mind as well, or Hexe would have to be called to once again try to move further inside her mind, and dig deeper into why she was having such strange nightmares. Nina got up from her chair, and moved closer to the doorway to have a peek. Arddhu had done his best to keep her safe inside her corporeal form, as she slept down below after spending the night deeply hallucinating, while up above they tried to get the dream sorted and move her further in to the Goddess realm for safer keeping.

"She is just dreaming child, the medicine worked. See? Look at her face, the bruising is almost gone." Horae moved up beside Nina, resting her arm across Nina's shoulders. The bruises at once seemed to fade away, as if Horae had ordered them to disappear. "See, all gone." She pointed to Sibrey as she turned towards them in her sleep, moving one of her arms so they both had a better view of her lovely face, now unmarred by the ugly shades of black.

"She looks like she is in pain?" Nina queried back.

"Honey, believe me when I tell you, you worry too much. She's all right, I promise you."

"So what do we do with her after the dream ends?" Nina found she had been thinking about this silently for a while; it was only as she was thinking about it, that she found herself actually speaking the thoughts out loud, and was slightly surprised when Horae answered her back.

The voice echoed in the silence of her mind, coming to the surface as she muddled with the questions inside her head. Horae's words came out to reveal the reality of the situation that was about to reach the surface of her thoughts.

"Well that won't be happening for a while now. Before we have to worry about it, and I know we all are guilty of doing just that, there is much more to be done elsewhere on the home-front." Nina sighed as she turned to follow Horae across the room, listening as she continued to talk to her with encouragement, while taking her away from Sibrey's chamber walls.

"So, shall we go and greet our friends who are just starting to settle inside the castle's meeting chambers? Besides, if we hurry, I have it on good authority that Tamerk has been spotted just along the outer-edges of the barriers, and will be coming in soon to join us as well."

"Tamerk, here?" Nina was surprised. Tamerk's appearance in the middle of all this was an event, and to have their old teacher amongst the Oracle crowd was a rarity along the fringes of the Goddess Realm. Horae glanced at the young Goddess before continuing on.

"He has agreed to give us a hand with the calling of the order, to help with the new coven that has been arriving since dawn." Nina sighed.

"I forgot that had already begun to fall into place. I've been too busy with Sibrey to notice the extra celestial signatures permeating the castle solars for the last few hours." Nina looked longingly back in Sibrey's direction one last time. "Has Tamerk found the Bowl of Kalmayta then?"

"That was what we agreed to, I believe," Horae answered, knowing full well that the bowl had been given up for lost after the last calling of the order. Moraig had been to blame for that. But stranger things have been accomplished in the past; however, this was Tamerk we were talking about, so the odds were good: Either way, it would not have been easy for him if he did actually locate it drifting in the stellar winds, deep among the String Nebula's many home-worlds.

Horae moved toward the pitcher of water Hexe had placed on the small side table, taking a goblet and draining some of the elixir before examining the contents with an affirmative eye. Triduana, their compére, had brought it up specifically from her secret grotto where she resided beside the Sacred Oak tree. It was the same Oak tree near the spot where Sibrey's actual body's Fey particles still slept, way down on the surface of the Planet where a certain feline entity guarded her actual sleeping form.

She held it up to the light and watched the bubbles slide from one side of the glass to the other, reminding her of what it would look like if she was on a boat rocking on the water.

"This never seems to taste the same each time I drink it. It's really quite wonderful. This one tastes like Pandora berries. It really is outstanding; would you like to try some before we head down?" Nina turned away from the time locked window, to watch Horae pour herself a second mug full of bubbling liquid and raise it up once again, to the filtered light streaming in from outside.

"See, this one has turquoise threads filtering in and out, like little fish trying to swim up rapids in a rain storm." Nina giggled, listening to Horae's description of Triduana's majikal waters.

"No thanks, I haven't got any more room left inside my stomach for fish. Besides, while you went to check on things, I had a nice full goblet that was equally fascinating. It never gets boring; I simply don't know how she manages it. Mine blew air bubbles, sounding like a series of underwater hiccups, turning it a bright pink as they exploded into my face, and now I feel like I've got the whole damn river inside my gullet, guts and all!" Horae nodded, and laughed at Nina as she held onto her stomach in a series of mock explosions.

"Triduana likes to add a bit of majik to all her potions, especially those that she knows we will try." Horae still held the mug in her hand and swirled it around in the air, watching it gather more colours, before drinking it down in one swift motion. "Ah, this one is exceptional; we must thank her for the effort she put into its creation."

"While you're at it, why don't you ask her to slow down on the fizzy bubbles in the next batch? I'm sure that there is something just as spectacular in other ingredients she could get her hands on, somewhere down in that cave of hers, that wouldn't make my stomach jump through hoops every time I try to drink it." Horae burped rather loudly, unbecoming of a Goddess, as Nina looked on in mock horror at the air bubbles that came into being from out of her mouth.

"You know something that has always made me wonder about?" Nina held out her finger tips and watched as she blew the bubbles across the tiny air currents that danced along the edges of her thumbs, letting them take to the air currents which moved about the window sill. "When I was just a small little Goddess," Nina started, "you know at night, when I was learning how to improve on the way I could manipulate and change the dreams of the young Fey children, I often wondered how Arddhu had been able to live among Humans on the world of their Earth for as long as he did." She sighed, looking at the bubbles as they continued to dance across the room. "It just seems so impossible, to not have the freedom to do our majik like we do here." When she didn't go on, instead simply stopped, transfixed by the bubbles moving around the room, chased by the Mauntra light moving down the walls, Horae answered her in hushed tones.

"It's something that isn't even thought about much, is it?" She tuned briefly to Nina as her sister caught one of the bubbles, and proceeded to lure it down her fingertips. Horae smiled at her dream twin. "I guess it's like breathing for us, and isn't even registered inside our brains that it is something special. I'm sure it must have been difficult for him." Nina, now lost in bubble wars, simply shrugged at her, popping several bubbles that had landed on her arms, not really listening to her twin talking about what she had initiated about Humankind and their critical beliefs of majikal ways. Then, as if by design, all the bubbles seemed to pop out of the room at the same time, as Nina came to her senses.

"Hey, I'm not finished yet; dumb bubbles, always in a hurry." Horae ignored her as she moved about the room trying to see if there were any stragglers hanging about, as Nina realized there were none to be seen. She walked back to Horae, picking up the conversation as if she hadn't strayed from its content.

"Truly it really makes me thankful to have never visited that planet until after my schooling days had ended, because I'm not so sure that I could have refrained from having majik in my everyday life." Horae laughed, thinking about the uproar it would have caused, while Nina, slightly preoccupied, went for another peek at the window to the room Sibrey slept in.

"I'm sure it would have scared the bejeebes out of the entire race." Horae continued talking as if Nina had stayed, now attempting to throw small bolts of light around the hallway that skittered off the stones and bounced along the floor and out of sight. Several small creatures that lived within the stone yelped, coming out of their holes to yell at the time Goddess. Horae stuck her thumbs in her ears, and used her mind to give them little funny feathers along their eyebrows. The feathers sprouted quickly, growing into a second line of long eyelashes above their brows. The creatures, who had been minding their own business when she had sent the lightning bolts crashing along the floor, yelled their displeasure, now trying like mad to pluck them out before they majikally turned into long wings along their foreheads.

Several had already taken to the air, and were flying about the corridor with feathers sprouting all over their little bodies — the air filling with tiny Elemental Stoney Mason Bee bodies, floated with no rhyme or reason to their flight patterns, then crashed like mad into whatever came into contact with their new appendages. Madness ensued, and each tried like a maniac to remove what was in reach, before they crashed headlong into whatever came into contact with their upper face, making them all look like a bunch of crazy canaries covered with feathers too long for their bodies.

In a majikal world, nothing was too outlandish. Their language grew colourful and their heads came unattached from their bodies, while they screamed at Horae, floating down the corridor pecking away at whatever came within reach, trying like hel-buckles to hold on to anything that would stop their sudden rush down the middle of the air currents that had arrived, just in time for Nina to turn back around to talk to Horae.

Her face said it all. As Horae raised her goblet to her young sister Goddess in salute and drank it down, thousands of tiny little bee bodies ran after their heads in all directions, bumping into various things that got in their way, finding themselves in a bonafide pickle. All the while, they were further complicated by the second Goddess's movements towards them, creating a secondary motion in the air currents they were floating in, reversing their trajectory. They blew upwards right through the stone walls to another part of the castle, many floors above and kept going.

Nina began to laugh, forgetting for just a moment Sibrey and her little Shapeshifter body, was still sleeping in the other room. Her laughter rang out in the corridor, expressions of glee echoing throughout the entire structure. Horae joined her as the last of the bubbles from the water she had drunk were absorbed inside her skin, making their way down towards her inner esophagus and exploded outwards in a rather unsavory belch.

"Funny thing was I needn't have worried. You see, being a time Goddess, if I had to actually go down and live with Humans, I would never have that problem. I'd just erase the memory by moving about in time and changing the event to suit the moment when the majik proved to be too much, for either them or myself."

Nina stopped laughing. "What?" she asked, looking at Horae, perplexed.

Horae groaned, and smacked her in the arm. "You know, the not having that majik thingy you were obsessing about earlier."

"Oh, right," Nina said, finally getting it. "Funny girl, but what does that have to do with headless Mason Bees?"

"What, indeed, my little Princesses? Are we a wee bit bored?" Someone had entered the room silently, behind both of them, as the laughter had distracted their normally acute hearing from detecting the approach. When the voice actually spoke, both Horae and Nina nearly jumped out of their skin, launching themselves skyward before floating back down to the ground landing in a pile of fluff and feathers. The voice laughed at the two of them, as a few Stoney Mason bees instantly reverted to their former selves some-where deep inside the bowels of the stone-walls with yelps of something foreign sounding in their buzzing language, all mixed in with a couple of swallowed feathers that were still coming out of their mouths, as the spell lost its potency and they scuttled away to safety.

The Goddesses finally regained their footing. Just as they came back down to solid ground, that familiar voice started to regale them with his version of events of Horae's childhood years. "You my dear child, made just as many mistakes as any of the students I taught." Tamerk smirked, as he came into the room just in time to hear the banter between his Time and Dream Goddesses having a little fun with their memories of growing up in the arms of the Divine.

"Tamerk!" they both shouted and moved towards him, after brushing themselves off, leaving the occasional feather to float above in the air currents whenever it came crashing into their celestial energy. Each Goddess, upon reaching him, almost knocked the poor old soul into the next room, after the big Fascuin Centurian hug they gave him landed him in a puddle of Goddess and Stoney Mason bee molecules, all blended together to make a fine kettle of divine stew. They picked themselves up, smacking him in the arm with Goddess strength punches that made him try to block their movements and duck for cover.

Their individual strength behind those punches would have sent the local Fey populace through the castle walls and into the watery sea, back out where it stood just outside their door. But Tamerk was able to block them without a second thought, as he smiled at each of their distinctive laughs, and grinned wildly. "Now girls, I haven't been gone that long, and it's not like a little Troll like me could actually write and tell you all about my day in the middle of the woods." He laughed wildly at the hilarity of his own remark, being that Horae was a time Goddess and all; one with the ability to manipulate the quantum doorways of time at her discretion. Why, it could possibly have only been a few seconds since last they had seen each other in the shadow of her true ability; however, it always came to mind when he travelled to see each of them through the years, what she was capable of achieving.

"Now, what was that all about?" Tamerk pointed to a few Mason stragglers that had not yet found their flux, and were floating away trying to gather their parts; somehow missed as the majik had disintegrated around them. Nina turned to watch, as several rolled around different areas of the room muttering away wildly under their breath at the turn of events. A few had reverted to sliding the sides of their heads against pieces of stick or stone shards they had pried loose, trying to retrieve some semblance of order in their little minds as they loosed the last of the stubborn feathers that had been locked into place, refusing to budge. One moved towards Tamerk's side, and jumped onto his shoulder to whisper something in his ear, then realized his head was continuing on down the corridor. Tamerk retrieved it much to the happiness of one confused bee, and after screwing it on as tight as he could get it, he carried on with the original intension of Fey-narking on them.

They watched its eyebrow rise up at one end still covered in feathers, making him look even more hysterical to the Goddesses, who cupped their hands over their mouths, trying not to begin laughing once again. The Mason turned to Horae with his hands on his hips, and spat at the air in her direction. It moved towards her and then stopped in midstream, just sort of hanging there, as she looked pleased with herself, while the substance looked all honey-like and gooey, frozen in her time link. Tamerk listened to the little Mason, nodding with each interpretation of his whispering tale.

"Hmm, is that so? Really truly, my little Horae did that to you? Such a bad Goddess; I'm sure I will have a talk with her, and she will be punished accordingly. Yes that is true; she really should have been born a Witch. But you know how Goddesses are; that was simply not a factor in her birth rite. Yes, that is true, I am sorry that I didn't get here sooner, and I think that in the future she will try to do better." The Mason stopped talking and looked in her direction, suspiciously. Although he was quite finished the story, he wasn't by any means letting her have the last laugh; instead, with one final sentiment, he gave her a nose flicking salute, and popped out of sight just as she went to knock him off Tamerk's shoulders with a flick of her fingers, causing the goo to retreat back into the walls and follow the little creature as it made its escape.

Tamerk laughed heartily at the both of them, catching her hand just as she came to bring him back within her time dilation field, and connect with its little body. She let him go in relative peace, smiling weakly at her teacher.

"Nothing ever changes. What else have the pair of you been up to?" To look at the two of them, they appeared innocent enough; however, that was far from the truth, as both shrugged simultaneously, offering him a drink of Triduana's brew as a peace offering, then kissing him on both of his cheeks, making him blush while trying to change the subject. Right, he thought, true to nature, nothing gets spoken that incriminates the deity.

He took the water and drank it down heartily, gazing into the clear liquid as it swirled around in his goblet, making him burb rather loudly, much to the glee of the ladies standing at his side. Horae looked back at Nina briefly, and then laughed.

"See I'm not the only one who can fart through my nose." Everyone started to laugh, including Tamerk, who almost blew the entire batch right out of his right nostril upon hearing that remark. It brought Nina to the floor in hysterical giggles, as Tamerk finished the remains of his nectar in one final gulp, and Nina's hair burst into long flowing curls.

"Ahh, now that's something isn't it?" He grinned widely, saluting each of them in turn. "Now back down to reality, my sweets, what is happening on the Sibrey home-front? Is my little one still sleeping in the dream-state, or has she found the doorway that has been put in for the removal of this challenge?" He left the girls when they pointed towards the chamber that Sibrey slept within down the long corridor. He whistled a brief rendition of Dante's Prayer, belonging to the Song Goddstress Loreena Mckennitt, as he moved towards the viewing port. The recent smash song seemed to be sticking within his memory for the moment, coming through the airwaves of another side of the galaxy in the time differential Horae had opened up in her brief excursions to places unknown. The tune seemed to move through his body, sending small electrical charges of nostalgia, with its emulating moans of pleasant harmonious rhythms. The Goddess was fabulous at her music, and could be heard long into the starlight hours along the furthest reaches of Sopdet's space, drifting within the shift-point doorways to old Earth.

The doorway they had erected for Sibrey was not far; he recognized the telltale blue electrical zapping noises sizzling away in the background. He peeked within the energy field that housed her sleeping form, and smiled at her through the curtain of its waves.

"One day, sweet shippel, your dreams will come away and you will be able to see your Panther again. Sleep well, and remember the doorway has been set in place so you can find it." He watched her breathe for a moment, and then, kissing his fingers he slid them towards the electrical padlock, placing his hands along its edges and listening to the added charge of particles he provided for it. They sizzled and slid into place, allowing his molecules to be added to their precise fluctuations, and then reset after he removed his hand, settling down to their normal range. He was silently glad to see the youngster well, despite the recent bruises he could still detect from her recent fall.

"What happened to her face?" he asked. Nina smacked Horae.

"You told me they were gone, and showed me so. You tricked me and threw us into that thing that you do." Nina wiggled her fingers in Horae's face in that way she did to make a point. Horae smiled, shrugging her shoulders as if she hadn't a single thing else to accomplish except her moment of fun.

"No harm done." Tamerk replied, looking between the two and grinning. "Nothing ever changes around here. You girls make me laugh; after all that has gone down, you still need to be guarded from each other like little mice with tiny little pieces of honey thrown into each other's line of sight to sweeten the pot. Really, I'm sure Horae only meant what was best for you my little dream weaver, and I'll bet the Goddesses of Queen Sopdet's little band of musketeers will always have that in common with each other; right."

He nodded at the two of them to make his point, then, kissed the tops of their heads as he scolded their little minds. He knew they didn't mean any harm with their little bits of fun, but it made him wonder what might be the latest antics that had gotten mixed up inside, a Goddess brain that had grown up while he had been away. He had always spoken to them like that, even though they were not of his blood. But blood or not, he had been there since their inception, and for some unknown reason they seemed to treat him as the patriarch of this realm. He wondered what they would actually do if any of them actually got a chance to meet his real offspring. He was sure they'd think twice about his status within this realm and head for the hills as they ran for cover. But, that would be for another day; right now he chastised both of them lovingly, like a father who has found his children to be slightly misbehaving.

"So again my sweets, what happened to her face?" He looked from one to the other of them.

"She fell out of bed when she first arrived and woke up briefly before her time. We had to go back in and disturb the time-locks to get her up and back into bed." Horae spoke softly to him.

"Humph, fault or real?" he asked, looking between the two of them for the answer.

"Fault." Nina whispered, looking at her feet. "I went to bring in Horae from the outer-doorway and while I was gone, she must have found a way to wake up."

Tamerk flicked his fingers into the air, and pointed for them to move in the direction he wanted them to move, leaving the goblet behind him. It dissolved into thin air, returning back to the hot springs of Triduana's caves the moment it became no longer useful.

"We shall have to work on your timing then, shall we. On the bright-side she is stronger than we thought, no?" Horae looked on, grinning, and then laughed. "See, it's all my fault Nina, and you're off the hook at last. I told you I could fix it with time, and these little fingers you seem to be so nuts about." She wiggled them again as Nina moved around her to the other-side of Tamerk as they walked. Horae followed behind him without a second thought, catching up fast. Both moved just out of the others' reach, as they repeatedly tried to whack each other on the arm. They walked with his direction down the hall, shoving each other to get out of the way; as he rolled his eyes towards his home-world wondering just what he had got his own-self into.

It was nothing he would not have expected of the pair, and more often than not they would get themselves into something that either Hexe or Triduana had to bail them out of, far worse than a little fall. Time would heal, whatever it was that arrived within its wisdom, and the Shapeshifter would in time come to be a part of their own lives. So, in reality it would be like having two older sisters that constantly got you into trouble.

He smiled again with that thought; who could have wanted what one never had in the beginning. Poor Sibrey, she may not want the pair of them, when she got to where she was supposed to be in the coming times, and seri-ously why would she, when she got to know the lot of them and realized the Panther would be far better company. That made him laugh heartily, as both looked up to see what he was doing, while down below a definite growl was distinctly heard. The worst of the pair of them was no better than Sibrey on one of her good days. If he didn't know better, he'd have thought they were family. However, sisters these two were, and if either one of them actually got themselves into a bind, you could be damn sure the other one would come running to bail her out at a moment's notice. Hum, maybe Sibrey would be better finding her own friends, he thought.

All three marched towards the corridor Tamerk led them to, taking them away from the scene of the crime. This war was far too long in coming, and had made the inhabitants of the Goddess realm much too jumpy in the past few years. Each had grown older and the ageing process was far more unkind than either one of them would care to admit. Even he had aged during those years, and yet he felt far too long in the tooth to actually be the age they thought he might be. His hair had grown significantly whiter along the edges of his face, and from the back he had a perfect white streak that had occurred when the Sling had touched him the last time he had moved on through his woods.

He was older than time, at least he liked to think he was, time being the fleeting beauty that she was. It could take a perfectly good life, skirting around the edges of reality and waiting along the fringes until you aren't looking, then twist back around and bite you in the ass. But at the very least you know you've been bitten, which leads to the next question, who lives within the confines of deep space for going on a millennium, and isn't somewhat old? Seriously ole boy, he thought, you need to find another hobby.

He sighed and moved the pair of them deeper into the main quarters of the castle, passing several rather large tapestries hanging from the upper balconies along the main castle turrets. Each was intricately woven and held the life cycle of each of their inhabitants woven within its threads. All were held inside the world of the weaver and their competent hands, forever caught up in various scenes of castle life, among the village inhabitants of the off-worlders. The tapestries were alive with living beings that got up early each morning and generally wove their lives into the tapestries each and every day, creating their lives as they went. It was extraordinary to see, all fixed within the Goddess world with brilliant watercolours of long since extinct civilizations, that were completely unaware of what this realm could actually visualize in their silken threads.

They couldn't see over here, they just wove their tiny worlds without knowledge that the Goddess realm existed, each having been caught up in their own private universe far removed from the present. They were now lost to the others that ran parallel to their own, drifting aimlessly when the wormholes became crossed, frying their shift-point doorways from anyone opening them ever again. It was a damn shame really, but the Goddess realm continued to watch them from this portal for the time being. Maybe one day in the future, the mechanics of the failure could be revisited; however, not before they fixed this little problem still fluttering about in their own skies.

The world of the Goddesses was full of life at every angle, one that moved and turned within these old walls with relative ease. Some still lived among the trees outside, while others lives were recorded and played back, to be repeated time after time, for whatever means they had discussed upon their own individual umbilicused soul, before that arrival and untimely demise.

Tamerk agreed this world was starting to unravel at the edges; he could feel its breath slowly decline along the inner-core. It would only be a matter of time before, like the phoenix, it would burn itself out, and then rise again from the ashes, gloriously new and Balor free. He only hoped this time the same Balor stink would be dead and gone for the new millennium, which found itself right around the corner waiting for the newest phoenix's to emerge into the newly formed world of another age of the Fey level of life.

With that in mind he shook his head to unravel the cobwebs, and stepped forward to finish the day with what he had cooked up. They all needed a bit of entertainment to hold off the coming times of uncertainty, and this was something he was sure would fill that need. The calling of the coven could wait one last minute while they waited for the last of its members to arrive; the stragglers were filtering in one at a time from various access points around the different Nebulae. Sopdet would, in time, find the reason for its beginning, but in the meantime Tamerk would have to bring everyone involved together at the right moment in time, to find the endgame; however, giving them something to do for the moment, stood between him and a night out with a warted frog. Eeee Yewwwh! And that, my friends, was seriously not on his agenda for the entertainment he had in mind.

He shivered with the thought of having to wade into the old tallow pond full of Jellyfishcals that guarded the entrance through the surface reeds, which led into their underwater city. He really didn't want the gig; he hated those things, all slimy and nosey, following you through the vestals of reeds that hung along the edges of all the shallows, deeply entrenched in muddy foot-prints. It wasn't until you actually got deeper into the pond's weedy bottom, that they stopped their advancement into the world of the weeds. Having the pond flora blocking their ability to advance further into the realm of the warted frog was where they stayed, hovering along the edges of their world of reeds, unable to follow you, was good news for him. Unfortunately they would be waiting for him to come back out, and that was usually where they stayed, for he always took another route out, leaving them unaware of his departure. Good for him maybe, but not always for those souls around him, unaware he had taken them along for the ride.

Well, at least it had asked him to join him, while others had just assumed he would attend whatever function they had decided to call him to. Maybe next time someone got a little card game going, he would get his friend Moraig to come with his Salamendrium, and Tamerk could introduce the little mare he had won at the last Penndersnagen game of Flagernutt Tuttle cards. At least they would have something to entertain themselves with, while they played along the air currents of the Elemental worlds, darting between the inner-realms of the space in-between while he took all their attention away from his cheating at cards.

He really ought to get out more, this all sounded rather like some old snot taking his body out for a test drive in a Nebula full of sand. If he was that bored, he had better get the girls occupied with something that would keep them entertained, before either got too bored and ventured to places unknown within the shift-point doorways on either side of the outside battlements. That would be dangerous for all involved, as their Goddess molecules also had signatures, and could be traced far out into the planet's outer-rings. If the Sling happened to be in the right place at the right moment, when his little divas decided to step into the night air, he might be able to hunt them even into this realm. Which could very well expose the truth before its time, and all their hard work would blow up in their faces — let alone a certain card game that had yet to happen.

Hobbernaut stones, a mouthful at best; looking after Bairns was hard work. Unfortunately, the real problem lay just up ahead, and was about to begin again, despite all the preparation he and Kashandarhh had invested into its destruction. This time at least both offspring were older, in protective custody, and had their powers just under their little noses, unlike the last time when they had to deal with wailings that had to be quickly hidden from

Balor and his minions, upon their birthing. At that time their molecules had trace lines set inside their newly formed codes, and before they could be removed they had to get them away from Balor, replacing the old ones he could track without his knowledge.

The girls then had proved to be excellent caretakers, and had followed his instruction to the letter. Maybe today, with his recent find, it would keep them from playing tricks among themselves, and center their attention on what lay ahead. That is, if they didn't wrap their brains around what indeed was hovering on the fringes of the doorways; then it was a different ballgame, and potentially could prove to be disastrous for everyone involved in the days to come.

"I brought a surprise for all of you. Come, you're going to love this." He stopped and redirected Nina as she momentarily turned to look back where Sibrey was starting to toss and turn in her sleep. "Come Nina, don't worry this will settle her down, I promise sweet girl. You won't be disappointed." He winked at Horae and put his arm around both of them, to move them faster in the direction that he was heading.

They heard the others moving about in the Great Hall, dragging something heavy to the central Damesk`ka. Triduana could be heard even at a distance, singing in a deep baritone voice, as Tamerk kept them moving down the hallway towards the huge room. It wasn't until they moved to join the trio who were already in the room, that the reality of what Tamerk had brought to them came into full view, standing in all its ancient alien glory, right in the center of the main hall.

The moment both Horae and Nina viewed the thing, it made both of them gasp in utter astonishment. Tamerk enjoyed the theatrics of it all, stepping in front of them and walking in backwards with his arms wide-open in a sweeping motion. He formally bowed to them, as every bone in his slight frame prickled from the bowl's extremely high energy.

"You've brought the Bowl of Kalmayta. Oh Tamerk, how did you find it?" Horae couldn't believe her eyes. Nina had her hand over her mouth in shock. She actually had tears flowing down the sides of her face.

"It's been gone for such a long time," she hiccuped. "We all thought it was lost forever; especially when the fires of Falias had tipped it into the

String Nebula, and the fires prevented all of us from advancing into them to retrieve it."

"Oh Tamerk, its lovely!" Horae finally said, choked up with emotion; finding her voice, as she fanned her face with her right hand and fingers. Tamerk laughed and pulled the two of them into a bear hug.

"Happy now girls, no more tears. This is a time to celebrate. Triduana, bring us some of that damn water that you like to fill us all to capacity with. At least until it starts to come out of our bloody ears." Triduana turned briefly and stopped what she had been doing with the pedestal along the Damesk'ka's base. She frown slightly as she rose up with exaggerated emphasis on her lips, and waved her hands in mock surprise.

"I thought you liked it, ole man." His response was telepathically sent through her energy waves, unheard by the others in the vicinity. He nodded to his hidden flask and winked, pointing it in the direction of her overflowing water fountain. It was the same flask which held the Santarian Brandy he stole from Cian.

"Never said I didn't old girl, just want to get your attention away from Hexe's ears." he said telepathically, in her direction. She smiled and nodded without moving her head, in true Triduana fashion.

"We need to celebrate a bit I would think, and that would be just the right amount of kick to add to the majik I had in mind with this new batch," she answered. Tamerk grinned and passed it over to her under the table, where the water from her hot springs seemed to be hovering in mid-air without any kind of container to hold its pure essence.

"Don't tell Hexe or I'll get my ass kicked." She grinned back at the old Sprite, who started to whistle a dance tune, taking the attention away from what Triduana was actually doing. Hexe didn't buy it for a second; she had heard the two of them speaking her name in the middle of squeals of pure glee coming from the twins, and cursed loudly at the old fart.

"Hey, one of these days ole man, you and me are going to have a dance with my fists, and something tells me your kin ain't going to find all the little pieces I bury around the galaxy." His eyebrows went up in a kind of oval shape as he flat out snorted at her, not believing for a single minute, a single insult she had to say. He pretended to ignore the entire rant. To be fair, he adored their sparring matches. They both continued to learn from previous insults they had incorporated into their last encounter. Hexe was a bright Kiffersnitt, always finding new and unique ways to keep him on his toes. She wasn't just bright, she shone through the star system with a blinding bloody light that Tamerk had actually adored from the moment he had met the little snit. She wasn't finished yet, and continued to berate him with feet firmly planted wide apart on the ground, in a fighting stance.

"Then we'll see who has the final word on who puts what in the damn water." He started to smile, as something started to erupt into a full on roar inside his gullet; he shook his head at the little terror with a full on belly laugh. She would one day, in the near future, be a very dangerous Goddess to not have on your side, especially with this megalithic war that had been started so long ago by another deity, who had no business interfering in Fey matters of the Tuatha De` Danann.

He needed to start with all of them in one way or another, to gather the energy required to get all of them good and mad at him. It was not to cause strife among his little Goddess crowd, but so they could keep it relevant for the day they would need the energy, sometime in the near future when it erupted and breathed its breath along the Fey planets and their home-steps. It was with this bantering he had started to tease Hexe on another level much sooner than the others, knowing full well her response in kind would be far more dangerous than the others'. He needed that energy to move through him, so he could absorb its toxins and use its poison when the time came for the Sling to attack along the edges of the Goddess realm. He could use the build-up, to replenish the molecules he would need to use when the time arrived.

If he could just get her temper to flare off and on in the coming days, he could feed off its molecules long enough to sustain the level required; all the healing proteins from her inner systems would flow outwards into his Spriteish shell, and the Sling, when it attacked at a future date, could only do so much damage to his outer-core. The energy that he took from her would heal and replenish in a few seconds, each time he acquired it, and he had been doing this for going on a few hundred years now. In the future it would heal the wounds he would undoubtedly sustain, getting him closer than the others and reversing the ritual back on its ear, should it go sideways.

Having the ability to heal anything no matter what it was, was something that needed to stay within this side of the darkening realm that lived just outside the Goddess occlusion. If it got to the other-side through the corridor, which would be opened only long enough to pull him through, they didn't stand a chance when it hit.

He drained the goblet Triduana had passed to him to taste, in mock indignation, snickering away at the false threat Hexe had made. She wagged her fingers at him. "You and Moraig ought to get together and go blow something up. Maybe this time you can find the little bugger, and get him to return some of the other junk he's taken from us, along whatever little Quasar he pretends to have lost it into."

She wasn't finished with him quite yet, as she continued on with her rant, while he continued to calmly drink his spiked water with a slice of Hexe yelling at him on the side. "And while you're at it, persuade the little shit to bring it bloody back to the hall of antiquities, where he stole it from." She shouted at Tamerk's head, looking along the floor for something to throw at the old Troll, who hadn't responded in any way to her biting comments. Maybe this time she could turn his nose into a black hole and he could suck his face into himself.

"Alright you two stop it; you're no better than the Sling moving around the edges of our outer turf. Now, isn't that why we've all come to be here in the first place, not to act like a bunch of cracked monkeys out on a whiskey run in the Goetutonias Nebula northern rings?" Horae started towards the pair of them.

"Hey, I'm not that bad; he's the one that stole the Bowl of Kalmayta in the first place, and then really threw a fit and almost blew it up." Hexe looked on with indignant exaggeration. Tamerk laughed again, repeated the conversation, and added the rest of the story that she had left out.

"You mean Moraig did this, because really I was just an innocent bystander when the whole thing went south. Besides, don't you think Assha should have a role in this as well? It was, after all, partly his fault the little snake. He was the one, not me, that ventured too close to the rings of Falias in the first place," Tamerk remarked with fainting innocence from the entire debacle, picking his teeth with his fingernails, as the others simply rolled their eyes at the response.

"Truly!" He looked at all of them with feigned innocence, when they started to laugh at the lie.

"I think," Triduana said to them all, looking mostly at Tamerk as she said it, "it was what happened to the actual bowl that got so much attention; not when Morfesa refused to allow him to move the Fires of Osiris into the fields of the Cauldron, Tamerk." Hexe shook her head at Tamerk, who still tried to feign innocence of the entire ordeal.

"Through the doorway that Assha and yourself had already made arrangements to fit it into, you idiot. So, I'm not quite sure how you make the comparison." He shook his head at the truth.

"Nope; can't say that is how I recall the thing at all."

"Truly, your memories of most things suck!" She shook her head at the Sprite as he slung it back in her direction.

"It's not like there's going to be a test on what I'm currently holding inside this noggin, you little freak, and when the time is right I'll know exactly what needs to be done, my little healing snit, so why don't you go out and play in some far away Nebula, and get off my back before I sling you into the path of a comet." Everyone groaned as he proceeded to make a spectacle of himself, until he finally moved to add to the commentary and brought another level of insanity into the room. "Let's see, ah yes, there it is." He pointed to his stomach and illustrated with exaggerated glee as he pulled the invisible story from out of his gut, falling over as if the thing was sucking the life out of him.

He continued on until he had finished his last dying scene, and looked up to see if they were all still in the room after it had grown quiet for longer than he would have liked. He opened one of his eyes to see if maybe he had accidentally thrown himself back into another doorway, but it was Horae who had stopped them all from seeing his theatrics, and had frozen time around the entire group. She looked at him with her hands on her hips, cursing him silently with her eyes.

"Are you done? Or shall I just slip everyone away to another realm while you finish the kill shot on your own?"

"Ok fine, bring them back and I'll find the strength to tell the story without the theatrics. You really are no fun anymore you big baby, and how come you're able to do that without me knowing it?"

She just stood there silently waiting, not even dignifying that with a response, while Tamerk got up off the floor and brushed himself off. He caught her eye and nodded, while she unfroze everyone around them and the noise level returned to its former volume. He gave everyone that famous smile and started to tell them the story that he knew to be the truth, without adding or leaving the rest he wanted to add into the tale that gave the mixture of his colourful version of events.

"It was around time to host the festival of Fire, and as usual both Moraig and I had been in cahoots finding new and unusual ways to entertain the masses, before something always happened and put a stop to it." Triduana had come up behind the two, nodding in agreement with the tale, as Tamerk paused to look at her and put up his goblet to refill its contents.

"This time we had tried to bring the bowl into the festival, disguised as something else. Up till then Moraig had been an active participant, until Triduana accidentally filled it with her majikal waters, straight from the caverns below where the hot springs run at their clearest points, thinking that it was nothing more than one of the ritual goblets. If I'm not too far gone in my understanding of the ordeal, it was at this time she became aware something was very wrong."

Triduana nodded at the storyline and he continued. "It had at first been perfectly innocent, until the water started to steam and boil out over the sides of it, and they had tried to make a run for it. But it was Moraig who rushed in and sealed the deal as he tried to make it past the old Druid that had told him previously that it could not be done within this point of entry, being too powerful to make it through the thinning walls."

"Now, not to be outdone by the old Druid Morfesa, who Moraig had not really cared a wick about, they decided as a group, that the fastest way to get it through to safety was through the front gates, where the old geezer had been directing the masses to their individual tables. Most of them had been gathering on the far side of the festival grounds, and were not in the way of the bowl and its entourage when Moraig had originally tried to pass it off as one of the bowls from the sacred trinity, alongside another of our other recently acquired relics called The Selmathen Stone of Anthros. Morfesa had been directing mostly off-worlders, when they had tried to sneak it through the assembly, and both Moraig and Assha had been approached by Morfesa telling the pair of them to get it out of here." He looked up at Triduana, and sighed. "More?" he asked, she nodded and spoke quietly to him.

"So, you were visibly absent in all of this, and had nothing to do with it? Sounds a little suspicious to me." Hexe looked towards him, shaking her head while he ignored her and continued on.

"Before Triduana had poured the water into its containment, Moraig tried a different approach, thinking he could use a disguise to make it through the barrier. He had only just brought it over to her side to ask what she could do, when something unforeseen took place, changing what should have been an easy fix into something very different. The story goes that her back had been turned, as she was filling several other goblets for the festival with her majikal waters. She turned briefly with her hand letting the spigot go, and filled the container to the brim thinking the pair of them had come to help. It had taken a few moments to get the majik to recognize this was not what should be inside the vessel, and as it started to boil and bubble out, she quickly sprinkled the surface with Sliverdust-Sulphur Sage after she realized it was about to blow up."

"All true," Triduana confirmed to the group, snickering at the thought of it.

"Thinking it would hold the explosion for the time it would take them to fling it out into the sea, they believed there was enough time to make it through the crowd of Fey around them, when the old Druid Morfesa arrived on scene, innocently waylaying them in his hunt for a goblet of her water. It hadn't taken long for the old Druid to smell the sulphur that escaped around its edges, even though Triduana had tried to divert his attention elsewhere when the pair of them had tried to enter the main doors with the bloody thing smoking along the passageway."

"He really was relentless when it came to that batch of effervescence. If only I had made something else that day, none of this would have happened." She smiled at Tamerk who looked at her, smirking away.

"What is up with you? Have I got something on my face or something?" she asked him, looking in the mirror to see if something had landed on her skin.

"Not now, you funny girl, then. Seriously...," he looked at her, shaking his head. "Right, that might have worked," he said with a sly smile.

"I have no idea what you're talking about Tamerk; please just spit it out instead of beating around the tree."

"Bush, Triduana. It's beating around the bush my darling, not the damn tree." She glared at him with a quizzical stare. "The little weasel had a thing for you, and anything you had salted it with that day, the creep would have said the same thing. Seriously Triduana, how did you not see that?" He grinned at her.

"You're kidding me, right? Augh, that is just gross, he's like twice my age. Remind me to trip the old shit next time we see him," she declared, offended, she pretended to stab herself in the heart. Tamerk stopped halfway through and took a deep breath, as he looked at the younger Goddesses who had gathered in fascination, to hear the telling of the tale of Triduana's suitor. He centered his attention on Hexe, who seemed to be riveted to his version of events.

"How am I doing so far?" He looked straight at Hexe and tried to flick her mind with his fingers, making her jump and yell back at him.

"Stop it! That's not fair; you cheated. I wasn't ready," she growled at him.

"Then pay attention to the story Goddess nitwit, or somewhere along the line the story will become the tale of the disappearance of Hexe the reluctant healer." he replied with sarcasm as she tried to reach inside and scratch the itch he had created.

"Come on you two; let's hear the rest of the story." Nina groaned at the two of them. Tamerk grinned at his little dreamer, and carried on talking, with Hexe still glaring at him in the background.

"Yeah, tell us more about Triduana and her lover boy." Horae flicked her eyelashes at Nina and the two of them roared. Triduana started to groan louder.

"No, stick to the storyline, or someone is going to find Mandrake Root in their water the next time I make a batch."

"Ah, you're no fun. Just when it was starting to get good," laughed Hexe, looking at Tamerk who stuck his tongue out at her. "Seriously, you have a flare for the dramatics. Maybe someday you can embarrass each one of us, and we can beat the snot out of you. Oh, pick me first; I'm dying for a fight." She grinned at him as he went to reach for her; just as Arddhu arrived on the scene, picked her up and placed her on the other-side of the room, sliding her sideways to the wall and knocking her to her knees.

"Hey, that hurt!" she yelled at him.

"Then quit it, or next time I'll not be so gentle. What is wrong with you Hexe? Can't you see he's baiting you, and that you're going to need more than your healing energy to replace what he takes from you?" She looked across the room at Tamerk grinning away at her.

"Yeah but..."

"No buts. Just stop harassing him, or I'm going to take the damn energy he needs from you, and give it to him just to hear the rest of the story," Arddhu growled at her. He turned to Tamerk. "Now finish the damn story; we've got company waiting." Tamerk looked behind him, and Hexe nodded in agreement at the two males, while Arddhu, satisfied he had made his point, silently walked away.

"Ok, so where were we? Ah yes, the fastest route around the area was to go straight through the room they were all gathered in, so they could get it to a safe location. Morfesa had seen what was happening, and disentangled Triduana's arms from around his neck, catching the tail end of Moraig's shirt just as he went to pass on by, turning him around again in the other direction and pointing him at the door." Triduana added a slight touch of sarcasm all of her own, at that moment.

"Did he ever do anything halfway?" Horae laughed with the others at the sentiment. It seemed that within her lifetime around the Elemental he either really had bad luck with things in general, or he just liked to blow things up, much to the delight of all onlookers. The others that seemed to get caught in the zone of his destruction had a very different point of view, and the moment he came on scene, Fey became necessarily nervous.

The story had not ended, but a hesitation in the telling had appeared. Tamerk sat down momentarily in a sort of intermission, not actually caring that he had become somewhat of a prat. Triduana shook her head, chastising him for his actions, then continued to prepare the bowl that rested on the Damesk`ka she had centered in place. Her hands prepared the herbs she had brought up from her storehouse of unique potions, and incorporated a new mixture into the waters she had prepared from her subterranean world that the others had not seen before. She sprinkled Dragon-Scale Whiskers into the mist, and smiled as they dissolved beautifully, creating a rainbow of celestial colours to dance along the ceiling. She glanced around the rook of a room at her collection of Goddess begotten mynah birds still chit-chatting away in the background, briefly frowning at the two nearest ones who had momentarily stopped trying to best each other. She coughed, drawing their attention. Each appeared to be trying to play nice, moving to opposite sides of the room away from direct contact with each other, while she began the final preparations of her majik, and moved to start the ritual.

They followed her movements with their eyes, trying not to get too close to each other as she walked setting things into their proper position around the apparatus she had before her. Arddhu wouldn't have to come back for the interim, but his mind was opened to their whispers if things changed before the ritual was completed. Instead, she ignored them, choosing to actually let Arddhu separate them again if they chose to continue with their incessant chitter chatter. For her, she had only a few moments to make the ritual her own, before the mixture became unstable and blew everything sky high, taking all of them with it.

She decided today was not that day. She moved lightly, not touching the ground with her feet, as she chanted the final words needed to fix the potion into its newest formula. It lifted her effortlessly and floated her backwards. She skimmed the surface of her majikal circle in a Widderschynnes direction, moving from left to right around the Kalmayta bowl hanging slightly above the Damesk'ka. This was done to undo any previous majik that might still hang about in the air from its arrival into this realm from the last batch, before she would be able to start fresh with a new circle and seal herself inside.

Triduana loved adding majik to her waters, and had such a talent for creating different tastes and textures in the small quantities that were harvested by her own hand, that what was presented here was simply an added rendition. Many different kinds of majik had been brought to the surface from the caverns down below beside Arddhu's little tree. You might recall that it was neither small nor little, in my description of it in the previous tale, but for now in the telling she was simply making a distraction of that division to the storyline to which the others would have to agree, it was simply the easiest spot at which Sibrey could actually have entered their realm, without having to attract attention from the Sling; the very creature that was presently making its way across Water's Deep in search of two offspring that were similar in age to the Aelflet that ran with a Shapeshifter fold.

How it had broken free from its restraints was anyone's guess. But for now, they needed some extra assurances that they could this time finalize its completion. And that, my friends, was exactly what Triduana was in the process of achieving.

Timing was everything — Triduana, now fully protected from further interference, took her hand and passed it over the goblet she had transferred from the table to her coveted circle. The stones beneath her feet began to melt away, leaving her hanging several hundred feet in mid-air, allowing her to levitate and float in the breezes of the cavern's warm air-ducts high above the mineral water-bath far below.

From there she created a portal that opened up beneath her, joining her in her protected circle as it moved upwards changing the previous wind's direction. This new Deosil direction flowed forward from this water source, which ran clear through the main chamber of her private quarters, creating a vortex that moved the air all around the new tunnel upwards, spinning her slowly around. They watched as it began to change its bearings, whipping madly like a curtain blowing in the breeze as it slid up around her body, fed by the wind she had created from below.

The sudden change in temperature where the others stood near the rookery opened up the final locking sequence beneath the floor under her feet. Once that happened, the movement of air changed the molecules from her fingertips, sending a fine trickle of energy downwards to penetrate through the newly opened fissure she had created; reaching down below to where her water's run their deepest. The others came closer and stared at the image that was beginning to form out of the mist. It began to bubble slightly as it broke through the surface barrier, producing an opaque cloud amongst the warmth of mineral and whiskers, while the story Tamerk had started to tell became lost in the majik, removing anything in its path.

What she had done was simply transfer the existing pattern of molecules in their downward decline; currently flowing beneath her chambers, and with a flick of her wrist reversed its triangulation to send it upwards. The waters below ground stopped moving for a fraction of a second as it froze in place, then recalibrated, letting her take what she needed from the majik that filtered from her fingertips.

They watched as several water molecules began to lift and become airborne, as tiny amounts could be seen from her streambed below ground rising skyward in the bubbles of air, and then forming into a fine mist that quickly reached the energy field she had created above. Once reaching the mixture she needed, she sent them towards the projected image of an empty goblet, and they filled the vessel with an unusual blend of her newest tincture.

This form of transference was used in some of the most sensitive of majiks that are still wildly used in most kingdoms of the Fey. Hexe knew their significance and looked with vested interest at this newest formula of sighted elixir, as it made its way from the safety of the caves below, and entered the cooler air of another world far above, where she herself currently lived. She momentarily forgot her war of words with Tamerk, and conceded to enjoy the majik that flowed all around them, revelling in its texture floating across her tongue.

Down below ground, its source once released, would continue on down the darkened corridors and fall sharply over the head of the falls into the shadow waters of the underworld. She shivered, thinking of its destination, but quickly turned her attention to what was happening in the realm that she had grown accustomed to breathing Goddess lungs into, rather than thinking on what was waiting for her one day down below ground in the caves of her ancestors. She knew there would be time enough for the fellowship of those who would take on the quest in future endeavours, but for now it needed to find rest inside the back of her brain, until she could stranglehold the memory and return for it later.

As soon as the water came into the goblet Triduana held aloft, she closed off the entrance into her world below ground and stepped softly onto solid ground once more. The stones melted back together again, leaving no trace of where she had pulled their molecules apart, as she closed off the circle and brushed its molecules into the wind. She then poured the contents she had accumulated into the curved bowl on the Damesk'ka, and instantly the water began to turn into a form of greenish mist, which swirled around the stone bowl like a whirlpool riding the currents of a Waterhorse.

"It's beautiful," gasped Nina as she looked into its depths. She watched as the water turned and spun in all different directions; first turning to one shade of the spectrum, then back to another, and then changing its mind, reversing its decision once again, and back again. She watched the strange dance, as it twisted and turned collectively pulling apart each of the molecules, while the water began to boil the colour away along the surface.

It started at the edges and gathered itself towards the middle, pulling the entire greenish colour it had collected into the center of the chalice, and then yanked it below the surface of the water from their eyesight. The exterior sheen that was left, then formed what appeared to be a mirrored image, which they could see reflecting the things around them; including themselves, as they peered into it. It still had the occasional ripple effect from Triduana's hands moving the chalice from its position high up in the air, and then in a slight hesitation, like a hiccup in time, its motion became quiet and clear, as the mirror that found the sanctuary of its clarity, finally stilled. Not a single ripple moved on the watery surface, except for one final bubble that floated up like it was thumbing its proverbial nose at them in the last few seconds and then thinking better of it, released its hold with a tiny hiss; it floated away into nothing.

Tamerk grinned at the spectacle that the Goddesses projected. He laughed out loud as he watched the girls all leaning into the mirror at once, holding their breath.

"You can breathe now, ladies, and stand back, as the majik flows through the void into where it can show you what has come through to visit." He threw one last ingredient from the pouch that hung around his neck into the bowl, and they all watched the mist turn a brilliant shade of violet, and then erupt momentarily into a full raging boil before growing uncommonly still.

Everyone held their breath, as a single moment in Goddess time became a few short centuries in the world of others. Then the air began to stir, creating a movement in the mirrored image that started to form into something they couldn't quite see. It was just a small shadow at first, and then as they watched it began to grow in its clarity, they saw it grow into something covered in the colour red.

No, not red in its entirety, but something worn around its shoulders was covered in red. As it grew closer, they could see it stood on two legs and moved in a slow gait, coming towards a ruined castle. That castle stood in the foreground of a lake that looked familiar to each of them, and as the picture cleared completely and they watched this male approach its walls, they knew what water source had appeared in the background.

"Hey, that's Killchurn Lake," Arddhu exclaimed, peering through the crowd of young females who smiled with the knowledge that the figure that now stood to the right of them had nailed it on the head. Tamerk threw up his hands, laughing at the Tree-Spirit.

"See, we are all trying to heed your advice by playing nice. Ask the others if you don't believe me." Arddhu looked perplexed, just as Triduana was wrapping things up, coming in behind him.

"Hum, when did you get through?" she asked him, smiling. Arddhu looked at her with the beginning wisps of understanding to what Tamerk was talking about; then snickered in his husky lilt.

"You used my shade again, didn't you?" He said, looking at the astonished faces of the other four of them beside her. Triduana nodded slightly, humming away.

"Well, for only a wee bit. They had it coming, and I just got tired of listening to them fight and you were nowhere to be found," she whispered to him.

"I kind of thought things tasted a little off down by the lakeshore," he spat out a Brumble Cricket from out of his mouth. I believe this one belongs to you. It keeps trying to burrow itself into my teeth! It's one of the reasons I came up here to find you." Triduana reached for it and quickly sent it back down to its home where it had crawled away from.

Tamerk looked the most offended while the rest of them looked slightly confused, and just when you thought he was going to strangle her, he started to laugh out loud in delight.

"Seriously, you can do that?" he said to her, amid the theatrics. She nodded, winking at him. "That is so cool. I haven't had anyone in such a long time try and trick me."

"Tricked us," said Hexe in the background, rolling her eyes again at Tamerk's confession.

"What, who is us?" Tamerk looked around at her.

"You know us; the one you were fighting with. You know, you and me you idiot." she remarked, rolling her eyes again.

"Hum," said Tamerk, bowing to his colleague in the most humorous of ways, and pointing to Hexe. "Who is she, and where did you find her?" he asked, pretending not to know who Hexe was.

"Ok, stop it the both of you. Right now the two of you are on my last nerve. Now, shall we play nice, or should I show you what else you don't know I can do?" Triduana looked from one to the other. "Ok, fine," she started to roar, when the two of them continued to stick their tongues out at each other behind her back, then begin to advance to smacking each other behind her back. Within a fraction of a millisecond, both were on opposites sides of the room, sitting on the floor with their mouths clamped shut.

"Whoa!" yelled Horae, grabbing onto Nina and backing up away from Triduana. "Seriously, you can do that? You always seem so calm. Bad momma Goddess, everyone needs to try and breathe before we all end up on the back-side of Sopdet's naughty list." Arddhu started to laugh at her words. Then she did something the others didn't expect. She reversed the time dilatation, and they found themselves back in the beginning of the ritual just before it had all started, and Triduana had created the fictitious Arddhu.

"How am I doing so far?" Tamerk repeated in exactly the same format just before he went to flick Hexe's inner brain like last time. Instead, this time when he went to flick her mind, he was locked out of its arrival. He shook his finger looking at it closely like it had something wrong with it. "What is wrong with you?" he said to his finger. "Come on, not now, just when I'm starting to have a little bit of fun." Nina started to giggle, folding her fingers along her mouth, trying her best to restrain the sound. For some reason Triduana had brought her along for the ride into the reversal dilatation with her memory intact. Tamerk looked up and glared at her.

"What's so funny little one, never seen someone fail at their little surprise before?" He was still flicking his fingers, trying to get them to work. Nina laughed harder, pointing to Hexe who had stopped to watch the movie, unaware of what was happening. However, one of them realized just what Horae had done, and was staring right at the two of them back and forth, away from the others still residing in another time dilation away from the three of them.

Triduana voice suddenly appeared, sharp and true in Horae's ear, "It's not nice to fool someone who can put you into the dream Sibrey is currently looping inside, little one. But since it's happened and no harm done and the two of them have stopped fighting, I think we'll just call it a day and let the image carry on as it is. Now, change it back before the Sprite finds out, and decides to take us somewhere we really don't want to be, because you know how that one ends." Triduana glared lovingly at Hoare, smiling a little too sweetly.

"Ok, but remember, if they start again I'm not responsible for the outcome," she said dejectedly, having been found out so quickly. Triduana spoke briefly to her.

"No, little one, I'll deal with that one when it comes down the pipe. However, thank you anyway; it was the thought that counts. So, if you don't mind, shall we?" Horae groaned, nodding to Triduana, who spread her arms wide, directing her time dilatation majik to the position she wanted her to move towards, and reverse the spell she had set in place.

The rookery once more began to move forward, allowing previously happened situations to move back into their correct positioning. Things around the room began to move like the pieces of a puzzle, folding back into their proper times, leaving behind certain unanswered questions that had already left a Sprite's mouth to hang out in the open air, while it reset. The moment everything was as it should be, those words seemed to fall straight out of the air, and come crashing down onto the ground, shattering into pieces without anyone the wiser.

Hexe tried to answer him back with another sarcastic comment about not knowing who she was; however, she suddenly stopped in mid-stream, shook the cobwebs out of her head and tasted the air with her tongue. She frowned, whirling around inside the new environment like a Banshee alerted to the wailing of another.

"What was that? Something tastes like sulphur. Who just did something that we don't know about?" She looked suspiciously around the rookery at each of them. But, Triduana had this under control. She waved Arddhu over and pointed to the bowl. Arddhu broke the stalemate of the previous time-frame as he cried out suddenly in disbelief, pointing to the very thing they had all come to see and had surrounded their bodies around, when he had first come into the room.

"That's not possible. How in the world did you get it back?" He was looking at the stone bowl currently being balanced by Triduana, majikally hanging weightlessly in the air above the central Damesk`ka.

Arddhu turned briefly, nodding at Tamerk with a sense of awe in his eyes, and clapped him briskly about the shoulders. "Good one ole boy, I'd have thought it would have taken an entire coven to release this one from its resting place." Tamerk grinned, showing wide white teeth, slightly curved just around the fang hooks, forgetting what had just happened. He didn't even get a chance to respond, when Arddhu leaned into his ear and whispered, "We'll get her next time, old boy." Out of the blue Nina cried out, leaning into the bowl, peering deeply into its depths with her hands locked on the sides of its outer-edges.

"Look, it's the Shapeshifter's Father," she exclaimed, pointing to the figure that had quite suddenly appeared much clearer in the mirror, while they had their little quarrel. "How in Corpeous rising of the mauntrated skies did that happen?"

"Tamerk, what door did you let him in?" Triduana spoke softly to him, as everyone turned towards him to get his response, but before that could happen, Daniel could be seen shifting into another doorway along the outer-fringes of that very castle, the same castle that Sibrey had first entered when she was being chased in her dream, without having any visual aids to get him through the door that they could see, as they watched him land outside those broken down gates.

"And how is that even possible?" Arddhu spoke out loud, as the others watched the Togernaut clansman move slowly towards the stone escarpments of the old battlements of ancient Tameron. Tamerk grinned at the entourage, gathering in the old rookery.

"You said she was having nightmares. I thought she might need some help in that department. So I sent in someone there to calm her down, so she won't set the alarm bells off again. Who is better at that than her own Father? Waa-Laa!" Tamerk grinned, watching their faces. Actually, he smirked, but that is neither here nor there, with the thought on how this would play out. Especially with regard to the other-side of the coin, and the fact that neither one of them had any idea what was about to go down, if it actually landed.

Who better than her own father, indeed!

CHAPTER TWENTY-EIGHT

The Warriors of the Capourian Wolf-clan

To Daniel's men, it appeared as though he was the one who had disappeared; which was what indeed did occur. But, as far as the elder Shapeshifter was concerned, it was everyone else who had vanished, and not the other way around. He was, oh so very, very wrong.....

That small difference of opinion all by itself, took some doing. Tamerk had to use Hexe's arrival for the time dilation to mix it into the fold just right. If Horae had been off by even an atom, it would have been disastrous for the Shapeshifter. This left him to complete the mix, and bring it into something he could use. If for some reason he was off by even a fraction in its centrifuge, the image would have come undone and the other that had been left to sleep inside their chamber would not have arrived into the matrix and moved to safety. There was a brief moment of breathable uncertainty that had actually occurred. It was when Daniel had been dreaming and had not heard the Sprite call his name at the beginning of the shift. But he had rectified that by taking him anyway, and becoming the creature Daniel believed was the guard captain, in the illusion that had been fixed into place inside the dream.

He had taken the bait, removed himself from the quarters of the billeted Shapeshifters, and gone across the fold, talking to one that he believed to be of importance in finding his daughter. It had taken some doing to play the role of all the Fey he had come into contact with along the way. But he had to laugh at the expression on Daniel's face, when he finally realized he had never spoken to any of them at all, since their arrival into the city. If the men had not been angry enough to travel from their village in search of their lost Shifter in the beginning of this quest, it would have taken a great deal more planning on his part, to get them in the right place at the right time.

To get them into the trigger point of the doorway, which had been kept open long enough to allow him to walk on through, was another story. Getting them all here alive had been harder than was expected; especially after they had accidentally come into contact with the blue headed Gorgon herself. That was something Tamerk had not foreseen along the pathways and, had it gone any other way, all his little Goddesses would not be looking at the bowl in amazement, as Daniel made his way across the stone case-ment heading inside the ruins of the ancient castle. Instead, they would be currently inside another timeline within its walled history trying to figure another way out of here, for the events about to transpire.

But, it had worked out after all, and if he hadn't knocked the creature out mere milliseconds before their arrival, it would have taken him a lot longer to get the Shifter to trust him, with one or more of his company killed by its poisonous heads. However, he could rest easy knowing that he had achieved success, and while the others weren't looking, he had shifted the remaining Shapeshifters back home to their village and removed the memory of the journey from each of them, and then watched with vested interest as Daniel made his way into the old castle with the others up-above.

The Goddess crowd peered deeper into the waters that relayed pictures of the past and a few current events in the castle's history, and tried to concentrate on his latest acquisition. The Shapeshifter's father made his way towards the palace compound; the very one that had brought Sibrey into the antiquary below ground, and one that stored the information and its belongings of the ancient House of royalty to the reigning Fey family and their ancestors. However, this time, the time lock had returned to the crumbling ruins of the majestic castle and its fallen rocks and mortar.

Those still thrashing about inside, closer to the great room were cur-rently unaware of Daniel's arrival. He found them as he came around the last corner of the outer bailey, tearing away with vested interest at one section of the remains of the once Great Hall of Aelven mythology. They stood among the ruins, along with the usual creatures that sometimes wandered through the long since abandoned rooms, hosting nothing but dust and a collection of bats nesting high-up in the timbers.

He heard them before he moved through the outer chamber, and at first thought they might be his own clan. He was wrong. What he found as he followed the tracks were three big burley unknown clansmen, who had resorted to smashing the latching system of the hidden chambers below ground, trying to coax the sentient lock into revealing itself once again, thereby giving them access to where Sibrey had disappeared inside.

Daniel became suddenly aware that something other than the warriors had been in the entrance to the solar. High up above them, hovering without one of his tentacles and standing as big as life, was the Earth Elemental Japonagus, who was still guarding the entrance to the underground chamber. This was the creature that had originally dragged Sibrey below ground. It was guarding one of the inner-gates to the Goddess realm, far below where she lay fast asleep up in one of the chambers closely guarded by the Cloud People now watching this. Daniel hesitated, trying to think of the reasons why he was going to come crashing into the middle of that fight. Cobwebs seem to filter in and out of this brain, from Tamerk's shift, and although he could see no way around it, he still wasn't completely sure whether he shouldn't just back-track the hel out of there, and make his way back up the cliff-face to freedom.

He didn't get the chance, as a twig snapped beneath him — he swore under his breath and gave away his location. The trio, who would occasionally fend off the creature with their swords as he dove around their heads — causing them to take a swipe at the Elemental from time to time, heard the intrusion. However, just then, Japonagus made a wild dash at their heads, diverting their attention back to him. Just when they thought they had him, he vanished into thin air and their swords came into contact with his ethereal mist. He reappeared somewhere further away, taunting them back and away from Daniel's position.

Tamerk released the Elemental with a slight wave of his hand. The creature acknowledged the Sprite's arrival and removed itself from sight. He instantly dissolved into the background of the crumbling rock-face where he had held his ground for so long, and vanished into the sea-foam far below, diving into the ocean swells.

The molecules of its position were still hanging thickly in the air for the Shapeshifter to detect, and although the others had not detected its whereabouts when it had disappeared, Daniel could still see several large bubbles coming up from the saltwater across his shoulders, far out on the left bank of the bay. What it was, he could not tell, but the thing had disappeared too quickly for it to have been anything else but a majikal retrieval.

One of the warriors came to investigate the new noise that they had heard from the battlements along the outer bailey walls behind them, as the creature disappeared above. The others watched overhead, trying to judge where it would reappear once again. But it didn't, and as the mist seemed to melt away right overhead with nary a whisper as to the reason why, they didn't take too long to ponder the cause behind it.

The warrior who had gone to investigate the noise began to see falling rocks along the pathway. Daniel silently cursed, thinking he had started the slide that now travelled along the area he had just come down, but the outline of a rabbit appeared over the rise and quickly bounded away into the hedgerow to his left. A whistle from the other Aelves could be heard as they too spotted the rabbit as it scampered away. One of them signalled the others back with a single nod of his head.

Unfortunately, Daniel had thought he was in the clear with the sighting of the rabbit, and would have been if he hadn't moved. But, he moved too soon, and as he watched the rabbit bound away, they noticed his slight movement among the stones as they came across his shadow. Another whistle stopped him dead and another smattering of stones broke loose beneath his feet. He cursed, thinking that maybe he could turn into something they could not see, but it was too late as all three warriors found his molecules and began to move into position to stop his advancement into the room.

Daniel was tired of playing games and, with the appearance of another apparently inevitable threat advancing towards him, he moved into position to meet it head on. He was in no mood for games, and when Muijalaa had signaled the clansmen to cut him off, Daniel was way ahead of them and moved to meet them halfway.

Nina clapped her hands in glee, watching as if nothing like this had happened before and it was all new to her little Goddess brain. Tamerk understood, sometimes she got a little bored with their celestial lifestyle. He had arranged a full on viewing of the events that were about to play out in the coming battleground of the Tantaris race of Fey who lived and breathed on this young planet beneath them.

Eurgerus went towards the noise he heard from the rear of where they had been trying to pry the huge rocks away from where Sibrey had been dragged beneath, and listened with the others for any sign of his arrival. He signalled the other wolf pack to keep to either side of him as he went up and around the Shapeshifter he still could not see, and thought was an Aelf. He was mistaken, as the creature's energy reading showed him to be a Shapeshifter belonging to the western villages. He did not, as of yet, know who the creature was, but something familiar about his hunting skills allowed Eurgerus to know he would not need his sword for this one.

Pharonis and Muijalaa followed his lead, and came up in the rear of whatever warrior had tried to follow their boot prints along the path, that had led him down the ravine from the horses they left high above on the cliff-face. The occasional whinny from their mounts above alerted them that they were still grazing high above them, undisturbed, and a simple band of thieves, were not coming down the cliff-face behind the original Shifter, on the edge of the energy readings that could very well have been hiding from them.

That simple slide of rocks shattered the silence Daniel had been able to maintain down the steep incline up till now. They listened to him curse lightly under his breath when he realized his location had been detected, and, listening quietly to his breathing, they moved away from their former position into a more secure location, to protect themselves from what lay ahead.

Tamerk had moved in to watch with the others still crowded around the bowl, as the slide show had just started to get interesting. He held his mug up for Triduana, when she made the rounds to pour another snippet of spiked water. Each of them drew closer to the scene below that was playing out on solid ground below them. He wondered how long it would be before something alerted them to the fact that each of them where old friends. Not friends in the usual manner, for these old acquaintances had never been formally introduced; in fact, they had never met each other in any lifetime. But friends they were, despite their differences, and each belonged to the one that would bring them together for the first time since Sibrey's hatching.

Sibrey had told her father about these warriors ever since she was little. When she had been old enough to repeat the dreams in their vibrant colours and brilliant clarity, it had been what 'scared of the dark' had been all about to her and her little demons, and Daniel had finally been able to comprehend. He had sworn an oath to protect the Bairn, and even he had a difficult time explaining why they had continued to haunt her waking breath, long past her infancy.

But, they had, and after one night in particular he had had enough, and in a moment of absolute clarity, he had decided one late evening when she awoke from a more volatile dream not recognizing either him or his mate, he would do what it took to get the dreams under control or die trying. This time had been different from the others; this time it had left her breathless to the point of fear, and she had run towards the trees in a desperate attempt to flee from those that seemed to still have a very real presence within her actual line of sight. It had taken every one of her brothers, as well as many friends that had been staying for the festival of bonfires, to actually prevent her from reaching the trees. Once she had been caught, she fought like a wild boar, and still to this day one of his sons bore the marks of her teeth in his forearm, as he had picked her up before she had lost consciousness and grown limp, while a big Black Panther, had watched them from the edges of the trees.

Who that creature was, still had not been explained. Stranger still, it had not advanced on any of them, and truth be told it could easily have dispatched each and every one of them, if it had tried. Instead it had watched, seemingly just as worried as they were about Sibrey's behaviour, with its head bobbing to and fro, following her brothers trying to get her under control, pawing at the air. It seemed strange at the time, for it had only appeared as she reached the most volatile of her fits. As they tried like hel to get her to calm down, he noticed a thin line of energy pouring off its hide and moving gently in her direction, just as she was knocked out and ceased struggling. They had been too busy to notice it leave, but Daniel recalled briefly looking back at the edge of the clearing where it remained during the struggle, to find it had vanished in the thick of the trees as they moved away towards their village with Sibrey tucked safely in their arms.

On the short walk back to the cottage and after they had lain her down on her cot near the fire, he had vowed that it was time to speak to Manannan about their unusual recurrences. His family had agreed that it would at least make him feel better, but then apart from his mate no one knew the significance of who Manannan was to her. The Sea God had simply reassured him the dreams were nothing to worry about, but still to this day Daniel couldn't quite find peace with their continued occurrences. The Panther they had not seen again; however, whatever it was that had arrived within the world of her dreams that continued night after night to plague her, was not something that could be simply explained away by someone who looked after the sea creatures out on the reef far away from the land dwellers, who currently lived among his kind.

Nevertheless, whatever it was, it continued to grow larger and expand its reign of terror and the dreams became exceedingly worse throughout the long nights of that summer in the times of the Moondogs. He wondered if for some reason, that phenomenon had something to do with it. However, they came and went, and the dreams went from bad to worse, carrying on long after they had left the summer skies. It went from a few nights at first, and then turned into weeks, much to their dismay. And then it followed a nightly pattern for months on end, before the dreams turned into full-fledged nightmares of some sadistic Dream-God, bent on claiming her as one of their own. Daniel had then, much to their own healer's reluctance, been forced to take her to the Dream-Witch who lived at the edge of Lucidity Lake in the beginning of the season of the fallen mare.

They spent three turns of the full moon of Fieldmarr, during the remembrance festival of Kalieas, getting her to remember that dreams were just scattered thoughts and couldn't hurt her, and that someday one of the bits she remembered would surface to show her that this was indeed all that they were, and nothing more. Then the moons shifted and went their separate ways, continuing their long arduous journey away from the rotation of the winter axis, and the dreams seemed to slow down a bit, leaving her in relative peace and quiet for a time.

But the memory of the dreams, was about to become very real for him. Daniel picked his way through the destroyed pieces of the old bailey's iron

gates, which lay twisted and bent along the shattered stones of the legendary ruins of the ancient fortress. It was here that something strange caught
his eye, arriving in a technicolor reminder of those long nights of sleepless
worry, blowing the hypothesis he and his mate had right out of the damn
water. For, only moments away, he would find himself doubting everything
that each one of those brilliant minds had said in trying to assure him this
was nothing to worry about, and she would soon grow out of it. Now standing before him, it reared its ugly head out of the land of the dream world
and found its place in the land of life.

What happened next would shatter that summer of restless nights, and
the words the Witch had spoken of comfort, as he was about to come face
to face and meet the demons of her nightmares up close and personal.
Daniel had never in a million lifetimes thought that what she had spoken
about to him on the mornings after each dream that had terrorized her
waking moments, could actually hold some form of realism.

Had he put coin on this one, he would have lost everything, and he
wouldn't have heard the end of it for many moons. It wasn't 'til they got
within about three strides of him, that Pharonis recognized who he was,
and their facial expressions changed from those of someone they had not
known a moment ago, to one of familiarity and ease.

"Daniel, is that you?" Pharonis said in a shocked voice, as he dropped
down out of the air from above, where Daniel had been hiding, almost
landing right on top of him, making the Shapeshifter jump clear out of
his skin. He began to morph into a bird so he could fly around the large
Aelf, but never made it past the feathers. Something prevented him from
completing the change, and all he got was a mouthful of flight feathers
trying to sprout through blocked passages that suddenly sealed themselves
over. Instead, without knowing the reason for the failure of the hawk, he
continued to try for his freedom and reversed direction, trying to project
his body away from where the other had moved to.

Up above, Tamerk hissed at the Shapeshifter's quick movements,
keeping just barely ahead of the molecules he had tried to change into.
As Daniel began to morph once again — Tamerk blocked that change too,
and in frustration Daniel gave up and came outwards, throwing a punch
in Pharonis's direction. Tamerk orchestrated the molecules like a director

controlling a Shakespearean play, and redirected his Shifter energy into butterflies that moved with the molecules out of his hands, never making contact with Pharonis's chin.

They flew upwards just as they were met by several pairs of additional hands, which appeared out of nowhere to block the punch, and instead found them-selves covered in butterflies as both Muijalaa and Eurgerus ducked out of the way of the mass exodus of wings. Both riders, who had joined in the fight that was about to erupt, pulled Pharonis and Daniel backwards up against the nearest wall, to wait out the insects that had appeared out of nowhere. They too had been well hidden when Daniel's footsteps had originally been detected, and had come out of similar hiding spots, moving to take up positions on either side of Pharonis in an armed defensive posturing, to defend their brother warrior against this new winged intruder.

Before they were able to stop themselves from getting involved in the fight that was about to explode, Pharonis got sucker punched through the hoard of insects still making their way through the castle grounds. Both of them moved together to prevent another occurrence from dropping their friend onto the stone floor, by shoving Daniel up against the crumbling wall, hanging by his boot heels, before they too realized just who they held tightly up against the outer-bailey swearing like a Troll.

They immediately dropped their hold on Daniel's arms, grinning wildly and saluting the Shapeshifter while Pharonis nursed a bruised mouth, saying something about at least it was only a fist, and not the famed Mercorian blades of the Togernaut clan taking his head off. The others grinned at the joke, and clapped him on the back as Daniel backed up, trying to stay out of their reach, visibly shaken by these strangers who acted like long lost friends.

What he saw next shocked him; they each reached for one of his hands, placed it firmly in their own, and knelt on the ground, putting his hands to their foreheads in a form of peaceful greeting. They had been far too close for Daniel to have not known they were there. As he tried to catch his breath, the scene that played out in front of his heaving chest, was nothing short of extraordinary. He freed his fingers from their embrace, trying to stay that much further out of arms reach in case they tried to use force after lulling him into a sense of false security, and caved his skull in. With hands free, he wiped the spittle off the sides of his mouth, gasping for breath, bringing huge amounts of oxygen into his expanding lungs, not quite knowing how to proceed or what to do next.

They continued to kneel before him; odd behaviour for warriors who had appeared on the hunt. While he watched them from a distance with suspicion in his eyes, Daniel was not in any way prepared for what was about to happened. At first glance, he didn't realize what he was seeing with regards to who they were; after all, he had never met the trio in the dreams Sibrey had encountered for most of her sleeping life. All he had seen was one very large warrior coming towards him out of nowhere, and then, as fast as a Dragon got caught in the shadow of the Draconian moon, something changed all that — confusing him even further.

Both parties had arrived simultaneously in the same small amount of space; when they first dragged him over to the central chamber's oldest wall, but it was Daniel who recognized the tattoo on the closest warrior's neck when he called him by name, and bent down to offer his hand in ceremonial deference. Daniel might have been forcibly stopped from doing any further damage to the warrior's face, but he had the element of surprise on him when they hadn't been looking. Now he was wondering whether that had been a good idea.

He knew that tattoo well; any of the Shapeshifters within Manannan's kingdom worth a grain of salt, would have known that tattoo. But those of his clan had special memories of the inking, which resembled one of the highest ranking Capourian Mountain Pack-Wolf clans that roamed the mountains and salt marshes along the shores.

"That's not possible; you're from my daughter's nightmares, not from flesh and blood," he cried out in shock, looking at the three of them in sheer astonishment; trying unsuccessfully to back up — realizing he could go no further with his bones already against the hardened stone surface behind him.

The clan of the pack wolf was older than time; most of them were only known in legend, and not as actual beings that still existed and lived today along the fringes of any of the existing Capourian Mountain meadowlands. It suddenly dawned on Daniel what this meant and he shivered at the thought of how he had taken her to that old Witch, seeing the truth of the matter staring back at him, right down to the three faces she had explained in fascinating detail.

The three warriors that had been chasing after Sibrey for only a few days in this realm of the Goddesses, now quietly conversed with each other. They looked at Daniel and grinned, rising to stand on legs that seemed to bulge with muscles far superior to those of any normal Fey Daniel had ever seen before. They spoke to Daniel with absolute certainty on their faces, and removed the grin he had taken as a half-ass sneer. They looked at each other then back at Daniel's face, while shaking their long manes of hair — giving the majik of their molecules over into the wind, offering him complete scrutiny of their minds. It was a gesture known well in those of the Fey clans, and one simply done to show they had not a single ounce of deceit in their bodies.

"That is who, she believes us to be, but it is a little more complicated than that. That old Witch you're thinking about knew very well what we were. We just got to her first, before she was able to speak to you and reveal what we were to your young charge. Had Sibrey found out too soon, she might just have high-tailed it back to the Panthers that run wild in the hills, and we would have found it harder to protect her inside their territory. It would have cost us time that we could ill afford, and we would not have been able to protect her from the danger she now faces; especially when she moves in different molecules with the one that travels with her as one of their own." The nearest male to Daniel continued to speak softly on be-half of the others.

"Yes the Panther that you saw belongs to her, and he was there that night to make sure you were able to subdue her before she made it into his realm, where the danger was at its peak; she was still too young to manage that transference. We as a clan, have known about her our whole lives; it is what we have been born into within your realm of energy beings that swim on this side of our mountain homes. Many centuries ago it was what was done to protect one that moves within different pathways of old Wulushian majiks. And in this incarnation it is your shippels fate; the very shippel that was given over at her wailing years.

We were created for the one that is called Sibrey, and it is her that we were sent to protect, and will do so by the blood-oath that we took upon our passage of birth into this realm. Had you been told what we were, something would have stayed within your memory, and that information would someday prevent us from fully protecting the female in the capacity she would allow us to follow, and our existence would have been for naught when the danger came to a head and claimed its heart."

Daniel's skin began to prickle, and a wave of fear came over his tensing muscles, as Muijalaa continued on with words that were creating havoc inside his visual cortex. He tried to breathe through nostrils that moved inside some form of thickening jelly, which simply refused to move out of the way and let him formulate new breath.

It stayed there momentarily, simply remaining stuck in place, and he felt he couldn't formulate the correct thinking patterns that would allow him to breathe without disbelief, leaving a far more bitter taste inside his mouth than what he currently had been experiencing. He had always been taught to trust no one, and Tamerk himself had made it plain to him in simple language even a slaw could understand. 'Be on guard with those that appear to have your daughter's best interest at heart.'

Tamerk had been specific, and what Daniel saw in front of his face now resembled all that Tamerk had warned him about, stuffed into a pretty convincing package of warrior testosterone. Alarm bells could be heard sounding off in the distant recesses of his brain, as Daniel began to reach for his sword. He had only gone as far as finding its handle, when Pharonis interrupted briefly, staying his hand with a kindness Daniel was not used to, and each of them handed their own swords over to him hilt first, in surrender.

"The Tamerk that appears as a Wood Sprite is not the Tamerk that is, Daniel. It is with that knowledge that we are bonded to succeed in the task at all cost, to the very essence that we are formed to breathe in this hiccup of a sheltered timeline of her soul. Should you choose to end ours, that is what we must endure; for anything else would betray who we are and all would be a secondary quest for another that would take up in our place."

Daniel's words were quick and to the point, still beating silently within a brain that found no reason to listen to what the dream-warrior had to say.

"What do you mean Tamerk is not Tamerk? That in itself makes no sense. I don't understand the words that make up that contradiction. And how come you all still keep smiling at me? It makes no sense to follow the words that are hollow and without substance. The very example of this notion of someone being not what he appears to be is exactly what I'm talking about. How can one be one thing, and be something else at the same time? There is no logic to that way of thinking." He tried to raise his arm with a sword that would not budge, as it lay loosely against his side, unable or unwilling to move, he just could not tell. His head began to feel like the world that he had grown up within was about to be rewritten, and everything that he had been taught was completely without texture or colour anymore. Still, he was not convinced of what they had become, simply because a child was born.

What happened next threw Daniel further out of sorts and deflated the anger that had been quickly rising — with all that he had seen in the past few Quadra-seconds. All three bent to kneel in front of the Shapeshifter and bowed their heads, giving him an honour-bound oath that took his last train of thought, right out of his damn head. To make matters worse, he dropped his sword and it clattered loudly on the broken stones, having no life left for fighting — he couldn't have reached for it, even if he had tried. They spoke quickly and without malice, directing their thoughts upwards to where Daniel currently stood over-top of their heads.

"There is so much that we need to tell you, from the date line that was programed into the time-stamp of our memories. It was to be delivered at the appropriate moment in your linear age differential, and it will take some time to systematize all within the brain-stem of our shifts, as it is still supposed to be a few moons left before that was to be. However for whatever reason it has happened now — so now it is."

Daniel watched the recalibration of all three warriors as their movements seemed to go into a kind of frozen state of automation, and time itself stood still around them. He held his breath watching what was unfolding, and the wind could be seen drifting along the linear lines in front of him — about one arm length off the ground.

Nina hiccupped as Horae swore, and smacked Arddhu on the back.

"I knew it; things have been far too calm around here to be not hiding something big within our ranks," Nina yelled, as she turned with nervous hands, to move in the direction of the room that Sibrey was sleeping within. "Do I have time to check on Sibrey before they begin the show?" Tamerk shook his head.

"That won't be necessary doll; you watch, I'll go. It's important that you stay."

She jumped back into line with glee, clapping her hands together until Horae smacked her in the back of the head, and she instantly stopped and glared at the other Goddess, biting her tongue in the process.

"Hey, what's wrong with you; that hurt?"

"No, what's wrong with you? Snap out of it you dingbat, this is not an amphitheatre set up with wine and grapes to be visualized at your leisure. Really Nina, get it together and start acting your age. Your acting like one of their Newbornling, instead of the full on immortal Goddess you are supposed to be!"

Nina stuck her tongue out at Horae, just as the mirror began to fade into a darker shade of metallic grey, and splintered along the outer-edges. Each of the replicas of Aelven warriors slowly began to find their hands, and deliberately moved their fingers to the next one's throat, placing them on the collar bone of the warrior in front of them in a process that looked like they were about to choke or at the very least strangle themselves.

They moved almost as if they were moulded together, and cocked their heads a bit to the right, closing all six eyes in unison. One by one, they moved together as if they had been tapped on the shoulders and began making a noise that neither of the Goddesses had heard in a very long time. It was one of those metallic clicking noises that could be heard when the blacksmith banged his anvil on the iron rods he used in his molten fire pits, back in the old smith village of Sombreia's forges. As soon as the rhythm reached a certain decibel, they opened eyes that had turned coal black and started to speak as a singular unit, staring off at a point of interest just above Daniel's shoulders and a little to the left. Whatever they were seeing now was not within Daniel's line of sight anymore.

He looked over his shoulder with great reluctance, and had half expected something to actually be there. It was not, much to his great relief, but looking at the trio he could only imagine the terror a young Aelflet would have had, watching the group of them as they proceeded to speak as a single entity, using vocal cords that belonged to something other than the three individual warriors that were now standing in front of him.

Around them things began to slow down, and the air became thick with a feeling of heaviness. Each single sound became intertwined with the next, as they drifted and curved around the other and attached themselves to the solid form of what would have resembled a vine growing skyward along the Anforian Sugar Maples. Once firmly ensconced, they spoke in small clicking noises at first, then it changed slightly and began to grow inwards, joined by musical humming sounds from the outside, which formed the ancient dialect of another time lost from down the ages, in a galaxy that hadn't been heard from in several million years. They adjusted the volume and let the accent intermingle with the mind of Daniel's vocabulary, formulating sentences to curve into those that would fit the language of the one that would be listening to the meaningful tale.

Daniel, still recovering from the fact that he was no longer on a Tameronian plane with his Shapeshifter clan, seemed reasonably calm for one who earlier appeared to be a little bit freaked out by their appearance. He drifted along the edges of what appeared to be a region that few Fey had ever been invited to visit, while all around him the sight before him changed. Feeling oddly out of sync, he dusted boot heels along the fray of the spaces in-between the two worlds, as they moved simultaneously with each other in the same space and time, showing him the visual side of what their story had to say.

He listened and watched the warriors who sang in this strangely familiar haunting language, which seemed almost musical in its dialect, and much to his delight, rather beautiful in its soulful texture. He closed his eyes to ignore the appearance of the trio who spoke fluently with its alien tongue, watching with his mind's eye as it approached a more colourful tone than anything he had heard before; that is, until he saw the picture they had given him to see, and he moved through the doorway to join with it.

The words, although alien in texture, still remained similar in their triangulation of the Aelven dialect. But his surprise came, when they corrected the slight variance of their voices possession, and he was still able to make out the words even though they were being spoken in voices that were definably not of Aelven symmetry, and not even close to the Shapeshifter vocabulary.

They spoke of solitude, and how one came through against his own volition. Their words flowed along the borders of musical song, and came together as foretold in the great plays from the royal compounds where the theatre would be filled to capacity on those warm evenings of the long harvest nights; during fire festival time. All of this he witnessed, as though he himself was actually standing in the exact place they were talking about.

They spoke of sorrow, and then redirected its direction into another being, one that was dedicated to that of the hunter. There was always a hunter in almost every battle this side of the greatest storytellers. But, what was told about this creature surprised even Daniel in the extent of its telling, and as he listened closely, completely engrossed in the tale which he had heard when he was still a child, long ago, it changed. Then he heard the child above that belonged to another start to wake from her sleep — he heard himself breathe, but she was still full of nightmarish dreams and didn't answer.

"Sibrey, where are you child?" he heard himself speak softly, into the outside air again.

The story stopped and one of the warriors looked directly at him, speaking in his usual voice, which was far removed from those of the storytellers who had previously spoken, and he lowered his voice while the others continued to sing, so that only Daniel could hear as he reached over with his palm planted firmly and touched his heart.

"She will stay and will be there when we finish our tale; she has always done so in the past, and even though we seem to be actively hunting her ourselves, it is for naught, and has never been to trap her where she is, but to trap those that search for her who do not belong within this realm. This, I promise you." He stepped back and returned to the others to continue the song that had stayed in its tale, while the others simply waited patiently for him to return to their side.

"For now there is much to learn and had we been allowed we would have given this tale to you sooner. But now, we shall try to rectify that wrong. Before that is done, we must warn you of the content of what is about to be exposed for eyes that may not be your own." All three looked around the perimeter of the broken battlements in affirmation of what they were speaking to Daniel about. Their eyes glazed black for just a fraction of a negatron as particles collided and formed a barrier Daniel had never seen before. The negative and positive particles came together and began to form an electrical charge that surrounded all four of them and circled around the area they were standing in, sealing them inside one of the most unusual protection circles Daniel had ever seen.

They looked around the rim of the new enclosure and their eyes returned to their former colour, as something slid back into the rocks and disappeared from sight. Muijalaa nodded to the others, and they continued on with their tale of Sibrey's soul, fully protected from whatever had tried unsuccessfully to penetrate into their domain.

"For now you must remember this, and all that is spoken before you today, be it given in a different tongue or shall it come from a source you are not familiar with in its strange dialect. For it is important to the telling, and even though it was not clear even to our own-selves, the reason it was not forthcoming in the early years, it came with others that bear that load still today and was not ours to give."

Silence remained, while the voices recalibrated their vocal cords to suit the tale they would tell of the unspeakable danger that still lay ahead of Daniel and his young Panther Spitlet.

He listened to other things that ran alongside of this silence, and thought of the wife and son who had remained behind, while his band of Pickadeum Stormknockers gathered together in the main square in Sombreia, and started out with head held high, and revenge in their hearts.

The voices started once again and came out with another dialect even stranger than the first; one that previously was not presented in its initial calling. As Daniel listened to its words he discovered that the song brought with it a haunting remainder of yet more problems that lay ahead. He discovered things he had not known were standing upwards and coming towards him with great velocity, formulating the truth inside his brain while his living mundane world came crashing down all around him, and landed smack dab upon the ground at his feet.

"The animal that waits along the borders of the trees is called a Sling; it hunts the children that belong to another world, that rest their minds on the soil of this land, until their shift. This one that is Sling, from worlds not known to the planet Tantaris, has travelled from another place, coming to this world and forced to join in tandem with one that keeps it tormented even to this day, even though its breath can no longer breathe the air around us.

That thing will continue to search for her and one that is of the blood of kings, until their energy disperses into the void, or he is taken and killed. But even in her dream-state that has yet to be decided, for she has slept far longer than was thought, and for some reason he has been able to track her even in that slumbering state, despite our precautions.

The warriors of the Trithogean wolf pack were called from inside the rings of the Siren's Stone Monoliths, out along the paramour desert that drifts along the quatrains of distant sands. They are mostly gone now, buried deeply within the volcanic activity that runs through the different drift-points along the shadow of that dune. But recently one resurfaced, and it still stands deep inside the desert sands along the rift that was opened by one that does not belong to our world. It was as the shadow grew in the far reaches of its arrival, that we found ourselves as a single soul forged together in a united front. We came together to form a protection around the one that forced us to ride along the fringes of her unconscious mind, just to keep her moving slightly ahead of its field of search."

"You mean you pushed her forward in her dreams?" Daniel interrupted, watching the warriors nod in unison and continue on with the story, undeterred by his hypothecation.

"It was not a push by your understanding of the standards of actual motion, but a conscious choice to continue to move her forward without actual touch. In doing so, it kept her from remaining in one place for too long, as it hunted along the fringes and its searches broadened, becoming exceedingly more dangerous the closer it got. Unfortunately, she became stuck in the continuum and tried as we may, couldn't find the reason to get her to move forward in her dreams. In doing so, she repeated the dream sequence over, and over, since the beginning of her childhood, while we continued to find the meaning of its nucleus to release her back to normal dreams."

Daniel remained silent as the story continued on, ignoring the fact he was far more exhausted than he first thought. There was no way now of finding his sleep; now that he was invested in the tale, sleep drifted away along the edges of the stone casement that lifted its crumbling head from the ancient walls of some forgotten castle he should know it's naming.

"The thing that is coming is called Symbya. He was not a dark entity being when first he was formed. That only happened after he was pulled through a Dark Matter Star when Balor did not have the knowledge of how to cast his circle, and protect the creation of its energy when it came through the vortex."

"Balor!" Daniel woke up shouting without having slept a wink, when the name came to the forefront of the conversation unexpectedly. "What does he have to do with this?" They turned in unison and spoke quickly, without moving their mouths.

"You must wait Daniel, we shall tell you as fast as we can. The real Symbya was nothing like this creature, and was something to be revered on the world he was born into. The creature that arrived in your lands was a very different being; one that remains strong even in the face of uncertainty." They continued.

"This entity, as we like to call him, which was conjured up out of the darkside of the home-world Star of the Sirens, is made up from the essence of what Symbya originally was. And the being that he was, no longer moved alone within the circle of his Siren brain-stem, creating a very unique and much more dangerous being than anything that lived inside him before. Long ago, he was sought after by the Fey royal Herders from many arenas of space, and even some in the Human worlds felt its presence along their borders, and sought out his energy readings from their side of the Milky Way constellations of those far off stars.

His unique abilities gave him that edge over those whose strength was always been lacking in the social graces, and many of those creatures sought his audience in greater numbers as word of his abilities grew by word of mouth, throughout the known worlds. It was foretold at this time that his race could see the future, changing its structure to those times well sought after within the realm of the Fey that had existed in times of antiquity.

Symbya was a natural in this field of visions, and his gift was especially clairvoyant in its visionary quest. His gift could actually visually and theoretically put you directly in the middle of where your ancestors had lived, back in times of their living breath. You see, Symbya's race were visionaries of their kind, and came with many different sights that bled into the vast antiquaries of Fey nobility. Their uniqueness was unparalleled in their beauty, and many so enthralled by their spectacular sight were lost from their own worlds when their wishes came to fruition, never to be seen again.

Each of the Siren races has, in one form or another, a secret that is hidden and lost behind the walls, which separate the species from each other and its revelation. Some were divided equally among the clans that lived and breathed out in the open arenas of outer space, while others simply belonged to family groups that moved about in the vast expanses of Fey worlds that ran parallel to the current Fey colonies. Symbya's clan had the rarest gifts of them all, with each following along the shamanistic lifestyles of the nomadic tribes of their homeland, and having a wanderlust that was unparalleled within their race.

His tribe refused to accommodate what was unusual; instead choosing to use the access to open up this knowledge further, one that was hardwired in the frontal lobe of their intelligence, and hosted the shard molecules that made up the arenas of spacial flux inside this area of brain matter. That knowledge made their souls more giving than those of their parent race, and gave over their findings to those true gifts of ancient majiks that have been stolen throughout the known universes, and following down another path that lead them away from the mainstream of the Siren race.

Symbya's clan maintained that knowledge throughout their lives and were able to hardwire their gifts and hide them away from the oracle crowd, finding ways to give them openly to the races that ran along the great divide of Sopdet's vast expanses of open space. So it was to become normal for them as they grew in age, to move between the old worlds, finding strange and alien objects hidden from the eyes of others. And once in a while they were able to obtain pieces of ancient artifacts, which had been hidden from the main Fey culture by ways of old majiks, and they would then take them back whole in their original condition, and return them to where they would be best suited to the needs of the races that had requested them. This is what Balor discovered when he moved to destroy the Tuatha De' Danann.

Many still had the original binding spells, which still harnessed them to others that lived within the depths of even the deepest caverns of the dark

Fey and their Ferrishyn hosts. However, his race also had a secret previously unknown to the remaining Fey races that lived on the other-side of the divide. That secret was the very thing that started the war to begin with, and what made what is happening today with the hunt of your kit, a very deadly gift to have.

You see, Symbya's talent was discovered to be very unique even among his own kind. That gift gave him the ability to do other things not previously known outside their borders of space, and was the very reason why he was so important among his own tribe. You see, he had the ability to remove the signature of those old binding spells that attached themselves to the ancient artifacts that the Sirens had been finding of late. With Symbya's talent, they could be removed and forever released from those that held them attached to their own kind, and away from those that sought them out. Balor had need of this gift, and assumed that this gift was a by-product of all the Siren species.

This gift had many of them nervous in its discovery, for it came with a price that others of ill repute found to be extremely tantalizing on many sides of the faces of power. They knew that the doorways would eventually be breached, and the factions of Fey led by those like Balor would find them far too valuable to pass up, as they in turn began to formulate an attempt to retrieve even a fraction of its majikal power for them.

It would have been catastrophic had it occurred, though many had tried, none succeeded to date until that faithful night when one of the doorways was accidentally left open, and someone allowed its arrival to go unchecked as something drifted inside and moved out towards the breeding grounds where the Sirens had been gathering since dawn. He was tracked down on one of the darker sides of the Siren's home-star, in the depths of the wastelands of Paramour, by someone that had knowledge of the thinning doorways, and used one of the deadliest evocation rituals that had ever been discovered to have been used by any of the races of Fey that lived today.

The practice of evocation was highly frowned upon, and was always considered to be one of the last resorts in any ritual that was performed with any majiks, no matter what the calling was intended for. Evocation in itself was deadly, and always had a price attached that others not familiar with its ritual realized all too late in its making.

This one was especially bad, and had the highest councils of the Siren home star fearing the worst, as its molecules of intent became known to them with its signature drift as it came into being. It came in thin, and then expanded, moving along the sands at such a high rate of speed that all that were present watched with horror as it swallowed everything in its path, moving out towards the breeding grounds.

Nothing could be done for those caught in its flux, and those that were only stung as it moved along the edges of their bodies became insane, as it searched the field for the one that it had arrived to claim.

Many Sirens died that day, and many more followed in the days and weeks to come, as it stayed and hovered along the recesses of their minds, claiming their souls as it tendrils moved inside their molecules and began to nest. The spell was intended for killing those that had been born with evil bled into their hearts, and was one of the worst ritual evocations to be found to exist in any of the majikal realms that moved along the borders of Fey space. It had been locked away and held in a safe place for centuries and most Fey didn't even know it existed until it arrived and moved in for the kill that horrible day along the Siren's home-world.

How it was released is still a mystery even to this day, how he changed the directive to kill at will was also unknown, and it will take the entire Goddess community a very long time to realize how it was even possible to find, let alone steal away from the depths of the locks that held it in transitional solitude. But stolen it was, and though it was never intended to be used outside the Goddess realm, it poured through the barriers that held it in check, and moved with an evil intent not previously programed into its matrix.

The original spell was created by the Cloud People, having been born out of necessity in the off chance that one would come into this world and need to be taken down before their true gifts could harm any of the Fey and their simple ways of life. This one in particular, had been always used by those of the Priestess caste, and not by individuals that knew nothing about its real power or true manipulations and the power that it controlled.

The one that stole it from them held no barriers and released a pre-defined circle that had been programed to protect those that moved within its flux. The particular conjuring that was noticed was without those safeguards, and was done without any of the protections commonly used to protect the one from becoming them-selves part of the energy transference.

What they had done was something so horrific, that it actually removed the Siren energy signature from beyond its homeland, and created an energy sting that picked Symbya up after he was located, not recognizing it as one of their own, and basically shoved him through to the other-side. What arrived to claim his signature, left Symbya to virtually claw his way across the sands and through the opening, trying to grab onto whatever he could before the string could completely engulf him and he was lost to his homeland and those that he loved, forever.

It was written that he was pulled out of a desolate area of the backside of his normal hunting grounds, and by all accounts as it was recorded by the scribes that placed its occurrence in the book of the dead, he mustn't have gone without some kind of fight, as all that remained were blackened scorch marks burned deeply along the loose sand, containing some sort of alien vulcanized glass; smelling highly of sulphurized hide, to mark his crossing as he passed through the containment breach.

When others of the ruling class of Siren chieftains came to visually witness the disturbing evidence after the disappearance of one of their own kind, it was recorded with deep sadness by one such scribe that came to witness the terrible scene for himself. What they came to see and had recorded in their text had not done the travesty justice, by the words that were used by one such high chieftain undeterred by its occurrence of this outlawed tribe.

What had been a definite scarring of the land had been excluded from the history books. This scribe had included such known occurrences as happened over the course of many instances, in the written laws of the tribal leaders of other clans, and could no longer formulate and hide its endeavour with this one. So he included what he saw in a small overlay on notes that were included as notations he scribed along the bottom of these historic novels that the ruling class had fictionalized throughout the times of their individual reigns, and gave them an invisibility spell so they couldn't be read by those who might have taken offense to his clarity. After all, the Sirens most affected were those of the renegade tribe and not of any great significance to the ruling might.

Included in this particular rare document that they had not bothered to read in its entirety, was one such inscription that showed the passage of one of the outlawed tribes to have succumbed to an unknown threat — which they deemed to have been hindered by the Goddess realm of Priestess writings. The scribe noted that the markings that were left were too defined to be excluded from the original text, and in leaving a huge trench which ran from one side of the divide to the other in its entirety, thereby splitting the region right down the middle; was more than worth the mention; not excluding the station of who Symbya was, and how the evocation seemed to target him and him alone.

This new scar in the landscape was something so catastrophic that for the others not to have included evidence of its passage was telling of the split in the clans already. For the evocation spell had caused many boulders that had been shifted and carried great distances by some unseen hand, to be moved across the breeding grounds in a sight of phenomenal feats of strength unknown to those of the Siren class, leaving the ground toxic. Whatever had opened the doorway, our Siren was not able to pull himself free, as Symbya had been literally dragged through the opening kicking and screaming; more than likely in a great deal of pain. Furthermore, it seemed to have left some form of energy behind as it continued to pull additional boulders and loose stones through the energy transference, as he made his exit into the void.

It fluctuated as it drifted, and wedged them into the open doorway, jamming several huge pieces along the edges of where it apparently left its mark. It sparked and spewed huge energy clouds that took several weeks to contain and remove from the mess it left behind; rendering a rescue from this side largely impossible.

This section of isolated landscape ran primarily along the fringes of several barren deserts of black-sand energy lines, and several of them ran in conjunction to similar shedding grounds that each of the Siren species used to replenish their energy matrices, causing the species as a whole to redirect their energy to another section of the desert far away because of the volcanic sparking's from the violent uprising.

His species could often be found lounging along the hotter dunes, shimmering in the sandy soil as they rolled about scrubbing the meteor dust off their beautiful hides, grooming their leathery skin to their inner-cells until it shone a deep golden bronze. It was this ritual of arrival that Balor used to hunt Symbya's energy matrix along with their cycle of molt. Unfortunately, it was not Symbya that he had tried to reach, it was another that he had been instructed to pull through by the Sidhe Queen and Balor, knowing no different, could not differentiate between the two.

It seemed that Balor thought he had grown wise in the ways of black majik, had not listened to the evocation. However, that was soon to make him careless in his dealings with creatures that were best suited to staying on the darkside of the void. For some reason the one that he found to have arrived in his study one cold and windy night, was one that should never have been allowed to come through the doorways he had opened, without having had more information about its history in the first place.

You see, Balor had not learned from a Wizard or a Witch, as he thought this creature that appeared before him had been. When first it arrived in the dead of night some years ago, Balor believed it to be something other than what the creature really was, and his assumptions on its lineage were far from anything he had seen in the past, so he had nothing to base his findings on.

Had he used his wits, he would have known something was wrong. But, having no former experience in his studies, and having never dabbled in dark majiks of any kind, his own arrogance drove him into believing he was better off dealing with it, than leaving it to the Sorcerers that worked inside his temples For they would have known instantly that this was no Witch or Wizard kind within two shakes of a Gargoyle's tongue. And Balor, too blinded by ambition to succeed in his hatred of the Tuatha De`Danann, had no intention of letting anyone know he was about to destroy the Aelven army and its newest members — who still had yet to be born, high up in the tower where he himself had played a big part in imprisoning their own mother until they were.

No my friend, what had arrived in the dead of night, was far more dangerous than anything the Fey had dealt with in any of the coven trials that had come and gone through the early years of the Fey kingdoms of Trithogean warriors. Balor, having been too blind in his anger to ask for help from those that could have prevented what came next, probably wouldn't have lived through the night the moment they witnessed the arrival of this creature in Balor's study anyway. Looking back now, it seems the Sidhe Queen had other criteria on her agenda than Balor's diabolical ideals of ruling the continent of Water's Deep. Her goal was far more extravagant, and included Sopdet's lands far away from a little old planet. But, we digress.

It appears, from all those that were in attendance upon its arrival, that Balor had been bragging and drinking heavily while he dined with a rather elite group of warrior thieves, who had been called to council with the impending war with the Humans; the very Humans that had been recorded to have come within reach of the outer-rim of the Fey worlds, and were about to breech this planet's shores.

His boasting voice could still be heard by those in attendance, bragging about what he was able to contribute to the cause, and how he singlehandedly was about to make history and become the next King of the Aelven hordes. But words were only sounds that rarely came to fruition, and much of the renegade Aelves who had been part of the supper he had catered to remembered a completely different story. One that was written down without his knowledge, by scribes that moved about in the darkest of nights beneath the chambers of his own castle walls.

They tell of a peacock that believed only in hurting others in his aspirations to get to the top, and would crush anyone of them had he the chance, in his hurry to become something he would never be able to achieve by his sheer violence and arrogance alone. Their words told of someone who cared very little for those not willing to help him with his grandiose plans of ultimate succession, and had he known that they had moved to record a very different recollection of events, he would have surely killed the lot of them right then and there. But that, was not to come until much later, when he moved alone to destroy all those that were present during the times of his incompetency; when in his arrogance and illiterate ways of majik, he had inadvertently left his ritual unguarded while he bragged and bellowed to those generals of highest military rank, who had unexpectedly arrived after he concluded this speech.

What came next was written in absolute secrecy and was not discovered until very recently, in one of the older texts that had been discreetly hidden and placed within the Goddess realm of records. It describes a very different view of the Formorian leader and his ability to open up a world previously unknown to those of the planet realms, and one incident in particular that caught several eyes for its ability to be unusually stupid in all things Fey.

It would appear, by all accounts written; that Balor had opened a small portal to another world and invited what came through with such reverence of pomp and circumstance, allowing several of those beings — not of this plane, inside the threshold to cross the barrier into this realm. To those in attendance of the dinner it looked like he had tried with what he thought would be something impressive, to show his reverence for a darker ritualized majik. What happened was something entirely different, and the creatures arrived in full force through the barrier and moved to take the chamber the old Formorian leader and his band of thieves were currently in and dining inside.

A fight ensued and the creatures were quickly outnumbered and rounded up, and during the remainder of the evening, as drinks were passed around in large numbers and gaiety of the evening returned to what had transpired, Balor grew exceedingly moody. Something changed in his eyes during the course of the evening when the bragging reached its peak, and all had lain upon the chamber mats, passed out from mead. It seemed they were too drunk to completely follow blindly what Balor had invited them all to see. Disgusted with the fact that he had not finished his demonstration on dark majiks before his guests had digested enough brandied mead to kill a bull Cathor, he had returned all the captured creatures to their own dimension without being able to demonstrate his ability to control their every movement with what he had been studying in the old manuscripts he had found in some abandoned cave, deep in the heart of Mangoesa Island.

The moodiness stayed for many months, and just before spring came, and the planting festival of Ostara had found its fingers and started to stretch warmly across the land, Balor discovered what he had wanted in an obscure scroll hidden in a dusty old vault that the Cloud 'People seemed to have left unlocked. In that vault was an old manuscript that spoke of a ritual that was founded in dark majiks long since discarded as being too dangerous, and found a way to summon one of the beings from that star system out across the rolling seas of stellar space without actually being there in the flesh.

The rarity of that actually occurring is along the lines of minuscule proportionalism. But, it did indeed occur, one deeply cold day along the fringes of the wetlands within the boundaries of his island, somewhere deep in the bowels of that Formorian stronghold as the waves rolled in and slammed loudly against the stone ramparts.

It is said that Balor went ahead without thinking of the ramifications of his actions, and hadn't learned his lesson from the previous evocation he created. Someone inside his own tight clique had not informed him of the necessary means to achieve the desired effect of the spell, and neglected to remind him that there would be a price to pay for the deed. To those of us who know, it is said that his own Druid Carpathious had no love for the King, and hadn't included many things in his instruction on delving into the art of majik, and therefore, rather pissed, he decided to go ahead and do this without including him in his plans, basically setting Balor up to fail.

Everyone who is anything in the world of ritual majiks knows there is always a price to pay for doing such a thing and nothing is ever free in its undertaking. For those of you who do not understand this thing, it is important to know that any form of majik, dark or light, must have an equal payment in kind to replace the atoms it would displace in its conductivity. The karmatic repercussions of that payment, can still be seen today along the shores of Balor's private sanctuary, and if you look really hard out in the water to the north of the castle moat, those scars that the shallows have swallowed up have several sulphur based aquatic creatures that do not belong to this planet.

In the advancing waterline along the far shore, these creatures live and breathe in another realm, and have modified their soft caustic shells to acclimatize themselves to the water environment that currently houses their little bodies. Now they are slowly eating away at the underside of the very rocks of his Formorian fortress; soon that too will fall into the sea, and his kingdom of perceived greatness will be completely invisible as it disappears beneath the waves, never to be seen again."

The warriors took a small break and became quite still, letting Daniel move about the old battlements, stretching his arms to take the numb feeling out of his muscles from remaining in such a rigid upright position for so long, as the story had proceeded and left him wanting more.

It made him feel somewhat strange, looking around at where he actually was, moving slowly amongst the broken stones and pieces of this once mighty fortress of some lost and forgotten kingdom of another age in the world of Tantaris's constant rebuilding. Along with bits of dread and a bad taste in his mouth that came with unfinished business that had given into feeling as if he was on the outskirts of something surreal, it occurred to him that what Balor had accomplished by greed and extreme narcissism, had created a time dilatation in the waters that were not used by the races currently living within these spacial waters.

That darkness of what he was able to use was something much more powerful than previously known, and that made him very nervous as his mind played out different scenarios that the Fey from Balor's selfish pragmatic attention to detail had excluded within the known races of the Siren home-world.

The trio of warriors moved again, and waited for Daniel to come back to their story, starting to hum slowly, almost inaudible to Daniel's ears. He found the sound soothing and was once again pulled into their tale. They surrounded him with words in much greater detail to the telling, that told of the exact arrival of Symbya's broken shell into a realm he had not given his permission to be in.

"We do not know as of yet how it went undetected by their guardians, but the moment it was cast, it filtered through on the threads of a Faden-strand that easily slipped through their towers, and went in search of the one being that could be of most use to Balor's diabolical needs. It appeared to us that he did not at first understand who he had come for, and that Symbya was mostly in the wrong place at the right time, and simply dragged with the energies of thread, being much closer to the search area that opened up, protecting someone else near their breeding grounds he had been talking to.

Balor did not have the knowledge, and had not been trained as a Sorcerer like we said, and would not have known how to predict which way the thread moved as it hunted through the sands of their desert environment. After all, he had started to use the manifestation crystal in its purest form, knowing that what he wished to find would be brought forth in its entirety, or so the book had told him. Unfortunately, he had not read the fine print of the scrolls. Had he done so, he might have chosen an entirely different route.

But either way, the crystal would not allow him access to his wish, after it was discovered that he had selfish reasons for the event. That particular safeguard had been built into its matrix by others of the Cloud People when the crystal was first shaped in the molten forges of the Wulushian desert tribes. That did not deter him, even after it was discovered he had failed with its complexity. His complete disrespect of the art of the Witch brought with it the consequences of doing things that you have no business doing, without the knowledge of the actual ideology. But still he continued on, feeling the taste of victory just inside the inner recesses of his insane brain. He threw it away and reached for something far more dangerous, and less picky. How it happened to be alongside a certain book was anyone's guess. But sheer luck or not, what he held deep within his pockets resembled a stone Kartouche of a previous Siren king; the very Kartouche that had been found alongside the book he had stolen out of the antiquary of the Goddess realm."

Hexe immediately looked at Tamerk, who in turn looked at her. All of them spoke simultaneously....."Morfesa! That little thief. Seriously, who else could it have been?"

"I'll be damned, and here I was thinking I was going to get blamed." Tamerk whistled. Hexe looked directly at him.

"Were you there?" she asked

He looked offended. "No! I don't leave a trail when I'm taking something that doesn't belong to me".

Triduana looked at him and agreed it had to have been Morfesa; who else would have forgotten to close the door? She turned her attention to everyone in the room. She didn't get very far when the wolf pack started to talk once again, and Arddhu shushed everyone into silence.

"We'll deal with that later, now listen, this is where it's going to get good." He spoke softly to the others, just as the warriors continued, and the group of them above turned their attention away from the accusation of the open door.

"He then did something that was unconscionable, after finding the one creature that was further away from the electrical field than the others, evoking its soul and yanking it back to Tantaris's realm without the safeguards put in place for both himself and the other he had found.

Once he was tagged, Balor dragged Symbya through the entrance point at the velocity that he called him into being, without any kind of protection, before the creature had time to react. It was not only reckless, but dangerous to the ones that lived along the edges of Toraigh Island and its beaches. The shock-wave that hit the coast sent massive underground shifts along the Mer-colonies that lived around the reefs. Many things died in Balor's karmatic repercussions that occurred on this side of the time-link, where he had outgrown his mind and grew exceedingly deranged along the footsteps of his own tribe.

But that's nothing to the actual spell that was used to bring Symbya forth without the protection of a Time Star Circle that is needed at all summoning of that distance, let alone the kind of magnitude of light transference that he had created with its wave, and the destruction that followed.

That particular form of derangement made him mad with power, and when the energy circled back, the wave didn't just hit Tantaris in its arrival into this world. When it arrived in all its fury, it first hit the Catacombs of Naunas, as it travelled down the chute and closed one of the more significant doorways into the darkside of Leberone; one that had been used by the Selmathens for centuries as a travelational point-module. The Selmathen became momentarily stranded upon many different worlds as the wave gained speed and moved out into the far reaches of space. Still to this day, the damage that he caused has not been completely calculated, and there are still unknown variables to what he created that might hinder the development of future Fey colonies.

Nevertheless, Balor wasn't done yet. He transpired to allow the field to yank Symbya's whole energy in its entirety without leaving the umbilicus attached, which was needed to release him, once he had accomplished what Balor needed him for — basically severing the link that would allow him to return home, once the deed was done. It's the law; all things taken must be returned. For whatever reason; he didn't think that applied to him. That stupidity cannot go unpunished. Because it is a crime of hate; one although

Fey in nature, but nonetheless something you cannot do here in our world without payment in kind. You see, that vortex created irreversible damage to the membrane of the Siren's soul, and fragged its nucleus from the world of corporeal form, then changing it into a fragmented scene of chaos that molecularly changed it into the destructive essence that now hunts your daughter relentlessly without a true reason or even structured form!"

Daniel whistled loudly, catching the warriors off guard momentarily as each of them changed the colouring of their irises, returning briefly to the world of broken stone. Each followed Daniel's gaze then smiled questioningly at the Shapeshifter and waited, motionless while he continued to navigate through the words they had just given to him in all their complexity, to catch up.

Daniel started to pace between the shattered stones, but waved them on to continue, as he made his way out to the edge, kicking the occasional stone under his boot in frustration. They skidded across the bailey then disappeared over the embankment to scuttle away many feet below his feet, out amongst the pounding surf. A few brightly coloured lights could be seen winking on and off again under the water — where the stones had made impact, and several pairs of eyes glared back at him as he darted his head back into the stonework of the old castle interior, hoping they wouldn't decide to scale the walls and come after him. He wondered if the alien creatures in the wolf pack's story had migrated this far south and had set up colonies on this end of the continent. Apparently, anything was possible.

The warriors merely stared blankly at him while he shrugged it off, and waved them once again to continue speaking, while he explored several broken stones that seemed at one time to have been some kind of face belonging to the statuary all crumbling around him. He looked back over his shoulders at the ledge, again hoping none of the blinking eyes made it over the top out of the surf. He shuddered at the thought. Toraigh Island was Northwest of Fomor, and if they were as acidic as the three of them had indicated, it could very well put the entire Island of Water's Deep into jeopardy of sliding into the sea if they indeed, had made it to these southern shores.

The blinking eyes stayed put, and he carried on asking them to continue once again, when they had not. Nodding, they returned to their hypnotic state, continuing on with the story as if they hadn't been interrupted, and were formulating their speech as they gathered themselves into another continuation of the same story, but with a different song.

"This displaced energy full of dark-star matter was originally created by some of the strongest majiks this side of the two worlds that exist in the Fey realms of yesterday's biospheres. Each of those life-forms used them at various times, to virtually destroy the essence of a Star Point Collision that sat just on the edge of arrival, down near the end of our galaxy. From time to time they would drift in and get too close, and someone would have to challenge its existence and follow the strict guidelines that the Goddess realm commanded, and bring in one of the star-point rituals to steer it clear of another collision.

What Balor and his little Sidhe nutter called into formation, was not done by invocation, but with evocation. Its essence was not used in any way, no matter what shape or form it became, to call forth something for your own purpose or gain. If you should proceed and try to force it to do your bidding in majiks of the ancient practice of the Shadowland Fey, it would simply fold up and refuse to work. But that creature who called herself a Queen tampered with its creativity, and shoved it through a seemingly innocent strand and tricked it to do something that should never have been unleashed. Their rituals tended to be a bit darker than the one that was created in symmetry to prevent Cataclysmic collisions within the Faden Corpeous and Goetutonias Nebulise. Those rituals had stronger majiks, each of which circled around each other in the same close rotation of worlds, and had similar shift-points that were shared openly with the other planets of the Selmathen species.

The evocation that Balor used destroyed that bridge, creating a number of single point collisions that occurred along meteorized pathways, which had come into contact with its destructive pyroclastic wave as it passed into each of their vocational ranges of gravitational pull. So when those tell the tale of how this thing came to be, remember that all was not as it first appeared to be. There is far more to the story of the arrival of Symbya than what others have been led to believe.

First and foremost, the creature that is hunting is Siren born. That in itself is noteworthy; not to mention incredibly dangerous.

It was then that Balor, having instructed the Sidhe to receive the shattered husk of Symbya upon its arrival into this realm, began to significantly manipulate its fragmented state of mind, and chained its screaming form to the walls of the Island of Toraigh with the help of the tormented Vermorbian he already had captured in his dungeon. Once this was done, he then sent Symbya on a systematic one way directional transference assignment, allowing him full access to use at his discretion — with any means available, to slaughter the offspring of his daughter Eithne, who had become impregnated with triplets and given birth, not two days earlier.

But Tamerk got there first, much to the anger of Balor and his Sidhe Queen, who at the time blamed Carpathious. That particular Druid had a mean streak, as it was. And even though he had not done what Balor said he had, if indeed he had been part of the original plan Balor hatched, he would have taken those kidlets and skinned them whole, before releasing them to the creature that Balor unleashed below the dungeons of his castle, as he drifted in and out of the winds, pacing along the shoreline. Had he actually caught them before Manannan supposedly turned them into Seals, as was foretold by those that had been there, this story would have had a different ending; one that would have been disastrous for the Fey living on this side of the great divide.

But that never happened; each of the children was taken by Tamerk in an effort to conceal them from the Sling that had been foretold by Sopdet. Tamerk and the coven of Ka'afrey split them into different areas of the Fey realms, hiding them from not only from their own grandfather, but from each other as well, hours before the actual ritual was performed.

Symbya's inability to execute his violent slaughter uncovered a fairly small glitch; one that to this day he has never been able to fully succeed and execute, due to the Coven of Ka'afrey's ability to mask the signatures of the children from their source blood, which was needed for Symbya to actually track the little mites.

One of the children had been taken to safety immediately after the birthing, and was raised by Manannan the Sea God and his Wife Tailtiu, in the other realm of the Merfolk on the Island of Vaukknea. That stranglehold of unusual plant life had a unique way of protecting itself with its massive reefings of ungrounded land; floating as it drifted with the tides, thereby holding no fixed address for one searching for its mass.

That island is the home of the Selkie Tribes, and having no ties to the Fomorians Races or their ancestors, Tamerk was able to hide one of these sons from the dangers that occupied his Home Planet, where he as a young-ster would have had the freedom to grow up in relative peace.

The other two have always remained a mystery on the Tantaris Home World, and until recently had never even been heard of, let alone imagined to have lived through the Dragon Wars. But they were alive, and very much within sight of the Sling, as it made its way through the lands trying to sniff through the ancient majiks that held their true signatures, and not those they had attached to their souls to hide them in plain sight from its relentless hunting.

Another thing happened that was not recorded in the happening of this unfortunate event. And this that came to pass was something that, had the telling been told within the world of the Tantaris Fey, it could very well have created an even greater war than the one the Humans were involved with the first time around. So it was kept secret, and those that knew of its truth were given majikal refuge within one of the in-between places of existence, to keep the secret from spilling out into the Fomorian villages that Balor still held power in.

Now that you are not within the realm of Tantaris the Real, your knowl-edge can be expanded on its arrival and cannot do damage to the ones that do not know of its fact. So, with the tale we are telling, and the fact of point you will not be returning quickly to that other universe for the time being, it is now given easily to you with an understanding of the severity of the secrets that are held closely to our chests within this Goddess realm of souls."

Daniel looked back and forth between the three of them, with a look of Goddess-smacked uncertainty. What he had just heard simply made him want to go back to Sombreia with the best intentions and fart. I mean truly let it blow, through the back end of him and make his intestinal tract reboot itself and kill him dead. Things had just gone from unrealistic to complete disbelief, and back down to shit.

Having the triplets here on this realm, alongside this hunter thing they called a Sling, just became very dangerous for anyone living within his homeland. Tamerk had not included the rest of this little bit of horror into his original request of taking on the child that had need of some form of refuge. Instead, he left her among those that would have protected her soul because of love, as this creature that could have ripped apart the entire village where they lived, with just a flick of his wrist, roamed free just outside of the village wards.

He simply gave her over with explicit instructions to her keep; like it was nothing out of the ordinary, and gave Daniel and his family sole care of her, before disappearing for long periods of time without word as to what to do with her. He should have warned them with an entire arsenal at their disposal, and they may have at least been able to maim the creature when it arrived, before it killed the lot of them. At least then he would have satisfaction of the actuality of having tried, before he took his last breath.

"His leaving you for long periods of time was because his energy had been detected, and he was trying to steer them away from where he had hidden her. Had he told you more, the energy from that strand would have found you instantly with his molecules, and the entire village would have been slaughtered, even with the extra things he taught you about the Mercorian Death Blade." They spoke to Daniel, not waiting to hear his surprise at them answering the question that had just popped into his head.

He shook his head with the image, not even noticing they had done so, as a shiver ran up his spine. What the hel was Tamerk thinking, he carried on with this line of thinking; this could have gone so many different ways, and all of them not ending in the way that would be good for his health or that of his clan.

"Damn Sprite, wait till I get my hands on him," he said out loud to anyone that would listen. Hexe started to roar, causing Tamerk to turn and glare at the Goddess.

"Seems like you really have a way with the locals Tam, maybe next time you should just send a big old bull Twicken to guard your doorways. Maybe then they'll just eat the locals and that way you don't have to listen to the babble."

Tamerk smiled and shot an electrical charge in her direction that sent her head snapping back, rocking her slightly in her tracks while he stuck his tongue out, and everyone howled with laughter before ducking for cover. She turned it back and slapped the air around the vicinity he had previously been resting in, only to touch nothing but air as he showed up slightly to the left, and pinched her cheek.

The war began in earnest, as each Goddess brought into the fray whatever they had to add to the mixture, and the fight was on. By the time it was finished, no one was left unscathed, and everyone was lying on the floor panting with laughter, as feathers and purple dust drifted down from above. Sometimes the simplest thing was all everyone needed to finish an all-out war, and both Tamerk and Hexe could no longer refrain from shaking hands and calling the fight a draw.

Down below, Daniel was unsettled by what the wolf pack was telling him. What the warriors told him next, while the group of Goddesses and whatever being Tamerk was, in his current incarnation, simply left him speechless. He took in a deep breath quite by accident, as it accidentally stopped him in the middle of what he wanted to do to the lot of whoever was behind this kerfuffle, and try to find the nearest exit point and run like hel.

The warriors didn't even react to the hesitation of what they had been relaying to the older Shapeshifter, and simply continued on as they had before, without much in the way of emotions; Daniel on the other hand was beginning to seethe with emotion.

"It seems, and I put it lightly, the Balor that was witnessed to this within this world, was taken as payment for what he had done to the Sirens, and the one that replaced him, well... his mind was not from the world that the Fomorian race believed him to be a part of.

You see, when all this was going on, the most important part of the story was that the moment Symbya came to this realm, the Sling was able to do one last thing before his Siren-self completely dissolved into insanity. Although it had done massive damage to his memory, it also provided him with one last molecule of retribution. And with that particle, he was able to absorb the signature of Balor the moment he came through from the other-side, into himself.

Sirens, although part of the Fey species of creatures, are mostly made of energy. With that series of chemicals and atoms, they have a unique variable in their DNA that allows them momentarily to move out of their current situation in times of dire trouble, and pull the nearest sentient creature who was responsible for their pain and merge their life-force with their own, to create a new being. However, Symbya was too damaged to go into Balor, so he did the next best thing, he brought Balor into himself. In doing so, Balor's life-force was instantly drawn in to Symbya's Siren self and he took the consciousness of those particles, and dissolved the chemicals of his brain into his own.

The real Balor mind, now securely inside him and safely implanted, could not escape. Outside, he left the husk with the horrible scars of the evocation he had done and pushed it into the empty body of the Formorian king, letting go of some of the pain he had endured coming through the dark-star meteor. At the last moment, as he started to lose consciousness, he gave one last push, redirecting the body husk of the old Balor and implanting some of the fresher memories of his previous deceit inside this old husk, so it wouldn't interfere with his own memory cycle, and sent him on his way as insanity took control. The Queen hadn't known the difference.

What he had created inside his mind by transferring this essence inside the Aelf's original body came with an unexpected variance that he had not anticipated with the Siren DNA. It came with an insanity that was tempered with rage, which could not stay within the host that was created for him to permanently reside on this side of the tidal barriers that had been set out for him to live.

As a matter of fact, it couldn't stay within any husk belonging to another race on this side of the barrier, for its very core was not suited to the environment of this side of the divide, being that it had to maintain itself in a temporal flux most of the time. You see, the home star of the Sirens had high metallic concentrations of Formediso to rectify that problem, and when it came through the void, all of that coating was destroyed in the dark-matter star, as it poured itself in through the threshold it had been forced to collide with.

It had taken several days of the moon to wear itself into being, and by that time Symbya was completely incoherent to what was happening on any level, so he couldn't have stopped it even if he tried. Eventually, it began to deteriorate further and the Aelven husk of Balor's genetic Siren DNA that had been placed inside him began to break down.

The Sirens tried to get to him, but it was useless. Balor's little evocation had destroyed any means for them to get there quickly and retrieve him, and the nearest star corridor for them to travel through would undoubtedly have been damaged with the destruction of the Dark-Star corridor. So, it left them only one choice.

Tamerk had a coven here, and he and the Witch Kashandarhh worked in tandem to find a way to safely remove the original without warning the current Formorian Race. And now, as they returned in force to reset their mistake before their actual deed had successfully completed its goal, they discovered that someone had gone into battle with the husk, thinking him to be the real thing, further complicating matters that made a real problem far worse than first thought.

It seems, when they destroyed the eye that umbiliced the two together, the link was severed and the original being's energy was blinded and could not reset the particles that would send Balor back into the vastness of the vortex, returning to his own body."

Daniel looked horrified as the three continued to talk, and had just picked up his jaw from the floor yet again, when this next revelation came into being.

"Tell me you did not just say that? You're telling me that the original Balor that stayed here was not the one that was born here?" The three nodded in tandem. "And the Balor that was here living on this planet from the time of his birth, is still bloody alive?" Daniel cut in briefly with a bit of stunned unmitigated screaming.

"Well sort of. He still resides in Symbya, and the struggle that currently resides inside the Sling is starting to break down after all these years." Daniel was not happy, nor would most of Water's Deep be were they to find out that little bit of information.

"There are two of them then, and he still lived through that?" Daniel was gobsmacked, he had heard otherwise, and had also been told he was dead before he hit the ground. All three shook their heads. "So, if that did not kill him, how did he supposedly fake his death and die?" The three continued on, in complete synchronicity, not even batting an eye as they followed him, pacing along the edge of where the three originally had been trying to gain entry into the corridor below ground.

"Tamerk's coven called in the Vermorbian from the Carthanthien Nebula that Balor had locked up in the Toraigh Island dungeon, which was only too happy to drag his energies into the Mauntra and disperse the true atoms of what he had become into the backside of a black hole. Unfortunately, by then Symbya had fled and they had to trace him out the backside of the Ocean of Souls near the Trench of Talon to catch him. Then the Goddess Horae replaced the time-lock and reset the images that Lugh had believed he had killed his grandfather as an older version of himself, and the whole thing was locked up in a nice pretty package, without the older Lugh having lifted a single finger to hurt him."

Daniel looked at the three warriors whose very essence that appeared to be blood and bone were simply nothing more than an enigma of alien origin. It made him shiver with the realism of it all, coming into contact with something unexplainable to many, let alone having a conversation with an Aelven replica that was initially a being that was created by majik.

The image that they created was still hard to fathom, as he tried to maintain his cool in the face of what they actually were. It became exceedingly harder to admit that he knew so little about his charge, and far less about her nightmares. He knew they were not born into this world, but created to perform a blood oath akin to something so strong that they would give their own lives for that which they were created to do. He smiled with the thought of them looking after his little hel-raiser, who would rather be more at home with the Panthers than her own kind. That must have been difficult in its entirety, for them to even try.

Funny how that had arrived inside his mind's eye at the moment, as it crept inside his brain and moved within the filaments of his memory cells. It was a different animal that had made her its own, when she was finally able to walk to them in the middle of the night in the darkest of hours. He remembered it well; choosing to give his brain a break from whatever revelations was yet to come in this mad world of Wolves and Sirens.

It was an extremely foggy night that brought to mind the thunder-storms that Daniel believed this world had never seen the likes of. They seemed to take on a life of their own, and surround each of the village's individual hovels where the Shapeshifters sat near their inner cooking fires, trying to stay warm and out of the storm that approached from behind, that cold and miserable night.

It had taken its time to wrap them all into a very unusual damp mist, obscuring the view from neighbour to neighbour, even sending the wild dogs to find shelter amongst the village barns and the domesticated animals that huddled inside.

He remembered with complete clarity, the very night what that had felt like, and it made him shiver with its appearance. To taste the sulphur tang that permeated the night air smelled of familiarity to the brewing majiks of the old world of Witches during the coven years. Had he been running with the Goddess crowd he would have thought that something huge was brewing, because it was so out of character for that time of year. It was a time of things to come that had sent him thinking of how it was, to be able to raise this child of mystery without the ability to tell anyone who she really was. He liked to think that they had done a good job of being able to raise her in the strictest rules of the land which the Fey had set upon them, but he'd be wrong. Tamerk's were far worse, and even down right outrageous when it came to protecting the little minx.

But it would have been another day he knew soon enough, when they would have to release that bond to her own destiny. That had not as of yet been even considered, never mind written within his own mind; until the Black Dragons showed themselves overhead in their skies.

He now moved about the rocks that had become the new floor of the old palace, and fidgeted with the markings of a long lost former kingdom that had been decimated during the old war.

"So you are the Guardians?" He scratched his face, thinking, letting the pause catch up with his words; then speaking with his mind in the direction of his Shapeshifter roots. "How long have you been searching the old battlements here?" He hadn't really needed the answer to that question; it was more a point of thinking aloud that brought the words to the surface, as he needed time to think this through.

"Why did no one think to get me involved? I could have been more of a help in finding a solution to tracking her." He immediately transformed into a Flight Monkey, showing the possibility of his ability to be versatile, and then returned to his original form to continue. "Or the very least get her to understand that you were not going to harm her when the night terrors had become rampant with tears." He spoke with frustration, mixed in with annoyance.

They watched him move about the ancient ruins and had remained silent in response to the questions they could not answer; the words were uneventful in their mind, as Daniel carried on fidgeting with the loose stones, looking around the ruins he hadn't had time before to do. But their hesitation quickly brought to the surface another response, formally planted there to respond in course.

"You have been involved, just on another kind of symmetry. The daughter that you claim without the ability to follow lineage from the line of the royal family, has been given true sight, and with that sight she seems to be able to change her body without help from the teachings of the Santherian religion. For some reason she has learned that all on her own, without our help, and you were able to achieve that." Daniel looked between them.

"I didn't teach her that; it just showed up one day." They continued, not hesitating at Daniel's negation of their claim.

"Either way, without you it wouldn't have surfaced. No one has been able to do that before, and since neither one of the old Gods was given the opportunity to find a Santherian in time to take her into its City of Light, she has taken it upon herself to learn things that only someone of the highest order has been able to achieve in the past."

"I doubt," Daniel thought aloud, "they would have even been able to get close enough to her, to explain any of this had there been the time."

Sibrey could be difficult at the best of times, but faced with any form of instruction, be it Goddess orientated or not, she would have simply run for the hills. It made just a little bit more of the Panther that she had been hanging out with, shine through with the movements that she had created with the pride — she had picked over family. He smiled now, thinking of her elusiveness. She had been definitely up to something from an early age; he wondered now if this was part of it. They interrupted him again, before he could speculate further.

"Every time we seem to find her, she manages to either wake herself up before we can begin, or she disappears like she did this time, and we cannot for the life of us find out how she could have done this without help."

Everyone in the chamber heard the small click, as the rock below them seemed to force itself apart, and the staircase below opened up to the rooms below. The guardians turned around in unison, coming discombobulated as a whole.

"What did you touch?" The voices instantly reverted to their former separate entities, as they scrambled forward and followed the sound that had reached them from deep within the far side of the chamber below.

"I didn't do that." Daniel turned to them, looking just as stunned as they did, just as another face emerged from the depths below, sending rocks falling through the blackened hole. The form moved into the above ground battlement, where they had been gathered and looked around with blinking eyes into the daylight.

Before any of the group inside the old battlements and up in the cloud realm had a chance to speak, the creature emerged, and they all immediately realized it was someone they knew very well.

"Ah, so that's where you've all gotten to." Tamerk said to the four of them. Nina clapped her hands in glee, smacking Horae in the arm.

"I told you, this was going to be good." Horae's jaw dropped as she bent closer to look through the stone, turning around to each of them in turn, looking at a now empty space that previously only moments ago a certain Sprite had been standing in.

"How in the Klifferdesh did he flipping do that?"

CHAPTER TWENTY-NINE

The Selkie Stronghold

The waves had finally arrived, after having been predicted for weeks to coincide with the conjunction of Naunas's stellar planetary drift-points. Creatures of both worlds used the unusual tidal fluxes, which came with the astronomical forecast of the high Fey ancestry, to find power in both ritual and ancient majiks. It was a time for those of the underworld to rise up and find the storm from the sea alive and full of life, and use that energy to retrieve those lost in times of tribal war from beneath the salty waves.

Tantaris could be seen moving in perfect synchronicity with its familiar orbital twin, which, from both worlds, could be seen shining brightly high up in either skyline. Leberone, the planet's moon sphere had also slipped into the dance the others had started, alongside every bolide that had come loose from the foothold of the Starshaper meteor.

They were close; as close as they could be, relatively speaking. From the cliffs of either shore that fed the stellar winds, high up into the mountain ranges of the continents, they appeared to touch each other briefly during these wonderful celestial occurrences, with more of a lover's embrace than that of something full of rock and volcanic dust still deeply embedded inside their inner-crust.

The casual brush of particles was followed by several large eruptions in the energy patterns seen from each other's skies, and if one cared to take the time to star gaze, they would see perfect blue energy strands following their outer atmospheres electrical charges, as they made their way into their individual places high up into the morning sky.

These occurrences always happened this time of the season, drifting and flying along the tidal currents of the Elemental colonies, which simply floated above in the airways the Sylphs and the Zephyrs called home, after finding themselves caught in a turbulent tidal flux of another world very much like their own.

They twirled inside the vortexes and moved in perfect symmetry with the stellar winds as they moved along their worlds, untouched by the violence of the storms below and drifted much more quietly along, now that the embrace no longer held its electrical frequency.

These days each of the quarters that fed the Elemental regimes with a fullness that rattled even the smaller Fey doorways, found peace and solitude within these strange tides that filled the sky with new life, shifting straight on through into the other quarters' guardianship, along where the Fey hierarchy had ruled for centuries, and beyond any normal scope of what Humans call time.

This particular one was ruled by the guardians of the air based world of eastern majik; now far removed from either planet's life cycle, which shone in the cartography of Faden Corpeous's skies. Its unusual flotilla of smells could be felt melting across your nostrils, floating almost sideways into the stellar winds while it ran in rivers, overflowing alongside the bogs like melted chocolate, and growing into a full on whirlpool of tantalizing taste and exotic texture.

It then spread through the star field which became the birthing grounds for similar quadrants and their Druid companions. These could be seen along the Fey doorways of other worlds, as they hosted their own Air festivals and feasts that contained many Fey beings not familiar with such widespread star-energy, with the stratigraphy coming inside the conjunctions pathways, which had moved and opened certain doorways within the star-charts through their own homes and villages.

The planet called Naunas was exactly in the middle of the flux of planets which ran with the celestial winds that moved throughout this side of the Faden Corpeous galaxy. Its natural environment was in every way a complete copy to our own atmosphere, and if you had a mind to look, after the Mauntra made its final bow into the night sky, you would see both planets high up skimming the edge of the same Nebula, swimming in and out of the stellar drift of living planetoids which now made this area of space their permanent home.

There had been another moon in the early years, which made up this small but majikal universe far away from the Human worlds that no longer exist today. Its life cycle had moved significantly into another rift-point, and transported several of the lesser Fey life-forms in its wake to its current address, which had not the proper authority to override its reversal, and return back home to its initial registry before its time.

Their arrival back into this area of space was not due for almost another ten Mauntra rotations; yet there had been whispers that they were already on their way, through several of the star systems that were between that compass point and our own particular arrival point, and would undoubtedly arrive before the storm had shown its teeth for another season. How I knew this, I cannot tell, I just without any comprehension as to the why....did.

Along the edges of the rift, Tantaris's sister planet Naunas, could be observed sending out fingers of gaseous filaments that joined the many waves of molecules Tantaris had already shed a day or two earlier, as they floated in the vast depths of space between both planets, and moved along in perfect symmetry with an almost sentient form of life.

These filaments would drift along out of range in a few days, and find themselves in distant arenas of outer-space, if they didn't get caught up in some of the asteroid belts that circled several of the outer-stellar drift sights, along the fringes of Sopdet's spacial infractions.

Tantaris had been covered in several layers of these spidery webs, when first she was formed. But somewhere during the time that the genesis waves hit its shores, they had dissolved through the different fracture zones, and melted into the oceans as they sank beneath her depths, along the ocean subduction plates.

Tantaris was the larger of the two main Fey worlds in this galaxy, and with the tides that Leberone blew their way, it could be seen dancing high around the many coloured energy threads she continued to produce with her coming of age. Each shimmered like a curtain which could produce several new layers during this weather occurrence, as she shimmered in the Aurora Borealis of another majikal sphere. They touched and manoeuvred along that line of entry, now covering every inch of space as the energy moved on through and between the layers, towards her shores.

Occasionally, they would find each other momentarily in some form of majikal embrace, and then break apart with a distinctive hiss in their magnetic couplings, as they drifted alone for many months on end without coming in contact with the other again until the following year. At that time it would begin the dance once more, when the conjunction shifted them back into position once more, and the timing was perfect for its happening.

This season one could see several larger threads not normally seen in this stellar drift point, moving quickly alongside the rotational compass just out of range of Tantaris's own movement of drift. They seemed to follow behind the others in an awkward game of tag, as Tantaris slid further away, and swam in the moonlight that shone with a strange purple hue produced by its movements, and then floated back into its own embrace.

Several loud booms accompanied the strange colourings, but nothing was detected out of the ordinary, as one of the Selkies of Vaukknea Island challenged the surf, and moved closer to the edge of the reef line, surfacing briefly to smell the air.

Tonight it will light up the horizon and drift with the currents along the Trench of Talon in the Ocean of Souls, finding its purpose during the fullness of both moons high above. Then it will find its place and guide an unusual huntress along the strange stellar seas, as it steers her in below the majikal wards with only the hint of a whisper, as she moved between the energy beacons without setting any of the island alarms off, that someone was here inside their rings without having being cordially invited.

She landed with another on this strange and hidden sanctuary, where the Selkie population had hidden from the world of the Fey for almost ten centuries. This island had life inside its own molecules, which fed the entire structure with the genesis codex, and filtered pure majik into this watery realm, keeping it sated.

Both planets had always been there, shining in the sky, and shadowing each other as they created the pathways the Selmathen race could find. Each followed a certain star chart, and kept up with the currents that Leberone controlled from high above, with its strong hold on both orbits within its proximity that chained it to both Fey-worlds. Sometimes it could be felt crossing in the shadow of each other's orbit, but it never found the exact threads until the following conjunction reached its stellar fingers along the currents of Leberone's stronger tides.

It had evolved quickly in its early years, and breathed itself into being, all the while producing sentient life in every stick and leaf that filled the land and beaches up to the high-tide line, with things that strangely never found time to sleep. They were alerted to the new arrivals, and woke up as they slithered towards both of the travellers the moment the island shifted into solid ground beneath their feet.

Kashandarhh had watched the night skies since she was a small tripe of a Witch-fledge. She had been able to see each of the planets while floating in a kind of equilibrium that shadowed her patterns of flight, as she passed through several star-fields along the borders of the meteor field that streaked across the night skies and into obscurity.

She had been on this ride many times in the days of her youth, but the visual effect was far more beautiful on the pathways that paralleled those of the higher tides of the conjunction. It's very scent fed several of her inner-senses with beautiful smells centered around those star-fields, which ran with the magnetic forces that could be seen trailing along through space like some form of Elemental creature swimming fiercely along the interstellar seas on its own intergalactic journey.

She wondered if they ever found their peace among the stagnant worlds the Humans created on the far side of the continental drift-line, without anyone to bother them in their own private worlds of hushed sorrows. But, then again, she was creating something that never had life in those early years of majik, and something always had to move with the symmetry of her unusual energy fields, if any of them had a chance of letting her see its skeletal soul.

The planets themselves now moved in different quantums to the thread movements than they did back then. Each had to be able to run in tandem to the flux they had created, along a much broader spectrum than what was created in the beginning years. Now that the years had transformed those spacial seas and given them new life, it breathed in the milky atmosphere of the meteorites she had played with in those thin times of majik, and allowed them symmetry as they glided along the solar array of stars. They now rode high along the edges of life, and skimmed the stellar tides which had become attached to that rotation which breathed new life into its own planetary bones.

The quadrants of Kashha's imagination rang true in the sightline she had created, and then moved along drift-points that rode the wave clear through to the other-side of both gateways. When Leberone came into the mix, the meteorites had formed their matrices further along the evolution of the Selmathen rift, and what she created with majik suddenly felt its breath along the shadow of another moon that no longer held its molecules in conjunction to Leberone's larger orbit.

Still, its shadow may have been darkened by this phenomenon that moved along the threads of its own pathways. But its remains were no longer made of bones and still full of a high concentration of Laurel stone from deep inside the moon's inner crust. It was with this that it created its own natural light in that darkened world so far removed from those that had memory of its actual existence. She instantly looked up to watch its darkened outline, still visible here in this space in-between, and although the light could not filter into its atmosphere, Kashandarhh knew it hung just above the horizon, as she wrestled her body through the majikal crack, and helped Soren step into her family's world.

Kalieas was that moon, and had only just come to call this place its own, as it moved alongside the space in-between where the Selkies had taken their island after the Dragon Wars. It had followed her in, not wanting to be left behind as she had first brought her father's coven here to hide. Leberone had never been approached by a similar fate, as it shone high above in full view on the continent, but here her light was gone, completely untouched by its own forces, and the destructive pull it created on the Fey colonies below.

She always had her suspicions as to why they picked one moon over the other, but it was still a miracle that when Kalieas was hidden, they had not chosen to inhabit Leberone while it had been laid open and bare for the picking.

There was a small inscription in the passage of records in the book of Selmathen shadows, which had been stored in the lower chambers of the Aelven Queen and her consort's ancestral home. 'Leberone had never known of its disappearance, until after he had been gone for almost a full turn of his lunar orbit.' How funny that such an event would be recorded in such a way.

There had not been time to go further into its revelation, and as time passed and the trail grew cold, no one ever thought to delve further into its disappearance. She of course, knew very well where it had travelled to, but that was as far as she was willing to speak to those that had their suspicions of its whereabouts.

The tale had been started by someone that the Humans had taken him with them when they retreated back to their universe in the cold and frozen Milky Way galaxy. No one had bothered to correct the fictitious tale, and it was not for her to set the record straight, even though every Water Elemental this side of the great divide knew it had been driven into the space in-between and hadn't left a single degree from its original orbit. But, then again, the Selkie race had also more or less disappeared inside Manannan Ocean of Souls at roughly the same time, and they too were rarely brought up in conversation with the younger Fey that had been born since the new awakenings of Tantaris's re-birthing. Neither of these new-borns knew the two were as a direct result of one another going together, which allowed the tale to be told and redirected by those that couldn't let it lie.

She came back into focus for a moment, and pushed Soren forward into position, moving his line of sight upwards, as she pointed to the rare sight of Kalieas swimming along in the skies, like fish moving along the sea of Sopdet's own creational vortex. He gasped quietly beside her, as she began to close the doorway behind them.

Soren watched Kashha's skills as a hunter take over immediately, when they came through this side of the veil. She merged with the ritual of the Shamanic tethering when she popped them through the hole she had created. He watched now as it changed their direction smoothly, without moving them through the storm at the foot of the reef that had descended out on the waterside in full fury. Had she come without its thread protecting them, it could very well have been a different story.

He immediately sniffed the air around them before they continued on, and his eyes grew wide with the realization of what the inner-rings held inside their majikal hands that so vividly stood out before him, ten strides away. They were amazing, and full of sizzling blue strandlings that made his hair stand on edge when he faced them, reminding him of his own stones back in the village of Tameron. He quickly went to move backwards, but Kashha stayed his arm and held him in place, grounding his Aelven energy into the soil at their feet. The sound vanished from his auditory perception, as she placed her fingers along his back.

Ok, not quite the same; had he been standing at this distance away from the Panthor stones, they would have melted his eyebrows. She smiled at him and nodded for him to remain where he was, then he watched her start to close the bands as soon as he got his bearings. She then ever so slowly released her touch from his skin, her fingers drifting downwards along his left arm, leaving it tingling with her energy. The rings of pure light that Kashha had allowed them to travel through, changed direction with her movements as she manipulated the pattern with Selkie majik. It followed her flow and merged to match what she was doing.

Soren watched with fascinated interest as her skin seemed to change and slightly flow into the landscape around them, forming patterns he had not seen before. Selkie majik was fairly unknown to the land dweller, and not easily witnessed when it was performed to those that happened to come across it when it was. She was standing not more than a few foot prints away from their energy, as he watched her take a bone handled athame, move along the doorway she opened on the other-side, and began to ritually close it. Her image was somewhat blurred, but the grounding she performed allowed him to somehow join in with part of her Witch molecules, allowing him access to what others would not have been able to see.

She moved Widderschynnes with the patterns of the rings as they started to close slowly, becoming smaller and closer together. Once that began to formulate, the rings changed direction, moving in a horizontal wobble and spinning in the direction around the opening they had come through, slightly sideways. Somewhere along the third rotation, the rings seem to merge, only hesitating slightly while she reached in her pouch when the words she was speaking reached their peak. She then added a tiny drop of Dragon-blood Sage as if it was waiting for her herbs, then it sealed off the final locking mechanism and formed the closure around the hole just as she removed the knife. They were in, and the shift-point door closed from the continent side of the wormhole keeping the doorway intact and untraceable.

Smiling, she turned to face him and stepped to his side as she returned the blade to its sheath on her boot, then dusted her hands off on her hips. Her image was covered in silver light as he bowed his head silently with a whispered oath at the sight. Behind them lay what was left of the molecules she had presented to the island's sentient breath, while they both moved silently into the realm of her father's clan.

The final looking mechanism had closed like a ghost, without making the slightest of sounds — except for a visual poof, and as Soren turned his head away from the sight above them in the skies, he watched it shimmer behind them and disappear slowly dissolving from sight.

Kashandarhh touched his arm briefly and his eyes grew wide as she directed him to an open pathway that had suddenly been cleared of all plants and fallen stumps with a simple wave of her hand. They both moved silently towards the coast — somewhere off in the distance, as she steered him through the opening in the pathway through the trees.

It suddenly occurred to him that he was in the company of one of the most powerful Witches in all of the Fey worlds. As he stepped quietly along the pathway she had cleared, it made him shiver just the slightest, at the revelation. Never mind the fact she rarely allowed anyone to travel with her in any capacity. For this, he was both honoured and a little sceptical as to the reason why.

He shook the cobwebs from his brain that had arrived inside the transference of the jump, then tried to comprehend the levity of what had just happened over the space of yesterday's world he still had rattling inside his reeling mind. He was used to travelling around in more or less dangerous circumstances, but what had transpired since his swim almost a week ago was mind boggling. What she had introduced him to, was going to take some getting used to. Witch kind was not overly generous, and he still didn't know whether he was exceedingly lucky to have met her, or a puppet in the show that had yet to be presented to him.

Kashandarhh smiled with her eyes, as she watched him quickly adjust to the new environment inside the inner-rings of the Undinecis reef without having to knock him out first. He shook his body from head to toe, as a vibration of the previous atmosphere left his skin and dispersed into nothing. It would take only a few moments for his Syann-Clan molecules to adjust his equilibrium to that of the inside flux; while others had not so easily been able to adapt. That is why she had allowed the rider to come along in the first place, when she decided to go in search of her father and his kin — far away from the shores of Tantaris's other realm. The other reason was about to come out of the shadows somewhere between here and the beach. But for now, they needed to hurry before it met them in the higher sections along the ridgeline.

The Dragonlord clan was strong, and his kind had always been able to withstand the constant changes in their bodies when they came across many of the different atmospheres that were presented on this plane of the Fey equilibrium. She wouldn't have even considered taking another through the void, especially at this time of year, when the Selkie home-world was not viable to anything not of Selkie origins. Her own genetic makeup would protect him for the amount of time they would be here, in case the approaching storm was faster than what she was led to believe. Both ways they would not stay long, and her father's cottage could give the rest that she could not provide, when she moved in sight of his home.

Tantaris was usually hit with higher than average tides, being more often than not, higher up, and right in the line of fire of Leberone's rotational wrath. While Naunas, her twin, always sat behind her sister planet at this time of year, and only her southern land-masses were attacked with the meteorite bombardment, she moved along the line of sight towards her winter hunting grounds in this unconventional tidal flux that Leberone's fingers of thread continued to shoot their way.

Down below, and moving faster as the rotation vibrated its unconventional tide through the spacial flux, Tantaris's land Fey fought with the usually high tides the infraction created on the mainland, as the sea rose to the height of fifty or so metres, and fell with each wave that hit the beach, dragging the occasional home along the shore back out into its reach, and drowning whatever constituted for what we call walls in its salty claws.

Out on the water side of things, the creatures that lived in this element thrived in the liquid environment, and even though their homes were not directly in danger as were the ones on land; they could be seen crashing along like mad Leviathans on steroids, as they made their way along the ocean floor, dragging themselves into the inky blackness to another part of the reef, and crawling back to safety.

Meanwhile, through the hidden jungle of the Selkie homeland, Kashandarhh and Soren made their way towards Vallmyallyn's watery-home in relative peace after the light show. Although they did not come through the regular route one might take to complete that journey, there was no doubt in Soren's mind that they had arrived without having awakened the watchtower guardians that always accompany these modes of transportation; otherwise they would have been met with a full accompaniment of armed Selkies, with knives at their pale throats.

All around him the sights and sounds were vibrantly alive and full of wonder, as they walked down the opening that moved and slid sideways revealing a perfectly preserved forest pathway, covered in moss and smooth rock. He was lucky to have accompanied one such as her, for had he arrived by other means, he would not have got the opportunity to see the island for what it was, instead of the illusion it gave off to an unsuspecting traveller.

This island was peaceful and full of life, with a weather system untouched by the giant waves that could be heard and not seen out on the coast. It was almost immediately apparent when he felt the sandy soil between his toes inside this microclimate she had once called home, that he was one of the luckier ones to have found its beauty intact and without artifice.

It was completely in reverse inside these spectacular rings, compared to the active one that currently was kicking up a raging hurricane out past the point that ran directly into the much deeper underwater trenches this island found its bones within. Inside, as he advanced down the path, he heard noises that resonated around several larger trees, which squealed with some form of sentient life that Soren still could not see with his Aelven sight. Something seemed to scamper in the upper reaches of the top most branches, and the moment their little party passed underneath their trunks, they quietly stopped and settled without a rustle betraying their whereabouts. Soren continued to look around, and wondered where the rings were in the upper atmosphere, and how they could encircle the entire island, preventing an entire race of Fey from knowing this place was here and full of life.

He had many questions that ran through his mind, but there were so many things for him to see all at once, that the questions basically left his mind's eye as he marvelled at the sights that stood all around him. He stepped lightly over the occasional stone that found its way into the middle of their advancement down the path, as Kashandarhh pointed out that each of them were not merely inanimate, as he had always been led to believe. Point taken, as he accidentally kicked one with his boot, and it scurried into the undergrowth, pissed at his intrusion. He stopped walking to watch its centipede-like legs take it to a safer place away from being squashed by the leather soles of his boots, and almost started to laugh as it burped silently, squirting out clouds of orange vaporous goo into the surrounding area. This in turn caused the flora that came into contact with it to quickly move away glaring at his passage, as Kashha grabbed his arm to get him to move.

"Not a good idea to dawdle, my friend. That goo will envelope the surrounding area and make its way down the path as it hunts for a new location to live." He turned back as she pulled him along, just as it had started to roll down the path she had cleared, heading straight at them. They quickened their steps as she cuffed him on the arm. "Please refrain from pissing them off further, Soren; we don't have time to fight all of them as we make our way to father." He turned to her as he continued to drink in the sights and sounds, forgetting any of the questions that momentarily arrived inside his head, while the storm front with its intensive winds out along the beach head ran parallel to the outside reefs.

"What do you mean all of them?"

"Keep moving; I don't have time to explain the what's, and wherefores, of the Selkie wildlife. Let's just move before something else rears its ugly head." She pushed him forward and out of range of what was coming in behind them. Soren was too busy to hear the noise return and grow to exuberant proportions, as they continued on around the bend and out of sight leaving the strange creature to veer to the left, looking for another place to put down roots. It was a visual reminder to Kashha that they were in the thick of whatever was about to explode through the surface of the ocean waves, out on the shoreline beyond the rings.

It would be here that she would find her family swimming and diving during these particular planetary pilgrimages that her father's clan turned into, amongst the Water Elementals. However, she still had to get to them before they made it past the barrier, which would leave her defenceless on an island full of creatures that had no love for the Witch inside her bones.

CHAPTER THIRTY

The Island of the Tryilamores

Naunas's rotation was also experiencing similar tides, as they moved in perfect symmetry with Tantaris's own climatic occlusions, high above in the morning sky. It may be Tantaris that got the tides, but Naunas had been known to produce even larger storm-fronts of the Air Elemental variety. Those had been recorded soaring wildly about in all directions, as they headed for the inland sections in the higher terrain causing greater rift points in their movement, which could find their way further up into the deepest sections of the highest mountainous peaks.

Nothing would be spared from this season of storms, crashing further and further inland every year. This year would produce some spectacular frequencies along the upper air colonies of the more mountainous Fey, after they had slammed ashore and lay to waste whatever was in their path from far down below in the kingdom of the Water Elementals.

Instead of worrying what kind of damage they would cause, most creatures in the Fey worlds moved to embrace the energy in ritual majiks born out of legend. The covens themselves would produce some fellowships with others not normally seen at other times of the year, as they chanted the storm rituals to search out their muses from the majiks of the guardians that would run with perfect symmetry to their own kind.

Kashha told him all this as they walked quickly through the unusual looking trees that made up this sultry forest, on their way to the shore. They moved along a familiar pathway she had walked down many times in the days of her youth. Both could feel the tang of salt on their faces, as the smell of the ocean filled their lungs with fresh air much cooler than Soren had experienced in the past, and much saltier than that which he had grown accustomed to alongside his own village shoreline.

When they finally reached the rocky coast, Soren realized they were not where he thought they would have come out of, from the trail in the trees. As a matter of fact, he was completely turned around in his head, and he felt slightly sick from the altitude as they came out of the jungle above the beachhead that Kashha had directed him to. He moved slowly to the edge of the rocky outcropping, and was surprised to see the sheer drop off that sent several large stones skidding over the edge, landing on a set of stairs that were built right into the cliff face previously hidden from his sight.

In his mind's eye he thought she was directing him to the actual sandy beach that he could just make out far below and to the left. He whistled at the image that stood before him, and could only marvel at the sight he was witnessing, while his Dragon-riders were off on another quest he had yet to find the time to think about.

Far below he could see the monstrous waves crashing into the headwaters, and several birds appeared out of the mist flying strongly, open wings taking the currents sideways along wingtips and quills, as the low clouds hung just slightly off from the area to their left. He watched them fascinated, as they flew in and out of the clouds around them, moving higher up in the upper thermals, combating the high winds with each tip of their wingspan; each perfecting their manoeuvres around and through several high gusts that threatened to take them down into the raging sea below.

Kashha turned to him and smiled showing brilliant white teeth that betrayed no trace of the grimace she had shown the Llyach clan when first he made contact with her, almost twelve slips ago. The birds recalled his attention to their aerial display, and continued to call to each other above the noise from below, as they manoeuvred with incredible agility through and around several thunderclouds, far above the maelstrom of the twisting turning sea that was crashing into the lower staircase.

The storm was coming from every direction, and swallowing the lower steps whole, then receding into the embankment of seed waves that rolled backwards before it sent the volume of water crashing headlong once more towards another level that had previously escaped the onslaught of water, leaving the wetter step beneath it still clinging with dripping foam, sea water, and the occasional piece of something with a very colorful voice.

He breathed in deeply again before he whistled through his teeth, causing a flurry of wings that added to the visual effect he continued to take in all around him. The ocean had always been something spectacular to witness. Even for a Dragonlord that had been born in the heart of the mountainous terrains of the inner continent. He loved this land, and wondered how Kashha could have left it, when all around him was so filled with wonder and exceptional beauty.

She ignored him, instead watching several creatures battling the open ocean down below in the upper trough of several huge waves, barking away. They could be seen attacking the ocean waves with gusto as they swam out into the atmosphere of the Water Elementals' realm, away from the safety of shore and into the raging open water. He imagined they must be rather brave to be outside in this kind of storm front, as they battled the higher than average tides that continued to pull the creatures further out into the complex line of foam filled surf. He couldn't quite make out what they were, but judging by Kashandarhh's smile, they could only be the Selkie clan of her father's herd.

Several shrill cries could be heard over the crashing surf below, and two beautiful Phoenixes arrived on scene to occupy the space the winged Osprey's were fishing in. Soren marvelled at the winged creatures, as they moved like a beloved instrument sliding across the thick of it, just out of harms reach, as the waves seemed to stretch their watery fingers skyward towards the aerial display overhead, trying to pick them off one by one.

Their screeching language rose in contrast to the massive sounds that the ocean created as it smashed headlong into several underwater reefs. Each wave crested and fell, crashing inside the one before it, and followed the other inside the loop from what could only be described as a storm cell out of someone's own wicked imagination.

Phoenixes were known for their wicked sense of humour. And these birds had clearly mastered that craft with a specific frenzy that the Dragonrider had never seen performed in such a daring way. They flew head on into the careening Osprey, and shadowed their flight, moving them closer to the storm. Soren watched in horror, as they tried to drown them in the oncoming waves down below, and just when it seemed all hope was lost, they plucked them from its icy grasp and brought them back up out of harm's way, much to the shrieking and horrified cries of the innocent birds.

They disappeared into the rain that rolled in offshore with hollow ringing laughter, as Soren swore loudly, watching Kashandarhh ignoring the whole play that had been not so innocently set up before their eyes.

"Try not to take anything seriously Soren, this island has ears, and all that stands before you is its way of seeing a Dragonlords reaction. It is not what you are first led to believe to be true, or the reality of their ways and the true comings and goings of the scene that plays out before you. They are just testing your emotions before they drag you into the heart of it."

"Well it bloody well looked like it was real. And if you ask me, I would undoubtedly answer that it was pretty realistic to these Tameronian eyes, and I can't imagine how they can top that." She turned away from the scene below to look at him.

"Don't try to understand it, for it is their way of making you feel out of sorts. It is really me that they have come to claim, but truth be told it will never happen and they know it to be so. However, it is only the beginning." She snickered as he rolled his eyes.

"It's beginning to sound like we have our work cut out for us, here in your father's realm." This time she didn't look at him, and simply replied.

"You don't know the half of it." The waves continued to crash in perfect unison with the music of the Phoenixes' unspoken language, and rolled like a Pelican diving into the sea. It would remain unscathed by anything in its pathway as it continued with incredible velocity towards the landfall of the continental shelf. Soren could no longer detect that land-mass where his home lie, but could only imagine it to be hovering somewhere out there in the mist, where it was more than likely hanging sideways to this upside down topsey turvey flight, of what could only be the Phoenix of Manannan's ancestral homeland.

Just as he was thinking about the unusual bird that made this waterway its home turf, something brought him back to the present, coming into view from out of the corner of his eyes. One of the waves had changed shape below them and was different than the others he watched, roaring ashore with the velocity of a hummingbird. No, this one in particular was different, towering over the others as it moved along with the tidal winds pushing from behind. It seemed to grow in size to enormous heights, much faster than others he had seen before it.

It was as tall as one of the huge Anforian Sugar Maples he had grown accustomed to seeing out on the coast, back on the continent, near this place called Lucidity Lake. He watched it grow as it crawled over and through all the others before it, towering well over them as it made itself ready to cascade up to the very area of the cliff face where they currently were standing watching the surf fall from its sharpened edge.

Several rocks skidded out into the chasm below them, breaking away the moment he tried to back up, and disappeared into the mist. Several creatures screamed as he kicked the stones over accidentally, sending whatever they were into the drink far below. He heard them go, and listened with horror at the length it took before they actually reached the bottom.

"May the Goddesses forgive me!" he shrieked, looking at the edge they had disappeared over, and then to Kashha. She looked almost amused at the deed.

"I thought I was klutzy. Well, that is a new record from the one that I previously held." She laughed as he looked horrified back at her. "Now you've just made them mad." She shook her head at the mistake, clucking away at his reaction. "Mother will undoubtedly hear about this one," she snickered.

Both Kashha and Soren had felt the energy of the wave's roar long before it came into full view, and when it came within a hair's breadth of crashing headlong into the upper steps of the stone escarpment carved out of the sheer rock below their feet, they felt its sting. It slammed into another outcropping that came out of nowhere just under the surface of some kind of hidden reef, before it hit them full on, and the water from the direct hit soaked them to the bone. "Yee Haa!" Kashha yelled with enthusiasm, absorbing the energy it created and taking the brunt of the force away from Soren's delicate Aelven bones. "Isn't this great!!!"

A hollow thud echoed in the distance, slamming just short of the intended target and dissolving into pure undulated salty spray. The one after it dissolved along with it, and took out several others in quick succession that tried coming in at the same angle. That huge wave crashed headlong into the reef, before disappearing for about the count of twenty Arbuckles, then launched itself into the air in a spectacular water spout that had all the markings of the geysers that ran wildly on the mainland near one of the old Selmathen fire tunnels.

"Holy crap!" shouted Soren as the wind from its launch hit them square in the face, marring their vision for about a tenth of a micro second, as both of them laughed hysterically, clinging to each other in case it washed them over the edge as it receded down the stairs and back into its own element. "Your right, its freaking awesome!" he yelled back.

When their vision returned with the saltwater sting still in possession of their tear ducts, and water streaming down cheek to chin to their necks, he could see that another wave of a similar size had formed once again miraculously much further away. Kashandarhh pointed to still another in the beginnings of that growing swell that had only just reached the outer banks.

"They repeat themselves like clockwork once more or less about every seventh wave," she told him, as the next one moved into position in perfect symmetry to the smaller ones beside it, making it smash further than the last one up the bay towards the beach.

He was completely entranced by her rendition of the events that the ancestors of the Water Elementals told the little ones during the telling of the water almanac's teaching times, for all those that lived and hung their hides along the shores of the Ocean of Souls. He knew about some of their teachings from his own schooling, but nowhere was the truth about the actual Selkie Island that ran inside that area of ocean, included in any of those old musty books.

This ocean was well documented by scholars throughout the centuries, and waves of such gigantic proportions were copied and sketched in many an artist's painting, before landing in the houses of the ruling race of nobility. For these huge seas were well known in this part of the ocean currents, where they churned almost at a hysterical volume of Elemental guardianship, largely imparted by the deepest parts of the ocean current, down on the sea-floor.

It was written that its birthing was far out at sea within the deepest parts of the Trench of Talon; the very trench that bore these salty monsters into an almost sentient kind of life, like everything else that lived and breathed on this planet. Soren ducked as another wave came ridiculously close to the ridgeline they were standing on. Judging by what he saw in front of his own nose, they had not lied about its unusual behaviour, as it threatened once again to drag them into its own element, with its salty maw.

It was known to be an area of Majikal Seas and mystical storms, giving birth to similar seed waves in past centuries that could feed one's imagination with mystical beasts long dead and gone, suddenly finding life as they stormed ashore, wreaking havoc everywhere its fingers found their footholds. But this one had no life other than what had been produced in its molecules from that angry sea. When it did reach the shore and burst forth on the sand, one could see that it was just a huge mess of salted water, filled to capacity with various flotsam and jetsam it had picked up from the currents as it moved towards the shoreline of a similar sea.

Kashha surveyed the spectacle and reminded herself of the whispers she had heard during her last visit to her father's world. It had been foretold for many moons that the coming celestial event would be one of the strongest the Merfolk had witnessed in several hundred years, and they had not been wrong in its velocity, as she watched it roar down the coast and find its way through the shoals and shallows of Undinecis Reef, trying its best to obliterate everything in sight.

But that was not all of the atmospheric events that were taking place within this section of space. It also coincided with the comet called Lyra; a very strange piece of spacial rock that seemed to move with the speed of twenty shift-point doorways with its arrival in pretty much any arena of space in the time distortion field.

Lyra's arrival here was no different than those other planets whose very shores could still bear witness to its molecules of string technology, which had been drenched with spacial dustings, along the shores of some forgotten lake-side, deep in the wilderness of another time.

It was known to cause havoc when it arrived along-side any of the planets it visited, knocking things a bit sideways then leaving in a huff while everything moved and shifted all around it, trying to piece itself together again like a jigsaw puzzle, from what had been the initial entry point where the tear in the quantum had entered its orbit.

Soren felt rain hit his face, and turned to see the rain had arrived as tiny droplets of what could best be described as the tear ducts of the sky clans. But it was only the mist overhead forming into bigger clouds in the cloud seeder's atmosphere. Finding teeth in their consistency, they now felt like the damp edges of a vacated sponge left to drip high above in the tree tops.

Kashha stood on the precipice overlooking the migration of the Selkie population, scanning the waves for traces of her father's clan among the other factions that moved with the coming urgency. They had not as of yet been detected by her inner senses, and only distant cousins had been felt to have entered the water from the shelter of their cove.

She still had time to get to the water's edge before they moved fully in their Selkie forms, moved away from her line of communication and the ability to understand her words. They needed to move quickly down the slippery staircase, and as she turned to tell Soren to head down, her senses picked up another movement that was slowly making its way around Soren's ankle, that confirmed that hypothesis. They had begun the hunt.

Soren felt it touch the edge of his boot only moments before he could kick it away. He yelled and shivered at the sight, and before he could do anything about it, it found the steel edge of the double sided blade of Kashha's knife. Then the majority of it retreated back into the jungle, without parts of its entirety coming along for the ride.

Kashha went back and picked up the quivering appendage in her left hand as the head turned around and sneered with huge yellow teeth.

"Flipping hel...what is it?" Soren shrieked above the wind and took a step back. But she ignored him, and pointed to the stairs, urging Soren forward down the stone steps ahead of her as she blinded it, and flung it over the abyss. He shivered at the unknown, but trusted her judgement. It was, after all, her world and nothing he could see would have been able to change his mind, when he agreed to join her here in this strange and unpredictable place.

"There will be more of them; best to head down now," she whispered lightly behind him, looking backwards, daring the rest to follow.

With them being so close to the actual center of the storm, she couldn't use the majik that lived inside her body unless she wanted to destroy everything within sight, from here to the shores of the continent. They needed to keep moving. Now that the natives were starting to awaken to her presence, there would be several more attempts before they were able to find the sand beneath their toes. If they weren't careful, there would be a full on assault before they reached the final steps just above the beach.

The huge weather system now reached the edges of Undinecis reef, and became fully entrenched in its arrival, as the Ocean of Souls far out at sea continued to cycle these monsters through in rapid succession. Each new storm system backed up on to the one in front of it, drenching everyone in its path. It had all the earmarkings of one that would undoubtedly cause some damage to other parts of Water's Deep and not just the west side of the continent. Its arrival inside the reef's inner ledges was warning alone; not including the formation of the enormous cloud that moved like a ferrous demon, riding with a Valkyrie high on its back.

They needed to move now, if they wanted any hope of getting to the bottom of the stairs in one piece and seek the shelter of her tree from the next set, of oncoming waves. She pushed him forward with caution, and reached for the blade in her boot, pressing it tightly into the palm of her hand as she made her way down behind him.

Soren stepped carefully down each hand hewn step, half expecting to have it pulled out from under him, only to sigh as it stayed intact and non-threatening. Kashandarhh watched with Witch's eyes, their slow descent, but knew that in order to get down safely she would have to be vigilant or both of them wouldn't make it down alive.

The storm cell must have started around daybreak, along the mountain ridges to the south; it seemed to be sliding on the lee side of the cliffs towards the inner most reefs that started to pull in other land-masses included in the chain of Vaukknea's Archipelago of Selkie inhabited islands.

The storm's very nature changed everything inside these rings, and its very existence was full of majikal transformations that brought the most stationary of beings to life, inside the inner most sections of the rings; normally being so far away from the storms outside, which battered their doors, gave the inner creatures a sort of protective barrier. However, with these particular seed storms, those wards didn't always play fair the way they were supposed to, and inside the entire island was beginning to move and get its feet wet, as the majik of what this paradise really breathed life into, woke up and began to hunt.

This particular system came with a weather pattern all its own, and with it the island residents now had the ability to shed their solid forms, and move into a more corporeal molecular transference, would let them create new forms for their Fey signatures that had previously been rock or fauna. With that in mind, there was a big possibility that they could be swimming in the actual ocean, if the rocks under their feet had a hankering to dissolve into something along the lines of any of the water based creatures; then they would be swept out to sea, treading water in this new inherited trait of what the island of the Selkie miracle was really about.

There was no need to alarm the Dragon-rider walking down the stairs besides her; that might very well lead them to their demise. At least he would not stand idle should their transformation arrive before its time, and she could be assured he would stand firm alongside of her and fight. That was unless something actually knocked him out and he actually arrived unconscious at the foot of the bloody stairs. Then, unfortunately, all bets were off, and she would be left to fight it on her own.

A small smirk arrived on the corners of her mouth; she watched the high water line move in and out, with high fluctuations along the tidal current ebbs. Too bad she had not known him when she was younger and a student in the school that had given her that deadly sense of humour. They could have had a lot of fun at the expense of teachers that seemed to collect their sense of adventure from the rocks and dirt around bare feet and barnacled toes.

She needed to pay attention to what they were doing, and stop daydreaming about things she could do nothing about. She drew herself back into the situation they were moving into, and scanned the skyline to feel its threads. Kashha could see that nothing had the tang of anything sinister along the shore line of the bay as of yet. But that could change in a moment's notice. If something decided to pick a fight over something she had done to it the last time she arrived for a visit, then at least it would feel the blade of one pissed off Dragon-rider before it found its mark in the Witch it wanted to sink its teeth into. Hum, she wondered if he could swim?

She memorized many things in her years with her father. This was one of the more interesting landscapes that stuck inside her brain. This particular bay was home to the biggest Selkie population this side of the rings of

Goetutonias meteorite field, and if her family realized she was actually here inside the space in-between, surely someone would have alerted her father to her whereabouts, and the general entrance point she would find past the rings would be alive with activity.

But he had not been there when they came through the void, and as luck would have it, both she and Soren had made it this far without having to call for his help. She really hated to call for help, even if she knew she was about to be eaten alive by something they could have stopped. She was spoiling for a fight, and by the feelings she got from this Dragonlord back in her own woods, he was just about as feisty as she was. That would prove helpful when the creatures arrived to claim their prize. Crap, he'd better know how to swim!

This was something she had always prevented from happening in the past. But right now if the island decided to fight her arrival, it would have the upper hand without her father's energy keeping it at bay. It had taken on a nasty reputation during her last few visits, and she had ridden the wave on her own, matching their attacks with ease when its continental land-masses ran with the energy fields of several larger ley lines that lived just underneath the island's toes. Any other day, she would have welcomed it, but today she was not in the mood to play.

For several years now, they had recruited several factions of Elemental incursions from various star systems to try and outwit her chemistry; they had all failed so far, and with Soren moving ahead of her, anything could erupt out of the mist below their feet and give her the feeling of well-founded satisfaction, as he was able to help her kick its ass, back into whatever hole it crawled out of.

She knew, without a shadow of a doubt, that it had never made arrangements for this scenario, and that by having Soren in her shadow when they came through the veil, they had no time to adjust their plan of attack with the added signature of the Dragonlord. Maybe this time she would have a reprieve from their constant ambushes. However, something inside her brain doubted it, and it wouldn't take too long, before they arrived on the beach, for the world to fold up around them. And with this Dragonlord, no matter how notorious he was this side of the Fey worlds, something would inevitably try to take a bite out of them, even if it was just for a taste. She smiled almost cruelly when she thought of how Soren was going to react to their plan of attack. She was betting on finding his sword embedded to the hilt, inside its sandy bones.

She knew her arrival came at the hardest time for the Selkie race to detect her signature, as both her fingers had shifted the curtain fabric and replaced its silken length, when nothing breathed its breath along the outer-wards. For that, she would have to move even more silently inside the heavily guarded rings; for a surprised island was a dangerous island. She knew she was basically all on her own, even with the expertise of one of the notorious Black Dragon trackers, and her fingers itched for a fight with the fabric of her father's home-world, which still insisted she was not one of their kindred spirits.

She had never enjoyed the contact from any species that lived on either side of the void, and this one Dragon-rider was proving to be a little on the volatile front when it came to having her energy signature detected in the Selkie home-world. The island still to this day, had maintained that she was on her own, claiming a combatant life-force inside her Witch's signature. Each of the individual patterns that lived with sentient life bubbles of the water elementarianism philosophy, were never comfortable with those of the Air Elemental planes. She, unfortunately, was part of their little watery clique, even if they refused to believe it. But the formulation of their watery brains had not been able to fathom her hereditary generics in its energy battle for the long haul, and as she moved with the fast approaching waves down the slippery stairs, she smiled with a wicked thought. She was at the heart of many of the creatures that still struggled to bypass their contaminated little minds, and had another soul of equal quality to her airy-Faery roots. Her world of air gave them breath, even if they refused to breathe her molecules down their damn watery Elementalized throats.

She had done this many times in her lifetime, and yet still they resisted her genetic ability to withstand the storms that each of them contributed to in their own unique way. The Merfolk were known to follow all strange forms of ritualistic weather phenomenon, while any other Fey species could only find sanctuary indoors, from its catastrophic effects, which had begun to rattle the doorframes in earnest.

As the storm threatened to blow apart the dwellings that rested upon the land-masses, they quickly sought refuge inside. While the water creatures and their element of expertise raised their heads...or what appeared to be of that persuasion...to the stormy skies, as several lightning strikes touched different areas of the water and the creatures that had been only moments ago on solid ground, moved en-mass towards its welcoming fingers and scurried away.

A true catastrophic storm front arrived in Water's Deep once in every hundred years. And this one was sure to out-rival those that had come before it, packing a punch that only that caste of the Water Elementals could withstand. During this time as it grew in density, many of the land Fey would find nothing short of death should they try to withstand the energy that was needed to help those with the ritual of the Selkie shedding.

Down the centuries, only the Selkies and their brethren water-creatures knew of the significances of its violence, and the turbulent sea foam that twisted the wave tops almost crimson, deep out amongst that violent sea. Kashandarhh could visualize some sort of majikal being off in the distance, turning the patterns of innocent waves into the grotesque forms of monsters and silhouetted shades, then sliding them into the ghosts of their ancestors, as they spun the whirlpools into a full on storm-cell undetected by others of similar systems.

Although now dead, and living in the underworld far from this world of Sea Serpents and Mermaids, it was often said that those who crossed through that veil in times of death, found the one true day when they could once again return to the world of the Fey, should there ever be a need to have such creatures roam the land once more. It still sent shivers down Kashha's spine, the thought that one day it could very well be her. She had no love of this life, but truth be known she had followed the dead on secret pilgrimages when she had need of their energy, when they had been taken to the grave without proper preparation.

She wondered if her family knew anything about her secretive life. At the moment, her paternal cousins seemed to be only interested in the storm, as they languished in its tortured movements, and found exhilaration in each of the cresting monstrous waves, as they fell from their great heights and crashed their angry jaws into the nesting of the next crusade of moving water.

The water changed direction once again, drifting with the currents towards the shallower areas of the nearest land-masses. It produced huge foam columns of salty spray, as the waves crashed into each other from every direction in a confused sea of turbulence that was unyielding to anything that stood in its path. She passed Soren slowly as he fought off another attempt on his life, thinking it wiser to have him move in behind them, instead of watching the next set of waves from offshore begin to form. And it was during this set of events, that she almost missed him taking a nose dive over the edge.

She turned to catch him when he lost his footing on the slippery steps, and as his arm came into contact with her own, she was able to hold him steady. Both watched as several tall Water Elementals moved towards shore, in precisely the same area that they were currently moving awkwardly down the set of stairs.

"I'm ok," he said letting her go, as he found his balance and they continued to pick their way down the rougher sections that held their booted feet firmly planted on its base.

The wind had picked up sometime during the night, and found itself in warmer than average waters. With this added into the mixture of wind and waves, they seemed to be changing direction, in a more unusual angle than that of the offshore flow. With Soren and Kashha continuing to make their way down, it could be seen moving towards the southernmost point of Undinecis reef, far away from any land-mass that the current Fey races lived within.

Soren was still feeling a bit queasy from their unusual arrival through the veil, and had really tried to not look down at the steeper sections of their slow descent to the beach. It had been explained that there was need for caution, but until now he had not really thought anything of it. Kashha had given him a crash course in what to expect from the waterfolk, but until his arrival on the stairs and visualizing the dizzying heights and the blackened dots floating en-mass, it had not really occurred to him that they really were not within Tantaris's boundaries anymore. At least not the Tantaris that he had been led to believe was anywhere near that extra pair of boots, under a certain cottage's bed, in a far off land-mass that no longer felt its threads on this side of the pond. He wished now, that he had thought to shut his bloody door after their grand migration to the stones, three days hence. No, he shook his head and tried to steer himself around the bits on the stairs, it was longer than that. He was losing track of the days now, and if he came home and that bloody beaver had moved into his damn sink again, he was gonna be living on the sharp end of his flipping sword! He hated the over grown rat that had been threatening to evict him every time he went away.

He swore softly under his breath, as once again he almost lost it and went tumbling over the edge into thin air. It reminded him of the early years of learning how to fly on Tansar's back, and if he wasn't careful, not even Tansar would be able to pick up the pieces that would be spread along the sandy bottom of whatever the hel this island claimed to be. Well, there was one good thing about that, at least he would be feeding the crabs and other crustaceans that scurried in the water as it once again retreated back into the sea.

Crap, he needed to really pay attention to what he was doing. He hated the thought of becoming fodder for some damn sea creature as it ripped chunks of this flesh apart with teeth the size of his own head. He started to laugh slightly at his own sense of awful humour and almost fell again. This time Kashandarhh smacked him full in the arm and almost sent him for real, over the edge.

"Stop it you fool, I can't save you with majik here. If you go over the edge this close to the vortex, you're going to really hurt yourself when you hit the bottom."

They were about halfway down when off in the distance several new Phoenixes could be seen coming out of the mist, flying straight towards the cliffs that they were descending, heading straight at them. These were not the ones that had harassed the Osprey before. No indeed, they were an entirely new set of helions. For these ones shone with a bright bluish hue that continued to alternate that colour scheme from one side of the light spectrum to a slightly newer, never been seen before shade of cobalt; the very cobalt that glistened from one side of their lovely feathers to the tips of their shiny white fangs.

This time they didn't bother the osprey who flew away from where they were currently moving towards. This time they came towards the place on the stairs that Kashandarhh and Soren were actually stepping down, landing several feet below their current location and eyeing the two of them who remained frozen in place.

Soren retreated one step back, and came past the very place Kashha had just put her foot down to steady her foothold. Both melded together and stood on the narrow ledge watching the pair of inquisitive birds, as they cocked their heads back and forth, letting out several hisses in their direction.

Kashha heard it first, and turned her head slowly, realizing they had been followed by a rather large reptile of unknown descent, down the incline of the stone steps. It was only six steps behind them and was hunched up watching them, set to sink its teeth into the backs of their heads if they moved even a muscle in either direction.

They were trapped. There was no way around it, and she had not heard a single sound over the crashing of the waves that would have sent her senses into overdrive had the water not been smashing the hel out of their current location on the stairs. Soren felt her tense up, and for the first time in his life, he didn't react the way he thought he might. She was talking to him with her mind, and for the first time he didn't freakout; this time he was only thankful.

He listened to words that had no meaning to him, and yet he understood them absolutely, without hesitation. She was talking in old Lemurian, a language he had never heard a single time in his entire life. And yet, he understood her meaning and what she was trying to do, as if he had learned it as a child and lived with the language all his life.

Her words grew louder along the cliff face, and gradually they were spoken out loud blending in with the two Phoenixes who blinked their eyes at each sound that was spelled out, shifting their feet from one talon to the next along the rocks. Meanwhile, behind them the vibrations of the words were having a definite effect on the creature, as the meaning of Kashha's words unwound before it, becoming all too direct and crystal clear.

Two things happened almost instantaneously, and ran parallel to what was about to transpire, had they not seen the birds and continue their advancement down the stairs. Both birds took to the air, and brushed past the Aelves, who leaped into the air the moment the birds took to wing. Concurrently, the reptile launched himself like lightening and aimed his rather large teeth just around the area where their spine would have connected with the points of their shoulders.

Now, had both Soren and Kashha been habituating on said stair when those fangs actually entered their bodies, the necks of both of them would undoubtedly be sunk up to the depth of her athame with razor sharp needles, which would have pierced the skin and bone and come out of the front of their necks almost a full six inches, decapitating them and ripping their bodies from their spines. Now, with that visual aid, things could have got rather messy. Instead, something quite opposite and rather miraculous actually did happen. It was wholly unexpected as far as one bloody Dragonlord was concerned; that is upon finding both of them to be part of the air and the space in-between at the very same time, and falling at the speed of light crashing like a mongoose through the trees when he missed his landing site because of a sneeze.

You see my darlings, travelling with a Witch had many benefits that are not ordinarily given to the average Fey. For one, she spoke many different languages, and had many ways to create things that others of lesser sight would have not been able to achieve. But Soren found it very difficult to trust her like he did his brothers. For one, he had been living with their idiosyncrasies for almost five thousand years. With her, he didn't really have much of a choice. Coming from an Aelf who was always in control, this was something he was still having problems adjusting to.

What happened was not something for the faint of heart. As she yelled for him to obey her, he, for a moment in time, couldn't actually fathom what she was trying to tell him. I could say that they basically jumped over the edge into thin air, but that would be a lie. You see, since she could not take the time to explain to him the justifications of vaulting off into thin air, without giving him assurances that this was indeed the right thing to do; she instead threw him off! She not waiting for him to begin screaming dove into him, and both went off the stairs basically at the same time and found themselves back-peddling their legs, with nothing to keep them airborne but the bloody wind and it wasn't helping!

Soren continued to scream, as he went down cursing several different oaths in several languages that he didn't even know he knew, while Kashandarhh whistled between her teeth and bit her lip not once but twice. They found themselves floating within the upper air thermals along the sides of the cliffs for a second in time, before they crashed headlong into the realization they were falling faster than their minds allowed them to comprehend, she had actually done it. Before long, gravity took over and they began to fall with the open air rushing through their hair, while their screams now an inherent part of the landscape were drowned out by the storm that had arrived without prejudice, and laid claim to those foolish enough to join its ranks. Then, just when all hope appeared lost — and Soren already had seen the beginning threads of his life pass before his eyes, a solid bluish smattering of feathers arrived out of thin air, and blocked their downward hurtle into an almost certain smashing of heads into the side of the bloody cliff.

They instantly took the lifeline, grabbing on before the wind knocked them further sideways, sliding down blue coloured feathers until they found the bone spurs that allowed them to grip the sides of both Phoenixes, which had miraculously moved underneath them. The great birds coming to their aid produced several shrieks, echoing their objection on the matter, as both Aelf and bird screamed their bloody heads off with the insanity of it all — careening away from the brutal teeth of Vaukknea's latest missed acquisition.

What proceeded next was something similar to a ride on a drunken night at the Ferrishyn fairs; they felt themselves being lifted slightly in the updraft that the wind was moving towards at the edges of the cliff, and they crash landed — although a little askew, but safely on the backs of both Phoenixes. It was still up for speculation to how that happened — as far as Soren was concerned, as they crawled upwards towards the birds' backs; the very ones that had previously been on the stairs; blocking their path, as the wind tore through their clothes and flattened their faces in a terrifying ride to the bottom of the cliff-face.

The wind not happy with the unsuccessful attempt at capturing another creature to fling to its death, caught them full in the face rather pissed off. Feathers and wet rain drops co-mingled along the edges of their fingertips, and they caught themselves from falling as the birds went into a steep dive towards the beach. Where they landed with hissing beaks and red blinking eyes, which showed no trace of domestication whatsoever, much to the astonishment of one very shaky Dragon-rider, who immediately looked at Kashandarhh with suspicion and yelled above the noise of the storm the moment they landed on the sandy ground.

What the hel was that? I thought you said you couldn't use majik this close to the storm?" The birds took to the air in flight, soaring higher up into the air, squawking away and thoroughly pissed at the loss of their dinner, further ignoring any attempt Kashha made to rectify the problem they thought they had covered at the staircase only moments ago.

She was brushing the sand off and pulling loose feathers out of her hair, which had slid out of their sheaths as they careened down the sides of the huge birds, and then casually looked him over with a whimsical expression of mirth.

"No need for majik my dear boy, when language works just as cleanly and much more efficiently; especially when you're about to be eaten bloody alive by birds half the size of your War Dragon!" She spat the last of the feathers lodged in her teeth, and laughed at his shocked expression. "Finally something has got your tongue, tracker. Shall we just call this even in case next time it is my ass that needs saving?" Soren shook his head and cursed loudly for all to hear.

"Flipping hel, even Symin would haven't have tackled that one head-on, and he likes this kind of a freaking challenge on the best of days. Nonetheless it appears you have a way of getting us into trouble without any help from me. Maybe next time dear Witch, you will try and at least give me a warning before I decide to throw myself into the jaws of some living piece of Selkie insanity."

"Tsk, tsk, tsk, ye of little faith, dear boy," she laughed, clicking air through her teeth. "I think you and I will do just fine, in all that we encounter on this bit of floncified rock." She turned her back on him and moved towards a safer place away from the stairs, up near the cliff face, and over by the far side of the beach. He followed at her side, as she continued on with her train of thought. "My father would be proud just to see that you haven't got me killed before he has been able to speak to us."

He pushed her towards the water as it flowed higher towards the area they were walking in, and picked her up while she squirmed, and mimicked throwing her into the surf. Just as a piece of kelp tried to whack them in the knees in a mad dash for freedom, a wave swallowed them whole. Soren turned his body to let his back take the brunt of the water just before it hit, and they both came up spitting salty water out of their noses. He held Kashandarhh in his arms and almost split his mouth wide open when he bit down hard on his lip as they landed on their backs.

"Oh, shit!" he yelled, coughing up small specks of blood around his gum-line.

She turned and smacked him on the head until he dropped her and they both laughed until the tears ran down their faces, all the while choking on the seawater. He put his hand on his lip, as she went in for another hit. "Hey stop that, my lip freaken hurts," he growled at her.

"Well at least I grabbed the feathers that were attached to its head and not it's ass you fool. You're lucky it didn't drop you on your head after you tore the remaining intact ones out of its tail." She said, laughing so hard she didn't see him smile and show a big wide sloppy grin on his big ole Dragon-rider face.

"Dragons are my speciality, not big blue birds that try to bite your finger, while they're saving your hide," he said with a bit of sarcasm laced with admiration. "Next time just bloody warn me that we're about ready to launch ourselves into outer space....Holy crap what now?" He turned, pointing his fingers towards the trees as the blood continued to come out of the wound. His face suddenly turned a ghastly shade of white and Kashha thought he was talking about the cut. She was wrong. The shadows of what appeared to be their newest threat arrived in greater numbers from the edge of the jungle, as hordes of creatures big and small were heading in what appeared to be a mass migration into the tidal surge, along the water's edge.

He ducked and hit the beach as their images moved in and out of his visual cortex, constantly changing shape while moving from one phase to another, and then disappeared altogether as their bodies morphed and moved into the surf. This was the time of year that all residents of the Island of Vaukknea and the surrounding smaller water rocks, moved into the ocean towards these violent storm-fronts, giving over to the ferociousness that transcended all other things they were currently preforming in their solid formations on land, at the time.

And the reptile on the stairs may have been no different than those that had already changed into something water born to join in the festivities. She had suspicions about its true nature, and felt somewhat vindicated in the assumption that it may just very well be one of her anti-Witch foes, but there was always the chance that indeed it was nothing more than a simple lizard out for a stroll, and had accidentally come across a readymade food supply, all dished up and randomly waiting for consumption on the stairs.

There was still some doubt as to the likelihood of that happening, while they were advancing down the steps; for the simple reason that she had not heard or felt its arrival within the vicinity, as it made its way silently from out of nothing but rock. When they had flung themselves into the open space over the stairs, and she had a split moment to look back from her precarious perch, high in the feathers of the phoenix's back, there was no trace of the creature or its long teeth, which confirmed her suspicion to the letter. There should have been some form of subatomic particle tracing of it, if indeed it had gone over the embankment, and she should have been able to track its passage to the beach below. There were none.....as if the creature had been majikally induced and the moment she left the vicinity, it had dissolved back to the ritual it came from.

Whatever was tracking her this time had perfected its attack. Her father needed to know they had crossed a line. For here many of the island creatures had come from far and wide, to make their pilgrimages to the sea. If indeed something had arrived without their knowledge, they needed to know about it before one of them got hit in the crosshairs.

Now this new threat was really nothing more than the local fauna moving into the next phase, one that Soren really had never seen before on this scale. Witnessing this, Soren faced the truth of the land that was solid yet Elemental all at the same time. Still, his mind found it difficult to conceive of their true nature, and he had to verbally ask her if indeed this was what he was seeing or another illusion set to trick him. She answered him mentally, trying to stay inert as they watched from the sidelines, until they had to actually move towards a loftier location, away from the twisting turning sands that threatened to drag them along on their migrational run into the deeper surf.

They chose the larger of several trees that had their root systems planted just above the high water mark, and firmly planted in the cliff face above. They were joined by several other mammals who had also taken refuge there, scurrying along the bark and getting out of their way. They watched those creatures of legend he had come to see, which he had never seen in the final transformation end of transmorphication. They moved amongst the mass migration, seemingly skimming overtop of their bodies, as they made their way down to the water, and sank their feet into its gravitational pull, disappearing into the surf as they shed their skin.

They were almost Aelven in appearance, walking on two legs into the water, and then transforming right in front of him the moment their skin touched the molecules of salt. He watched, fascinated as the oil of their skin made contact with the genetic makeup of the other creatures that lived in its environment, triggering the change. Then, right before his eyes, skin turned into fur and the creature morphed into the animal that breathed through mammalized gills in the shallows of the bay that her father called home.

This was what Kashha had been waiting for, and she pointed to Soren to follow her gaze as the creatures made their way down to the water's edge. It was their true love of the sea that gave every one of their species the migrational rights to this voyage of sheer ostentatious pleasure. And Soren could feel it in the air the moment they came into view, among the thousands of other creatures that moved along the sands. Their belief was that these very waves, at this time of year, were directly created for them and them alone. The pairing of their transitional state of transformational solitude and their vanity would not allow them to think otherwise, in any other term.

The moment each solitary creature came out of the jungle, the other creatures would part and let it by, as if they were revered in this environment for their sheer beauty alone. These creatures, walked on land and swam far out in the depths of the sea, came from the same folklore of creatures as the mermen and their companions, the Mermaids. Unlike their brethren, however, these creatures knew both worlds of water and earth equally, as they came to live upon the rocks and islands they called their home.

They were known as the Selkintramblay Capatofic Tryilamores; Selkies, on the shorter tongues of land-dwellers. These were the brethren creatures of her father's clan, who had the ability to transform into ocean going

Seals the moment they harnessed the power of the waves and used their movement within the waters of the massive storms that accompanied the higher tides.

Each twisted and slid fluidly under the water element, into its newest formulation, finding their energy inside the watery refractions that shimmered wildly in the depths of ocean currents, along this side of Water's Deep. Many that swam within the surge they could see belonged to several outer clutches within their own family units, and lived their entire life cycle out in the depths of those huge waves, never touching foot upon the land in their solitary lives far out at sea.

They were called the Narn, and were from the deep sea homeland that found its molecules to mix with those of the trench dwellers of another creature, which made these waters their hereditary sanctuary. Each of those individual creatures, of the wilder race of Selkies, had no love of the land, and used another form of majik to bring the land dwellers home to the sea to join in the mass migration, that allowed them to fight another day within the land-walkers' circumferences. Each could be seen beckoning the others to join the ride, barking and yelping their greetings to their long lost friends who joined them with the approaching Auicks already eagerly awaiting their arrival.

These solitary Selkies, were not particularly friendly, but would on occasion join up with those who belonged to a more social grouping, and although the waves were now coming in huge droves and wracking the sea floor with thousands of tiny particles, obscuring the vision of most any other animal, they all knew each other by memory alone, touching each other in the dance that the sea allowed them, gliding around in the wateristic thermals the sea offered only to them in this wilder form.

On the shore side, more of the land based mammals that created beautiful villages deep within the forest of their Is'lantic home, moved towards the beach where the waves had started to form a surge. The rocks rolled and fell into the saltwater around them, moving many of them up the shoreline, giving the appearance of a thousand pieces of shrapnel exploding in a stellar cartographied mine field of living tissue. It was to here that the large Elemental creatures Soren had first noticed on the height of the stairs, seemed to be swimming.

Smaller pieces of beautiful coral that had come loose underwater coloured the sands in a multitude of beautiful shapes and colours. They glistened along the tidal flats with the sea water, and ran in rivulets among the rock granules of sand and loose stones as the water moved back out to sea with each surge, forcing them farther up onto the beach. These creatures, now newly formed, only came to sentient life once in every thousand years, and followed the nutrients of the ocean currents in their molecular photosynthesis as they made their way towards the Selkie colonies on shore to join in the energy they needed to survive while they were awake.

The once bustling village that the resident Selkies now lived amongst on terra firma, had suddenly become a ghost town; when only a moment ago, it received the first morning rays sliding across its edge, as the orb moved slowly up into the early morning skies.

Word of mouth was not the normal trigger for exodus in the arrival of any storm that graced this coast, but this one definitely would be arriving quickly, with the arrival of the wild Auick formulating and calling them home. It was here that the larger Elemental creatures called the Auick came for those that lived on the land, and directed the land dwellers like a conductor, as they made this new element their temporary home. All that belonged to the world of the Selkie needed their attendance in the cooler waters of the sea, and those who chose to ignore its calling would find themselves suddenly alone and without a single creature who would answer their call on the desolate shore, before too long.

The mass exodus had made itself known around the Witching hour of the past nightfall. Each family group had silently prepared for their own departure, with no more than a nod of agreement among the elders of their clan. The gathering that commenced was all up to the individual home clutches. They took no more than what was needed to drop their Fey forms and transform into the beautiful big eyed creatures that swam with the oncoming tide. The Auick greeted them individually, out along the deeper edges near the shore, and directed them forward to blend with the majik of the waves and the sheer drop-off where the surface waters dove deeply into its open trenches.

The underwater topography at the shore was similar to that of the larger mountain basins that rested their feet along the continent's sharp escarpments. Only this was turned upside down, and ran its peaks along the bottom of the ocean currents which now housed several thousand metres of rock formations, all glistening in the morning Mauntra from below the water's surface.

Black skinned coats of oiled fur, jutted through the currents moving them smoothly to the outer depths of the deep water channels. The tides by the shoreline had a hold of the eddy, whose very aquiline structure moved them without any resistance, into the open waters, minimalizing the volume that was needed to transform them fluidly into that other shape of fish and fin. Once they reached those silken shapes, they had ease of mobility to perform the amazing manoeuvres that enhanced their creativity in these majikal waters of life sustaining molecules. They could be heard vocalizing their intentions with the yelps of several newly formed pups following behind them, while they swam past the reef entrance and out into the open water swells.

As they moved further out into the open, the salt spray battered their whiskers in their now fully Selkiefied forms, while one of the group swimming caught the shadow of the Mauntra's light that had just broken through the trees and shone along the sands to their position. His face formed a slight curve in its placement, as it fell across the shadow of a lone being out low on the high tide line. Vaal smiled with recognition of the two legged form placed solidly on the beach, with her hands planted firmly on her withy hips. Her form rendered her unable to move with the others that had gone before her, who were already thriving in the high surf and relishing its watery surge.

A tiny twinge of regret filled his senses, that he could not have found her before he attained his Seal skin, and he smelled her scent through enhanced nasal passages that filtered those that flitted around her and moved into the sea. Her signature filled the air, as she nodded slightly in his direction and came no further than her body would allow her, to keep from being taken by the tidal currents. She changed position slightly, as he watched from his vantage point, shielding her eyes from the sudden change in direction of the clouds up above, while the sea battered the coast line around her.

The Selkie blinked large black eyes that held no visible iris, also watching the clouds get darker up above. He had felt her presence when she first moved through the doorway of their world, and would have waited longer for her silhouette to show by her favourite spot if he could. It was one she had picked long ago, when she was still a young kidlet, along the beach head she loved, with toes stuck firmly in the sand. For whatever reason, she had taken longer than normal to get to their home, and he had sensed another presence alongside her signature when they came through the small channel the Selkie world had secretly set aside for her own entry. Hoping this was the reason for her delay, his eyes scanned its energy to find it higher up along the tree's solid roots. He frowned at its signature, confused by the images he was seeing.

She advanced along the shoreline, walking sometimes along the water's edge as she followed several large burls from the Rayoola Tree that jutted out into the salted lagoon, while the other stayed firmly planted along the bark of the huge trunk, watching the creatures of the island turn themselves into the sea.

Kashha had first come to the base of the tree, and stood watching the behaviour of all that resided within this village, moving off-land with the surge at the beachhead only moments ago. She stood with eyes shielded from the brightness of the day, watching as it carried them further away from the shoreline and out of sight momentarily, as they floated and bobbed with the tidal ebbs into the deeper waters of the bay. She did not hold the genetic transference to transform along with the others, as they swam freely, dipping beneath the waves, and disappeared from her sight once again much further out. Her father's clan felt her briefly as they passed, but the pull of the sea was much stronger than their curiosity, and they disappeared individually into its midst.

She watched them go one by one, headlong into the surging sea, with nothing but a slight of hand to witness her thoughts to their parting. She raised a hand to her mouth and kissed the wind, sending them off on their journey with the blessing of the Ka`afrey coven set into the air, that would give them speed and protection in case it was needed. She had other things in her destiny more important than worrying that she had not the gene that allowed her to join her Selkie family, as they made their way into this weightless environment of pure fluidic joy.

This was not the first time she had been left alone, nor the first time she had been left on this island by her Clan, as they made their way to the shedding grounds in the open waters. But, it was the first time she had been left with a stranger in their world, and one with an uncanny ability to get them both knocked off with relative ease.

Her heritage did not make it any easier with that thought in mind now; when she watched them disappear from view, diving below the surface with utter joy and moving within the pure essence of that liquid that sustained their lives and not her own. They became one with the salted molecules of unfamiliar territory while she, land-bound, could only watch and wish them well.

She had been born not of purity, but of substance, and today of all days she wished she was able to reach them before their journey took the last of them into the water and out of her reach. But she would have to wait. The way time moved about the Selkie brain, it would take many days — perhaps even weeks before she would have the opportunity to see them again. She smiled with a tiny bit of regret at their playful manoeuvres, and watched them one last time before the final tail splashing slowly disappeared. When they surfaced again in the distance, they were too far out for her to recognize the differences between mammal and created illusion.

She hesitated briefly, and then sighed.

Her parental lineage was on a much higher level of understanding than those who were left of purity of the species. She would come to understand that as she grew older, and time itself would find the way to correct her thoughts. She had more to do as a creature that was more adept at land based life, than her kin of the seas.

She had watched her family grow into strong beings that harboured only love of her, even despite her inability. The sea had held them together for more than 100 thousand centuries; at her birthing she had broken that hatching and come untethered into their world. Its very majik grew further from her grasp as time went on, but never came to rest within the species that bred her form into existence all those long years ago; in another time, when she grew up from the outside in.

Kashandarhh sighed and uncrossed her arms, which she had been holding tightly across her chest. She had been fathered by the same creature that was now pounding through the waves at such a high velocity of speed that she could no longer visually distinguish him from his own family clutch. She watched the lone Selkie turn and hover in the tops of the waves for a moment, fighting the foam that smashed into his finely oiled fur, then silently disappear beneath the water as it continued on towards the energy field, deep within the cold edges of the oncoming storm. Kashha knew his face and watched from the beach with knowledge of the shedding that happened at this time of the season. She didn't hesitate, or think that it might be another; instead, knowing it was her father from memory without even having to ask through mental telepathy: 'is that you out there?' It was an unspoken agreement, each time they met throughout the history of her arrivals on the island. There had always been that between them, ever since she was a young child of the land Witches, living among creatures that knew her for her heritage, and not her paternal lineage. Even before she was able to walk, she had always known his imprint within the texture of this world that she now lived within; that was their right.

She did not carry the chromosomes that held her father in form along with the others of his kind; she had been given another way of life that became the norm within the clan that taught her how to swim as it was needed, while she had come to rest in the early years of her life alongside the herd. She had not come with that particular knowledge in her genetic handbook when she was born, like the others of her family line, and it had been a labour of love to give it to her once she arrived in all their clucking glory, and they had revelled in its quality.

This particular activity had not come without a struggle for her, and proved far more difficult than she would have expected, coming from the molecular heritage of being from a creature of the water. But she had taken to the task with nothing less than sheer determination and a lot of swallowed water; add in much swearing to boot, and you had the young Kashandarhh down to a very loud tee.

Nevertheless, she had kicked her way into their hearts and almost drowned several of her cousins, and one particular elder who had given the others the day off, immediately having regretted volunteering his teachings, after she turned even his boisterous opinions to shades of a colourful blue tirade. But soon, it had finally given her some form of peace, inside the body of a child that had no flippers along her non-webbed toes. And she finally found some sense of semblance, as she felt her way like a blind castor-bean floating in liquid jelly, and it had gone no further. Sadly, they had decided it was best. For, anymore teaching her was going to end up with one or more of them getting seriously hurt, or for the most part damaged; as her Witchy molecules tried to sap the strength out of even the strongest males of Vallmyallyn's tribe while her father had laughed with enormous gaiety watching the proceedings from the beach, in all of its insanity. Unlike the others, you couldn't have paid him any amount of coin, to try!

But try they did, and as the long arduous days turned colder, it too had gone to the wayside — much to her own relief. It had not the slightest effect on her mindset at first, as her Mother's new Kilrenean family had given her everything else that she required to transform into the Kanoie bonding, away from that elusive branch of Witch branding the Llavalla clan had refused her. But it was unlike anything they ever had seen before, and every time they began to know what she had become, she expanded their vocabulary beyond their limits and reason, and they would leave in frustration, leaving her to wallow in the shelter of the saltwater lagoon, floating like a stuck pig, as she dipped her feet into its salty brine.

Days turned into months, and still they had not completed the task. And with her coming of age, she had learned most things on her own from the voices of the ancestors that dared to cross the folds of the curtain, who still remained now long since dead and buried at her side. On occasion, when she visited her Fathers Clan, she wished she could just once experience the bonding of those huge salt filled waves that always seemed to elude her curiosity. But nothing but cold hard sand had been felt between her toes, during the storms of the shedding. This was one thing she was now absolutely sure of, that she landasticlly needed to stay grounded and deeply rooted within.

The rain began to pelt the shoreline much harder now, and she was finally forced to run for cover, joining Soren who stood alongside the trunk of a Saltwater Jacobien Camiforean Elm. He had been resting in the overhead safety of its lofty over-protective leaves. It was her tree, one that had an attachment to her in the most oddest of ways.

This one was one of the larger varieties, and had the added ability to keep the rain water from reaching those who stood underneath its limbs in need of shelter. She had to admit that shelter from the rain that soaked every inch of her clothing was the very thing that she was currently in need of. And by the looks of the clouds that were wrestling with several rather large Sylphs out on the water side of the cliffs as they climbed higher up into the thermals, this was going to be a very long day of drenching the skin off their hardened bones.

She turned her attention to the tree, remembering something that her father once told her about their arrival here on this small land-mass that constantly kept changing its location. These huge trees grew primarily within climates of a salt-water ecosystem on only Selkie Is`lantic fauna particulates. This particular tree had made its way onto the sands above the tide line, and arrived for the sole purpose of this very spot's peculiar climatic condition, which still ran wild with the chaotic storm surges that came up onto the reef each few years.

Vaukknea Island's compass bearings were unique in its topography, and the large Elm which had been often called the Rayoola tree by many of the elders of the clan, found the island suited its needs, and could be seen playing in the water of the sheltered lagoon on calmer days, chasing the fish that swam close along the tidal flats until it was sated and couldn't eat another. Kashha, on the other hand had made fast friends with it in the days of her youth, and each without the verbal apertures of conversation, had become blood-Fey in record time.

Living in the Fey worlds, nothing is what it seems to be, and this tree was a prime example of one of those elusive creatures that defied all explanation. The Rayoola had placed large root stalks within the sands of Vallmyallyn's particular beachhead one day, long ago, when first this land-mass had risen to the surface world above. The strangest of its life cycle was in part to Tantaris's actual location, and not the direct correspondence to the debris field of its home-planet, which still had the occasional relative moving towards the many different shift-point doorways, as they travelled along in space looking for suitable breeding grounds.

However, the island itself was a living breathing being, made up from other such creatures that breathed life into its own existence, after having swum up out of the sea at their feet and created the island from nothing but their own backs and a lot of hard labour. It was old then; so imagine how, as an adult, Kashandarhh felt as she touched its familiar bark and welcome herself home in its extended branches.

Another smile started to escape her lips, but she held it back as she bit her lip to allow the pain to finish the smirk. She needed to not let the Dragonlord see this part of her, as the inner soul was starting to rear its ugly head. It was difficult to let anyone see her feeling this way. And if she had any say in the choice of its arrival, her vulnerability would not be allowed to see the light of day.

Soren was still hovering higher up the bark, looking amazed at everything moving along the high tide line. He had not noticed her discomfort as of yet, but in time he would put two and two together, and then her secret would come to light and she would have to do something foolish to hide it's like.

She needed the rider here in this place for many reasons. Without him to wait out the storm, there would be no other she could use for protection against the ones that were hidden and waiting for her to misstep. No matter how hard she tried to admit that this was not so, she had to concede that she indeed was fallible and that the extra energy that the Dragon-rider brought with him into this land would ground her in this insanity and keep them both alive. She was, after all, Fey, and soon she would have to find her sleep, along with everything else that stayed island bound. That is when it would hurt her, and she couldn't stay awake for the time it would take to bring her clan home. For that she needed Soren.

For, along with her senses being somewhat filtered from the enormous amount of energy from the storm, somewhere out there something was hidden within the waters of the island's molecules, and before the day was done, it would rear its ugly head and show its teeth to one of the two that kept away from the water's edge, where it lay in wait.

She could just feel its presence slightly, as it filtered in and out of her senses then darted into the shadows to become once again undetectable. She closed her eyes to redirect her senses out there just above the water line, out past the headwaters along the shore. It had an unusual signature combined with a tiny filtration of evil that could be felt even on this side of the space in-between. She wondered if the Selkies felt its stink out on the reef, before the storm had redirected their instincts into another more important activity. Or had she brought it through when the veils ionized the moment she opened them with her knife?

She wondered had Soren not moved through the veil along beside her, would it have affected her intuitions differently, prompting its discovery sooner, so she could have moved it out of the shadows. Or would it have appeared with that much more violence, had she come here alone?

She had many questions, and very few answers. The fact remained that, had she not come here in the first place, her father may not have been told of the comings of the very thing she had an urgency to warn him about. This new threat to her body, here in his own world, was nothing new, but gave her reason to pause. Was it something new, or just the island once again taking offence to her arrival? Whatever the cost, there was nothing left to do but wait for her family to return, if only to let them know of the imminent danger they were all about to come face to face with, on the outside of this protected realm.

Her brain hurt with the intrusion of the search, and her head pounded its annoyance as she gave up and retreated back into her own body. She focused on the tree Soren was so fascinated with, and gave over to the here and now for the time being. There was still time, before her father's kin could break from the storm, and return to hear the story of Symbya's return. Then, at least she could use his energy to redirect the charge she would need to cut through the darkness that had not allowed her access to its signature. There were ways to get through the barrier, but without the added molecules of one that lived here on a permanent basis, it would be useless to waste her energy.

She moved her head to rest it on the trunk of the great tree, as she listened to its heart and felt the vibrations of what it had become. Its very placement on the windswept archipelago of older rock formations with its ideal growing conditions, were far more advanced than what the tree had moved away from, deep within the underwater home.

A long time ago, when it had first arrived within this realm, it had spun out of control through the atmosphere of Tantaris's upper rings, and crashed landed in the sea somewhere out in the Ocean of Souls. It was there that it had first made an appearance within the underwater caves that dotted the outer reefs that the Selkies frequented, while they dove and swam those channels in their Seliki-amphibious state.

Here it recharged the bodies of its florafied chemical makeup, which filled its sap with beautiful golden liquid it acquired during its entry, and descent into Tantaris's outer orbit. This golden fluid was a by-product it harnessed within the debris fields of the Lyra comet, as it circled through this arena of space on one of its worldly destinations, along the surface worlds of the sky-planets. And it was here where it came to house the elusive Shapeshifter organism that propelled its DNA into something particularly unique with regards to the very essence of any of the sentient life-forms that it came into contact with.

It was foretold in Shapeshifter history, which had been studied by Kashandarhh intensively in the latter years of her training, that this organism was a direct descendent of the Shapeshifter fold which moved between the Wulushian worlds of ancient Fey. Anyone that possessed this molecule in their DNA was capable of many things not directly associated with their particular species. The tree had grown strong and flourished within this new element, and grew enormous limbs in the underwater home, which lived and nourished itself just under the surface of the waves during its many years as a water-based Elemental.

The adherents to this ancient signature within Sopdet's spacial infractions were few and far between. The actual transference of mutual genetic structure was reserved for one of the most elusive and powerful of the Shapeshifter warrior clans, and this tree had somehow been able to transmogrify itself into something belonging to the Shapeshifter clan's capabilities and not of a space faring tree.

Had any of the other less trustworthy races of Fey been able to switch this into their own chemical makeup, it could have been catastrophic within the hierarchy of the known Fey clans. It had repercussions that would cause significant damage to those that chose to use it unwisely, and for this reason and this reason alone that may have been the purpose the fold had allowed it to hitch a ride inside this spectacular species.

The tree had another unusual factor that was unknown to those who would try to steal and use this particular genome, and try to incorporate it into their own body chemistry. It had been held a secret since the first trees had started to appear on this side of the galaxy, and only until recently been explained to a select few that were good enough to be there when the teaching had commenced.

It seemed that Kashandarhh had many allies in her quest to better understand the reason she had been allowed to remain here on this tiny world. And it was to them that she owed many other discoveries that had been brought forth into the open for her to be a part of, and much too many for her to really consider the ramifications of further research, into letting her Dragon-rider companion in on its secret.

She also knew that this tree had come to her rescue on several occasions, and for that she gave it her undivided attention when it came to hearing its story. The tree had told her this once, when she had spent the afternoon in hiding from others that hunted her on this ever moving landscape, which would eventually in its living years, have redirected itself into all of the four Elemental realms before it completed its life cycle here on this planet, and then would retreat once more to the stars.

It was on this day that she had learned it had come from the generation of Fey that had found a way to stretch itself from those pockets of darkness, and become another creature, that used its' photosynthesis in additional ways.

It told her of a time, back in its arrival here on Vaukknea, when only a select few had seen it slowly rising up to reach the surface world of the air-breather Fey. It had proceeded to arrive in the Tryilamore territory far from the darkness of those things that had tried in vain and failed to attach themselves to its outer-bark.

It said it had tried continuously to find another section of the watery world where the sea creatures were not so thickly intrusive in the constant pressure of the lava tubes. However, it had been unsuccessful in its endeavour in the early years, and had been forced to endure them as they had continued to feed and live with their tiny little brains reattaching their suckers and claws into its subterranean bark.

It spent the waking hours pushing the little creatures away with huge geysers of water it drained from various pressure valves built right into its sodden wooded exterior walls. The very thing, over time, which gave it the ability to move some parts of its gigantic trunk upwards, in the sulphuric atmosphere it still held roots within, as they followed it sideways and upside down in its desperate attempt at fighting them off.

But through time it would become exhausted from the fight, and spend several days at a time remaining absolutely still, as the silt accumulated thickly on its trunk and the creatures settled in for the long haul, wiggling into whatever hole they could find. Every now and then it would shake them loose, in the never ending battle that never amounted to anything more than a temporary achievement, as they constantly returned to fight another day in this battle the tree could never really win, deep on the ocean floor.

It took its toll over the years, and it soon became apparent that the tree would need a different heat source to grow and expand; having extinguished the energy of its arrival through its descent, and the constant fighting to remove their exoskeletons from the outer layers of its own thickly scarred trunkified hide.

Time became blended into centuries, and one day it would find those illusive rays of energy it required to exist through other means necessary; as it wound and stretched its extended limbs through various cracks and fissures that some old volcanic Fire Elemental had grown by sheer madness, when he had become too old to move through solid stone.

These fissures had been made from the formational arrival of the Genesis Fire Elemental; one of two that had arrived when the planet was still a very young stellicular asteroid, and wobbled into its stellar drift right behind its sister planet Naunas. Both planets were the end result of what was spit outwards in the explosion of the collision that almost never happened; and at that it was only just a nudge at best. It was near the northern rings of the Goetutonias Nebula, where several bands of meteorite dust particles collided with the edge of the Faden Corpeous Galaxy that happened to be just on its closest rotational shift-point, during a time when the Zedrith Mordea Kippsen Comet passed along the fringes of both star systems.

The touch and drag orbit of what came outwards from that result, more or less dragged several huge chunks of debris from several larger asteroid belts that had been drifting along in the vicinity. As they made their normal rotational twist, it freed one of the creatures that had made that body of drift its home. It jumped willingly along for the ride, and arrived to formulate the makings of this virgin planet that soon would be full of new Fey life previously untouched by any majikal hands.

This unusual creature was both Elemental and Selmathen, and once belonged to the same Elemental family as the fire Brands that ruled the southern spawning grounds, and ancestor to all the fire based Elementalistical creatures that still were alive and breathing today. Kashha knew this with clarity, as each of the Elemental tanks of various factions had been part of her illicit training when she had moved through the Elemental worlds, after being invited in kind to its library of scholars.

That had been a long time ago. In the years since, she had passed her last degree of Witchnical testing, and had learned many things during those early years as a student along these waters, previously home to another Elemental creature she had not seen since the Dragon wars ended. But her favourite had been from this field of learning, and the teachers that had given her many hours of fascinating conversation through the late night hours, when she should have long been in bed and fast asleep, had long since returned to the land of the dead where one day all that lived upon this chunk of rock would follow.

This particular cousin to the current ruling family was recorded to have choked forth a great many of the tunnel formations that rested beneath the oceans of Water's Deep, in those early spawning years. And, judging by the tunnels that were in the area of Vaukknea Island, there must have been many factions of these fire creatures residing in the bowels of the planet's core, in the early years of the continent's early formation.

Part of their history is told in the Elemental ages of all Fey nursery legends, and all that have been part of the worlds of Sopdet's reign of worldly space know how they move about, by spewing rather hot volcanic breath along certain ley lines that lay invisible to the naked eye, while the stone fragmented and turned into beautiful crystal shards below its crust.

That seeding spread their energy through the vast columns that were quite frequented in this area, by many of the genesis creators at the time of the Capilictic Period of Tantaris's own birthing. It made her smile with the memory of one such hatching, and with Soren still higher up and completely unaware of the memory inside her skull, she let it slide into her conscious thought without fighting its arrival, as the wind tore through her outer jawline and he was left marvelling at her father's world, momentarily without her.

She had actually watched the birthing of one of these young saplings that had floated along the brine one warm summer day as it made its way onshore. Visibly unshaken by its arrival into the Air Elemental quadrant, it had blown skyward its underwater breathing apparatus out into the morning air, and snaked its way through the shallows one summer afternoon of her youth, like a water snake hunting greener pastures.

She remembered it vividly, as it waded ashore dripping seawater, covered in parts of its gills still clinging to the outside of its sodden trunk. It had risen from the depths of another root system from a similar tree that was deep inside another of those watery trenches, out in the dark depths of the reef's coral boundaries, just off the middle channel's naturalized underwater tidal ebbs. Truth be told, now that she looked back at it, the trees most likely reason of its change of scenery, was probably more because of what I'm about to tell you and not from the normal migration of its shedding movements.

When he finally reached the tidal currents that gave him the last mechanical push towards the world of air and earth, he had broken through the surface of the mirrored image he had seen as he ascended upwards from the depths. She had seen it move towards the shallows directly in the path of this one, currently sitting in the very spot it had decided it would like to be in and directed itself towards the shore like some kind of cocky sailor.

The tenacity of this species was recorded by quill, in the pages of most of the ancient relics which were housed in the libraries of those that kept the words alive, but she had never witnessed its arrival from its host birthing until that day, and smiled at the memory still embedded within her brain. 'Apparently this little one was simply an ass, in both worlds.'

You see, It had crawled through the rough surf and accosted the older tree, rooting itself within the sands that occupied the very land it had decided was in need of new ownership. The fight had been altogether brief, but memorable to watch, as she had witnessed the teeth that showed through layers of hardened bark shattering the youngster in half, only to have it rise up time after time and try again, refusing to admit defeat, snapping away with his open jaws at the more mature and definitely stronger tree.

It had been a short lived fight; followed by the older and much wiser tree holding both pieces of the sapling firmly in its grip. She remembered hearing a kind of low whine from deep down in the elder tree's throat, as the sapling stopped its assault, lulled into a sense of incoherent stasis, while the older tree quickly repaired the break, using vines it pulled out around its lower branches, then spitting some form of thick sticky thing from its own bark to join the two pieces flawlessly together. The immature creature lay almost hypnotized, cradled in its limbs, healing the wound with the nutrient rich sappy concoction that ran openly from a wound the ancient tree had opened up for such an occasion.

It could still be seen today, although older, chirping away to the other step-trees it had become a part of, as she looked skyward along the main stem; still very much a mouthpiece with his slightly bent stature still evident even today. She smiled slightly as she looked upwards shading her eyes in silent thought to the location where it had grafted its salty bark high up in the reaches of the upper canopy. She found it sitting rather stoically along a main artery where other youngsters the tree had given birth to were to be found alive and happy, enjoying the squabbling of its fellowship to fight another day, in the very tree that sat grandly just above the area that they were themselves sitting on. Then as if on cue she watched it basically wait till another little one was within range, then try to knock off the newest member of the trees youngest addition, until it too joined in on the squabble and the fight was on. *'Yes, I would say that qualifies as something of an ass; apparently once an ass, always an ass!'*

Kashha laughed at the audacity, for even today, after all it had been through, it was still giving the elder tree a headache with its constant chatter and bigger than life personality.

'Sounds like a Witch I know,' she said to no one in particular. Soren heard her speak briefly, and turned to see who she was talking to. Seeing nothing, he carried on sightseeing from aloft, while she reminisced about the days of her schooling years on these Selkie shores.

She had heard from one of her more favourite teachers, that there had been much territorial fighting in the early years; the Fire Elementals fighting alongside the other Elemental factions that had dared to set foot upon this new meteorite of micro-tubular formations. This particular rare find of Fire Elemental tunnels, had the ear-markings of what appeared to have been seared through the air of the wind Elementals' own breath; one that moved in-between that of another race of Elemental Fey, as it reached the Earthen Elemental shores along the water breathers' domain.

This tunnel system, which stood open to the wind at the current moment, was hidden to those that had not the need for its use, and was the only entrance to the original tree's first arrival when it initially broke from the surface world below, to the molecules of the world of air.

Some of the trees that followed the original tree's route into this realm, came through one of the shift-point doorways, and also found refuge inside one of the bigger tunnels that the Fire Elementals had carved outwards from the inner workings of the core below. To this day, the mantle of these unusual creatures could still be found to house one of the old original Shapeshifter factions, as its heart still beats away, deep within the very crust of Tantaris's surface world, inside these strange giants.

Much later water had taken over those caverns as time passed, and the origins of the original tree had grown rapidly within the depths, breathing through gillified bark for going on near a century before its ancestors had broken free into the surface world above.

Sometime in the coming years, after it had time to adjust to Tantaris's atmosphere, it would need to find a proper passage through the tunnels of the Fire Elemental's breeding grounds, before it would be able to make its way to the surface world far above, and find another place to plant its roots within and shed the tectonic bark it had grown accustomed to. For now, its lower limbs would stay below the surface of the waves, keeping its leaves and branches slightly above the water in the air breather's world. It swayed with the surface winds, giving the tree its necessary nutrients from the land of the skies, as time down below filled in the breathable air with seawater.

In times of old there had been many animals that lived within the sea calling this Fey-aquiline structured bark home; and as time advanced, and the world of the water closed in all around it, it had sent out several new shoots that had grown towards the surface world above. Below the Air Elementals domain, it needed to create a kind of armour shielding on its outer bark-like skin, to protect its inner shell from all that came to call it home. The scars were still visible if one looked hard enough and peeled back the surface to expose the bones, on each and every one of those older species of the Rayoola branding of new space faring arrivals up here on the surface.

Kashha scraped the moss growing along one said scar, and placed her healing hands inside its wound. The scar disappeared and the bark resealed itself, while the tree let out a kind of mild humming noise. Soren looked down at her momentarily.

"What did you do? The bloody thing is purring," he said, putting his head against the bark. She smiled and shrugged back at him, realizing he hadn't really expected an answer as he moved further up to hear another section of the continual thumping noise, deep inside its inner core. She concentrated instead, on the story inside her head while she searched for other scars within her reach. There would be too many today to finish the task in the way of completion; however, one day she would eventually complete her healing and the tree would welcome her hand when it came to asking something of it in return.

This shielding was done primarily for another reason, far removed from that above. It used that method as a kind of propellant, to transfer itself within the water molecules and to actively propel its motion through the vast depths it would ascend from, over the many years. These propellants would come to be useful, as they explored the ocean depths, and sent out feelers in the open water to others of its kind that had also migrated to this planet and made it through the transference as this one had done. But it would also have to find a way to travel through the different atmospheres it would grow and ascend to, as it filtered and rose up away from the shadows that moved down in the depths away from the surface world, where the rays of the surface heat could not be felt.

It would take many centuries for this to be attained, but eventually it slowly made its way to the world high above. As it moved among the fathoms, it guided its breathing to suit its needs, to withstand some of the integral design flaws it had integrated into its outer bark, when it had first arrived on this planet all those long millenniums ago. One such update had been to depart from the ocean floor below when it reached a certain age; to do that it had to survive through some of the harsher pressures from the fathoms of those watery depths, as it let go of the root system it had firmly planted. That would allow the entire tree to float in the currents, which held the nutrients it had grown accustomed to feeding on, as it made its way to landfall and shallower waters.

Once arriving on the surface world, it was here that it found the peace and solitude of the daylight it craved in the shinning other realm of air and burning heat. Its new oasis was far from the land of water and fire which had served its purpose in the early years. And none of the aquatic creatures from below had survived to stay along its bark as this creature began to meet and blend with the Air Elementals' realm.

Any of the creatures that survived the ascent quickly bailed out in the last troposphere under the water's surface, and could be seen zigzagging along the final barrier as they watched from beneath its trailing root system, far too unpressurized for them to follow into the new environment. Calling for it to come back, they stayed only moments when it was clear it would not be returning, then they swam back to the bottom to search for other arrangements.

Many of the younger saplings that had taken leave of their home planting grounds before their time had not been able to withstand the pressures involved in the accent. Somewhere along the way, many of the youngsters succumbed to the harshness of the strange environment, and drifted in with the tides as mere shells of hollow wood, and not ones that had at one time pushed lungs through water molecules like that of a fish.

The ones that did make it had much to endure before they could actually find solace in the sands of this other world. They had to also fight their way through the ones that had gone before them, and the older much stronger ones would not be as easily dispatched as they had down below, in the forest of the ancients that breathed with lungs through the gills of fire.

Kashha listened in the wind, hearing her name, and stopped to ascertain the source. Nothing remained left to find the signature of whoever had voiced its syllables. Strange, it had sounded almost Mer-like. She looked around to see if something might have sneaked up behind them, and found only branches and the few odd last season buds that hadn't been released into the surf. Her shoulders ached from this strange atmosphere, and hadn't found their rhythm as easily as they once had. Soon she knew, the time would find its fire, and the planet would start to embrace their new Queen. She wondered if maybe they were closer than she had thought to that coronation. If she didn't know better, she would say if that was true, she was off by almost ten whole cycles. Goddesses forbid... they were far from ready. She closed her eyes and waited for the pain to subside and her memory returned to the tree's story.

Once on the surface, they still had to reach the beach. As the waves crashed all around their armoured bark, shredding it to bits as the winds directed their root systems slowly towards the shoreline and up above the water-markings. Those were the days, much later in the time that belonged to the formation of these crumbling Clactonian stones which lay along the seams of a younger Acheulean fault line, living and existing long past the history of the Human fields that seeded mankind's arrival into their own galaxy of faraway stars.

So there it stayed this fine grand tree, whose bark they could feel alive with life among the world of the storm cells. And it grew stronger as time progressed with its new found land-legs, joining the ones that had already arrived to others that would come much later, to form this chain of reefs that gave them a brand new way of life.

Kashha once again breathed in deep, and cocked her head to listen, there were many living breathing parts of the forest that to the untrained eye would appear to be quite harmless in ones field of vision, on Vaukknea Island. She would have the time to teach Soren some of them, now that her family was gone from its solid foundation.

She would need that time if they were planning on staying here overnight while they waited for the shedding to find its wings. For things were far from what they appeared to be. Nightfall was coming and what stood around them was not something an Aelf; even one as capable as a Dragonlord Aelf, would be was able to fully function with on his own. She glanced at the Mauntra to gauge its ageing; she had about maybe four Zedfrens before it set along the western side, and they came out to play.

CHAPTER THIRTY-ONE

The Banishment of Kamera

Nothing was further from the truth on any part of the islands that the Selkies called home, than what appeared to the unsuspecting traveller once the Mauntra went down. Many of the actual inhabitants that walked in the dead of night could be seen in the daylight hours as simple plant life and nothing more. However, the lush beautiful jungle flora and fauna that occupied these waters and adjacent reefs, then pushed their little noses into the air-breathers' world, were far from what they appeared to be. Nothing could prepare such wanderers that arrived without invitation into the water realm on the Elemental side of this strange and forbidding world. Not many were alive today to tell the tale of what actually lurked in the moon of the dark times, on those nights. The island had seen to that from the beginning, while most daytime creatures slept on in silence, without ever waking to the carnage of the nighttime feast.

It was for that very reason that the Selkies first decided to settle on this very part of the unusual underwater mound that had called them home while it was building its land-mass deep within the ocean of a still very active volcano. The vibrations resonated well inside the energy of who they were, and there had never been any problems with it spewing its hot molten rock into the sea around the reef. The island took care of them; each Selkie born into this world of the water quadrant of the elements knew the land and its underwater coastline very well.

They had, after-all, been able to include one of the Fire Elementals in the actual planning of its location, as the island floated towards its current location, placing itself above that mound to take up roots. Well, roots were an odd explanation for what actually held the island in its place. But for now we shall go with roots; the rudders came later. Later the meaning will be self-explanatory, without me going into a boring account of the reason why. Nevertheless, I'm sure it will be well worth the wait.

The aquiline environment was well suited for their needs, and even with the clan of the Narns further out around the stellar reef of Undinecis, all Selkies were pretty much part of the arrival of its surface world whether they lived on land or not.

The entire mound had been nothing more than sand and volcanic rock, with a few barnacles which had been living just below the tideline, as it was thrust upwards out of the sea upon their arrival. The living essence of those creatures that presented their backs for the Selkies to live upon under the air-breathers world now lived in symbiotic harmony with those from the sea.

In the early days of its birth, the land-mass, which had been growing with each volcanic eruption, found the means to complete its dispersal, spreading its breath to find the surface world above lacking in life to sustain its arrival. Once the majikal spell transferred the life of the ocean floor into something more solid and weight bearing, it ran in perfect symmetry with the creatures that had been living in the underwater world and claimed this area on the reef their land based home.

During certain times of the day or night, as the Mauntra moved through the sky far above, the centuries changed the inhabitant's metabolism. As time progressed, the island came alive with creatures that moved and shifted the surface, thereby making it one big living breathing creature neither solid nor visible, to the one that wished to watch the transformation with their own eyes.

The island had its ways, Kashandarhh knew well, and moved as it breathed just below the surface core with mystical vibrations not previously known to the other Fey worlds, and creatures not born into its silent ruse. That movement as a whole allowed the land-mass to take shape on more of a permanent basis, and when the tides were just right one could see the land sigh just above the high tide mark, and shift into something neither animal nor plant based as it basked in the moonlight of a colourless sky. Thus, in turn it could be said that this island was more mythically alive, than one based of simple rock and sand floating elsewhere within the essence of a living breathing Liquidine Sea of salted mud.

For now, she remembered that strange day as a Witchling Bairn, and the story behind the reason she was taken away from the village that had been the only home she had never known.

Kashha had come to this island when she was just a small-ling. Her father, Vallmyallyn, had travelled to Llavalla to bring his wife Kamera to join his family group, after being informed there had been an incident there that had required an immediate change of residence. It seemed the Kanoie Witches had been horrified to find the truth in Kashandarhh's birthing, and even further horrified when Kamera had gone against their pairing of another Kanoie male, who was chosen by the elders to be the one to bond with her, many months previously. She had all out refused the joining ceremony, and had left just prior to its bans becoming part of her life, still drying with their plant based dyes within the trees of their village wards.

All in attendance of those early days of her family's higher standing within the tribal clans of the Kanoie Witches bore witness to her disobedience, and later it was told that they had suffered greatly because of her delinquent ways and left to travel the southern wastelands of Llavalla's desert, near Dragonclaw drift. Kashha had never met those relatives, having been separated from their signatures at such an early age, but sometime when this was all over she promised herself she would find them and bring them back to where they could once again find peace, within the village that used to be their home.

In the meantime, she had been told one dark night of the Fieldmarr moon, the story of their exile, deep in the mountainous terrain of Cydclath's secondary plateau, near Telpphaea Falls. The falls were the highest in all of Water's Deep's mountainous Elemental ranges, and became entrenched with stories of souls being lost in the sands along Dragonclaw drift.

She knew it was dangerous, and had heard many stories of those who had been found many days and weeks later, killed after being turned around easily in the dead of night, their bones scattered along the lower levels after stumbling in the darkness. The falls had since been diverted from their original channels and became less deadly with the coming of the second landing of Fey colonies in the surrounding area. They now fell over the 2000 foot cliffs that made up the backdrop of the falls' sharp rocky outcroppings far below, instead of making their way through the narrow channels deeper inside the caverns that ran straight into the mountain's core.

She shuddered to think that was the fate of her own kinfolk, but as time had come and gone throughout the years without word of another set of bones showing its teeth beneath the high cliffs, she had her doubts to the actuality of the meat of its exterior telling's. Her mother had found peace in the absence of any form of communication over the years, and had given Kashha the gist of what had happened once she had been able to comprehend the full extent of the actual truth behind the rudeness to the Kanoie indifference to her birth.

It would seem that Kamera had tried to explain things to the caste of her Priestesses, when the time had come with the travel arrangements both Vaal and herself had agreed upon: The very proposal that would find him by dawn, waiting at the shoreline to teach his young daughter how to swim out beyond the breakers and to meet the clan that had travelled with him hanging out in its swells.

But that had not gone over as well as she had expected. She had been so busy with the spells that were needed to prepare for her journey, and the time that they would be floating within the sea, that she had forgotten how dangerously contemptuous this tribe of Witches could actually be. She had, after all, been part of their inner circle and had believed herself to be somewhat immune to most things concerning what her birth rite implied. But they chose to ignore her high hereditary standing, all of a sudden treating her with a disdain fitting for one that was below her station, as if her being one of the high Priestesses of their own coven meant nothing to them.

She discovered their horrible behaviours quite by accident one morning when Kashha was only newly born, as the Mauntra poked its big broad nose out of the shadows, and moved down the almost invisible limb lengthways, out along the upper branches of a Lucreous Tree. Something seemed to catch her eye, as it suddenly shone like crystal in the reflection of those filtered rays, and the deception rose up all around her in the air, leaving her with a clear view of the events that were about to play out.

She could see something had changed in the morning sands. It was mostly a feeling that had arrived, as the air moved just above the sand pit that had lain outside the Priestess quarters of the old city. Kamera always visited the sight when things troubled her, and today, when she had stretched and awoken in the still dark morning, was one of those days that seemed just a little out of place and needing that rite.

The sands were located above one of the fissures that ran directly through several quadrants of the leylines that ran perpendicular to the avenues of the older buildings that had been built by the old stone masons. That clan was no longer here on Tantaris, and was mainly part of the old tribe of Trithogean warriors that had moved through these spacial waters in years long past.

Their brethren had played an integral part of everyday life here in the strange village of the Kanoie clan of Earth Sorceresses. There were many Aelven clans that had led the way in their tribal teachings, but never had the actual lessons been taken and shifted into a working map of the times ahead. It was done according to the universal format with regards to foreseeing the day's events through the sands of the Paracleese, as each household had taken the oath within the branding times, to endure its rites.

Kamera had prior knowledge of other healing ways that had been used in the past; ones that would help her to see things that others were unable to foresee in the sands. But, this was a secret and had never been verbalized as being part of their sacred ritual, as it would have repercussions somewhere down the line if they had any idea she was able to tamper with those old ways. In a few moments, she was glad she had not shared that bit of insight with any one of them.

She moved quietly, doing her best not to disturb the others that were close by in other cottages and watched it trickle in slowly. Then something moved towards her and wavered in the hot sands along the strongest section of the leylines' crossing. It shimmered just above the surface of the molecules of silica, out along the pinker pieces that had bits of tektite granules mixed in with the finer grains. They moved in perfect symmetry around the grounds in a deosil direction, placing several letters in plain view of where her eyes could see them. *Beware*, it read, *they are coming. Protect yourself!*

These sands were used by all of the Witch Clan and most days could be found to have a heckle of Priestesses from various walks of life surrounding the elongated boardwalks, as they also prepared their day and found strength in its council. She watched other members of her tribe arrive to retrieve their own messages for the coming day, unaware of what Kamera had witnessed. This time she didn't even hesitate, there would be no chance now of a peaceful settlement with the tribe; she released the message holding lightly in the sands, leaving no trace of what the warning had been for the others to see.

Her time was limited, and now her time had run out. She had thought she would have time to pack, but that too proved impossible, as she made her way around the sands taking an unfamiliar back route to her cottage, surprising Kashandarhh's nurse who was in the middle of some kind of retrieval chant. She used her own majik to knock a hole in the ritual as it failed to be delivered, sending it back in on itself so it would fail to cause further harm to herself and her newly arrived Witchling.

The old crone cursed her intrusion, vowing others would take up where she had left off, as Kamera pushed her ritual molecules through a Wulushian destruction chant and locked the old bitty out of her home. She hastily grabbed a few ritualistic herbs within reach, which she had already prepared in case the trouble found her before she was able to get to the village wards and one little wailing that still had sleep in her eyes; then she was off.

She had endured many similar responses from other tribal members who had got themselves into trouble in the past, and she had been avidly outspoken on their behalf, when something they had done had gone awry. Until the moment they had begun the wailing call, she had been under the illusion that she herself might be forgiven for this small indiscretion, thinking some of the more seasoned Priestesses whom she had taken under her wing, would help her out.

She could not have been more wrong.

The alarm sounded, not long after she had reached the path that would take them to the wards, having been informed by one bellowing old crone of a bloody nurse. It would seem the old Druids too had been busy; having the inner-sight that gave them advanced knowledge of events, and prior knowledge from the old books that sat high on the shelves of the Priestesses' temple walls, still covered in cobwebs and full of ancient revelations that spoke of fanciful dribble. Put that together with one very interesting tale of the rise of the Witch child that bore the markings of a Selkie King, and she knew they would stop at nothing to hunt her down.

Kashha smiled through wide teeth and half smirked at the thought of them poring through those pages, now coloured yellow with age and smelling of musty old mold, trying to figure out which of them would defy the tribe. They must have been horrified that day so long ago when it was revealed that it was her mother who had been the one to give birth to the Selkie offspring, as the reality of the manuscript coming to life inside their very walls had arrived on their doorstep much sooner than had been predicted.

Of all of them, she was the most dangerous and the one most likely to be the individual that they would need a full coven to stop. Her designation as Keeper of Souls, gave her complete control over the entire tribe and made her the only Priestess on this side of the divide that bore some of the more unusual and rare Majiks, now lost from the Kanoie Witches who no longer had passage into their realm. Her majik was legendary, and with her relationship with the ruling family of the Tuatha De`Danann, it would mean disaster for the clan if they lost her.

Kashha had read it over and over again when she received the old manuscripts during her training years, many years after she first entered the sacred center of learning. It had been one of those times in the dead of night, when she had taken her black Rapier hawk, Spenkel, out for his dinner. He preferred to hunt out in the far fields, away from the noise and lights of the school. So she had stayed longer than expected that night, enjoying the air herself and leading him in the wind as she flew alongside him until they had reached the edge of the sea. There she waited — while he fished in the shallows and it was here that she came across several very interesting trinkets along that shoreline, just lying on the sand waiting for someone to find them.

They didn't return until after the moon was high overhead in the night sky. She put him in the aviary and started to climb the stone steps to her dormitory, bringing the odd treasures into the light.

One had been an old rusty key, set with black coloured stones, seemingly similar to the mineral called Jet. The other thing was a locket, and inside it she smelled the familiar scent of Dock mixed in with Greater Plantain. Both were healing herbs and, although the locket seemed ancient, the herbs were fresh and going by her nose, picked sometime that night.

She wiggled up her nose and had just finished a sneeze, when she noticed a book had mysteriously been set on the outside steps of her room. It was covered in a leather cloth that looked almost like the hide of a Selkie. If the legends were true, it made no sense that a Selkie would have parted with its hide, knowing fair well it would never be able to return to its beloved sea. She had just tucked the book and the pelt under her arm, when something had fallen and found its way onto her lower forearm, pricking her skin and making her yelp.

She dropped both of them the moment she felt the prick on the surface of her wrist, but found nothing that could explain how the injury had arrived. By the time she entered her dorm room, holding her wrist, and scoured the area where the injury had landed; her wrist had burned with whatever poison had entered her molecules. Her head began to throb, and she felt slightly lightheaded from the toxin. Then, to make matters worse, just when she felt the need to sit down on the edge of her bed, and right before she fainted from the pain, a tall silhouette had come in through the entrance, melting right through the doorframe of her room.

When she woke up several hours later, she was alone and whatever caused the reaction had vanished into thin air. It was then she noticed the hide was missing, and the perfectly clean locket that contained not a single essence of the herb she had smelled just before she fainted, instead had been applied to the injury on her skin. She rose to further inspect the bandage and realized it was adhered with a beautiful silken poultice that someone had applied with great care to her wrist, and the locket that had held the herbs was dangling from her bedpost, swaying ever so slightly with the movement of the bed, smelling suspiciously of salt.

Whoever had looked after her injury, had also moved her to the pillows of her feather bed, and carefully set her upon its feather-down, making sure she wouldn't fall upon the hard surface of the floor. Her jaw ached from the muscles she had torn when she fell, and as she glanced in the mirror she could see the outlines of a fairly dark coloured bruise beginning to form along her jawline. She had no memory of actually hitting the floor, but she did remember the silhouette in the doorframe as she lost consciousness.

It would take many years for her to gain an understanding of that day, but nothing compared to the surprise when she pulled the poultice off her skin to discover a perfectly shaped tattoo of a triple sided helix, permanently inked onto her fair skin. Feeling the raised mark on her wrist now reminded her of the day it had appeared; her skin branded by some unseen hand, without complete clarity of the structured arrival. It didn't burn as one would imagine it should have, instead it had been stinging momentarily like a bee sting when she regained consciousness, then faded slowly over the next few hours, disappearing into what appeared on her body today.

She brought her wrist up to her face, rubbing the mark with her left thumb, where the beautifully etched markings on her skin could be seen up close with Witches eyes. What had appeared as a simple dye the colour of a brilliant green emerald, now burned neatly into her right wrist then disappeared from view to the casual eye, caught in a majikal spell that the herbs had incorporated into her tattoo, marking her skin beneath her epidermis with this beautiful marking. The same mark hundreds of years later, which would be found on both the little Pantherous Shapeshifter called Sibrey, and a Human male of undistinguishable age.

She looked down at the diagram that resembled a slightly oval Triquetra, and felt the bumps that entwined each circle into the next. It hadn't faded in all these years, and only made her feel slightly stranger when she had read the words highlighted in bright letters on the torn and yellowed musty pages of that damn old book. She remembered picking it up and sneezing a second time when it reached her nostrils, as she had nursed her wound. But she could honestly say nothing had prepared her for what she had seen when she browsed through the pages and discovered that the markings of the children of the Quasars were the very same branding that permanently marked her own skin.

Another strange memory that still made her frown with its arrival. The Selkie rings must be closer than she thought; knowing that things seemed to come into her brain only when they were running along the back side of the island's banks. She shook her head to clear the cobwebs, but they remained and only intensified with the memory.

It seemed like a lifetime ago that those words echoed through the recesses of her brain, but the message had been clear and concise, and had silenced the wondering as to why the tribe acted the way they did, after she was born. The words had read as simple text that had been directed at her birth rite, or so she had been led to believe. It simply said everything in four lines, which she had memorized by heart and not forgotten.

It had been foretold of the flight of a vast Selkie arrival that was about to transpire on the shores of the planet that ran deep with water. A child of both Witch and water shall move between worlds to find the calling, and when the village within ran red with bloodfire, all inside would cease to exist from the lives they had known and their signatures held in the bubbles of death if they stayed to stop the shifting of the clan's newest arrival.

It had not made sense to Kashha as a child, and only quite recently had she thought that the words rang true to who she had actually grown into, and the story of her arrival into this clan of strange Witches and their adverse reaction to her birthing.

She moved away from her thoughts, ignoring the heart that beat with constant rhythm, and focused her attention up the sands along the breadth of a larger root stalk, tiptoeing through a mess of flotsam that had beached itself as the tide pulled it towards the shore. She was deep in concentration on the thought of what it all meant, when something caught her eye out in the surge off to her left.

She tried to see what was moving along the surface of the water, but nothing appeared to be out of the ordinary. Her senses were all over the map right now, and with the storm moving things around out on both water and land, she ignored her gut instincts and moved around the root to be with Soren. She continued considering what she had been thinking about before she was interrupted by the shadow that seemed to be nothing more than just land creatures taking to the ocean in times of the shedding, and carried on with her memory.

Back when this had started, the damn clan of her mothers had tried to stop the Tryilamores from advancing any further from their own shoreline, as the Selkie contingency arrived in force. They quickly shifted a runner to the coast, warning the advancing Selkies that Kamera would not be coming to join them. She had instead; they claimed, changed her mind in the final hour and would be remaining inside the village walls.

Silly Witches, Kashandarhh thought as she remembered the story in all its vagueness; however she remembered that it was none other than her mother who had arrived to explain the story once she had been summoned by school officials, when Kashha had nightmares and they could do nothing for her. What she described to her was not more than what was necessary to clarify that Kashha had done nothing wrong. It seemed what had transpired was something between the two males, and all Vaal had told Kamera was that they said something along the lines of words that sounded more like a glorified pissing match. The words, although clear to the Witch clan, must have seemed comical to the tall Selkies, who would have towered over the poor sod as he had stood their quivering.

Nonetheless, the message had been delivered and the general gist of what was said went as such. 'They could not permit one of their own to exchange her power with any water creature, no matter whether the child belonged to him or not. They simply, as a land-based clan, would not stand for it. And it was not going to happen within their village in the foreseeable future.' But, then again the males of the race tend to allude to the actual physical scuffle that probably accompanied the remainder of the storyline, and as far as her father's best friend, Ballynamullan was concerned, he probably decked the little snit before Vaal had time to pull him off, and sent him on his way screaming his little Witchified head off.

Kashha had to smile; she had no doubt in her mind Bally would have probably dropped him into the sand at his feet about two full fingers before her father would have diplomatically been inclined to remove him, as he ran back to some official nutter swearing up a blue streak. She snickered at the thought; the Witch clans had always been mentally connected to each other, so they should have known what they had said would never work. After all, all Witches had the sight; it was just depended on whether they used it properly, that it would actually help them.

Vaal had at first been surprised by their reaction, upon coming across their scout after scaring the daylights out of the poor shod, still dripping wet from the change and covered in nothing but land based Aelven skin, sneering away at them. The words had not made any sense, since his first encounter with Kamera had been nothing more than gentle and kind. But this member of her clan had been extremely rude and quite angry, and amid the facial tics of his trembling body, as he stood there listening to his lie, the Kanoie male moved away backward and ran for the hills, phasing in full flight. The rest of the Selkie clansmen heard nothing of what the Kanoie male had said, with Vaal blocking the conversation he and Bally had delivered to them.

But Kashha could only speculate as to the actual conversation, and was adamant in her assumption that he probably lifted the Kanoie Witch into the air with his mind and slammed the poor sod into the nearest tree. Turns out later, the male was none other than the Witch who had been chosen to hand-fast with Kamera, and had more at stake than what Vaal had believed. Kamera had told her he was just lucky to get away with a beating, and would more than likely of been dumped into the sea, compliments of his own betrothal commitment signed in community property to Kashha's infant hide.

She snickered slightly and turned towards Soren to see if he heard her; he didn't. That made her smile, watching the Dragon tracker shift his feet from root to root, still very much focused on the sights and sounds of the reef world. Kashha settled into the rest of the memory that wanted to play out in front of her with images that needed to dance.

Vaal had decided brute force wouldn't work, but a full contingency of Selkie clansmen might. He called them out of the waves with a hand signal. They advanced from the waves in his direction, making their way in droves up the beach, dropping their Selkie pelts and wrapping them around their shoulders without the mainland Kelpie pools anywhere in sight.

So, naked and dressed in all their finest, they had only just come through the trees when Kamera's energy pattern was met on the path, and he redirected his clan into the trees to hide. Modesty was not the issue here, as in the Fey worlds this kind of body imagery is often found in all different formats. What prompted him to direct the clansmen and himself into the trees was the child's energy signature, which had begun to show signs of an unusually high unstable flux.

He laughed heartily about it when Kashandarhh was safely place in his arms, and he swung her high with her infant giggling, later on that day. But the true gist of the story never got past his lips without howling laughter at whatever story he had heard of the telling. It would seem that Vaal had that way with everyone, when he first met them. Truth be told, when you met a full grown Selkie male for the first time in your life, you too would think twice about pissing him off.

But it had been foretold to happen, and nothing could actually stop its occurrence no matter how hard they tried. And many rituals had been pre-written in secret, away from Kamera's inner Witch-sight, to prevent this very thing from happening. No matter how well they were prepared for it, it simply would never be enough. It had been wasted breath and wasted time... For it really wouldn't matter how many Sorcerers they had called into the Priestesses' secret ritual chambers to help in the process. It couldn't have been changed, even had they been able to crack the stone tablet it had been engraved into, and then separate all parts, before burying them deep within some secret vault away from the world Kashandarhh lived in.

You see, the very atom of the ritual first written inside this side of the re-birth of Tantaris's rising was seared and carved in the stone, not simply copied into the pages of the old book of the dead. The engraving was then majikally enchanted. Which, until the actual spell played out, or the person who created the spell changed it, it could not have been exchanged for another thought without having an opposite reaction that was equal to the actual spell that had already been born and bred into being. And without that being done far ahead of the birth and arrival of her, it could therefore never conclude its written text and would have proved disastrous for the one breaking the stone.

Furthermore, the Witch it was intended for, who had been bred by both land and sea had already gotten her bloody wings. For once something began the long journey from thought to probability, moved by unseen hands into the temple of the Paracleese; it was simply something that would have to be waited on and lived out in its entirety, along with the recesses of the ones who gave the majik life from the beginning.

Nothing could change the outcome. The clan had no other choice but to use brute force in their stupidity, not knowing that what was about to happen was known to have been the beginning of the end to their race in kind. For, to have what they had at their beck and call, you would have thought they could have found another way to find a peaceful arrival; especially having a contingency of Selkies at your doorstep that were twice your size, and following the lead of someone in love with the very one that you were about to ban him and his clan from ever seeing again.

Not smart by any means considering how the book was written, especially with the child who now stood between them and the ocean, bobbing back and forth with fire in her eyes like a damn moth caught in the flame. They had immediately taken her into the water to extinguish that fire, and with the others of his kind circling the trio, she had been well protected by the tribe's Selkie majik around her, while her energy fire slowly receded and melded with theirs into more acceptable levels.

Kashha remembered bits and pieces of that far-off memory, now lost in the time-shift of when she was young. The actual moment Kashandarhh had come awake on that faithful morning all those years ago, something had changed in her chemical makeup, and she found strength building in her body that was not her own.

What Kamera had given her during the early hours of the morning had made her understand all that was about to transpire in her surroundings, even though she was still on the outside a very young foundling with filtered eyes that had not yet found their sheen. She remembered it filtering through her memory, as the rings today shaped its edge and the mist surrounded the picture and honed its center into her brain — out along the thread that centered on her environment that she now found exploding with new life.

Little fingers played with each amazing ray of the Mauntra that hit her young face from outside her window where she had slept, curled up in her sleeping sling all those years ago. It was alive with brilliant light that sparkled with diamonds as the movement inside her soul came alive with the essence of the warrior Queens who had lived on the fringes of Naunas's beacon of terrestrial light. It was here in this land of her father's clan, that her ancestors came alive along the edges of this particular Rayoola Trees' lower branches and touched her mind, giving her the glimpse she had forgotten of the story of what the infant had seen and done while others of her kind had tried to prevent the written word from playing out.

She gripped the tree harder to keep her balance, as she watched her birth-ing and marvelled as time fast forwarded and she could see her mother's quiet thoughts on what was about to transpire, and the things she was doing to prevent the coven from thwarting her movements to be with the Selkie king.

Kamera had been busy during the night, and had set her ritual into overdrive. It sparked and found life inside the barren room that had grown alive with runes and bones. Several markings of Bind-Runes were all over the walls, illuminated by the dawn, which moved slowly from the depths of the midnight stars, and gave birth to the ritual that held its course.

Kashandarhh watched the stars go out one by one, as the daylight filtered slowly from high up on the wall until it's sheen pulled the darkness back into its shadow, and kicked the greyness into one of the tiniest areas of a darkened recess still fighting to have a ring side seat in the fireworks that were about to begin. The door slammed shut as the bones rolled sideways and held them-selves about two stones above the floor; twin helix circles joined another that was drawn in sand on the floor by the firepit, where several embers held their own in the rising daylight.

Kashha watched her mother move towards the corner where she lay, and place several blackened marks from those circles, on her forehead, chanting some kind of Samhuinn Fire chant that was used during the Twintaea Moon times in the old Trithogean villages. The markings turned brilliant emerald for a single moment, and then disappeared, leaving only a slight dusting of charcoal on her face. Kamera blew the dust away just as new life in the child awoke; with the temporary replacement of her infant mind rattling inside the stronger bones of a new hereditary Witchlet; years older than she was.

The memory played out like a play of one of the greats, set in an open air theatre where others could sit and watch, as it played on in real time from a distance across the strings of that distant memory. The child's eyes would grow wide as the knowledge of what was happening came fully into her understanding.

Kashandarhh in today's world still watched her mother seal that long ago spell in place, by nimbly rolling the bones of a strange crystal sphere she pulled from her leather satchel, and then place it in the air. Not looking back she gathered up her child and left it hovering behind them, making her way towards the garden pathway that would take her to where her beloved, waited with his clan and the retrieval of one that was in imminent danger.

The path she took would provide her with a safe haven in the off chance of any ritual interference's arrival, giving her only a short distance to make it to the trees before the village would be fully aware that she was on the move towards the sea. That was all she would need; allowing the sphere to mask her signature and give her safe passage. She hoped they would follow her and not second guess her true intentions and go back towards her cottage where the sphere was hanging nicely sealed away. If they followed her they would not be able to stop it, as she would have been able to get far enough away from its signature, before she herself would be swept up in its majikal embrace. Nevertheless, just in case they got past the main barrier she had put up outside her door, she proclaimed upon the land another formula to finalize and break her ties to the Kanoie clan once and for all, and just before she left the old stoop of her doorway, she crushed the umbilicus that held it in place.

The sphere lost its tether and floated freely through her cottage, moving as one with the currents of a much older majik that had found the crystal and changed the molecules into something just a little more volatile and much more dangerous than the ones currently used inside the Kanoie wards. Kashha may have only been an infant at the time, but she remembered with clarity the instant she felt the shiver of strength move through her spine as the morning light moved across her window pane, and the Witch inside her genes took on a more sinister approach to an older majik that had not been used for what they were about to do.

This ritual involved a simple blood transfer, and had never been done before outside the Selmathen time jumps, and would only succeed if Kamera transferred all power to a younger mind not fully developed into the set ways of adulthood. Kashandarhh had been perfect for such a bonding, and Kamera knew it was so from the first moment she held Kashha in her arms on the day of her birth. Kamera gave Kashha everything she had learned herself in this life line, leaving nothing of herself within her own signature that stayed within the bonds that held her own unique placement inside the wards of the Kanoies' own energy flux.

The Witch Kamera went off the grid, and the Bairn, already part of the Selkie signature went undetected from the village minds that sought her out. They moved like ants crawling through an open field towards their burrow and the Queen who gave them life. The exchange would be absolute, and Kashandarhh would become all that they feared would exist within the coven that they had so desperately fought to prevent from coming to life, in the first place.

CHAPTER THIRTY-TWO

Kelpie Guardians of Vaukknea Island

Vallmyallyn was not of Witch kind, and therefore was seen to be an outsider within the ring of clans that resided in the wick before Kashandarhh was born. The Kanoie were a tightknit community, as Witches tend to be, and had lived their lives mostly alongside the edges of the Cydclath Mountains for as long as anyone could remember. It was rare to find anyone other than those of the wick moving through the north-side of the Cyd, as the cliffs on that side were known for their steepness, providing little shelter should one get caught out in the open when the weather took a turn for the worse.

The mountainous terrain was difficult at best, and the closer you got to the Telpphaea falls, the steeper the climb became. The Kanoie living here were mountain Witches, and moved around the mountainous passes where life was lived in relative peace easily. That is until the Selkie King arrived, and changed their way of life.

Vaal's clan had never set foot within the inner grounds of Tantaris's mountainous terrain, even when it was time to shed their pelts in the times of their stay upon the air-breathers world. The distance would have been insurmountable to one not accustomed to living up on the land, and much more treacherous to his species than to other land-based life-forms, living out among that Fey in similar ocean-faring communities.

The sea smelled of life, and moved with the never ending energy strings the Selkie tribes required to exist on this planet. Leaving its boundaries and its life blood was dangerous, if Vaal had need to move between the lands that moved in different atoms than those of the water-world he was accustom to, beneath the ocean waves.

However, the greatest danger resided closer to his realm, and lay hidden up among the rocks on the beach, not far away from the water's edge. This area was known as the Kelpie tide pools, which species could be seen frolicking among the shallower inlets and rivers that led its rolling sands out into the sea along the high tide lines.

They were the keepers of the Selkie pelts; each of the Selkies whose time on land was at its arrival would leave their precious water pelts inside this sanctum of Water Elemental boundaries, in order to keep them safe and away from the land-based Fey who hunted these prized pelts for a pretty silver Doubl' on for each one that they found just tossed along its banks or conned out of some hapless Kelpie not wise in the ways of the world of thieves.

Balor had an entire contingent of these thieves that specialized in the black market of Selkie pelts; some of which he would barter with the owners for coin to finance his hunting excursions, others he simply took and destroyed in retribution for the clans' dealings with anything Tuatha De'Danann related that he had found out about, through unscrupulous means...real or made-up.

The Selkies had need of specialized security for their prized possession, finding themselves far away from the Gargoyle home-world, where they had been able to provide that service to the Selkies, as simple guardians.

Now, before you throw up your hands and say how does a species that is primarily made out of stone in the daytime, maintain a security detail, on a race of water born creatures of the sea; remember on their home planet, things are not as they appeared to be in such matters. We shall, at another time give you the history of these creatures, but today we shall continue on with the tale at hand.

Some of the more unscrupulous Aelves that the Trithogean's allowed to remain near Sopdet's planets out on the fringes had hunted them down to the extinction level on many of the other worlds. Therefore, the entire remaining clans of Water's Deep were quick after the Dragon wars, to create a space that was all their own, and one that would not be so easily entered inside this realm.

It was called the space in-between, and it was not visible to those that hunted the species in the ways of the land bound Aelves. Many of the other creatures that sought the prize pelts of their unique oiled coats had not the ability to find the entrance through this strange and alien world that they had created from another situation, much different, but just as deadly were it to occur. This gave the Selkies a chance to bring back the species from the brink of extinction in this quadrant, and with the energy they required out in the open waters, they had no other choice but to find a new guardian to help with keeping their most prized possession safe and away from those that did make it through the doorways into this realm.

A majikal joining of another water-bound Fey was needed. The search leads them to another slightly more unstable and feared creature known as the Kelpies. The Kelpie was an animal that resembled a horse or sometimes similar to a small pony-like creature, once it made its way on land. Their historical pairing was long in the making on other worlds, and had been very reliable from the moment they had agreed to help in its ritualistic working to that of the present times. But it hadn't always been that way. Their mutual understanding had come through sources that had been handed down to them through the ages from father to son for as long as one could remember.

Each Harras or Kelpie string had attached themselves to each of the individual Selkie families, throughout the lifetime of their existence on this coast. They were paid highly for services rendered, and each species moved to work together as a complete click, instead of the ones that lived separate lifestyles around each other, and tested their boundaries along the water's edge. Had any of the Kelpies gone rogue and turned against the Selkie population for any reason, the deception would have been catastrophic for both groups, as the lives of Selkie and Kelpie were majikally intertwined as tribes of Manannan's water Fey. Deception would mean the spell that bound them together would no longer be one with the majikal formula that he had created, and the species which moved as one pairing, with that particular tribal being, would be formally evicted from the space in-between.

Should that occur, and it had from time to time, as pairings had been unfavourable at this time of betrayal, the ritual link that held the two species together could then be challenged by the other. The host that was wronged was allowed to choose the death ritual of the other in a mutual arrival, as both creatures would simultaneously disappear from inside the void of the space in-between, and the one that had been innocent of all crimes would be reinstated once again, with another host family outside the tidelines until such time as he could once again petition to return to his own waters without retaliation from the clan of the other.

This had only happened once, in all the time Vaal had lived here on this reef. And as far as Kashha had been told, it had not occurred again since her arrival into the clan. She had heard how a certain Kelpie had slightly betrayed one of Vaal's younger cousins in a similar but not catastrophic occurrence, and the clan en-mass challenged the Kelpie's own kin with the authority it had to swim the tide pools. It in turn ended somewhat in a rather long winded pissing match. And although it was their right by contract binding within the agreement they had put in place, it was a common practice to forbid those who had inadvertently caused a grievous wrong to pay such an exorbitant price for their deed.

The offending Kelpie was then subsequently barred from the Tryilamores' bays and waterways, incorporating Dead Monkey's Rocks to Undinecis reef, and the ill-fated family was exiled to another reef back in the realm, away from the world of in-between, to spend their remaining days away from others of its kind. It was a harsh reality, and one that needn't be repeated, but the others knew that one day if they betrayed the Selkies again, it could very easily be much worse for them.

If anyone cared to look down by the water's edge, the written contract was still there, carved in the rock cairns that littered the beach along the caves that Kashha had seen when she was a youngling. She might have been too little to read the words, but the unique drawings had fascinated her when her mother had shown them to her one stormy day when they had come to watch the mass dispersal of her clan into the ocean for her first shedding. Her Mother, at that time not wanting her to be alarmed as her father's clan had taken to the water and disappeared within its molecules, thought it would take her mind off the sudden disappearance of her Tryilamore family. True to form, she had spent the morning playing out near those rocks while her father's clan swam away, leaving the two of them alone with her none the wiser.

Kashha had spent many hours in her younger days placing her fingers along the ancient etchings, feeling the stonemason's blade mark the grooves as she waited patiently with her mother on the beach. The area today was home to a vast colony of sea asparagus that could be seen levitating and waving at the gulls on the gustier days. The majik that held them in place now could be felt to amplify with the approaching storm.

It was told that once the rocks became free of the majikal spell that bound the contract inside its molecular strands, the Selkie chieftain could regain their foothold on the underwater realm, and break the full power of its words. That would leave both the Kelpie and its cousin the Each-Uisge open to the Selkies' hypnotic mind without protection, inside the rings of their underwater domain.

What would then transpire along the underwater drift-point was anyone's guess, but surely not having the field in place which prevented that from happening in the first place would send the energy wave straight through the shoot and destroy the remaining rings left in place that had been held in perfect balance for so long, and bring the in-between world back into the present day before its time. Should that happen, the chain reaction would force the barrier that gave them calmer waters inside that protected sanctum they now claimed as their own to be excluded, and with a simple twist and recalibration of their minds, the Kelpie Fey would be amalgamated with the Each-Uisge and forced back into one being, and not the two separate individuals they had lived to become.

That had never come to be in all the years of their dealings with each other; for if it had come into play, not only would those Selkie lose the ability to return to the waves once they had made it to land, but the Kelpie and the Each-Uisge as well, would lose the ability to transform into their chosen form, and all three creatures would be bound to the land they lived beside for all time. However, the most radical change would come to the latter of the trio, and those Water Elementals would then be drastically changed on a molecular level. Their ability would vanish from his or her genetic transference that now occupied this space in time, and the world would grow up to not know that they, at one time, had been separate creatures when they had first lived and plied the waters along Tantaris's in-between shores.

So, both creatures chose to work in synchronicity with each other; bound together by mutual agreement and chosen to be part of that world as symbiotic allies to the Selkie race. Each held their own in the majikal spell that held the secrets of their being. The same one that held on to the closely guarded ritual now carved in stone along the waters of the beach head they swam in, while the high tide lapped its edges, now covered in small green like fronds, waving wildly away at the gulls overhead and having some insane conversation we couldn't hear.

The Kanoie were far from the drama of the Selkie worlds, and had always been landlocked into the head waters of both mountain ranges that had given them protection from anything thinking of attempting the mountainous terrain to reach their compound. They heard the legends of the Sea Serpents, and their companions, that lived in and around these horrible seas, but they had never worried that one of their own would defect towards the sea and test the theory, knowing that its waters were alive and full of very dangerous creatures related to King Manannan's underwater world of the wild and formidable Elemental Sea.

He had a vast range living in that medium and the Witches had always held their feet upon dry land; choosing to feel the earthen rocks beneath their toes, instead of the liquid brine of the smelly kelp beds. The Each-Uisge on the other hand, loved the sea, and each of Manannan's citizens of the world of water, were equally adept at plowing through the waves on a salty morning. But this creature was unusually skilful at causing great havoc throughout its environment, and was renowned for its vicious temperament. How the wild Selkies were able to tame its nature was still up for debate, but legend tells of the old Sea God and his minions harnessing their power and riding them like Dragons in and around the many islands that dotted the coast lines, just to cause fear in the hearts of those that might be inclined to attempt to steal their gold that lay buried somewhere out there, just beyond the farthest islands.

The tale morphs much further, and tells a strange story of several wicked Seelie families that had chosen to live along the coastal waters, which had been taken hostage and killed by such creatures as they moved towards some of the coastal villages the Drymiais had left behind, not too long before the Dragon Wars had erupted.

However, the village of Llavalla was so far away from where the sea met the land, as it moved wildly along the jagged coast along the Shapeshifter turf, that no one really knew whether the stories were actually true or not. So the adults of the clan had always taught their young that the sea was a dangerous place, and to move towards the ocean would mean certain death to any should they actually try.

Of course, we know that is just another Fey-tale created for sleepless nights, and a warning to kidlets of all land-based Fey to stay away from the water, and not just the Witches of Kanoie. However, it hadn't taken Kamera's appetite away from going and seeing it for herself one day, choosing instead to breathe the air and find the true meaning of the myth that continue to run rampant, through the telling of that tale.

Kamera had always had a strange desire to taste its salt beneath her tongue, and had moved towards its dangerous fascination without the necessary permission of her clan. She always had gone against the grain in most things that they had told her not to do, from a young age, and this was no different than the yearnings of a certain young offspring of hers, and the Shapeshifter of the Togernaut tribe, who chose very similar patterns in their young lives.

Ah yes, that would be me....hum I wonder if I'm related?

Kamera was, after all, forging the rebel bones from the onset, and she only followed their rules, when they suited her needs; to achieve something much more indicative of the prize that waited just along its salty shores. Its tantalizing betrayal was too interesting to leave behind, as she moved between the wards that had been set in place to protect all that lived within these village walls, and proceeded towards the coast and into dangerous territory that had been given to her on a silver plate, served up with an absolute unequivocal side of nonsense.

There had been a strange vibration when she first cast the spell that allowed her to advance past the guard. Her knowledge of those that lived near the coast was limited, and not knowing the majik of the Selkie King and what its molecules could do to anyone moving alongside their territory, hit her full in the face. But, it was nothing to compare with the image that she saw upon her arrival, when the threads of shift fell away at her feet, and her eyes scanned the horizon for anything that might be construed as a threat.

Kamera, for some reason, had been focusing on the land side of where her feet landed, as she arrived to taste the salt on her tongue when she first came out of her forced shift. With that little bit of appetizer, what appeared in the shallows almost took her breath away, as the salty wind revealed something she had not been expecting.

He had been swimming in the shallows of the small islands off the far beach, when he felt the vibrations of her thread as she came out of the shift. Her mind and attention had been otherwise engaged by what she had seen all around her in this new and exciting atmosphere of salt and brine, and she had missed the signature of another as he moved towards the shore watching her.

She tasted his shadow as he came within her line of sight, and moved slowly within metres of her, standing at the edge of the water. He bowed to her with a slight tick of his chin, as his ability to shift into something that could walk on two legs grew into its full potential the moment he rose from the liquid brine and morphed from the water-folk of the sea, still wearing a strange looking pelt along the skin of his spine. He shook his whole body like a wolf, sending salt droplets and spray in every direction, as he finished the change right in front of her.

As the transformation began, something resembling an outer Seal skin suddenly fell away from his body as his new shiny skin amalgamated into this other creature. It was at this moment the pelt of the water based life-form melted away fully from sight, and the creature's flesh was replaced with pure Aelven skin. She watched fascinated at this creature, which seemed to be equally fascinated with her.

Meanwhile, the sea had begun to recede and a strange calm had descended upon the rocky shoreline; birds that had never seen a Selkie this side of Water's Deep before arrived and welcomed the newcomers to their land-based nesting site, while he stretched and yawned in his new skin before moving out of the shallows of the water and into the more solid formation along the sand to join her.

Their connection was immediate and forever seared in her brain. The handsome Selkie male came to stand beside her out of the waves, retaining his balance with bronzed legs standing firm and wildly planted, completely naked for all to see, along this section of beach she hoped might be secluded. Not only was it not secluded, and was bearing witness to a very healthy adult male, he had smiled down at her with a beating heart that she could hear from outside his own chest. She marvelled at this creature that showed no signs of intending the violence he was so clearly capable of perpetrating.

Could the books have been wrong?

She felt alive for the first time in her life, and the village walls of the Kanoie Witch clan seemed a distant memory that had been more hallucination than a reality she had lived within. He spoke quietly and softly to her with an almost musical lilt that replicated itself inside her heart. To say she was stunned would be kind. The truth of the matter was that she was scared out of her wits. And to make matters worse, she could see that her heart had betrayed her, and as it fell and tumbled towards his feet, she knew without a shadow of a doubt that she was never going to be the same person she was when she left the village that morning. He grinned widely, a wicked smile plastered all over his face, and picked up the pieces from the very ground that betrayed them to his own heart, and laid them openly towards her in the palms of his hands.

"I have been waiting so very long to meet you Kamera. To you, my love, it is with great pleasure that I give myself unconditionally, to one that has risked so much to find me." He bowed his lean body forward towards her as she bent to retrieve the pieces of her heart, and touched the outside edges of warm skin that had only momentarily retreated from the cold sea. He winked and whatever dignity she had left was gone. He held them both as they fell to the sand, too weak to continue to maintain an upright position.

It was at this chance meeting that she knew without a shadow of a doubt that she would need to challenge these outdated and unreasonable rites that would not allow her to move within the sea that he had called his home. For he was no more ferocious and evil than the very bones of her dead mother, who was long since dead and gone for going on five thousand years.

She knew there was no present danger to her situation, and that the elders of her tribe had set these boundaries to prevent the outcome the book had spoken about many centuries earlier in a fabricated lie; which she had no doubt was about to be tested in black and technicolor Fey-gone bloody reality. She had read that old musty book backwards and upside down from binding to bitch Witchery, in her early years of training. Having known of what was to come down the road the moment she stood on those shores under a similar tree that Kashha now placed her feet upon, she would never have believed that the words were about her and the child that stood strong and full of majik in days yet to come. But I'm getting ahead of myself as usual...

Now back to the present that carries my tale.

He was hers; she had known it without thinking when he had taken her hand and moved her heart as none had done before. There would be no going back to the life she had lived without this gentle giant in the waters far removed from the village of the Kanoie Witches.

Many months went by and still she had not told anyone of their chance meeting. She was not afraid of what they would do, but more of how they would do it. She took an oath that when she was found out; she would leave the tribe she had grown away from in the days and weeks since his arrival into her heart. They did not know, as of yet, that she was with the child that would allow the prophecy to come into play; the very child that she would have to take away from this place before the prophecy arrived in all its majikal glory, to claim its soul out in the rain on a night of total darkness.

But that happened sooner than expected; at least the finding out part. It didn't take long on one winter's day, as one Priestess moved between the edges of her brain, and discovered that Kamera was with child and the prophecy was about to find its threads in words carved out of primeval stone that were locked away, deep in the bowels of their own fortress.

Even though they discovered she was with child, the identity of the father had been closely guarded, and the secret firmly locked away from prying eyes of a race of Witches that could destroy the life that breathed its breath along the recesses of her own womb. This she had done for herself in the beginning of the Selkie transfer, and Vaal had seen to its hidden recordings with Sea-majik much older than anything the Kanoie clan had spoken or written about, since the first elders of their clan had stepped into this world.

So the child came into this world with eyes that held onto her secrets, and it was discovered that her mother had been betrayed by one that she had thought was a friend. It was like taking away the home where you were raised, having it disappear from your field of sight never to know where it has gone, to experience the banishment of both yourself and your young Bairn from seeing its existence for the rest of your days. All because of the jealous behaviour of another who had other plans for your own life.

This is how the ancestors of Kashha came into play, within the homeland that she had only seen at the moment of her birth. The elders had called a Whenshi on the bans that had been proclaimed in the days of Kashandarhh's birth. But Kamera made it past the guardians that protected the village from all other tribes, without having the birth rites that gave them access to its lands, and simply floated away with Kashha firmly ensconced within her grasp, and vanished down the pathway into the trees. This is what Vaal felt when he had ordered his clan up into the trees.

The Selkie land-pup had grown strong in a mere whisper of an Elemental sneeze; about the same amount of time that would under normal circumstances have taken another kidlet many years of dedicated schooling with the hierarchical Priestess in order to achieve.

In another birthing of equal rulings, there may very well have been sulphuric majik at play, but that was not the only thing that played its hand in Kashandarhh's wakening. She had started the day as an infant, and by nightfall she had grown into a youngster of several years of age. A truly remarkable feat for anyone of another planet not being of Fey heritage, but that is how quickly the offspring of the Selkie grow, in the times between one of the moons to another. This is due to the fact that Selkie offspring are born at sea, and their young must be able to manage the swells of the huge rollers that come crashing in along the outer-rings, in case one of the predatorial Leviathans of the Sea Witch clans moved inside the rings and tried to steal the Seal-lits away, from the safety of the others and the bay's warmer waters.

Kashandarhh was half Selkie, and as she grew, her gift came on strong with a strength not previously seen to exist inside the continent of Water's Deep. The wind sparked many fires on that day, and when she came to leave alongside her mother, she took the power away from the coven of the Kanoie Witches who were left standing inside the village walls, scream-ing their little Witchy heads off and absorbing most of their majik, into her own.

That was something Kamera had not expected, nor did the ritual she performed have that direction; no, that was done by Kashandarhh alone, and still to this day lives inside of her, making her incredible strong. Even though she was still a baby, her power had been unfathomable to those not aware of what she would be capable of achieving, and it left them without the strength to complete their ritual to imprison both herself and her mother inside their walls; away from the father who she thought waited by the shore with others of his kind, simply floating in the swells.

Kamera had not known whether the child would have the strength she needed to break those bonds; after all she was still a young wailing. So Kamera not knowing she would do this, had set about another more power-ful spell to run simultaneously with the one that she presumed they had set in place. She had achieved this in the early wee hours of the mornings while her child grew stronger, and others of her kind had still been fast asleep.

This one had not really been needed, she discovered quickly after just a short time that her young daughter could take care of herself. But, had they not been necessary at the moment of their inception, they would never have been introduced to the world of the living. For wasted energy was something not easily touched on in the code of conductivity the Witches lived their lives protecting. Had the need arose, the story could have ended much differently, and Kamera would never have taken the chance on pro-tecting her offspring with anything but the very thing that proved to be, thankfully, quite unnecessary.

This one would sit on the sidelines, shimmering in the electrical charge of the sphere as it whirled and swirled inside her cottage walls, just above floor level. She watched the energy grow for a moment before she decided to carry its arrival to its intensity and wait for that brief second to see if indeed she had been reading the signs inside her child correctly. She found it easily without beginning to fret, as something else became apparently clear. It would be more than enough of a punch to break the bond which kept Kashha tied to the Priestesses of the Paracleese, the very coven which who would have been her destiny, had she chosen to stay.

So the daylight returned as though nothing was out of the norm, and the birds came out along the tree tops to greet the Mauntra as it lifted its face towards the new day. Then all of its secrets came into the light, as the unexpected majik claimed its prize with intense creativity, and all that the Kanoie had envisioned came fully into view. It was met with sparkling intensity, and the branded familiar smell of sulphur from the brew pots that bubbled and boiled in the morning dew, blended in with the meal that would never get a chance to be served, as all hel broke loose inside the village walls.

Kamera smiled as she shimmered in the energy pattern that filled the morning with glorious revenge. All the Kanoie could do now was send its shooting sparks onto the shadows of two silhouettes moving quickly down the path as the majik closed behind them and the moon fell away into the new day.

That morning was a day of firsts, as it made its arrival out on the land. And any attempt at retrieval of the pair was simply cut off in its initial creation, as it severed any chance of her arrival back into the territory of the Witch-line. Soon nothing was left but the mist the Priestesses conjured up in their wake; it enveloped and circled the area, creating a sudden burst of renewed energy that followed the fire play inside Kashandarhh's little Witchy face, and shot down the path ahead of them toward the sea.

It moved like lightning and screamed with electrically charged earth majik as it made its way to the beach. Both mother and bornling moved down the path, the mist sealing off the entrance behind them with a final and audible click. With eyes that shone like fire, the Kanoie watched the Selkie Bairn of Kamera fade into the mist until nothing was left but the shinning red orbs of those eyes that refused to blink. As they moved down the lane, they seemed to take an eternity to wink out one at a time, but eventually they all disappeared with the morning shadows that seemed to be in cahoots against their existence. Then there was nothing left, as both energy patterns went off the grid, making their way further down the path and out of reach of the ones left behind and forging ahead to whatever lay ahead of the lightning bolt of pure Paracleesan rods, fully charged with spent rage and fury.

Kashandarhh stared at the pathway without any remorse, as she balanced on her mother's shoulders, clinging happily while Kamera's footsteps crunched softly on the path as they walked away and made their way to the shore. She watched the strangers as they scurried like rats in a desperate attempt at preventing them from producing the majik that would awaken the guardians of the village wards. She felt nothing of this bonding she had left behind in the mist, as her child-like essence took control and climbed higher within its intelligence. Instead, she nestled smugly into her mother's warm milky skin, around her lower neck, and ignored them. What had happened could wait for another time in her schooling. Her mind reverted to the Witch-child, not understanding the true severity of what was about to happen further along their road of chosen seclusion, now fully enrolled into the Selkie lifestyle of her mother's choosing.

With no longer any home to call their own, she slept briefly with that fire still simmering in her veins like a tallow candle left to melt in the window sill. But that only lasted several hundred feet down the fire brandished energy thread that remained still half floating in the air. Their banishment would be final and absolute; of this she had no doubt, and cared little for its reasoning. There was only one thing left to do, which she would do quickly in its final instalment, and then her transformation would reverse without any lasting effects.

At this time she felt her mother's warm heart beating quickly inside her chest as several bands of perspiration trickled down her face. She moved with footprints that never seemed to touch the ground they were walking upon. Silent whispers of needing her father's reassurance correctly fell into place in its delivery, as she pulled in the last bits of thread they would need to make it to the coast in one piece.

She slid her dark eyes sideways, revealing an inner knowledge that had lain hidden and dormant until just the right time of her awakening inside a Selkies higher brain function, as she slowly drifted off into her own very old soul. The ancient majikal mind of that old soul smiled with the knowledge that she had arrived with her majikal energy intact; amid the crackling fire that accompanied them as they moved forward down the path towards the sea.

Several small and nondescript creatures scuttled away underfoot suddenly, unexpectedly caught in the crosshairs of their footsteps, while both Witch and Selkie pup entered into their new life as other majikal beings that floated along the brine and felt the sand betwixt their toes. They became this new formulation of Witch-kind; one not previously known to their clan as it suddenly became introduced to the continent and a place of new beginnings, inside the world of Water's Deep. The island sighed with the new arrival, and incorporated the molecules into the mixture alongside every other species that lived amongst its bones.

Kashha yawned, having spent almost all the energy Kamera had transferred to her soul, and blinked quickly just before she drifted off to sleep. She took the grains of the molecules that lay dormant but fully functional inside her memory, and shifted both her and Kamera for the first time to the sea. She did this, without thinking, accomplishing a thing that had taken most other initiates many more years of study, to achieve.

This was the last thing she had needed to complete, and she found herself reverting instantaneously to the little bornling who had never had these strange things happen to her, in such an early beacon of her newly formed mind. She slept without thinking as her cheek hit her mother's shoulders once again, and the Witch Kamera slid back into the world she had left.

Kamera returned to take the last part of the journey fully functional and without further incident; except maybe for a headache that lingered for most of the next few days. Kamera on the other hand, had never been back in all those years, but Kashandarhh's curiosity one day got the better of her. She had learned in her schooling in the latter years, the actual spell that had given her directions to the entry point of their city, and viewed the Kanoie Witches inside their new world without her mother. She had been shocked to see that they had been locked individually into the majikal spheres that Kamera had created for them on that horrific morning.

The particular timing of this event, must have happened some time later when they had left the shores of the continent, when the majik of the sphere finally burst wide-open the moment they were able to finally unlock the protection grid and entered her home. Kashha had watched the bubbles of their entombments, as they scurried like ants — constantly bumping into one another completely unaware of who watched them from the outside, as the Kanoie sect inside were virtual prisoners of their own making, locked away for the remainder of Kashandarhh's life on this planet in Kamera's time dilation.

In her study of the clan, Kamera hadn't told her that was what had been intended for her last ritual of the sphere that moved without its umbilicus inside her cottage walls. Kashha had found the means to clear the pathway and return the occupants to their former glory, should she need it whenever the timing was right. She hadn't tried.

She could have activated it at any time in all those years that she lived within the Damonian Woods, but she never did. She had not the stomach to relive the horrors they had set upon her mother at the time of her birth. Not that, she hadn't wanted to; she had really wanted to go in and watch their faces as they realized the prodigal daughter had returned to slaughter the works of them. And her anger had only grown during those early years she had trained and mastered her exceptional craft.

Instead, she watched them from time to time, gaining insight she would use in another way. This one let her excel silently, like no other student that had been bred into the line of the Witch, and moved her into the realm of the ancients like no other Witch had been able to do before her. With that instruction inside her brainstem, she found she could diffuse the more volatile situations that came and went during her schooling years, while it gave her the means to fight her fears in those times of nightmares that frequented her dreams long since the opening of a futuristic world of realms not previously visited in the times of the Fey.

Then finally one day, in the morning hours of the feast of colours, she had closed the viewpoint one last time, and kissed its wards with a poisoned lock so none could find its entrance before she did something that would have brought shame on her father's village. That one action had saved the remaining Kanoie clan, without having taken the knowledge skyward, and placed it into their tiny brains through the world of hidden shadows now living inside her father's realm of watery tombs. But loyalty to her Mother also prevented that from happening, and the village had not known how close they had come to being destroyed by the child they had tried to control with the line of the Paracleese Coven nestled deep within its roots.

So, for the time being she had stayed her hand, knowing where the old village still stood. Finding the strength was good enough for the interim of her mindset, and the coven she had worked so hard to collect in later years, when Balor had become more of a threat than their pitiful vendettas. Still, the coven had known nothing of the fire that simmered just below the surface coil of her seething mind, and soon enough things would change, and the Kanoie would feel her energy sting just slightly before the village would turn to dust, as it burned in the light of the coming end days when the coven she held tightly to her chest would once again rise up out of the ashes and breathe their first breath after years of hiding in their own death.

It was in her best interest that she stay away from her mother's former clan; that is until the day that she would need to find the individuals who had changed her life among the land dwellers. For that, she would need some help from Tamerk and his Goddess crowd. Down below their realm she wasn't known for her kindness to those who had not been forthcoming towards her Mother, and until now she wasn't so sure she could have remained without judgement to anyone that belonged to the inner ring of foolish Kanoie harpies that had brought with their lineage a certain kind of impending doom.

The Goddess realm would stay her hand, and keep her from doing something she would regret, should it happen too soon. The Tuatha also had a hand in keeping her busy, and had taken great care to keep her safe as she travelled from one side of the great divide to the other, in order to prevent it from happening before its time. They knew she was dangerous, and there would be plenty of time, when the world was reborn, to execute her revenge. For now, it was the time to keep one step ahead of their newly arrived guest, and that should have a much wider variance for keeping the masses alive, until the turning times.

So she was kept busy, and Kamera had also made strides in protecting Kashandarhh since her departure from the Kanoie clan. She made sure that both Witch and Selkie could never be challenged again, for they could not be seen as anything more than two separate beings, as the two now remained completely away from the merge that had been felt that faithful day. Although she was now much taller and hopefully well developed in her new skin, there was still the off chance that having the lineage of the Paracleese descendants still breathing inside her own skin would try to eventually break its bond, and return her to the other-side.

Kashha smiled at that thought as she walked along the lower bark to meet Soren shoulder to shoulder, up near the tree's protection rings. She knew without a shadow of a doubt that to have Selkie blood put into the mix made her both dangerous and more powerful than anything that the coven had integrated in the past. That alone, made her think twice before making her appearance known to the clan of her mother's kin, even in today's world of Fey calculations.

She would have to wait until the timing was correct. If she was even out by a Miladram, someone would die before she could remix the energy faunt that had been set in place by the Ka'afrey coven she had enlisted and recruited all those years ago. She didn't have time to play around with the current problem without help from Tamerk and the Dragons of Soren's clan. By now hopefully they had found the shelter they required to stay out of harm's way, before they too disappeared forever in its mist and fell through the stink of what was about to happen in the coming days.

The wind was exceptionally strong, and as it whipped her hair across her face she bit her tongue, climbing the last few yards that took her to Soren's side of the tree.

"Damn it!" was all that came outwards into the airwaves, sending several creatures that had not been there when first she had ascended towards Soren's location to come out of faze and move. They quickly darted out of her way, and skidded into the upper reaches of the tree where they tried to lick their tongues along its bark and were subsequently picked off by its extended limbs and returned upside down into the surf squealing away.

This world definitely had its collection of strange and unusual creatures, and judging by the trees' extra vigilance, this was only the beginning of what was yet to come. She knew she had seen many similar storms that ran with stranger tides, but this one had another element she had not seen before. Until she had time to sit and catch her breath, she still needed someone to see the shadows with eyes not related to the current species, which now had completely vanished from the surface world of the air-breathers' sight.

She should have brought Kamera with her on this journey, for she would have immediately recognized the difference in the air of what seemed to be stalking her inside this world of Manannan's sea creatures. But there was no way of leaving her home unguarded from the Sylmoor groupies that had crashed landed in her isolated world, and who, up to the time she had left, had still been a little shaky and not completely balanced after they had found their footings inside her woods, with only a Dragonlord to protect them. She might have done so, had Tansar still been there; for he had been there many times and knew the lay of the land. For that reason it made her nervous to have left them alone inside the protection wards without his majik to guide them through and back to the safety of Kilren; especially at this time of year when the Tuatha might have some emergency and they had been left alone to fight for themselves until Stephponias was able to walk without help.

For now she could do nothing about it. So her memory continued, as she had walked with her mother along a similar beach on the other-side of the sea, biding her time and digging into the rough edges with calloused hands that bore no semblance to the Rayoola's sharpened tree bark. She hung on...as the storm raged all around them, soaking them both to the skin.

CHAPTER THIRTY-THREE

Father of the Witch

Kamera, having just escaped from her village with her young child, had only just reached the sea, and had waited no more than a whisper before several tall dark haired animals began to emerge from the kelp beds dripping in sea water. She heard her name called softly from land behind her, and quickly turned to find Vallmyallyn and a few warriors already on land and coming down the lane they had just travelled through in their shift. She blinked, watching those from the sea move slowly forward, careful not to complete the change unless it was necessary and they were called to do so, as several strands of long bull kelp that were wrapped around their upper bodies where their shoulders should have been, were slowly untwisting themselves down their backs and swimming madly away back into the tide-line.

Vaal called to one of his warriors on land, alongside him, to take Kashandarhh from him as he quickly transferred the little one from his arms into those of his own healer. He needed to get both his young off-spring and her mother, who had been exposed to high levels of her majikal transfer into the water, to begin the healing process that would absorb the danger levels they had clinging to their skin. Those on land who had escorted him quickly moved into the sea to accompany the others that still waited out further, keeping watch while he moved Kashha and Kamera quickly into the shallower depths, bathing her body in the salty brine to contain the fire within.

The creature he had called healer, would not fully transformed while Kashha was in his embrace, made a musical clicking noise with vocal cords that were more accustomed to breathing through gills than any land-based creature, and gently directed Kamera to follow him farther into the sea, while the youngling was immersed in the cool lovely water away from the tidal surge along the shoreline.

Kashha, too tired to resist, grew limp in the water and the sea absorbed the energy that remained deep inside the molecules that had been hidden from her mother's sight. They dispersed, and the ocean claimed them as their own, as Kronn returned the infant to her Mother, clicking away to the others with his affirmation that the deed had been done. Vallmyallyn smiled at the child now resting comfortably in Kamera's arms, as she softly touched the Tryilamore's face to say thank you and moved towards Vaal. The Selkie returned to the depths, transforming immediately as he dove deeply beneath the waves. When next she spotted him he was covered in fur and retaining the large dark Selkie eyes with no trace of the body that had helped her daughter manoeuvre around the Selkie majik she knew little about.

Vaal moved Kamera onto her back, coaxing her gently to relax and let Kashha snuggle up to her still warm body, and pulled both of them beside him until Kamera grew tired. He switched places with her, cradling his offspring lovingly in his arms as his mate swam to the shallows of the beach where she could touch the bottom and momentarily find her safety. They sat at the water's edge while she regained her strength from the ordeal, as Kashha was rocked to sleep. He moved silently, shaking the water droplets out of his silken hair and smiling with eyes that spoke only of love and adoration for his mate and their small very sleepy child, full of newly formed unknown majik.

Kamera had always found him to be startling in appearance, but nothing prepared her for the words she would say to him face to face, as he combed through his tangled mess of black curls with his own fingertips, and brought forth something for Kashha that woke her up slightly, and made her giggle.

He looked at her and smiled, using humour to entertain her untrained thoughts. But to Kamera he had silently quizzed her mind and found out everything he needed to know of what had transpired when she had summoned him to the beach. But that would be all that Kashha would be given in that memory that her mother transferred to her young untrained mind. The rest would be something that only lovers inherited within the winds that whispered in the silent rain, while she fought with a depletion of energy still finding it low on its reserves.

What she did remember was that he had spoken shortly with her mother, in a strange and silent way, as he had entertained her away from their adult conversation and when that became exhausting to Kamera, he directed her to the others of his pride that had come along for the ride.

A few of the closest ones came slowly in out of the deep with eyes that didn't betray their fascination for her childlike charm. They were small and Seal like in their liquidine world, which contained several other creatures they pulled out of the surf to entertain her younger eyes. She laughed at their reaction to her small child-like voice, which must have sounded slightly alien in formation to their partly analytical ears. Then she further squealed in delight at their wide-eyed stare and large blinking eyes, which wrinkled with long whiskers at the end of their nostrils as they occasionally snorted, producing large air bubbles under the water that floated upwards and burst into the air.

They had remained in their Seal like forms instead of transforming as had her father; who had taken Kamera and himself back into the shallows to prepare her for the journey ahead. They swam slowly alongside several thick matted areas of seaweed she had seen floating just along the surface of the cold water when he put her on his shoulders and entered the substance, while her mother had taken a bit longer to recover from the ordeal.

Kamera, once again coaxed back into the sea, floated alongside them, laughing at Kashha's reaction to this new and alien world of the water-folk, almost drowning in her attempt; as she swallowed several gulps of seawater into her lungs when first they had descended into the deeper areas of the bay. She quickly recouped her breathing passages back to their original condition as Kashha's little body bobbed alongside them in the water, until Vaal was able to redirect a pair of larger Selkies towards her location to place her easily astride their backs.

She went under momentarily when the pair moved along the surface and came up underneath her, until they were able to balance the little one properly. When they finally got her positioned right, she was still coughing a bit of salty water out of her little Witchy nose, not yet realizing she was not of their species. However, the water continued to rise and fall alongside her like a drunken ship in a sea of gathering froth, as she continued to remain determined to flop sideways just to annoy them. The Selkie elders, undeterred, held her firmly in their grasp, floating with ease, while both Kamera and Vaal quickly moved alongside, to the unremitting glee of their offspring.

Vaal would have turned back if her life had been in danger, but Kamera urged them forward as he brought both of them all out into the deeper sections of the rocky shoal. She still remembered how it had felt, strange and exhilarating on her land-breather skin. The cold water had only momentarily caused some form of distress, before she realized others of his own clan's vast contingency had just arrived alongside him with big blackened eyes that blinked through the crashing surf, as they popped their heads up near her, one by Selkie one.

When the salt hit her lips and she tasted it on her tongue, it was more of a shock than finding herself among those creatures that were known only in legends that lived in the storybooks of the Aelven army of the Tuatha De'Danann. She had been thankful to them all, as they had arrived in vast numbers on that fateful day. It was something that only the Selkie themselves could have achieved. For the distance they needed to travel that faithful day would have been insurmountable for her young fledgling to move them through another shift with the borrowed majik she had transferred from her own body. That majik would only last so long, and for one that was still too young to travel those dangerous shift-points in the air, they would have fallen into the sea without the flotilla of Selkies to guide her through.

Kamera would have been little help in her weakened state, and would not have been able to do much once the majik transferred back to her, and she could have easily gotten lost in the connection of the different drift-points that rested inside the shift within the saltwater realms, even if she had directions into the space in-between.

So it was to be that Kamera of the Kanoie tribe of land-Fey arrived with a very young Kashha in one of those off seasons when the island had shaken itself loose, and taken on a more solidified formation. This allowed herself and her daughter to set foot on its sandy shores before its proper timings, far from the village that had almost stopped her mother from leaving its haunted halls, and removing the trappings of a future coven Queen.

That was the first time Kashha had seen this island home, and the first time the familiar trees had become her companions as she watched the rogue waves that her father's clan needed to stay alive crashing about as they blew into a full raging storm-cell. She grew up under their sheltered branches in times of the storm seasons that had sent him out to sea for weeks on end, leaving her to play at the island's edge as the inhabitants ran the gambit, returning to the sea to feed off the dregs that poured off the reefs.

It was here, should the island decide to join the foray of creatures having fun out on the shoals, that she could maintain a semblance of safety. The roots of this beautiful tree would find the means to keep her above water, and away from the dangers of drowning. It was also to here that her mother had gravitated, just for that very reason, and one that had directed Vaal in allowing them to stay in the storm seasons while he was off island and out of sight of their non-Selkie hides.

Something in the present made her sneeze, and brought her back to reality; as the bark once again moved around the area she was climbing in, and several land based fauna that had been hiding were disturbed, and suddenly flew up in her face and landed high up on the bridge of her nose.

She had walked this beach many times, and it never seemed to fail that the residents refused to acclimatize themselves to anyone not living here on a full time basis. Her arrival here was no different than with Soren's energy signature, and this time she hadn't the time to find a way around what they considered to be the new password of the day. Instead, small eyes looking straight at her larger ones, could be seen questioning her motives for being on its beach; the very beach that was beginning to become quite crowded, with the rest of the Island residents either taking to wing and soaring, or rolling and leaping into the roaring surf at the tree's feet.

Undeterred by the activity around it, the creature tilted its head in an awkward angle, looking down right comical in its exaggerated hooligan stance. She looked down at it in an almost cross-eyed motion, not giving in to its arrogance. It blinked twice, then, not giving her further scrutiny, it turned its attention to her companion further up, and hopped down from her nose in hot pursuit of the Dragon-rider Aelf.

It had only just vacated her face, seeing Soren as bigger and better game to play out its nasty tournaments with, when it merged like lightening up the bark to be joined by an army of similar beings hel-bent on achieving whatever goal they had in mind, for Soren's exoskeleton. They made it about half way before the apparently annoyed tree simply tossed them into the surf, much to the comical relief of Kashandarhh. Soren, unfazed by the happenings, carried on with whatever had fascinated him far above, not bearing witness to the event he had almost become part of.

The tree wiped away any lasting effect the creatures had left intact on its bark, scattering the last tendrils of energy into thin air, before settling down once again into the beach rock and directing the afflicted roots of the incident beneath their stony faces, becoming quiet again. Each of the small, now completely drenched, creatures popped up one by one further out, and swam to the other end of the shallows, cursing the tree for allowing the newcomer to get away scot-free, from any initiation ceremony they had had in their tiny little minds.

Kashha knew this would not be the last that she and Soren would hear from them, as most Fey creatures had terribly good memories for deeds of retaliation they felt owed to them. But luck would have it, the process was halted by hands not belonging to their own bodies, and a Witch they had forgotten that could have harmed them much more than some gnarled old tree. Still, that had not dissuaded them from at least giving it a valiant try.

She remembered a meeting on similar soil, so very long ago, of the same said creatures, who still muttered loudly along the far shore, shaking the water droplets from their furry backs and spitting several pieces of kelp and tiny shrimp antennae out of their teeth. But back then, during the merging of her mother and herself with the fauna standing along the shoreline awaiting the return of the Tryilamores, they had welcomed her with open arms when they had landed on the beach with a big Selkie contingency dropping their pelts in every direction along the sands, on their heads.

At that time Kashha remembered their staunch indignant responses, as her father's kinfolk more or less walked right over top of them, spitting sand and Selkie fur betwixt ears and eyeballs, as Kashha had watched them skitter underfoot, diving for cover. They had tried on several occasions to make friends with her, but none of them seemed really sure what was entailed with that simple gesture, and would antagonize her to the point of frustration. Instead they had found it easier warring with the little Witch, away from her Selkie heritage and her father's watchful eye. She made it into somewhat of a game, deflecting their advances with simple balls of energy, and both species would fall into exhaustion from a day of what could best be described as a game of wit without the actual brain having been involved.

So, this was nothing new; only their application of another set of rules to a new game in the life of the creatures of the Selkie Fey. You would think they would have grown bored, and moved on after years of being ignored and taken for granted every time they came out of the sea after the shedding. But that was never something that had come up inside their little brains. Instead they took it upon themselves to make a life of retaliation against those not related in kind to the Selkie fold, and having a Dragon-rider here was just new fodder for the old game previously played.

If Kashha was correct in keeping score, last time they had lost by almost two whole points. That meant Soren had it coming in the hours ahead, when they made it back to their beach. Hopefully she would be ready for them when the time came to defend him, and she wasn't distracted by other things arriving around her at the same time.

It had been another unsuccessful attempt by them on that first day of their arrival on the island, Kashha remembered with some sense of alarm. Back then the day came and went with several things the Selkies had allowed to transpire once touching soil after their long swim across the sea. They had to prepare for two that could not swim, when the island moved as a whole with the sea days, and find the correct tree that would allow their molecules to rest inside its branches during the up and coming storm season that was approaching. As soon as the Selkies left the area to replenish their depleted resources, and Vaal had moved away to attend other things for the day, the creatures that her father called the Krugs, had arrived in all their finest glory, covered in bells and forest paraphernalia and the initiation had proceeded without dire consequences.

At least on their part anyways: But that's not how Kashha, as a young Witch, had perceived it just coming away from the Kanoie stronghold and seeing the deviousness of her mother's tribe. She went to work on them, with Vallmyallyn laughing at her scheming little mind, and had been left busy for weeks planning something to get them back. That had gone on for many years, during those early times of arrival, and each trying to out-do the other as one would come back in some form of mass retaliation, leaving the other to untangle whatever the initiator had messed them up with, in the after days.

She had enjoyed those years of play, and remembered fondly the long months both sides had used to find ways to blow each other up, if only for a few micro-seconds before their molecules came back together again and replaced the ones that had gone missing. Even as a little child, her strength in her majik was legendary, and even that had not stopped the island creatures from making a fool out of themselves; time after time they fell in great numbers, until only a handful of stanch supporters remained to play havoc with a little Witch's mind, while the others slowly left to find smaller and fairer prey.

She knew Soren was in for it, and nothing would prevent it from happening, even with the majik that held her and him together. They would get him back in full, just for being in the same vicinity as her. She still shuddered to think what would have happened had the Kanoie actually made it to the island after Kamera had taken her and left. She would have paid good coin to see that fight at ring-side, when all the creatures that lived inside of the Selkie protection rings converged on their sanctimonious Kanoie hides. What would have been left of her mother's kin who had actually made it to the island, the Selkies would have been left to dispose of their carcasses out in the Ocean of Souls to feed the Sea Worm.

The whole island would have converged on them and the subsequent war would have gone down in the history books as something more than just a legendary excerpt in someone's book of shadows. Now, come to think of it, it would have been almost historic in nature to witness the battle that would have started. She laughed, thinking it would have been fun to see the outcome, as the Krugs got their asses zapped by things not directly related to island politics, and the Selkies would have sent the big guns in to bring all the damaged molecules back, and changed them into something they could use on the island.

The tree was larger today, and its familiar scent made Kashha smile at the memory. But Soren had never seen one of this particular species in this texture and size. So, when Kashandarhh returned from her silent vigilance at the water's edge, she wasn't surprised to see him looking upwards into the higher recesses of the leafy canopy, now creating a spectacle of itself by waving wildly in the storm winds. By the time she got within speaking range, he was so engrossed in what he was seeing that most things around him happened without him actually processing the activity.

"How is it even possible that it stays upright, when all else around it seems to be starting to move and shift around?" he asked as the storm all around them smashed the limbs from one branch to another, as he did his best to stay ahead of them, hanging on for dear life.

Kashha stopped and tilted her head sideways, looking the tree over for a split second as something familiar crossed the threads of her memory. She smelled the air and froze with its memory. Then, without thinking further, she moved like lightning towards Soren as the memory broke free, and she realized just what was about to happen. The storm was beginning to reach its velocity and touch the shoreline along the roots of the giant tree, opening up an inclusion beneath its underbelly, allowing something else deeply buried inside the old lava tubes to breach the world up above.

She screamed Soren's name and whispered silently to the tree, as the beach began to explode with particles of sand flying in all directions.

"Don't you do it without protecting him," she yelled aloud this time, when it blocked her mind from what it was about to do. "Come on that's not fair; he is not of our kind, at least give us enough time to get out of the bloody way."

The tree continued to ignore her, rumbling its intentions deep inside its buried roots stalk as the energy that was about to burst forth could be felt deep within its outer bark. It made its way to the sands of the surface world where the current could be felt along the water's edge. Then small electrical charges could be seen crackling along the upper recesses of the higher branches. Soren watched awestruck at the sudden display of electricity from far above, as it began its descent to their location below.

"Don't you dare, hurt him; he's not from this world." Kashha screamed at the tree, completely incensed. *'He belongs to me.'* Kashha whispered deep inside, as she continued to move towards the area Soren was resting his booted foot on, fascinated in his ignorance, and entirely unaware of the events that were about to play out as he hooted and hollered into the air. She turned as she made it around the last section of the now fully energized root-ball, which was twitching almost fully charged and ready to explode upwards.

She tried again, but the wind took the words from her lips up and away from Soren's ears, and for just one second she thought she would have to transport them through the shift and away from the looming tree, with majik tearing their molecules apart in every direction. This time he turned to face her just as she yelled one more time, as the beginning of a shift was trickling off her fingertips.

"You need to duck," she yelled at him.

"What?" he screamed back through the level of noise staring to rise around him almost deafening, as the shape of Kashandarhh started to go blurry and disappear from sight.

She had waited just a tad too long. Right at that moment, the ground became alive with living roots moving upwards out of the ground, snaking and whipping the air around the two of them. If she moved them now the chance of injuring the tree was too high a price to pay; it would explode outwards in a puff of broken wood as one or more of its madly whipping old roots would be broken in the shift, and come through the void she had created to move them, thereby damaging the tree forever.

She looked at the rider who would be claimed by her inability to detect the movement fast enough, because she had reminisced about the damn past and let down her guard. The wind began to howl as if in protest to the tree snarling through its teeth. Kashha ducked and skidded away from the vines that whipped about her, trying to trip her as she tried to reach Soren's position. All around her from the beach up through a fifty Yardlens area of well-placed soil was fully engulfed in the onslaught of ferocious vines and roots that would make their way momentarily to Soren's position.

It became impossible to hear any more words of warning from her, among the twisted gnarled roots that broke through the surface from every angle, deep within the sandy depths and straight through the middle of the storm around them. All that could be heard now was the sound of a cracking whip moving downwards towards them from somewhere up above their heads. Crap she had forgotten about the tree's ability to form the damn whip!

She pushed forward, trying to put herself in harm's way between the whip and Soren's Aelfan body. She only moved him closer to its heart as he moved closer to the other-side of the branch the whip began to descend towards. Before she had time to adjust her own body once again, she mentally heard another voice take over; one more familiar to the Dragonlord's physiology.

"She said move, Soren!" And the perfectly worded voice of Tansar could be heard above the storm, just as she pushed him out of the way, within moments of another huge vine crashing headlong into the area he was standing in. He went flying and fell about ten Yardlens away from a fairly huge piece of wood that was absolutely covered in razor sharpened teeth.

"Seriously Soren, you need to get your damn ears checked. I told you to pay attention to what she-" Tansar never finished. Instead Soren interrupted him, yelling in horror, coming instantly out of his innocent infatuation of all things related to this side of the void, and arriving fully with all the molecules of flux that still ran wildly through his veins, looking into yellowed wooden teeth that had turned into a bloody weapon of war.

The end of the vine's attached limb had grown almost exponentially sword-like in appearance, forming a very sharp dual-sided blade at the end of the extended branch. It still had its leaves attached, and they were jutting out in all directions with one thing added to the illusion he was forced to confront, as it came down at him hard and fast directly above him.

"Tansar, get me out of here!" he screamed, forgetting where in the Kepet he was. Tansar's voice was nowhere to be found, and Soren remembered where he was, looking wildly for the one who was with him among the branches.

He felt the wind from its downward spiral as the leaves parted right over his head, and for all intent and purpose looked like they intended to bite him in half with those bloody teeth, now perched at the end of his hair follicles. It stopped just shy of his eyebrows and stared at him with teeth sharpened to an inch of the blade he had still buckled high on his back.

"Please, my Lord tree, he is mine. I will vouch for him with my very life," Kashha said through clenched teeth, "Don't move Soren; don't even bloody breathe. I can't help you with majik here," Kashandarhh whispered, closer than he thought she was. He screamed inside his head with no words coming outwards, and closed his eyes as a face moved in and touched his brow. It licked his Aelven skin, then, without another moment to lose, shot past him and carried on, realizing its mistake.

He was not the intended target. Kashha moved in between her mind and the tree's and saw what the tree had actually perceived as a threat. Before she could warn Soren, another one of the huge roots rose up out of the beach beneath them, and attacked the sands that had arrived within the vicinity of their corner of the beach. The tree had felt the signatures of something moving underneath the sand, coming straight up from underneath its main roots, and moved with the velocity of a freight train on steroids, swinging down from the far reaches of its outer leaves, to sweep the sand away from attacking its stem and gnawing into its signature meteorized energy.

The truth of the situation was that these trees didn't really have a mean disposition, and would never have caused Kashha or Soren any harm. In fact, the tree adored Kashha. However, for some reason the creature beneath had not known she was there when it had surfaced, and had only been disturbed by the intentness of this storm front up above; deciding to take advantage of its molecules. When it broke through the surface world it detected Kashha's signature high up in the tree and moved to incorporate her majik into its own body to protect itself from what was hunting it below, unaffected by the chaos from above.

Unfortunately, her signature was all over the map, and the energy of the storm was making it difficult to decipher where she was actually located. However, that was not something that either Soren or Kashha had time to think about, as the tree was trying its best to manoeuvre around the two who were currently just inside the danger zone, and the face it created was directly in defence of the situation it had perceived as something detrimental to the little Witch's health.

As the image arrived in her head, she looked down in horror at what the teeth had tried to attack. It crawled near the branches in the direct vicinity of her right leg, apparently setting its sights now on the Dragon-riders bones. What she saw only exaggerated the image she had inside her head, and she tried to keep as calm as she could without forcing the majik to come off the ends of her fingers, and kill the creature that had just arrived in the open air around the base of the tree. However, the tree anticipated her feelings and redirected its trajectory towards the image Kashha inadvertently projected, moving toward the image she created inside her brain.

The tree's newly formed jaws, made out of rare meteor dust, struck again, as both Witch and Dragon-rider tried to move out of its way, and it hit another branch that the storm moved violently around below them. This time the tree screamed in pain as it's snapping teeth went deeply into its own bark, just missing what was climbing up Kashha's right boot.

Many things happened simultaneously, much to the horror of both Kashha and Soren, who had no idea how they had been dragged into the melange. First, in order to protect its outer shell, the tree needed to move the two creatures that belonged outside the danger zone that was currently about to become an all-out conflict. Second, it needed to stop the bloody creature from implanting itself inside its outer layer of bark, as it fed on the Witch's energy, all the while removing it from Vaal's daughter who had inadvertently arrived on scene, unaware it had just sunk its teeth into the outer bark of the tree's hide. Thirdly, and just as important, it had to prevent the creature from leaping through her veins into her actual bloodstream, preventing the tree from reaching it and disposing of it into its rightful place. And fourthly, but not least, send the creature backwards into the sand, down to the fire tubes where the Elemental from that realm could properly direct it to where it had come up from, and send it back down into the bowels of its inner planetary world.

The Rayoola Tree was nothing like anything that even remotely resembled a stationary piece of mainland flora, let alone any kind of giant Elm one had seen from the ancient climates of the continents. Most of the flora on Vaukknea was alive with sentient life, and this tree was trying it's best not to do damage to the creatures that were part of the mammalized life-forms that sought its protection from the impeding storm out beyond the violence of the world of the outer reefs. You see not all of them had a need, each time the storms arrived, to participate in the chaos, and most of those would simply find a place of refuge among the larger habitual formations, and hold on until it was considered safe to return to their own hovels.

In theory, anyways; that was what it had tried to defend, and if it didn't do something fast, the invasive creatures from the planet's core would have him defenceless when the brunt of them arrived in the coming micro-seconds, where the original scout still tried to bury its fangs into its outer bark and paralyse its precious sap inside its own veins.

Now, you must understand that it wasn't so much the fact that it didn't like anyone that took shelter within its shade as it stood in the edges of the waters of the lagoon, because it adored the attention that the tiny creatures of the land based fauna bestowed on its beautiful bark, unlike those of the watery domain that had tried to obliterate that particular piece of real-estate. But, by its own calculations, just as these very creatures were about to take shelter shielding themselves from the movement of sands that sandblasted the very daylights out of its bark, they were in exactly the very spot where the exterior of the underwater coating that had been shed from its outer limbs by the constant bombardment of sand from the storm for the last hundred micro-seconds, was now down to its final last section of nerve endings.

Kashha yanked Soren to the left of the root as it tried to stretch itself from underneath the pair, letting both teeth and sharpened swords hit the sand. They landed askew, arms and legs entangled alongside the flaming teeth, as each tried to compensate for the movements of the other, with the Elm finally winning out by virtue of being much bigger than the two of them. Then, as if on command, its limbs came outwards like a fist on a hot oven, and pushed them both off and out of the way in one great final explosion of barkticular emulsified muscles, as one of the creatures moved to advance on its fleshy underbelly.

That send a backward ripple of water through the beach head, and in a manoeuvre to compensate for its trajectory of misfired landings, the tree, trying to divert the incoming sand from causing more damage to its bark, overshot its trajectory by almost a full mile. In the end it almost drowned the pair of them along with any other creature within the vicinity, as the torrent of water it produced when the voided space suddenly filled up with sea water, fell onto their tiny limbs.

Now, torrent was putting it kindly; the wave that actually arrived to hit them full in the face literally drenched the pair of them, and sent them traversing through the slick water on their backs as it receded, moving them out into the surge of water that was moving back towards the edge of the tideline, as it pulled them further along the rip and out to sea.

Now, as luck would have it, a secondary rogue wave that one of the larger Auicks was riding on, mistook them for new arrivals and threw them farther out to sea along with several other creatures unlucky enough to have been in the vicinity, and all became caught in the violent riptide that started to swallow the entire area with too much energy and too much tree testosterone, alongside the migratory Auick who just happened to have gotten into the way.

Soren went under quickly, not having the genetics to run with the sea, as he was dragged into the violent middle of the surging water. If not for the quick thinking of Kashandarhh, who found his foot just as he became wedged in the center of its rotating motion, it could have been a very different outcome; one much more deadly than first anticipated.

"Quit kicking me in the head," she yelled at him as his foot found her cheek once more. His voice never found its mark as, the moment he went to respond, he found that he had swallowed a dear sight more water than first he thought. The squeak was drowned out with several additional gulps of seawater filling his windpipe, and he quickly sunk into the inky depths, as the Auick slid sideways and moved out of the doomed creature's way.

It moved back into the reef shoals, away from the lunacy that had arrived in its element. The tree on the shoreline had suddenly all but disappeared, and Soren, unable to stay afloat, began to move underneath the surface layers with the sheer volume of water moving around his body stinging his lungs. No longer was speech a possibility of any kind now, as it dragged him further into the icy depths of cold water and down into what he perceived as oblivion, while death hung largely on the final chapter of his life.

Breathe....

Kashandarhh couldn't reach more than just what was within her hand, and even that was beginning to slip from her grip as the paralysing effect of the water had started to inhibit her ability to hold on to anything Soren had left her with, as he slid under the waves, leaving her with only a silken thread that the Auick had shed as he moved out of their vicinity.

She dropped the strand as it tried to bring her into the deeper sections of the bay, not realizing she was from the continent, and not a part of the island fauna. She flicked it away about the same time she felt something move about her legs as she went under to get a better grip. Whatever it was, she wasn't going to be able to hold on for too much longer, as it quickly tried to move between her and Soren's body. The water was cold, and her fingers were losing whatever grip she did have, as the dark shaped darted around her. There wasn't time to hold onto Soren and fight whatever had decided to make a meal out of the land dregs pulled out to sea. She had to think fast, but no matter how hard she tried, she had a bad feeling that it wasn't going to be fast enough.

The underwater creature twisted amongst the movements she made as she tried to kick its body away at the same time trying to remain within the upper surface area of the fast moving water, which now tried to also drag her down in its inky depths. She made contact briefly and then it slid away. Fear had never occurred to her in all that she was able to find, deep inside the spirit that lived within the Witch.

But nothing made her skin crawl more than something that slithered and moved below the sight of where her vision could not provide the answers to what it was. She swore, as she always did, to take the high road of indifference, giving her the mindset to find the strength to not shudder and flinch, as she desperately tried to save both herself and Soren from further disaster while the creature moved off, leaving behind what best could be construed as the perfect meal.

She dove down looking for where the Aelf had descended into the depths, and came up empty. She panicked trying to fight the waves, seeing things that were not really there in her moment of weakness. Most times the things that moved along towards the creepy crawly end of the spectrum only did so in self-defence. And most things are in direct response to the actions that others created for them.

She had no tried and tested truths to weather the storm waters that she now found herself to be in. She began to laugh at the analogy, starting to surrender to the frigid waters herself, and becoming more unstable inside her mind. She needed to fight her fears and try again; she dove deeply, moving frantically, looking for any clue that her fingers might encounter of the damn Aelf, but once again her lungs ran out of air.

Being more from a land environment, this was harder than it looked. She started to grow numb along the vertebra of her lower back. The dark shape returned, from a different angle, sending shivers up her spine that were not related to her being cold, and the water once again dragged her down as she tried to regain her balance. She swore again, but this time when it circled back and returned for a third time, grazing her leg, she aimed straight for the creature with her own fist. She felt bone as she made contact, then the creature moved off and didn't return.

"Yeah run, you coward; next time I might just take a chunk out of you," she screamed at the retreating flipper, as it moved off.

At least she could swim, if that was saying much in a time of drowning. That domain belonged to her father's kin, and all who resided within it. It was only with those words in her mouth, before she had really finished with the thought process, when a large Seal moved to the surface of the water spouting a large stream of mist into the air, that she realized she was not alone in her ordeal. She sighed with relief, as others of his kind began to pop up nearby, coming to the rescue of both Dragonlord and Witch, as they became caught up in the tidal currents of the edges to their storm. It was then that she remembered Soren and shouted at the nearest one to find the Dragon-rider beneath her.

Damn, she just realized, she had freaken kicked one of her father's kinfolk, and to show that her fist had actually touched skin and bone, one of the Selkies was limping along behind the others just out of her reach, with an eye quickly growing to the size of one of her fists. Tiny squeals and squeaks of Selkie language echoed through the herd, as the images of her father came into her thought patterns, asking her if they might assist them into the shallows, or had she decided to continue the thrashing of another cousin just for the hel of it.

Kashha could not find her voice fast enough, and could only nod her acceptance of their offer of taking them out of harm's way. Soren was brought to the surface, right in the midst of two very large Selkie males, their razor fine whiskers brushing up against his death like cheeks.

He was not moving, and Kashha had only begun to swim towards him when one of the larger Selkies moved in a direct line between them and hit Soren full in the chest with his tail. Kashha screamed and Soren came to coughing seawater out of his lungs, still very much limp from the ordeal, but nonetheless alive. There was no time for anything but a silent nod in appreciation, at the realization that she too had almost become one with the deep.

They barked their strange and shrill language back and forth among the others that swam around the pair, bringing Kashha back to the safety of their sleek bodies, now fully in control of both of the wayward land creatures, and headed for shore. Kashandarhh looked behind her to see how Soren was faring in the high surf, looking to the entire world like a big old drowned rat much to her thankful eyes, and one very reluctant Selkie who stayed completely out of her range of fire, just in case she decided to give him another go around to match the last injury he had sustained from her.

There would be time to make amends on land; for now both of them would not have lasted much more in the depths of this stormy world. She might have, at one time, been a very strong swimmer in the right conditions of the lagoon, but out here at sea it was an entirely different story, and she gratefully accepted whatever the Selkies who had come to their rescue had to offer.

Then, on the flip side of the coin, this was nothing to the sight that brought Soren to the surface from inside the clutches of the water's inky hold. He discovered two or three of the Seal like animals darting in towards his sinking form, deep down in the depths that had begun the beginning stages of claiming him for one of their own.

It was one thing to watch them from shore as they moved within the water, and quite another to actually have them move around you, as the strength of the water had control of you in its grasp, and you couldn't fight them off if they had been hel-bent on your destruction. It freaked the crap out of him, and although he was more than grateful for the rescue of his corporeal form, he was more than happy to be seeing the waters of the shallow lagoon that now began to come into full view, as they swam him towards the lighter and shallower shoreline.

The moment he could feel the sand beneath his toes, and his body began to feel the warmth of the sandbars away from the huge swells outside the lagoons shoals, he promised himself that Quist would be getting off from anything he had planned to accost him with, the moment he might have got his hands on him. And no matter how much he pissed him off in future, he would never take flying in the air for granted again. Even if he was, a damn Dryad!

Bloody Wood Sprite, he started all this, Soren thought, still spitting up saltwater. But he was safe, with all his teeth, and moving quickly up the beach, or at least as fast as a crawling wet rat would be able to move with sand in his breeks and seaweed in his ears.

He was safe for now; at least he thought he was, as he continued to cough his head-off still unsure of what just happened. However, that tree Kashha cared so much about was freaken dangerous; she should have warned him. In future he vowed to give them all a wide berth. And next time when, she asked him to come for a short walkabout to have a friendly chat with family, he was going to have to formally decline. But that had not happened; as he caught his breath and his eyes surveyed the estuary, bringing him face to face with the beauty of the island that Kashha grew up within. He instantly forgot his temper as the surroundings within the inner-rings began to shimmer with pure Selkie majik and he lost his bloody mind to its magnificence, and then promptly threw up all over its beautiful beach.

He raised his face from the warm sands that attached themselves to every wrinkle on his drenched skin, and gazed with utter amazement at the splendour of what came into his field of vision as he spat out several layers of sand still caught in his teeth and the contents of his last meal.

Everything around him seemed to glow or shimmer, leaving nothing that wasn't tied down through root or fin to be excluded from its sheer beauty. Everywhere he looked, the same thing happened. It was like looking through a pair of majikal eyeglasses that created another world, as it finely tuned his Dragonlord eyes into its island's compass point, and made him feel like the continent was a sparse landscape of dreary old dead rock.

He watched as the land itself seemed to move in a symbiotic structure to the winds that, for some reason, no longer had any connection with the storm, which still raged on intensely out on the beach outside. Not even one single tree had a leaf out of place, and the grasslands that smelled of freshly cut hay, just lightly moved with what would appear to be just another normal summer's day to those living inside the protected zone.

Most of the herd of his rescuers had remained out in the reefs, and stayed with the storm that they called home during these moments of dual lifelines. The five or so Selkies that escorted them into the land locked lagoon had only stayed for the time it took for them to regain their footing on dry land, and disappeared with a flap of their tails beneath the waves. The others who had come to rescue the landlings alongside them, stayed farther out, even though they too had followed the others called in to help the air-breathers, who had found themselves way over their heads, in the deep water environment that wasn't their home.

They would have helped if they were needed, but when the group had arrived, everything was well in hand by the closest clutch already in retrieval mode, and after witnessing the incident with Kashha's fist, they decided to leave well enough alone and encourage from the sidelines. That was in a manner of speaking, and to put the story into it proper text, the moment the sea began to change into more of a freshwater consistency than the salt that their lungs craved, their bodies would begin to revert back to their land-based selves.

The storm had been due for weeks before it arrived, and some of the Selkies had been a lot more fragile than the others that Vaal had asked to give him a hand. Those individuals moved with the others as a clan, but Vaal would never have asked them to come into the lagoon, knowing that the fresher water could easily begin the transference with their weakened state, and further prevent them from reverting back into their Selkie forms when they needed to return.

It was hard enough for them to move heavy pelts back into position, without having to do it more than once. Then they wouldn't be able to absorb the energy off the reef that their deficient bodies craved, and some of the weaker might actually die. Vallmyallyn wasn't taking any chances. It was because of this that he let them float out along the outer shoals of the bay while a select few had volunteered alongside him to bring his daughter and the wayward Aelf to the inside waters of the lagoon's bay. The welfare of the clan was always paramount, so the weaker ones remained in Selkie form waiting for their brethren to return, so all could move along together out to the deeper waters of the offshore energy field, and back into the storm they needed in order to survive.

Soren gazed back in that direction for any sign of the retreating Selkie creatures, but there wasn't even a wake from their movement underwater. How they had made it to this particular location, Soren began to wonder, as he looked all around the edges of the aquamarine waters trying to see the pathway among the foliage he had seen that moved along the water's edge. But there was nothing to see, as the island claimed the passage and moved itself back into position while they passed inside the protection field. He knew that they had swum in through the channel that presented itself while the water was up to his ears, but nowhere could he make out the actual entrance when he arrived in the shallower waters, nor did he see any trace of the creatures as they made their way back out to sea.

Vallmyallyn had only just arrived, after leaving the others to take them inside the lagoon's atmosphere, while he made sure the others out on the shoals were safe. Finding nothing of concern, he had been able to transform into his land-self easily, the moment he returned and they had reached the warmer waters of the lagoon's mineral rich environment. He now swam with feet and limbs alongside his daughter as soon as both she and Soren reached the sandy bottom, with his pelt wrapped tightly around his middle girth.

The actual bottom of the lagoon reached upwards to find their feet, moving in amongst toes and tiny shrimp-like creatures that flitted slowly up and down their bodies eating the remnants of the energy they had absorbed from the outside waters. Once he made it to dry land — bone tired from the apparent drowning, it was all he could do to crawl out of the sea and watch the birds filled the sky as they flew all around the tiny lagoon, calling in sounds that were not always familiar to Soren who, as of yet could not even tell what they were, let alone believe what he was actually seeing. By the time he quit trying, he had made it up the embankment, dripping water-droplets wherever they fell down towards the warm sand, while Kashha lingered, following her father floating along the shoreline keeping a watchful eye on him.

His mind had been playing tricks on him since he had arrived here in the space in-between, of that he was absolutely certain. For he felt both drunk and sober all at the same time, as he walked and laughed aloud with eyes that could no longer tell whether he was awake or asleep. Kashha knew what he was seeing, as she had seen it many times over the years, when she returned home from distant planets. However, she was able to structure its behaviour, being part Selkie; whereas, Soren hadn't a drop of the chromosome inside his Aelven bones. For that he would have to remain drunk to its indifference, doing what he could to maintain his own molecules from absorbing any more than he could handle. She smiled with regret. He was on his own in this one; for in this she could do nothing to neither help nor do anything more to assist the situation in its final presentation.

Soren babbled softly to himself, as he moved in circles like a foundling Human in a Faery village, gazing at things that captured his wandering eyes. Everywhere he looked things were different here, and even more vastly altered than the middle of the Plains of Sheymoar, where he had moved when first visiting the Zarconian Falls in the northern part of the continent.

He had enjoyed that trip, watching the different landscapes move beneath Tansar as he flew over the Morphana River across Dragonclaw Drift. It was said by many, that the colours from the air were magnificent to watch, but even he had to admit that here on the Tryilamore's landslip, things were much more beautiful than anything he had ever seen before.

The birds here had some form of multi-coloured feathers, and sometimes they even turned into razor sharp scales as he watched and walked away talking to himself, now fully stoned with the rings' energy field. Their very nature always could be warranted to send off warning bells to the inhabitants in a musical way, letting the others know their wards had been breached. That way if an outsider found the lagoon by some fluke of nature to the actual discovery of the Selkie Colonies that were hidden by choice, it would quickly render them unable to continue further into their realm. Then one of their warriors could shift them away to another world, away from others that may have wandering ears, listening to the compass points of where they had found the village. Their direction of choice was usually through the Pin Nebula, where the memory would be picked from their memory cortex, and the image of the coordinates of the space in-between would be erased from within. However, no matter how careful one might be — occasionally, one might find themselves in another realm; one not so easily accessible in their search to return to this dimensional doorway.

This was Selmathen majik, which had been very effective over the years as Balor's spies had occasionally drifted in among the tides, on timbers of shipwrecked boats that had come into contact with the Sea Worm off the northern sections of Toraigh Island. It was here that the currents ran towards, and it was here that the border of the space in-between ran its offensive, up against the back of the continent's constant drift. But Soren didn't know all that, and continued his drunken stupor, stumbling through the beach head going around the bay towards another beautiful location he had visualized with overstimulated eyes, as the pair in the water followed him slowly along the shallows.

It was here, in the corner of the jungle that a small cottage rose and hung in the branches of one of the sturdier looking trees. Soren watched it sway ever so slowly in the now much calmer lighter breeze, unable to do anything but simply stare at it as his own body swayed drunkenly on the sands.

'Flipping awesome,' he whispered to no one in particular with his mouth wide-open in wonder. "Hey Kashha, where is the storm that we just swam through?" he shouted back rather loudly, unable to find the correct pitch that his voice could project, bringing his hands to his face as they appeared to grow expeditiously longer. He looked at both Kashha and her father as he spoke; trying to find them in his ever-changing vision, turning around to see if indeed he was seeing things and that what had appeared was not just a figment of his imagination.

"The storms do not affect any area of the land-masses within the inner-rings." Vallmyallyn replied simply, quite close by him. Soren startled, jumped with the noise of Kashha's father being so close. Kashandarhh smiled at Soren, as he looked on much more puzzled than before he had asked the question.

Vaal cocked his head as he followed Soren's inquisitive face, and followed the hand movements of a drunken rider who laughed at their changing shape as he brought them up to his face. Vaal grinned and winked at Kashandarhh in the way that he had when he always followed each of his answers with another questioning response. "Seriously Kashha dear, a Dragonlord?"

"So," she retaliated. "A Witch from Llavalla father, really?" she threw back at him in quick succession.

"I didn't know your mother was from that bloodless, clan." he said simply, smirking slightly. Kashha grinned at him, and Vaal continued on with his questions. "That is not the point child. How did you arrive without warning the sentries of your arrival to the old entranceways, with one that obviously does not belong — and a drunken one at that?" Kashha drew up one eyebrow and turned her head slightly, tilting it in his direction.

"He wasn't drunk when we arrived and you know it. Besides, that was the point, father dearest; had I warned you we were coming, you may have taken actions to prevent my arrival. As far as the stoned part goes, I'm sure you could help him in that department." She stood with her hands on her hips in a faintly indignant response.

"Notwithstanding; had the question supplied the silence that is required within another sentence I can't, and brought forward with I won't, until I bloody will," he said with as much sarcasm as he could muster. Kashha actually laughed, as she watched her father's animated hands; it was good to be home on the island again. Her father's fragmented insights had always driven her mad in the past. But that was in the past, and she had been only a half grown then. Now, as a full-grown, she relished in its formulation, and countered in retaliation.

"You bloody will now, you old fool, or Mother will show up and you will have to deal with her." Vaal sighed, and moved towards Soren, placing a finger under his chin, and redirecting Soren's eyes to his own.

"Stop it you Aelfan fool, the air is clear...so bloody see and quit fighting it." Vaal walked away, finished with his idea of an enchantment, and ignored his daughter when she threw up her hands in the air. It was the teaching of one of her father's kin that actually amalgamated the Witch into her true formation of the natural order of things, upon the sands that now constituted this form of land. It was one who let her mind wander into how she actually thought things through today, to get a response from those who swim in circles and think in sea- riddles.

"So that was bloody it, and you couldn't have given him some form of relief before he made a total ass out of himself?" She shook her head at her father. "Sometimes I really wonder if maybe both you and mother were made from the same mold." He grinned widely, almost splitting his mouth in half, in that oh so perfect Selkie smile.

"Yes daughter of my loins we are as one, but it is you, not I that has that mold." In saying, he dove deeply into the water, slicking out his long black hair, spitting lagoon water up high into the air.

This Selkie mind had melded the formation of both worlds into one, and gave her the simplicity of her own mind to finalize that reality into the world that both would be able to function within. Soren was a product of his own imagination, and if he had only sat still long enough, he would have seen that for himself over time. It had taken an enormous amount of head banging on her part to realize that she was a victim of her own undoing, and therefore, once that had been accomplished and she had stopped fighting it, it had come fluidly and without further incident. The same thing happened for Soren's sight; except this time they didn't have the time to wait for its arrival to correct itself.

During the father daughter uniting of minds, Soren had wandered towards the cottage that simply floated around in the branches of another much smaller Rayoola Tree than the one that had flung them skywards out into the surf.

"Its structure defies gravity," he said more or less to himself, after looking back when not getting any response from the others behind him. He realized they had not advanced towards the cottage as he had, and had stayed more or less near the water's edge while he strayed all by himself, much closer than he had expected.

He had felt Kashandarhh's father touch his skin only moments ago. But whatever he said was a mystery that still rattled inside Soren's loosely fitting memory, for the time being. How he had arrived from the water's edge to this area farther away from the pair of them was remembered sporadically, moving quickly from Vaal's side in a direct response to whatever majik the water creature had done to him, with that hypnotic glare that seemed to pierce him down to his very bones. However, he would have preferred to stay drunk....

Now rightly so; he definitely could see things better and rationalize his thought processes in a much clearer way than he had before; so maybe it was nothing more than that. However, if he started clucking and growing feathers along his outer extremities, things were going to go a different way when he met Selkie bone with Dragonlord fists. That was before he totally morphed into whatever new creature Kashha's father had changed him into, and one he would bet was not accustomed to violence towards the Selkie race as a whole, of which he was sure Vallmyallyn was capable of producing. After-all, Kashandarhh was not just her mother's daughter, and she was full of unusual things not related to the Witches folds he had become accustomed to in his line of work. So instead, he busied himself with the surroundings, preferring to stay clear of the fish until something started to bloody sprout.

He had seen the home in the initial stages of his world of crazy, but now, with cleared insight, he could understand the strangeness of its reality. The real oddity of the situation became much more apparent the closer he inspected the floatation that held itself upright within the branches. He moved to another angle to get another perspective, and came face to face with the very swollen and unusual looking tree's clarity, which held no resemblance to the other creature out by the beach at all.

Soren could see that the swelling itself was not due to anything that you would first believe to be the cause, but when you took a moment you soon realized it was withholding even more of a mystery than what it appeared to be from a distance.

The cottage was not stationary, as it first appeared. It had begun to move about within the branches, giving the appearance that it was sitting within another structure made of something more fluid. Nothing of his first assumption proved to be accurate, for what looked to be a clear watery substance actually turned out to be just pure and simple air holding it in the actual tree, like the hot air balloons he had once seen out on the fringes of the Saber Fennone lands.

Soren stood there in amazement, scratching his head, then walked around the edges rubbing his chin as the reality of the site started to find reasonable hold within his imagination. While the whiskers on his chin didn't move, the hairs on his head had found themselves to remain some-what upright, loosely resembling something more fitting of a Troll. His reflection was spotted immediately as it reflected off the bubble of air that held the tree in place. And, as he tried to lick his fingers to gaze into the air-bubble to fix the stray strands, something kicked him in the knees from behind and he went down briefly onto the ground.

He turned and rolled, coming upright with his knife firmly planted in his hand, to face his unknown attacker, but whatever it had been was nowhere in sight. He looked all around the area, even peering under the stems of several large flowers growing nearby, but nothing was spotted that closely resembled something that could have been able to do the deed. He looked towards the pair still floating away in the lagoon, thinking it might have been one of Kashandarhh's little jokes, but their soft voices were engaged in discussion about something not related to the actual touch he had felt. Instead, he turned his attention back to the tree, which was now vibrating as if it was laughing at him. But nothing seemed to be out of place within its structure, and if he thought things through, he would have realized he might just have fabricated the whole ordeal, and the hit had been nothing more than a product of his own rather vivid imagination to the Selkie flux running rampantly up through his damn nostrils.

He couldn't have been more wrong.

As a replacement for his senses being on high alert, he moved towards the cottage and inspected how it actually was able to remain within the branches of the tree, and not simply floating slowly up into the sky. He went around the thing twice, scratching his head, and still he could not find out how the majik held it in place. He poked it with his foot and watched as it floated to another location within the tree, resetting itself away from him and his boot. He grinned, finding sentient life within its matrix. That in itself was bizarre to watch, as it slowly shifted and looked like a pea-hen getting comfortable on her eggs and finding that sweet spot that she was happy with, remained perfectly still with satisfaction to its arrival.

He called to Kashha and her father, but they were even further out of hearing range, moving further into the waters of the beautiful lagoon, walking with their feet in the shallows and stirring up the white sandy shoals beneath its surface, oblivious to his calls. Small ripples of water moved along the edges of where they had stirred up the sand's actual cells, and he could see them move deeper into the warmth of its environment, settling nicely up above their shoulders. He watched them briefly plunge into its depths, coming up for air about thirty feet from their original location, then smiled at the water ripples as they turned different colours and made their way to the beach.

A huge conch shell floated to the surface, and a small group of feathers came spewing upwards into the air and floated away, then the shell righted itself and sank back down to the bottom of the underwater realm, satisfied with whatever it had tried to accomplish. Soren scratched his head and grinned wildly, as he saw father and daughter disappear under the water once more and come up further away, spewing simple water-spouts high up into the air, and not the strange sight of air-borne feathers as the current inhabitants of the shell had done.

Neither of them would have heard his words, having reverted to the unintelligible sounding clicks and words based entirely on dialects from the sea. They made no sense to him back then, and he had stopped trying to figure the strange pronunciations as they became well engrossed in their own unique language, leaving him further and further behind as they continued their fascinating conversation about why they had arrived.

He had no need to participate, he would leave that to her. Instead smiling, he watched for a moment alone from a distance, as they laughed and slapped the water with the occasional click, then without warning stopped in the middle of actual spoken speech and reverted to a kind of hand signal that made them look more like animated Trolls in a fist fight at ten paces. This could take a while, bringing Vallmyallyn into the actual reason of their visit, but what Soren didn't know was that it would not be in the time frame that he thought Kashha had first spoken to him about.

Time here in the Selkie home-world seemed to be irrelevant in the movement of the inner-rings, as Vaukknea Island seemed to refract slightly away from what he had come to know as real time on the continent. You see, there was no past inside this perimeter, and there would be no present as he had come to know things outside in the other realm of Tantaris's additional worlds. It would appear that inside the rings things kind of got a little bent, causing each timeline to run and coincide at the same interval as the one before or after it. This blended the fractures as they came together, uniting them into a single piece of unobstructed thread, allowing for singular life to breathe along a united breath of salted air.

But Soren didn't know that; he continued to breathe the same air as the others, unaware of the shift that was playing out around him as he moved with the same amount of muscles inside his own body. In the outside world, things around them moved much slower, as if caught in some slow rotational drift as they went about their day, and the moment they stepped back to the outside world, they would return to the exact moment they had left, as if they hadn't been away in the first place.

Inside the rings one also didn't age, as least not like outside the drift-point. The rings that kept this world in sync needed the power of the Selkies themselves to maintain their energy flux. And right now that energy flux started to cloud up his sight of the two of them out on the water, and make them appear to waver like the heat on a hot day out on the dunes where he had learned to ride as a young whelp.

He got bored and returned back to his inspection of the strangely beautiful home that Kashha told him she had been raised in, and watched fascinated as it floated among the foliage, changing colour as it moved to different locations within the branches of the nest tree. The cottage had completely settled in its higher reaches away from his ability to disturb its outer-edges. It appeared to change in its appearance, now finding colours in shades that mimicked the actual forest around it, as it blended into the background. Then, satisfied with its location, it crouched like a fat turtle waiting for the predator to leave.

Had he come across it without his companions in tow, it would not have even been visible to the naked eye; at least not his eyes. He wondered whether Tansar or Quist would have the sight to detect its presence, but then again they had also made it into the Witch's lair when he had been knocked out cold in the properties of Kashha's majikal doorway as they moved into the Damonian Woods.

He was starting to feel funny, and the chemistry inside his body tried to adjust to the new environment he found himself in. This world was starting to feel a little weird, as if he was slipped some kind of hallucinogenic herb when he wasn't looking. Whatever he was experiencing, things around him became even more animated as he watched the effects of the Selkie shielding on his unimpeded Aelven body up close and bloody personal.

The reason for this was becoming even more of a mystery as he watched with renewed sight and a lopsided grin. He felt drunk with the illusion set before him and, lifting his fingers in front of his face, found them to shimmer with an ethereal glow. Air danced around the tips and moved off his skin like the clouds moving over a mountain top. Even the winds seemed to have changed their forms, as voices he had not detected before suddenly found his ears and made him jumpy. Everything around him seemed to be moving at once in a bright magnitude of new colours he had never seen before in the colour spectrum. He got his bearings, and firmly planted both feet, grounding himself just as something caught his eye as it moved.

In the space of a single motion of breath that he inhaled and blew threw his nose, one of the boards of the cottage above him all of a sudden began to bulge and move out of place. Soren watched fascinated as something started unwinding the rope fastenings, and popping several of the wooden peg-nails out onto the ground without a single visible source that could have created the action.

He watched the tree foliage twist a bit, then unwind, extracting one of its odd shaped branches and transform itself into a single piece of what could best be described as a wooden arm with some form of hand attached, then pull out one of the branches alongside the outer walls within its reach, which appeared to have finished its purpose. The other, now dry and brittle, had no life inside its rather sad looking dried out foliage, and had begun to look a bit worn around the edges as it had been injured and hung loose from some unforeseen drama of a past age.

It spied a new branch that was covered in a maroon spray of leaves and feathers of another tree that happened to have fallen in the beginning of the storm, and floated into its range from out in the lagoon. It appeared to be sentient in its own organism also, and seemingly still quite alive, as it had momentarily been crawling onto the shore away from the beach to rest along the base of the tree, just as he had gone around to the other-side.

Soren jumped back as the arm that the tree had created rotated to the right, ignoring Soren altogether and picking up the branch to place it within its own structure, grafting it into place. While the original piece was flung outwards to the ground and landed with an audible thud, he heard another sound just below that level that soon made him begin to laugh.

Several unusual looking creatures appeared to scurry from underneath the roots and trunk from a narrow entrance that had opened unexpectedly at the base of one of its thicker areas of undergrowth. They moved forwards in a mad dash towards the new ground litter, shaking their fingers and heads in his direction as they clucked away. Then they dragged it and pulled it downwards into whatever hole they had appeared from, and slammed the old wooden door in his face after sticking their fingers in their ears and swearing at him. Not even a whisper of wind marked the passing of their movement and the tree reverted back to its original shape.

Soren started to laugh again, pointing to the creatures that lived inside the great tree's trunk. This time the pair out in the water heard him moving backwards along the high waterline, and met him, covered in water droplets that still ran down their skin. Soren turned as the two advanced up the beach, waiting for them to come within speaking range so he wouldn't have to shout.

The Selkie fussed with his hair, combing the occasional piece of seaweed out of his mane, then tied it up above his shoulders. Soren immediately moved to the left and placed Kashha between the two of them, just in-case he had done something wrong in approaching the rather large Selkie's home. Vaal moved an eyebrow up as he glanced at Kashha and smirked, before speaking to the Aelf.

"So, how is it that a Dragonlord finds himself within the middle of a Selkie stronghold?" Vallmyallyn towered over Soren by almost an arm length as he stood waiting for the Aelf to answer his question, water pooling on the sand, slowly dissolving into the loose stones where he stood.

Soren coughed, realizing just how tall the Selkie really was once he was out of the water, then shook the cobwebs that had formed inside his brain from the power of the rings and let them fall around him and answered the male without further hesitation.

"It appears we have a mutual enemy that has breached both our villages' trust. I'd like an opportunity to find a way to bring a resolution to the ending of its existence in any of the worlds that it has tried to seek refuge within," Soren replied, surprised, now speaking with complete control over his vocal cords. Somehow the effects he had been experiencing had reversed direction as the Selkie had arrived beside him. He now had a new understanding of what was at stake, and a lot of respect towards the towering creature that could easily stamp the very life out of him should he desire it, let alone pull perfect speech out of his muddled brain. But, it was Kashha who supplied the next question to Soren's response and her father's quizzing eye.

"Father, this is Soren. You really need to call in a few of your council members, as this appears to be becoming much more than all of us from the other-side of your rings can handle alone, without my coven." Vaal answered without taking his eyes off the Dragonlord, with nothing more than honesty.

"Your timing couldn't have been worse. Nothing will be easy to attain within respect to this particular problem; it will take some time with the storms just arriving at our doorstep. It could not have happened at a more inconvenient time for our species, and it may be awhile before I can get back in to you. We need to recharge our energy cores before any of us will be any good to you as such." He sighed, pointing to his lack luster skin that had begun to grow transparent, and turned his attention back to his daughter.

"You child, will be here when I return?" he asked, raising an eyebrow in enquiry. When she didn't answer, he started again. "It's not a question Kashha, it is a request." Kashha looked at him with a quizzical stare, nodded in agreement, and then watched him as he started to make his way towards the water once again.

"Just hurry father, it is beginning to make advances in finding the entrances to all of our wards. And, given time it will breech even your protected shores to find the remains of the coven and its allies."

"Give me what the Goddesses need, Bairn, and I will return with the others. We will both need that time to recharge our core molecules down to the bones for this." He nodded towards the cottage, making his point, as he moved further into the water without waiting for her response, and dove headfirst into its environment.

"I hope it is enough time before a breech is made to the old cities," she yelled after him. "Hurry back with all that you need for your clarification rituals," she added, as a last response to that thought, still watching as her father turned towards her and winked. He descended below the surface, facing her as the water slowly climbed up his skin, then disappeared without a ripple beneath the water with a Selkie smirk and a flip of his silken leather tail. The other Selkies slapped the surface of the water and moved towards the open sea upon his arrival. Then, as a clan they entered the entrance point environment en-mass, to reclaim all that kept their birthright in formation, as the Auicks continued to guide whoever challenged the waves, towards the making.

The thick of the storm would be continuing for most of the next three days, but the energy that they as a species required would only sustain itself until nightfall. Myallyn needed to return to the reef where most of the clan had gathered amongst the strongest of the waves to wait for his return. They would not wait for more time than he needed to reform the bond that he wanted with his child from the land. It was more than he could bear as he returned to the open ocean to swim as Selkie and not his offspring's other Fey reality.

The waters of the lagoon were reasonably warm, so when he was first able to return to his land based form, in order to save his child from the open ocean's clutches, he had done so without too much hardship. There would be a lot of aspects he would have to factor in, in order to avoid the possibility of not being able to return in time for the energy currently spinning out of control on the reef. However, he hadn't thought too much about it when Kashha had needed his help, even though he was almost spent in this old coat of fur and fin. It would be another story when he had to actually return back to his Selkie formation.

The Selkie molecules would not be too happy with the transformation on that side of the changing. They needed more than time, to rest their transmogrification molecules in the allotted frame of time that he had given them when he forced them to return to the former amalgamation of land particles. He had no choice but to return to the reef to start the process that his body craved; one that the others shouldn't have been dragged into because of an accident on land that was a direct result of his offspring coming in through the wards without their knowledge. It wasn't their fight, but somehow Kashha had torn a piece of their heart apart when first she had arrived with Kamera, and he couldn't really have stopped them had he tried. She was, after-all, part of their world as well, and that was an unusual occurrence in this realm of Selkiefied fir and Seal fin.

The Tryilamores did not mix with the land creatures from the mainland continent. It had simply never been done in the past. There really wasn't a reason as to why, it just was something that each of the clutches did when they moved among Manannan's watery realm. It wasn't a rule that Queen Sopdet had requested of the race as a whole, nor was it a reigning ruling of the ocean Elemental King who moved among the water-folk to make sure all followed the guidelines set in place beneath his golden trident. No, it simply had come to pass as the world evolved among the stars, and grew into the world in which he had been selected Sovereign of the Tryilamore finings.

Now that watery realm was calling to each of them to move quickly as a clan, the Auicks waited patiently for their final exodus to move them towards the energy mass that was becoming unstable without their colonies out in its waters to stabilize it. He needed to move his family clutch quickly, as he changed into the creature that was resistant to the constant bombardment that the land form had put on his Selkie molecules. The particular energy that his body needed to transform was usually done in stages. One with absolute timing, which had to be rebooted now that he had messed with the molecules when he returned to the fresher waters of the lagoon he had only recently departed from.

Its start and finish was triggered by their own body chemistry and the night-less time of a fully bloodless moon. To force the process was sometimes painful and full of hazards that could be lurking within the cooler waters outside the inner sanctum of the lagoon's secure environment. He started changing the moment he became submerged in the protected lagoon, and even that had been completed within record time, as he joined his water clan as something else in the shallows remained stationary along the edges, remaining perfectly still until he had done so. Had he not been concentrating solely on this, he might have picked up its energy sequence and the day would have ended quite differently. However, he had more important things to do, and a simple energy reading among the mass of creatures moving within the waters was nothing out of the ordinary at this time of the year. So he had inadvertently missed it in his rush to get everyone out to the reef.

The dangerous waters had always been a challenge to any of the group that now awaited his arrival before the transference of energy was completed. The very susceptibility that he had left his clan to face was nothing short of what could have proved to be fatal had the Sea worm decided this day to pay them all a long awaited visit. Its very passage into the Selkie home-world could have inherently been something history would have undoubtedly created, without the transference of the old ways which they had just returned to, to find life once more inside its ancient waterways. This mythological creature that Humans had said was only a Faery story had been spotted just outside the waters of Tryanafie Bay, which was not more than 100 miles east of the reef that they now waited in for Vallmyallyn to return. So, assuming the scouts were right, it was no longer something feared in the dreams of their young, but something to fear for the clan as a whole, being as vulnerable as they were.

It would take only a fraction of that time to reach the herd had it found them waiting outside the induction zone that had been directly linked to one of its wormholes. Several older holes still could be found just below the surface outside the bay's channels, but he had not heard of any of them being used for travel since before the Dragons had arrived on the shores of Symarr Island. But as luck would have it the wind was blowing away from the reef world where they were bobbing along in constant watch for its arrival, and they had thankfully remained safely out of harm's way as Vaal returned to guide them on.

Their challenge would not be encouraged this day. He moved them all en-mass to the outer rim of the transference point, where the old reef used to move the species inward on their movement towards the energy field. The storm had greatly intensified since he first found himself heading in its direction, and they would need to replenish their strength before the hour was out, or some of the younger females may not make it into the ferociousness of the shedding grounds.

Huge thunderous waves had begun to rise to dizzying heights as they continued their migration to the world of the reefs. From there, alongside other animals, they witnessed their unusual patterns which resembled previous formations that had collapsed whole islands in their wake as the Auicks led them through. Several had remained behind waiting for the last of the herd to make it out from the island shallows, and quickly sent them on their way past some of the stronger sections they normally would have had to swim right through. Vaal was grateful, and would have to pay them back in kind, for some of his clan would not have been able to steer their young bodies through the corridor they normally would have been sent towards, as the mass exodus had dragged them in. Even now, the extreme power of the waves tossed them around like matchsticks as they crashed headlong into the Selkies' sleekly oiled forms, sending several of the older males sideways away from the main group and into the ocean currents that had the audacity of keeping them firmly in its grip. The females moved quickly to form a solid wall inside the inner ring of younger male's bodies, to keep their own hides from being torn apart and brought back out where their male counterparts had been taken.

Vaal and his second in command broke free of the others, and skidded through the troughs of the foaming giants, diving deeply underneath their struggling forms and pulling them free, just as the current tore through the group, leaving pelt shedding's along its pathway and sloughed off Selkie skin floating in its wake. They drifted in the current away from their hosts, who swallowed more water into their lungs than they could expel, and rose to the surface in a shower of coughing spasms and hoarse barking, refusing to let it impede their progress.

All of them came into the slot with the help of Vaal and Ballynamullan's underwater motion, as they swam in circles releasing the current's pull on their ageing backs from the massive energy overhead. One Auick remained behind the pack, helped them skid back to the others through the undercurrents as they crested the surface heavy with foam and seaweed fingerlings, otherwise safe to fight another day among the dangers of the reef.

The Selkie language vibrated with high pitched squeals and yelps coming directly through their mammalized intake valves which, to the land Fey, sounded not unlike the shrill barking of a young land pup. But the excitement of the majik was about to begin; primarily made up in part of the unusual tones that could be heard amongst the younger ones that had never seen the stronger storms since the inception of their birth two arns ago.

The storm was starting to create havoc among the outer reef's underwater realm, and the grasses that the eels swam through on their way to the burrows of the Sangrinine Butterfluncal Trickells had begun to lose their grip within the sand filled rocks that made up the many lairs that they lived in. These were not the only creatures struggling in the high winds;

many of the underwater creatures were having a bit of a ride on this day of storms, and not all needed the intense energy it would provide in order to gain power, as did the Selkie Clans of Vaukknea Island. Many creatures of the tides used this time to surf along the edges of the storm, and one of those creatures now had both Kashandarhh and Soren in her sights as she cruised slowly out of the Selkie senses, and into the passage they had hidden in towards the warmer waters of the lagoon.

She had slipped into the cove easily after Vallmyallyn's departure, when it had finally been revealed to her, and swam closer to the area of the beach the softlanders had chosen to wait until his return. They were not at the water's edge when she arrived, and her passage would go undetected as she waited patiently out in the shallows of the warmer underwater dunes.

Nothing made a hunt harder than to be tipped off in the beginning. It would be hard enough to figure out the right moment to create a diversion without the element of surprise, and if she had any idea of what the creature with the softlanders of the Dragons had been, she would have licked her lips in anticipation of the kill with that much more vigour. She liked surprises, and this one was going to simply be delicious.

The creature had luminescent pale Jadquoius Oysterus coloured silken locks circling alongside her face and head, which floated amongst purple seaweed combined with tiny shell-like amphibians, encircling her moon shaped face. Green and silver sparkled scales shone incandescently in the Mauntra's reflective rays, giving them more of a reflection than any kind of mirrored image would have presented.

The waters were clearer than she had seen them in a long time, giving the sand along the bottom the opportunity to shine brightly all the way through to the other-side of the lagoon's edges. Her luxurious tail moved about with an elongated lazy appearance, as the warmer climate in the lagoon slid down its length, feeling unusually warm.

It wasn't the water that sparkled as she glided through its liquid salt, but her long and beautiful tail as she moved about, waiting for their arrival back to the water's edge. From the vantage spot that she had been riding within the waves, she hadn't been able to watch from the reef as the Saltwater Elm had first deposited both land creatures into harm's way. It was the actual splash that caught her attention in the beginning moments of awareness; as she followed it through; she then visualized what appeared to be the remnant molecules of a giant tree that had inadvertently brushed away other vermin at its feet as it set the creatures into her sights, and within reach.

The very thought of the more than perfect situation had been flawlessly orchestrated in dreams that were silently sheltered within her dreamscape. This was more than she could handle when the thoughts of abduction towards the female came upward within her brain. Before she could begin to move in their direction, the Selkie clan that had already begun to emerge into the storm turned around and snatched the pair returning her prize to the beach head.

Cruelness escaped her lips with the factual thoughts that she herself was something that males would give their own lives to possess. It should have been her that they came to rescue, and devoted their time with, instead of some ugly old creatures that shouldn't even be here in this realm. Even more of a reason to snatch the female, as she was sure she wouldn't even be missed. She hadn't tasted a Land-Witch in a very long time, and if she remembered the texture, it should taste a lot like raven.

Ah raven...she hadn't had raven in a very long time either. And now that the sailors very rarely had them on board when their ships went down, she had resorted to the same old fare as everything else within this damn old sea.....fish! She was beginning to feel like she was turning into a bloody fish, she ate so much of the crap.

However, tonight she was going to have something more palatable than damn old seafood. She brushed her hair with her fingers as she came over to a beautiful underwater rock covered in tiny shells. A shrimp moved past her, and she ripped it right out of it shell, devouring its succulent soft body and swallowing it whole. Others moved out of her range and she ignored their cries as she continued to preen herself, oblivious to what they had to say.

Her vanity was dazzling to herself, and to look in a mirror would have shown the true physical beauty of who she really was. For that reason alone, she hated the mirrored surface of the lagoon waters, for truthfully she could never compare herself to any of the females through most of the known Fey worlds that hosted her Watermite kind. She was different, and had been born with something the others had not. It was this thing that she had focused on the land dwellers of the continent. But she was not after the male of the land creatures, she wanted the female, and she could wait as long as it took to get her hands on the prize.

Kashha had taken Soren into the cottage by the back stairs she had touched to open, as the heart of the home moved within its clarity. The stairs did not touch the ground, as would normal entrances that erected themselves in the worlds outside of the hidden cities, but followed the flow of the essence that was created by the majik of the Selkie rings hovering directly above it.

This old majik had been well hidden from the other Fey species, which had long ago forgotten that they belonged to the water-worlds, and lived in the old ways. It now rested within the solitude of nothing more than quiet and complete solace of a calm race, perfect for the rest of one's soul in the insanity of the another world's chaos. It was here in these very walls that she had been raised; in a loving home away from the ridicule that the Kanoie Tribe of elders had inflicted in trying to enforce their lifestyle upon Kamera, as she grew fat with child in the months prior to Kashha's birth. Now she was older, nothing they could do would affect her again, as laughter brought her into focus, and she watched Soren explore her home.

She introduced him to the amazement of the interior living space of the strange home, as it came to life before his eyes. Its unusual flux amazed the Dragon-rider, as he gazed with wonder at things he had never imagined could be real, while they floated and passed him by and carried on their normal routine. Each time something new arrived in his line of sight, there was an equal and immediate response from Soren, who reached out and either touched, prodded, or poked it, as it continued to elude him to go about its day. She had actually laughed when Soren accidentally pulled a corner of one of the windows apart when he was inspecting its structural integrity, and it came away easily in his hands. The cottage walls actually slapped his head, then went on to repair the faux pas that had resulted in its damaged sill. Soren at once began to break things just to see if he could get out of the way in time to avoid the life-force that resided within its genetic makeup, and watched, while it was able to track his movements within the interior of its walls.

He lost, as the cottage literally threw him out one of the windows that it created just for the expulsion of his character. He fell down onto the sands far below. Then, to make matters worse, the creatures that lived under the tree had just begun to cart him away, when he came to and discovered he was being dragged beneath the sand — leaving only his upper-body sticking out of the thicket, along the base of the tree.

Kashandarhh had been laughing so hard that there wasn't even a chance to help his sorry posterior. She moved backwards towards the water's edge, watching as the spectacle in front of her was being carried out, with tears of laughter still caught in her eyes.

That was all it took, as a single flash of shiny scales and claws snatched her laughing ass off the beach and dragged her underneath the freshly disturbed surface water, leaving not even a single wave to mark her passing.

CHAPTER THIRTY-FOUR

The Makings of Dragonlord Soup

Recipe for the perfect bowl of Dragonlord soup:

A pinch of mangrove... preferably one with the highest
concentration of foliage...
Two breaths of a Sea-Scallpin's tongue...
Three sprigs of brain coral...
One extra-large Mermaid skull or hip bone if that is not available...
And a final whisper of ancient Zercaouse wood, slightly damp.

Place all ingredients in a large lagoon of warm water; add one pissed off
Dragonlord. Stir continuously until unconscious, and serve up on a platter
of vines and leaves that live within the area, and consume at your leisure,
or until the next unlucky traveller stumbles ashore and we have dessert.

Now go and enjoy, while the meal is secure....

The morning tide brought new meaning to the word un-catatonic. You know, what that word means: To not react to something that is happening. Well shove an un- in front of it, and you pretty much got the day that Soren was dealing with.

Soren, the poor Dragon-rider, couldn't have had a worse day if he had tried. As a matter of fact, he was so damn worried about how the Selkies were going to react to losing Kashandarhh, let alone what they were going to do to him when they found out he had not actually been able to participate in getting her back, that it never even occurred to him that the island might be less than pleased with his bloody Aelven molecules without one that had purposely been able to placate them in the first place.

That little piece of information had begun immediately upon her withdrawal from the beach, and out of his reach. He had been pacing all night outside the cottage, waiting for Vallmyallyn to return with his clan, sidestepping away from the building, hoping he wouldn't fall asleep so it would eat him alive. There wasn't even a glimmer in his thought pattern that he would wait out the night inside the now very alive and sometimes growling cottage, which floated just beyond his reach, waiting for that one false move that would take him into the clutches of its claws again.

It had taken him the best part of a twenty minute struggle to free himself from the clutches of that thing, which lived under the Nurse Tree, as it spat and hissed like a crazy animal in the dark. He had tried to use whatever came in reach from the tree, to free himself, but that proved to be more like a game of Coir Kat and Micecicles with a mixture of futility. The moment he tried to use it as leverage to gain his freedom, the cottage literally snapped at him. That also marked the first time the actual growling had begun in earnest.

He began to give thought to the idea that this endeavour was much more complicated than his off-hand first encounter with a snarly old Wood Sprite called Tamerk. Of all the things Symin and himself had gotten into in the last hundred or so years, this was definitely going to top his list of what not to sign up for again anytime soon; that is in the coming lifetime of his or his Dragons' own mortality. Ok maybe his mortality; Tansar was on his flipping own.

Actually, to be fair, this was something that he was not ever going to agree to repeat. Even with the smallest hesitation in the thought process of his entire lifetime of stupid stuff he did repeat; he wouldn't! Why in the bloody hel did he get himself into this crap? It's not like he had a huge sign carved into his backside saying: 'Please make me look like an idiot today, I think it might be fun!'

But, unfortunately that had not been the worst of it. He had watched the Witch get dragged into the water, after listening to her laugh her little head off at his own humiliating situation, and couldn't for the life of him get down the beach in time to give that thing something to drag out in the surf other than his newly made travelling companion. Had he been able to do at least that, and take her place, the creature would have had some serious damage done to its eyes compliments of a certain knife he had tucked into his boot. Unfortunately, it had happened so fast that had he even been out of the sand, which had been up to his chest trying to crush the daylights out of him, and dragged almost under the house, he wasn't so sure he could have been in time to be of any help to her anyway. At least he thought it would have felt better than sliding on one's backside, watching her disappear, and not being able to do anything about it.

That was really why he felt so helpless and just a little bit pissed at the cottage that stood beside him, watching his every move as he paced along the high tide line, just in case it came back for round two.

"Hey, stop growling at me, you stupid hunk of wood. I thought you and I had an understanding!" Soren glared at the home, and found that he was talking to it in the manner of one that was actually addressing a person standing in front of him, instead of something made out of timber and vines.

"I don't know why you're so bloody mad you idiot, none of this would have happened if you hadn't flung me out the bloody window. The very least you could have done was release me, so I could have gone after her. But no, you let me get dragged under your bloody porch so I was absolutely helpless, struggling away when I might have been able to at least prevent the creature from taking her out of the damn lagoon."

He threw a stone into the water and turned to walk away, like it was the most normal thing in the world to do in the situation. But something hit the back of his head, when he was no more than a couple of boot strides from his previous position. He was furious, and turned around just in time to see that the tree had moved position, dragging the cottage with it, swaying dangerously high up in its branches. It started to track his movements towards the high tide line, where he thought he would be able to sit out the storm and wait till they returned to send out a rescue party. Unfortunately it seemed the rescue party would be coming also, after him.

'Damn it, now what?'

"Hey listen, her father's going to be pissed if you hurt me, remember that, you hunk of...," He couldn't think of anything nasty that hadn't already been said.

"It wasn't my damn idea to come here in the first place. All I did was follow her in when she asked me to come," he shouted at anything that would listen. Everything on this rock had shifted with the tree's movements, and it soon became apparent, that he was not only not safe, beside the tree, but that the whole damn island was beginning to look unsafe to even be standing on it.

"Ok, all right I'm leaving. But I'm sure as hel that Kashandarhh's father won't be too happy with you if I'm dead before he gets back. Remember, he needs me alive. I'm the only one that can tell him what happened to her, right? Do you, even understand that?" *'Crap!'* It changed pace, and moved faster. He started running.

The tree wasn't listening. Instead it stalked him into the water and when he reached about waist deep, he began to think about swimming for it into the middle of the lagoon. His options were slowly starting to dwindle, as he wondered how long he would be able to tread water to wait for Kashha's father to return before he either drowned, or the sea creature changed direction, and returned for him as well.

He kept looking at the shallow depths, as he moved about as slowly as he could without trying to disturb the ripples of the surface any more than was necessary. He could see tiny fish darting by, as they carried on their daily activities underneath the water's surface, oblivious to the dangers he was facing. But the tree continued to stalk him, and it became more apparent that whatever was still in the lagoon must already know he was there. He began to swim, not caring that he was thrashing through the water as the tree continued to track him, putting him in an extremely defenceless position.

He kept moving, and after a while the tree let him go on without chasing him down further. Last time he spotted it, it was crawling back up the dunes and planting itself on a bluff, watching him as he continued on occasionally looking over his shoulder. He heard the distinctive sound of the cottage once again getting settled, and then turned his attention to what was beneath the water he was walking through. He spotted a huge Sea Tucker Fish that had one of the most colourful shells he had ever seen. The scales alone would have captured a tidy Draggert at the market near Tameron's Fish Palace in the main square, but for now all he could do was keep himself afloat, while all around him went to hel.

There were a lot of other very interesting things beneath the water's surface that he could see quite clearly, but none of it was of interest to him as he struggled to stay away from the beach. He stumbled on stones that caught his feet, yet still nothing found his ankles and dragged him down. Instead, he moved about the edges of the lagoon, trying to stay within touching distance of the shore line, as similar trees hissed and sent out air roots, whipping the beach to let him know that they wanted him to keep on moving. He became worried that if the creature came back and he headed to shore to seek shelter, the local flora would serve him up on a silver platter if he even tried to hit the beach. At least here he would have more of a chance than on land. Out here the local residents were mostly benign, despite the island's continuing attempts to knock him off up on the shore.

However, in the meantime, he was just going to not give them any cause to give it a go in the water, before he ran out of all his options. It didn't last long, before everything began to hunt his every move and he was forced to actually go out into the depths of the lagoon's waters just to keep out of whipping range of the vines that tried to ensnare his arms and legs. For some reason they seemed to grow longer and more dangerously efficient with each minute he stayed in the sheltered waters, and soon even the fish seemed to show interest in his limited knowledge of the area, as the vines moved closer to their domain pushing him further away.

It was about four hours later, with him treading water and seeing his skin start to shrivel into tiny little sunken lines all around his hands and feet, when he spotted what looked like something that could help him wait out the storm. It must have floated in on the outside currents, drifting just out of range of an old mangrove nook which was trying its best to hide its sight from Soren's eyes. Had he not been floating near that site, it could very well in the next few minutes have accomplished that very deed. But, Soren spotted it before the island could cover it over, and reached to pull it out into the open, pushing several air root feelers away from his arms, as they found his skin and tried to reel him in.

They broke free and the boat came away easily into the deeper sections of the bay away from the edges, without sinking. The boat was old, he could tell that much, and very battered, as if the storm outside had tried to crush its body with the waves, and only got to a small upper part of its structure before it floated into the tiny bay, and entered this section of the mangroves. The planks were made out of some kind of wood not indigenous to this area of Tantaris, and for some reason completely locked out of taking on a life of its own like everything else inside the space in-between. He could only thank those responsible for letting him find it, while the bay continued its offensive of trying to pull him ashore.

He guided it further away from the edges, out along the deeper pallet of the aquatic colours while visually inspecting its buoyancy. It seemed strong; he rocked the edges, testing its ability to hold him. Soren figured that it had been on the move for quite some time, drifting from whichever place it originated from across the great oceans of the Old Sea of Hioroques. He also could see that the island had no control over the watery surroundings that he currently was residing within, and everything around him seemed locked in some form of a protection field the moment he had touched the boat, further preventing the island from reaching him. No wonder it didn't want him to see the thing. Not that the truth of the matter signified anything but simple safety, but it was equally important to think that he might just have a chance to make it through until the Selkies returned to land.

He climbed aboard and settled into the bottom of the skiff, feeling much better as he warmed his body in the Mauntra's rays. He drifted towards the middle of the bay, and the flora along the shoreline ceased their efforts to eat him alive. He wondered how long he had been out in the water, and had begun to drift within his own mind, relaxing tense muscles that had been much too long used in keeping him afloat. He closed his eyes. It felt so calm that he now seriously began to doubt that the skiff was actually there. He shook his head to try to shake the sensation of the hallucination from taking control over his thinking process, but only succeeded in causing himself to feel more light headed.

He started to hallucinate, making him feel that he was still neck deep in the waters of the lagoon, and not anywhere near where he knew he was.

"What the frig?" he mumbled. The island was showing him strange pictures in his head that made him believe he might just not have found the boat at all, and had dreamed the whole thing up. The idea became a nightmare, planting itself in his head and taking root. It reminded him that if he didn't start for shore soon, and find out if the skiff was indeed a figment of his imagination, he was going to actually fall asleep sinking into the brine of the sandy bottom, and making fish food for whatever lurked nearby.

Something big bumped into him, moving him forward towards the boat he thought he just climbed into a few moments ago.

"What is this madness?" he said to himself, as his head began to sink beneath the water. Startled, he came up, half-heartedly coughing and spitting out water that he had swallowed in that short amount of time. But, try as he might, he could not seem to get himself to swim towards the safety of the skiff with arms that seemed to be getting heavier with each passing moment.

Another bump, but this time something was actually carrying him along the surface of the water; this time he actually felt himself beginning to drift downwards as he slipped into the unconscious world of dreams full of nightmares, deep down inside the Selkie ring of liquefied terrors. Yes, it appeared the water had found its new medium and spoke to the Dragonlord through its liquefied voice, seizing control of the creature that was responsible for taking Kashandarhh off the grid.

Soren started to dream things in quick succession. He had never been able to in the times when he slept during the night time hours. His dreams were fragmented, and flowed without substance until he reached a dream field that was more familiar to Priestesses of the old ways, than to the claiming of his own soul.

His dreams began to match the actual lifetime experiences within the coven clans of the old rites. He seemed to be moving somewhere, as if he floated about in the time of his race's history. But the molecules seemed to be a bit fragmented, as if they had no air to breathe, and couldn't transform properly to show him what he needed to know.

He could feel his limbs without the pressures of gravity pushing them inward, allowing his body to experience the rapture of nothing but time and never ending motion. His flight path through the actual space, kept him following in a more or less a direct pattern of approach and never faltered from the direction it carried him.

He felt so strange having no pain from the cuts he had received from the creatures beneath the tree. He knew they were there, for he had tried unsuccessfully to stanch the flow of blood from the surface wounds that threatened to feed the fish, when first he had entered the water. So how was it that these wounds, that he knew were there, and had been very apparent when he had entered the Lagoon, majikally disappeared the moment he moved to the outer atmosphere of what he could only describe as volumes of stars, instead of liquid water?

It didn't bother him for long, nor did it even cross his mind that he might not be in the boat at all, nor whether the truth of the matter was actually that he had climbed aboard it to reach safety. Whatever the truth was, he could not tell. He soon became so transfixed by the sights and sounds of the journey that he was moving inside, that he let the memory go without fighting it. It was something he had always wanted to do as a Bairn, as all the wee ones did within their own secret worlds in the dead of night when they hurt. So he moved to the stars, and pretended he was someplace else as the island took over his mind and he sank into the Selkie bliss.

He woke up on dry land, on the heels of what could only be described as a piece of floating rock. He felt the roughened stone beneath his feet and felt the wind of space move the air around him, as things began to form and shape the creation into real objects, which then floated and drifted by him, as he moved along the borders of wherever they seemed to be taking him for the moment. He watched whole star systems whiz by and felt the spray of comet dust fill his nostrils — with strange sulphuric concoctions he couldn't identify — alongside the smell of metal components not found in the air of Sopdet's planetary reign.

Then, there was this wonderful heat all around him and turning about slowly, he could see a star beam of light from some distant galaxy. He watched it settle around the rings of fallen pieces of floating meteor dust, as it wobbled in an unusual orbit and spun backwards in reverse direction from the other systems nearby. He couldn't quite put his finger on it, but seemingly it appeared to be almost sentient in its configuration; staying just out of the pathway of the collision course he was travelling on.

He began to realize that he knew precise directions in this vast expanse of deep space, and could start to see with his mind's eye that the Tuworg Nebula at this time of the year ran through The False Galaxy of the Crystal Horse. He couldn't remember having known that, but whatever it was, it gave him intimate knowledge of the pathways of stars and their galaxies, as he moved as one with the open space and watched its rotational shift. The two star systems had appeared to him through a hole in the rip of time that he was staring through. He watched them as they moved together between two other very large and distant star systems — through the same area of space — without tearing each other further apart.

Soren watched as the shimmer of silver moved like a curtain, and the two galaxies began to merge towards each other, folding themselves within the rip and coming out the other-side unharmed. They moved apart unaffected, as if the collision of the wormhole they had just moved through had no influence on their surface areas'. Amazing how that never seemed to get old — he mused, as he watched the old formation of colourful string tentacles making their way across the vastness of each orbit, touching the outside of their neighbour's electrical charges and grasping that energy into their own worlds.

It appeared to be more of a symbiotic fold, than anything else, with their reaction to the other's various placements within the energy field that was created between the two universes. Kind of like the relationship between the Selkies' energy transference within the Storm Waves on the Reef outside Vaukknea Island. Yes, that was exactly what it looked like.

"Wait a minute, how did that creep into my dream?" thought Soren, as he began to slowly realize he was actually starting to feel the effects of gravity on his own body again as it brought him back to the present day.

His fingertips moved, and he heard someone speak, but still could not understand the sound that reverberated in his eardrums. Apparently wherever they were, they were getting closer to him. He felt the distinctive impression of the boat rocking as someone came aboard. Whoever they were, he still could not see them; blinded by the strong odour that had produced the spicy smells that permeated the skiff.

Then he felt his body being picked up and moved by strong hands, placed on the weakest sections along his limbs, under his back and head. Instantly he felt warmer, as the sensation changed and whatever had moved him from his current position lifted him onto something much warmer and a bit oddly shaped. He was shifted ever so slowly forward, and the motion seemed to be rocking him back and forth.

Small clicking noises came into his range of hearing as he tried to fight them off, thinking beetles were crawling across his limp body. However, he couldn't move and whatever had him imprisoned continued to let the insects crawl around him; he panicked. He started to hyperventilate, as things were starting to swim within his brain and the effect was causing him to watch the space ahead of him that had been turning black. It now come crashing into his own body to devour him in all its strength and odd intensity, as he lost the ability to control even the slightest muscle in his body.

Soren once again lost consciousness, and when he regained himself through the lost void, he realized he was still swimming in the waters of the lagoon, reaching for the bloody skiff. *How many times was this going to repeat?* Apparently, his vision still couldn't comprehend what was happening, and the poison drifted into his veins, releasing the toxin further into his bloodstream.

Outside, the creatures watched the dream unfold, allowing it to take him wherever it decided to land, as the skiff in the dream drifted towards him. He reached out again to retrieve the edges and tried to hoist himself up before the jungle once again moved in to yank it from his grasp. Its interior was familiar this time, and the wood smelled unusually spicy for something that had been ornately carved out of a single piece of a Zercaouse tree trunk. The memory took hold this time, and it brought him to the time when he first became a Dragonlord.

Tansar had taken him across the Old Sea of Hioroques to one of the remaining cities of the Earth Elementals to be at a tribunal for the Cantons. It was here, as he attended their society's Dragon rituals, he was first introduced to this tree. The tree had been very prolific all around the Elementals' outer city edges, and he remembered how extremely beautiful it had been there, growing majestically along the tree-lined wards. But he didn't remember it having that spicy smell that now assailed his nostrils, and filled him with dread.

For over three thousand years there had existed a ban on cutting this tree down and this kind of skiff had never been created again in all those years. In fact, how was it even possible to have survived this long? There had to be something he was missing in the picture he was being showed. The rings above him collected the knowledge of what he was seeing and gave him the answers to the questions that kept repeating themselves inside his head.

The skiff returned and drifted towards him. Instead, of reaching for it, he let the waters take him with the current and watched the skiff dissolve into huge limbs belonging to the Nurse Tree as it dragged him towards the beach. Several shrill voices could be heard as something was crashing through the surf and the next thing he knew, something was reaching towards his frozen limbs and rocking the boat he seemed to be lying in. He tried to scream, but his vocal cords were paralyzed from the poison. A single Selkie face emerged out of the shadows momentarily, then disappeared; its lopsided grin turned into a snarl, making him frown. He tried to break free in a lagoon primarily supporting a very active Selkie stronghold of Sea Bearing Creatures, which seemed to be bearing down on him and not noticing the significance of the skiff floating along within their own port of entry — with him sprawled outwards and looking like a piece of broken driftwood.

It was just a tiny twinge of memory, but it began to form a small amount of something he wasn't fully activating within the cells of his brain-stem. The air smelled heady and the voices he heard before had disappeared. Where had the voices come from just moments ago and why did he feel like he was being cut in half by enormous vines clinging to every part of his Aelven body — pressing down to the very bones, along his flattened spine?

He felt drugged and completely immobile, preventing him from being able to move even a single eyelash. He tried to blink, but that too seemed to have been suspended. All the while, the yelling returned around him; high and dry in the bottom of a the very real Canton skiff that had majikally appeared right out of thin air, with the wayward bones of a Dragonlord Aelf — firmly snared and permanently attached.

CHAPTER THIRTY FIVE

Rescue from the Beast called Vaukknea

When the Selkies started to return to their various points along the coast line of their island home, a select few having already been sated and brimming with new energy, moved lazily ahead of Vallmyallyn towards his home site. They had chosen to update Kashandarhh on his imminent arrival, after the last of the energy surges ebbed, leaving him behind to enjoy the luxury. They had left him voluntarily, to follow through with the very last of the vast energy waves that still pulsated with minute amounts, fluctuating in and out at the lower reef edges that they had always given to those that ruled as their reigning sovereign. It was his customary rite of the elder passage in their ritual energy transference to receive the last fractional bits and pieces of their substantial essence within the tribe, and one that he found no pleasure in this time, as he stayed out with the Auicks, ploughing through the remainder of what the reef world provide for him.

He was worried, and reasonably so. With his daughter home on Selkie soil, it could only mean one thing. And that thing that brought her to his world was not far enough away for even him to hunger for the last bits and pieces that had strayed between the drift-points that the others had let drift by, which he had in times of past sought out and incorporated into his final molecules from the shedding. He needed to wait until the time was right, or he wouldn't have enough strength to help in the fight, but he grew more anxious with each passing wave, and finally, when he had thought it through and the waves had slowed to a more even keel, the Auicks released the last of the larger seed waves as they made their way down to the west side of the Island of Symarr.

He had only abandoned his fix and gone in search of what she needed, when he heard the call to arms, and by the time he arrived, nothing he could have done, hadn't already been tried by others of his family unit. However, that had been sometime after his clutch arrived back in Tryanafie Bay. And it was here that they had found Soren, floating in an antiquated Canton skiff, in the middle of what was once a very clear and peaceful lagoon.

When the alarm call went out, and he heard it above the waves as the Auicks were releasing the seeds from the umbilicus of the feed, he had gone back in due haste to find out what the fuss was all about. What his brethren had found puzzled them at first, as they reached the entrance point and saw that the surface of the lagoon had been covered in the forest flora that extended far beyond where the beach had been located in the past. As it revealed itself to them, and they slid underwater through the channel, they realized that high above them newly formed land had been created along most of the surface area of their lagoon, and when they tried to come up for air only a few patches of open water remained. The land was quickly taking over the remainder of the overhead breathing space.

They quickly changed into their land based forms, and went to investigate. What they discovered upon entry, as the freshwater invaded their saltwater doppelgangers, was anything but normal. As their eyes and lungs adjusted to the air, and their bodies fully charged from the storm waves, they used the new energy that was pulsating through their bodies to run with the last remaining drops of water to the side of the Canton boat.

It seemed that the island residents had a low tolerance for anything not directly related to the Selkie clans that called this piece of rock their home. The flora and fauna that lived alongside Vallmyallyn's home were known for their intolerance of anything not of Watermite kind or its affiliates, but this was going well beyond their defensive strategies than anything they had done in the past.

It was one of the reasons the Selkies as a whole had decided to build their home on this particular piece of majikal property. The island itself had a very strong affiliation for protecting anything that practised in the art of water and earth majiks. Kamera's kind, although strange, were of Witch decent. Both she and Kashha held a certain reverence for the island's protection, through the Witches' code of ethics that her kind had practised throughout their lifelines. It was the island itself which had adopted the pair. Through their rite of passage they were the only three of Tantaris's creatures who had been accepted into the exemption that the Selkie race had included in the bans of their kind, and two of these had always given the island no reason to evoke their exclusion.

So, with the protection of the actual island's entire population in his hands, Vallmyallyn had borrowed their severe restrictions and given his family true assurances that they would never be harmed, if ever they needed a place of refuge while the clan floated in its shedding grounds at certain times of the year. For this to have happened, something must have gone terribly wrong, and since the tribe hadn't been informed of what was at stake, and why their little Witch had returned, it had caused great concern for those who had witnessed the event.

For them, they had no idea that Kashha was no longer within the area their island protected. Furthermore, what had transpired to set the island on its warpath, which changed the very topography of their lagoon's previous land-mass, was still a mystery even to Vaal when he finally did arrive to join the chaos?

As it would have it, the Selkies that did arrive first, swimming under the newly erected carpet of jungle growth, found the density to be where its origins where centered towards the far corner of the bay, and went over to investigate the unusual departure of the original bay's creation. They could see off in the distance, the island flora was heading towards a piece of badly sodden wood, floating just barely above the water-line. Although they didn't know at the time, it would be here that they would discover the Aelf jammed into the far reaches of its lower gunnels.

As they crashed barefoot through the surf outwards into the newly created land-mass, to find the source of the infestation, the vines and branches of every part of jungle life that could fit into its badly creaking wooden shell were filled to the outer planks with extensions of newly formed roots, limbs and leaves, pulsating and groaning as the skiff was in the process of being ripped apart. For some unknown reason (and they weren't talking as of yet,) they had cornered the Aelf called Soren in the middle of the lagoon, in what could best be described as a network of vines that were growing massively larger by the minute, trapping him inside their thickening mass, and not giving him a chance of further escape.

As they moved to investigate the stranger who was being held captive in their bay, every kind of island vine that had taken up residence in the vicinity of the lagoon and then some, had either crawled or moved outwards onto the water and beneath its surface, entwining among each other to form a very strong and fierce matting of newly formed living land. It snaked its way around several large hunks of brain coral and right through the center of the occasional piece of volcanic rock dotting the lagoon floor, as the fish continued to move towards the open ocean in sheer terror of being left without a place to live.

The newly formed land actually pushed itself up and rested from the bottom of the bay to about six inches above the surface of the water. They broke and yanked the matting that was beginning to even find their own feet, as they tried to move towards the stricken Aelf's barely noticeable form in the bottom of the boat. The island had always been known as a living breathing entity, but that had never been tested in as great a capacity as it was on that day. The Selkies could only marvel at its creative capacity, and the land life that was indigenous to their culture base, as it gave them a glimpse into the stewards of that foundational support system.

They were in the process of committing to removing Soren from that living mat of limbs and branches, when Vallmyallyn had returned from the reef. It was unbelievable to even imagine something that could be so thorough in its remedy of an undesirable situation, but Kashha's father had only asked one thing at the sight of it, as he had transformed into his stronger island form.

"Where was Kashandarhh when this happened?" The Selkies who had been removing Soren, had not seen Kashha with the skiff, and had not even successfully removed Soren completely, when Myallyn arrived on scene.

"It would appear she is not in attendance to the Aelf, which might explain the island's reaction to her companion's placement within the matting?" Vaal nodded and joined in to force the stronger reeds apart to extract the stricken Aelf from all the twisted vines that had taken up residence along the upper canopy of the newly formed lagoon's floor.

They were able to actually walk on the strength of its newly formed root system, far out onto the usual crystalline waters, as its structure had combined so forcefully together, that it was actually considered to be new land. It was a shame they would have to remove its mass when they finally could reach Soren's in the skiff, as it was really useful in deterring others from making their way into their turf without detection.

However, what made Vaal really laugh, as they finally fully extracted him from the vines and got him out of the bottom of the skiff, was that the matting simply retracted all on its own like a ring on a coil of sphere line dust, when it was rankled to its breaking point at the end of its Quadramass. In simple terms, to those of you not familiar with a section of line dust pushed to its breaking point, it simply snapped and rewound itself back into the start position, as they stepped away from its retreating form, trying to not get caught in its departure.

This was something they could use in future land distribution of their tiny island's growing hydroponic population; however, if they didn't hurry as the vine continued to retreat back into the jungle world it had originated from, they, along with their reluctant Aelven patient, would eventually be dumped in the water and they would have to swim for it, with the now very heavy carcass of said Aelf that was not participating in the retrieval of his own ass.

It didn't take long for either species to return to shore, and Vaal was quick to hasten his steps as soon as he felt the sand beneath his toes. Unfortunately, nothing was left that could be construed as evidence of Soren's adventure of stupidity. He needed to find his daughter, or at least a clue in the area of the west side of the bay, as to how Soren managed to retrieve the wooden skiff from out of thin air.

How he had lifted himself into its interior, before the vines had been able to reach him and devour the structure in their leafy clutches, was nothing short of a Selkmordian miracle. It must have been dumb luck for these Earthen creatures to not have given his heritage of being an Aelf that belonged to the Earthen tribes any consideration. Especially with something that belonged to the Canton civilization, that for some reason had arrived inside their lagoon without notifying the locals of its arrival. Soren should have easily been able to spot the energy signature it produced when he had been hunted from the shoreline, but why had the island creatures allowed the skiff to be seen, when he was trying frantically to seek something to help him survive their attack?

Their usual format was fought with silence, revealing themselves only after it was too late to run. Another thing that was unbelievably lucky for him was the timing of his kind's return. The only thing that showed anything was actually still alive within the wooden structure, was part of a face starting the process of having the life squeezed out of his very existence, and one frantic blinking eye, moving without the ability to vocalize the silent scream; which had probably been the first thing that the vines had taken away in the stages of covering him up.

How long he had been in this position was anyone's guess. They had been on the reef for more than two full days, all of which had been in the time-shift wave-carrier in between their worlds. For Soren, that could have been all that the island needed to simply wipe the existence of the Aelven male from its memory banks, as well as his arrival with Vaal's daughter Kashha. But Vaal didn't think so; he really thought the island would have consumed everything there was of the still living Aelf by now, if that were the reason for its hunt.

If that had been its plan, it would have left nothing visibly alive that allowed them to even wonder what had become of either one of the two forms that were left on the beach when Vaal returned to the reef. As a matter of fact, the island was capable of erasing the memory completely, of their having had been here at all, if it had deemed it to be dangerous for the Selkies to have contact with them. There had been instances of that happening across the Fey worlds of late, and the island was capable of achieving that easily if that was what it had intended to do.

Meanwhile, back in an Aelf's slightly stoned mind:

In Soren's world; at the moment of the Selkies' arrival, they took over three tarns of their time clocking, to extract his painful very unlucky ass. He had decided they were only stills in his memories, followed by extractions of the dream he had been having in its flotational world of voided space.

Soren had to be knocked out, as his final limbs were removed from the boat with special tools, which could have easily torn the tissues, causing some damage to his soft Aelven eyes. Just before he faded to black, another voice that had been summoned within the world of their Dryad council; a non-resident forest Wildcrafter, was heard arriving close to him.

He had to be pulled from the mainland, after going to visit several colleagues, who had gathered to witness the resent rumblings of volcanic activity along the edges of the Llyach clan's turf. Knowing that the Selkies would be out at sea, and not wanting to participate in the mass exodus, he decided it would be a good time to enjoy time away from his nomadic lifestyle, while living on live energies of the recently active fire-tubes.

Vaal's wife had had many dealings with the Aelves of their tribe, and it was here that they shifted to retrieve their Sage. Soren remembered the whispers as they had tried to extract him out on the mattings, which had drifted in as mostly short dreams. Some he remembered well, while others were just jumbled up thoughts which made him aware of what he was dreaming of in a messed up world of living trees. It was here he saw the open island in all its majesty and although he was spiritually living momentarily in the ether, he watched the process by which they extracted him, as he lay dying on the mat they had committed him to.

In the next appointment, trying to get to the mystery of where Kashha had disappeared to, Vaal had sent one of his warriors to summon Kamera to the island to help with the collection of what they needed to get the Aelf into a position where they could talk to him. They had still been unable to revive him, once the majikal words of the Sage had passed between his lips, and all else they tried had failed miserably. So, against his wish for his mate not to be involved, they had no choice but to summon her to the island.

Back on the mainland, Kamera had been at Kashandarhh's home when the unknown Selkie male had shown up in Kilren, asking where he could find the Witch's mother in attendance. They had no way to release Kashha's Protection Wards to allow him to continue on his way, but Zheckarria of the Kilreneans did send Ganmole in the direction of the energy field that would allow him to find Coutinnea, flying under the movements of her wards because she had been allowed to travel through herself under Kamera's initial direction.

Kamera had been inside the greenhouse that Kashha kept well stocked with vegetables and other difficult to find herbs, watering them with a silver flashing of crystal dust to encourage them to produce the bigger varieties, while she waited for Soren and Kashha to return. Having been so occupied; Stephponias had been the one to spot Tinnea's hawk companion flying towards the barn, where she had been gathering eggs from the ducks that resided on the rails within.

It had been a few days since the pair had left on the shift-point energy field that Kashandarhh manifested to travel to the island of the Selkies, and they had not known truthfully when they would return. Kashha's cottage in the woods gave them a bit of a reprieve, not being affected with the earth rumblings of the Llyach earthquakes. When Stephponias had returned to their village shortly, to let them all know that the Witch was indeed aware of the Dragon situation, he then had shifted back to the entrance point and returned to wait alongside the road while his wife and Kamera moved towards its vibrational rift point to allow him back into their part of the Damonian Woods.

He had waited, while they made their way past the trailhead Coutinnea had first entered, when she arrived at the forest that Kashha had made her home. She felt a little more secure about walking through these woods with Kamera by her side, but Kamera still had to laugh as Coutinnea kept a vigilant eye out for the Tree Morrigan she had assaulted, to make sure it was not still hanging around in the area she first encountered it in. She didn't have the chance to tell her it was not one of Kashha's dangerous sentries, mostly out of respect for her own child, but also one that may in recent months prove to be useful in other respects, with the information needed from the occasional non-coven member. Either way, it had not been spotted, and they had continued on their way.

They would be returning home in another day or two through this same trail head, but that time Kamera would not be joining them as first planned. Mind you, if he hadn't heard anything that needed his attention directly from Llyach, he was truly tempted to stay here until Kashha returned. This was something that only having experienced it once, could you really begin to understand the complexity of the beauty that surrounded the inner wards of an incredibly complicated ecosystem; one that, had he the opportunity to provide assistance to the Witch in the future, he wouldn't hesitate to come back to again, just to absorb the uniqueness of her woods.

He loved the reclusiveness that the Damonian Woods provided to all who entered, allowing them to bask in its unusual energy flow. He would have to talk with Kashha in the future, to see about creating something similar in their own village, which could evidentially provide them with some beneficial properties as well. But, for the mean time it was still awfully strange to see Coutinnea's hawk come flying in over his head of its own accord, without either one of them having sent for it, as the wood he had been splitting echoed its cries to alert him of his arrival.

Kamera heard the wingtips flutter by the window as she moved towards the movement that the hawk had used to displace the air in which to fly through. By the time she had moved down the steps, Coutinnea had passed her a parchment with Vallmyallyn's signature seal on it, which she had retrieved from the silver flask attached to its leg.

She unfolded the document and grew slightly pale, reading it out loud to both of her companions, who had stopped to hear what the missive had to say. While Coutinnea stroked Ganmole, and the bird preened the feathers she had disturbed with her hands, Kamera stopped talking as the words began to sink in. She didn't say another word to the two beings that had stayed to wait, after the final words rolled off the pages. Instead, she seemed to be taken aback by the news, looking slightly worried.

Finally she sighed, letting out the breath she held in, not realizing that the two Llyach Aelves were still waiting for her to give them a clue to its meaning. She turned to each of them and nodded, smiling, giving into her sense of camaraderie; a part of her daughter's fire returned to her eyes, as her two companions watched her closely. Time seemed to be stopped, as each second she spoke, the words that she had read scratched on the Selkie parchment, seemed to almost come to life as they danced and vibrated in her hands.

She glanced down again, taking her eyes off the horizon she had been staring at, and found the parchment beginning to warm her hands. Soon she knew they wouldn't be just dancing, they would be burning all the remnants of the words that had been written, bursting into flame. As a last minute decision, she instead chose to return the packet up into the air, instead of dropping it at her feet where she hastened its demise with majik. It instantly burst into flames, and as it burned without a backward glance at her guests, she returned to Kashha's fire ring, walking right through the ash, as it settled along the ground and disappeared into the soil at their feet.

She planted both feet firmly along the burnt edges of what Kashha had used to call Tansar through the voided space of energy the Damonian Woods used as a protection shield. She cocked her head sideways to hear the wind, and then called forth the words that would allow one of her husband's clan members into the shift, which would grant him entrance into Kashha's hidden world.

This time the skies began to turn an amber gold in colour, sending a tiny whisper of jasmine flowers upwards to float in the solar winds along the invisible wards Kashha had put in place. It was Kamera's own energy additive that was her signature key that Kashha had entered into her personal drift point, so Kamera would be able to enter at will should she have need when Kashha was away. It wasn't used very often, but when it was, it was adequate to move the wards easily and freely when something was needed.

The volatile entrance point that needed to be created to bring forth anything through the divide would not open without having a tiny spit of powdered volcanic ash mixed in with meteor dust from the Hydrous Secular galaxy of planets. Kashha had brought plenty of it and it was pulled into jars in the upper sills of her herb pantry. Kamera sent to retrieve one of them with her mind, while she held the ring of amber fire in place for its count.

When it returned, the wind had just begun to swirl inside the fires edge, as she removed a minute amount from the contents of the jar and threw it into the edges of the flames before sending the jar through the last remaining opening of the protection grid and back into its proper nesting place on the sill.

Things began to change; stretching the molecules sideways and making things move in the direction Kamera would need to enter the ash-ring to sustain the volume she would require to escort the traveller through. Once having the ornately carved jar of Fire-Dust securely settled in place, the specialized sealings on the protection wards would need to be ritually opened without the Llyach Aelves watching her on the outside of the circle.

Kamera threw up one of the hidden ward walls that lay among the outer-edges of the ring, which one could see but not hear through. It gave her the opportunity to follow an old shadow ritual that gave the dust substance without endangering the Witch at the edge, as she entered its molecules towards the hottest parts of the burning flame and lit it on fire.

She focused her words on the rhythm, and not the wording; giving them full substance but not shape. The wording would be after, and that would require perfection without mistakes that would often change the flow without warning. Completing this would engage the atoms to collect into fractions, transferring the combination into its nucleus. She pulled the wall aside before it would be ripped apart by the energy it had sustained, and threw the field of volcanize dust outwards into the rune symbol of sec-ondary fire. That created the opening that she could use as a doorway to pull the Selkie through the barrier that stood at the ring of stones near the entrance of the trailhead, just outside the point of entry.

The brink of transference opened on this side and a single male land creature of Selkie design made his way through the doorway, shaking water droplets the colour of silver stardust from his lean framed body and cleanly sodden face. He didn't even hesitate with Kamera's words that continued without stopping to close the portal, and waited with her hand signals in the enclosure she had created to protect both from the dangers of outside entities following him inside.

Suddenly there was a popping noise, as one little nasty tried to sneak past the wall, and the ring of stabilized fire slightly wavered, and then shot forward, cutting off his progress to enter without invite. It changed him into tiny little particles of neutron caplets which dissolved into hot magma, and dripped down the circle edges into the puddles of falling water already indentured upon the ground.

Kamera watched to make sure it dissolved completely before she contin-ued, then placed hot Barbery Sage leaves from her leather pouch into their mix, transferring their substance into the ring of fire that sizzled with energy then softened with her words, and both Selkie and Witch stepped away from the ring of fire as it went to ground. They only moved about a Flagnard, when Kamera held onto the Selkie's shoulders and pulled him towards her, dropping the final pinch of Salamander Oxenberry Dust into his hands. He rolled it into his fingers, cupping both hands to his lips and blew the dust into the air that surrounded both of them. He smiled at Kamera.

"I am as free as what you thought could be of those not marked by my symbols of life." She smiled as he turned his forearm upwards toward her eyes and she saw the symbols of her husband's tribe transcribed in ink with the Selkie markings of his clan.

"I am grateful that you are indeed who you claim to be, for had you not been he who is the one that I remember, I would have had to use this." Kamera held up the other herb she had taken from her pouch within the circle that was just beginning to take its form within her fingertips.

"As am I," the Selkie said, upon seeing the deadly Monkey Barb that now revealed itself, coming into full view with all its deadly properties pointing in his direction. She released the majikal thread that held it in play, while the male of her husband's clan looked quizzically towards her.

"So, shall we get to our visit of importance, or shall we banter just a wee bit more?" His long eyebrows fluttered in mock teasing, revealing the silken feathers they were attached to, raising above the crest of his upper nostrils. The question had elevated the beautiful eyebrows, pushing them forward from their hidden location above his upper Ethmoid bone, producing something best described as comical elegance. Kamera laughed again.

"This is good to have my family of need once again, please, what can I do to help?" He got to the point, without sugar coating its delivery.

"Your Kashandarhh has been taken, and Myallyn has sent me to bring you back." Kamera waited for a moment in thought, before she spoke.

"She is stronger than any of us, she will survive; it is written. To have me come in-between to begin the font of tracing her molecules would bring many more challenges for your tribe to bear. How can you risk the dangers to have me implement my will on her behalf?"

"It is written that you must find your peace within whatever means available. In doing so, we can shelter our bodies from what will come," the creature said without any outward sign of emotion.

"Then what will be, shall indeed come to pass, but vengeance will be mine as the time approaches to the calling Sea that has taken her." The Selkie smiled softly, as he bowed politely to her, pointing the way.

"I expect no less; now let us be ready to travel."

CHAPTER THIRTY-SIX

Kidnapped by a Mermaid Freak

Kashandarhh woke to find herself alone, somewhere that appeared to be underneath the water, in a huge sunken cavern many miles out at sea. Where it was, she couldn't yet tell, but she was betting it had to be somewhere out between the Ocean of Souls, and the Trench of Talon; by the smell that the sea was producing. It didn't take her long to get her bearings in the darkness that breathed with some form of salty sludge, as it tried to hide the location the creature had brought her down into, through the depths of several fathoms of water that lay between her and the surface air far above.

She felt pain, but not from any injury that she could immediately discern. Instead it was based on the pressure of the ocean depths, which were pressing on her inner ears while she had no ability to release the symptoms as she was dragged beneath. Until she equalized the pressure that was caused by the pressing on her sinuses, she would remain partially unable to contain even the slightest awareness of her whereabouts.

The cave was able to, for some unknown reason, contain most of the pressure that had invaded her skull, and provided some relief from blowing her eardrums wide open and yanking them out by the bone shards. For that, she was thankful. She felt its dankness even before the small beam of light began to glow from the small oval crystal that hung around her neck, revealing the immediate area she had come to be lying in. However, it wasn't able to completely take away every fibre of evidence she needed to formulate an approximation of the actual area of the undersea world she seemed to be surrounded by. But as the telltale stink of the Sea Worm breeding grounds was still slightly detectable in the sea, she knew it had missed certain major aspects of who she actually was, and what she was actually capable of doing.

It left her to feel that the plan had not been well thought out, and that whatever creature had taken her, that was still somewhere off in the dark just out of her sight, was not all there in the final completion of its own mind. The thought made her groan with unnecessary random opinions running rampantly through her head. It hurt for many reasons, none of which were quick or random at the moment. Instead they were about something entirely different, and it was about to dawn on her in the following few seconds. But for now, she needed to clear the pain in her head.

She momentarily tried to swallow, which only seemed to open up another previously undetected wound in her scalp. Annoyed she moved to pinch her nose and blew to relieve the pressure in her sinuses; the blood undeterred, continued to flow. Before her brain could register that she was manacled around her wrists, she found the wound to be nothing more than barnacle abrasions that must have caught on her hair as she was dragged from the beach. Finally, the image caught up with her brain cells, producing the unmistakable imagery of chains.

"Damn it," she whispered, as her hands came downwards out of the dark to land in front of her nose again. "What the flipping bloody hel?" she spoke rather crossly to the sodden walls now also coming into focus around her, as she shook her hands to try and release them. They wouldn't budge, instead the manacles stayed, resting heavily around both wrists and indifferent to one another. She lifted the offending irons towards the dimness of the pendant's light, searching for the other stone she had recently acquired; one that was more important, than her very life.

The low light from the pendant revealed it safely tucked away and still on her person; although slightly colder and mimicking silence, but nonetheless safe from harm. She instantly breathed a sigh of relief only to have it dashed as several layers of heavy shackles could be seen wrapped around her lower body. She bent to find the fastening attached to its locking mechanism, groaned in frustration, as her fingers fumbled with the cold steel, while the sound echoed on through several other rooms that sat somewhere out in the darkness.

She felt their existence, even if she couldn't hear the echo that would have been ringing like a Banshee inside the underwater cave. Well, at least she had that. If push came to shove, at least she had more than one chamber to move around in, when the time came to fight it out. She cursed, sending a flurry of sea bats further away from their underwater roosts to parts unknown, while the light continued to give her the means to pick the lock and give her, her freedom.

Many times she had used a beacon of majikally induced brightness to light the dimmest sections of particular caves she had gone into to retrieve certain herbs that were found in their environments. Though never one that was aggressively alive with another life force still actively seeking to knock her off. For a second in time she thought to extinguish the light, or at least to lessen its direction as it scooted around the cave illuminating things better left unexplored. She thought better of it, and let the light absorb the dank smells giving her something she could renew her senses with, and give her some form of personal grounding that would normally take an infinite amount to time to achieve had the dark claimed her sight, and she was left to go by sounds alone. Her ears began to bleed.....

She needed to get her bearings and find her ground, or everything around her would feed on the feelings of fear that were beginning to arrive from somewhere deep inside her gut. That was strange; fear hadn't been part of her generalized range of feelings of late. She shook her head to clear the thought, and sprayed blood droplets along the walls. That small undertaking brought her back to reality and not some imagined horror that could or could not be real. It momentarily reset itself.

She found the shadow that had tried to filter inside her mind, and removed its roots as fast as it tried to elude her and plant itself among the stem of where her fear molecules had been residing. She grabbed it by its tail and sent it flying, retrieving it alongside something that seemed to have been tampering with her personal protection beacon. She was now fully secure from whatever had tried to implant the silly thread without being able to lock it into position. It scampered away down the darkened corridor where she would not be able to launch a full scale attack on its sentient majikal hide. Damn ears!

Checking to make sure no damage had been done; she was relieved to see that no harm had come to the cells it had been trying to worm itself inside. Her memory was still clear; for that she was thankful. Had it arrived in a foggy haze to re-enact itself from the time she had been snatched off the beach until her finding consciousness as she awoke among the slurry of the sea, it would have taken that fear to another level; one that she was not ready to give in to as of yet.

It was bad enough to remember sharp snapping fangs that would not release their hold, dragging her deeper into the water of the lagoon until she passed out from lack of oxygen, without the added attraction of memory loss suddenly having found itself in her frontal lobe. However, that was all she could claim; for admitting the truth of the situation, she had no memory of what had transpired after her drowning. It was after that time frame that her recollection ended and whatever creature had snatched her from her father's hidden sanctuary and moved her deeper into the open waters outside the bay — thwarting any chance of rescue that her father's kind could have formulated from their sentient piece of Elemental real estate — now was simply absent.

How her body had survived along the path the creature had taken, could only be presented as water-crafting, as anything else would certainly have ended in her demise. So, it would account for another undetected thought that had just joined the forum; this creature must have some knowledge of the dark water spells that had protected her from its death grip. This brought her to another assumption. Who had that kind of majik here in this world of the sea, other than King Manannan?

It hadn't taken more than a moment when the thought came through strong and clear, making her feel rather sick. 'Oh hel no,' she groaned again, with the answer coming into the forefront of her memory, moving simultaneously with another symptom that was about to explode outwards into her brain. The remembrance of the creature's identity had nothing to do with what she discovered was a rather serious headache. It came on without warning, splitting her head like it was a coconut that had just been breached; hurting her from the inside out, coming on relentlessly without her being able to contain it from pressing harder into her mind, and choking off every thought she had ever had from that moment on.

Without warning the catalyst that knocked her to her knees came on as if to thumb its nose in her direction, and the creature's identity came blasting through to the open air of the sea cave, complicating everything just before she lost complete consciousness. She let it come on without examining its creation. It was, after all, something she had no choice in, as she slumped into the position that the rocks had provided, choosing the deeper part of the dark to take over — leaving her helpless and alone, instead of dealing with the memory of what it had to be.

The nitrogen sickness came and went in the next few hours, and she remained at its mercy. There was no way she could filter the gasses that had inexplicably invaded her bloodstream, without letting them run their course. She lay heaving and in extreme pain from the spasms that infiltrated her body from the depths the creature had dragged her to, while all around her the sea cave did its best to release some form of mild sedative to save her life.

It moved along her skin at first, filling every centimeter that her entire body had needed, before it slipped into her blood stream to neutralize the reaction to the nitrogen poisoning. From there it filtered the poisons that had grown to such high levels of toxicity inside her veins, as they openly ran into her heart. This allowed the nitrogen bubbles to pass through each chamber without over stimulating it, and causing her heart to stop. Whatever was part of the chemical slurry of the seaweed she was lying in, had been engineered by nature and utilized by other creatures during their arrival into this undersea domain at various times in the cave's existence. However, none of these creatures had been sentient enough to produce a breath through living lungs like the land dwellers that lived high above on the surface world where Kashha had come from. So who had directed its arrival?

She had no time to question the motive; instead she let the dark move her closer to her death as whoever had engineered the slurry had their hands full with its composition as did its best to save her life. However, she did have luck on her side, in the manifestation of Selkie molecules inside her DNA. Those particles superimposed themselves within the particles of the sea bed, creating a new form of molecular structure that protected her life. Had she been any other creature of the land world that the Mermaid had captured and left to die inside these caverns, her life force would have expired long before the green algae had time to protect her as they infiltrated her pores, and sank her to the depths of her despair.

Now it moved and collected the nitrogen like a slug absorbing its prey, where it produced some form of a protective barrier, thereby neutralizing the nitrogen as it slowly made its way out of her pores and entered the atmosphere of the cave that surrounded her; joining with the rest of the muck at her feet she was lying in. Then, something seemed to drift over her unaffiliated with the cave, as it slowly made its way towards her head. It entered her ears to repair the damage that had been done while she had descended into the depths blowing out her ears, and the last remaining nitrogen molecules too stubborn to leave; then let her sleep.

She came to once again far from her home, or at least her father's home, waking to find the balance that fits inside her own equilibrium covered in seaweed and brine, chained within an inch of her life. Having set that into its proper functioning state, she found herself once again attached to the sides of a rather oddly shaped burrow of some undersea wall, covered in stinking weeds that proved against all odds, to have saved her life. To what end, was still out with the jury on its discovery. As to the identity of the beast, she could hazard a guess it would prove to be none other than the original tetrapoded Witch, of the Ocean of Souls herself.

She had heard whispers of this particular creature she was about to come face to face with, although she was someone not well known in the circles of those that had come into that breed of creature's tides. In fact the creature that had taken Kashandarhh was in fact the one hidden gem that the Sea Witches of the Mermaid tribes had ostracized within their own community. That particular creature had been long gone from their waters for going on a century or more, and most of those still alive today that had originally seen her had long ago forgotten the real reason she had come to be so hated among the water-folk in the first place.

What she had against Kashha was anyone's guess, but that wasn't going to bring Kashha freedom while she remained chained in this horrible darkness, unless she could bring light into the dimness of its interior chambers.

Once again she asked the crystal to do her bidding. Finding the crystal thread still attached to her neck after she had fainted from the pain had been a stroke of luck. It could just as easily have come loose, in those dark hours of pain, and rolled away never to be seen again, lost within the sludge and dripping rocks covered in Goddess knows what.

It quickly lit the interior cave much brighter than it had before, as she fumbled with the garments wrapped tightly in layers around the chain, trying to expose more of the light in her condition. This time the brilliance of its center came out in full, and brought forth things that were probably better left back again in the dark, as the illumination began to broaden her inner-sight into the workings of a very dark mind. However, she had no choice in the matter, and soon would rethink that strategy when the interior wall of where the creature had decided was somewhere she wouldn't be disturbed, had been revealed.

'Shit, this is far beyond bent,' she whispered from deep down inside her mind, trying her best to keep quiet, while all around her lay the trappings of what the old hag had stolen or received in payment from every wayward soul that had wandered into her turf, and fallen victim to her deviousness. 'You are truly one crazy bitch,' she said under her breath, bringing the manacles up to her lips to wipe away a piece of seaweed that still clung to her face. 'What the hel is wrong with your mind, you Mermaid freak? Even at my most vile, I couldn't have begun to think of ways that could compete with this,' she thought. She moved to rectify that now with renewed proficiency, while the chains continued to annoy her.

The air that lay drenched in darkness was tainted with more evil than she had seen in the darkest Sidhe caves, out along the meteor fields of the Gargoyle planet, as it floated above in this dank and dreary world — one that Kashandarhh was sure had never seen the light of day. Its toxicity was not yet tested, but in days to come if she suddenly grew a pair of horns she would at least know where the damn poison had come from.

She looked around to see if there was something that could give her leverage in removing the manacles, but for the most part, she was madder at herself than at anything left to actually blame for the predicament that she now found herself to be in. There really had been no time to protect herself from her sharp claws before the Witch had fragged her from the shoreline. As far as she knew, Soren would be completely helpless after seeing the ruckus she must have caused after being dragged away.

That brought a new unanswered thought into her mind, as she continued to try and unilaterally break free without using her powers. What had happened to Soren when she had disappeared off Selkie soil, and the island had realized she was no longer protecting him? And how long had it taken him to remove himself from the grip of the things that lived under the tree, before he too had been claimed? Too many questions and not enough answers. This was not going to be easy being chained to the wall, and however hard she tried, physical interference was getting her no closer to removing the hardware.

She resorted to majik, and soon after the room was bathed in a new form of light, concentrating on a plan to break through the shackles that chained her, giving new opportunities to further her cause. They snapped, then shattered with a majikal pop, and she threw them against the far wall, retrieving a strange piece of wood that floated upwards towards her from the sudden updraft in the stale air on the farside of the room.

The light from her spell quickly began to dim, just before she saw where the roughened shard had come from, and spied several other pieces of the same material lying heaped together around what appeared to be the remnants of several different varieties of shattered wood. They lay in pieces at the foot of the cavern floor, far away from the main entrance. It looked to be some form of railing used in binding spells that had been broken, and left in disarray from the cave's slimy creatures living in the sludge. Whatever it was, it would do for now, even though it was not going to be strong enough to hurt the Witch if she came for Kashha anytime soon. But it would be sufficient to knock her to her knees, until Kashha could reach for something else in the meantime that would make the Witch stay down; should she come before that find could justify the means, and then she would simply find Kashha's fingers around her damn throat.

The thought made her smile, as she formulated a plan, stepping carefully around the floor of the cave and away from the creatures living in the rubbish at her feet. The rubble seemed to be centered on this particular cave. As she reached another corridor that joined up with a third at the far end, she could see that the floor was smooth and free of what she had left behind. She moved without sound, just in case she would be heard in this almost hollow environment, but she had no need; following her own perceptiveness, she realized through her own senses that the cavern was empty of any other breathing upright life-form, other than her own.

It was in this other corridor that she found the old iron door. At least it looked like a door, sparking away with a strange blue electrical haze coming down the corridor. Once coming within reach of it, she noticed the door was old and looked to be extremely heavy. It had an ornately carved iron ring centered directly in the middle of the door, and along the outer-edges holding it in place, were huge dead bolt hinges, giving her the impression that it would be difficult to move.

However, once she began to move towards it and her body was still out of reach of actually touching its frame, the blue ribbons of energy moved towards her body, migrating like lemmings the moment she reached several marking on the floor. Where had these marking come from; because, they were not present when she first entered the corridor from behind. No, they had simply appeared as if they were hiding from her, and then for some reason decided to show themselves, just as she questioned her intentions.

Before she could jump back and concentrate on the etchings, the blue light reached her without actually touching her skin, grabbed onto her Witch's signature, and ran it down her arms until it reached the palm of her hands. There they stayed, tickling the hair on her skin with the energy flow, as they moved downwards along her finger bones towards the floor. They tripled their speed as she slowed her forward momentum, and pulled themselves out towards the strange etching she had just crossed over. Once they entered the ground, she could see the cobbled stones that made up the floor were set in an old runic pattern. She followed the blue ribbon of light that directed her onward, opening the door without her touching it.

She quietly slipped through the entrance and stepped into a corridor that beckoned her beyond, without a sound. The door began to close even more quietly behind her, bringing with it a fresh breeze of pure air in its wake, replacing the briny smell that had been left in the corridor that assailed her nostrils from the original room where she awoke. The strange blue lights started to disappear under the door, leaving her alone in the darkness, where she stepped back looking at their retreating slivers of phosphorescent light.

A single torch flared up behind her and before she could turn to focus on it, she watched several others flare up alongside it, sending off reflections throughout the corridor that led to somewhere dimly lit beyond. She turned to walk through the narrow causeway that she had been ushered into, moving towards what appeared to be a chamber in the background. Her senses picked up nothing alive within the new room, and she continued to move away from the old cave that had assaulted her senses until they were red and raw.

When she finally reached it, she could see the light reflect off a strange object in the center of the room. She moved towards it, leaving the narrow corridor that she had just moved through. But before she could actually move to inspect the object, as it sparkled and hovered in the center of the room, the corridor she had just exited began to close inwards and disappeared altogether, condensing in on itself and leaving her without any form of retreat. She was left with no way out, and the trap was perfectly set in place.

After cursing her stupidity, she now focused her attention to the interior of the room. The object seemed to reflect some kind of majikal ambiance from everything that surrounded it, while it simply hung in the air floating around the chamber like a balloon hovering above the ground waiting for the tethers to be released. She looked around the room to get a better view of what else might lurk inside, but found nothing but the amberlite bubble that had formed in a capsule around something, trapped inside.

She moved nervously around the chamber, feeling the walls to see if she could detect another way out. There was none; in fact the chamber was mysteriously empty of everything but this strange object; a rather sharp contrast to her previous location. She held up her pendant to catch a better look at the stone sarcophagus that held something large inside its prison walls, and found herself standing face to face with none other than Snickann-Freymyi; one of the most violent Valkyrjurs of all the known Fey worlds.

Kashandarhh quickly stepped back, and tried to move towards the corridor she had just entered, but she remembered it was gone. She remained confined, looking frantically around the room, looking to all the world like an ant caught in a bowl of honey, holding the piece of broken wood up before her, when it might really have been better left to those creatures living in the world of the sludge. She had only to go a few steps, but it was in those few steps backwards that she realized Snickann-Freymyi wasn't moving. At least she didn't appear to be from the angle that Kashha was at, when she had moved to find another exit.

It was eerily odd to be standing in the presence of this renowned creature, that only appeared to those who were dead or dying in the great Fey battles of ancient history. Was that her fate, to be fodder for such a creature as the one that would take her to her final resting place? And what in the dickens was such a dangerous creature as this doing in such a precarious position as to be surrounded by something that prevented her escape, deep in the bowels of some bloody ocean away from her own clan?

She had heard whispers of her mysterious disappearance centuries back, and everyone had thought the creature had simply died and returned to her precious underworld. Others had tried to replace her, but none had acquired the notoriety that Snickann-Freymyi had accumulated in her travels through the various universes she had chosen as her territory. However, she now saw that what the Fey world had mistakenly assumed about her simple demise, was in fact not true. How long she had been held prisoner inside this liquefied piece of amberlite was not apparent, but by looking at her surroundings Kashha could hazard a guess she had been here for a very long time.

She shuddered to think of what would happen should the Valkyrji ever break free of the prison walls that held her firmly embedded inside them. But having seen the remnants of nothing that had been used to free her, the Witch that had taken her must have also made the chamber impregnable to those that might have tried, or for the very least able to detect her from above; so in doing so, she had been left in the perfect piece of prison real-estate in the entire galaxy.

Kashha held her pendant up to gaze back in her direction, while it lit up the chamber in its entirety. Not only did the Valkyrji not move, but everything inside the room was deathly quiet as well. She scanned the chamber and followed the walls with her inner-sight, as they appeared to briefly shadow another energy signature not previously noticed inside the room. She listened for any notable factors, felt nothing more, as if it moved on or had visited the chamber recently and found another space to occupy.

She focused on the walls to see if indeed there was another way out of the room that had also been shielded by whatever lay inside this layer of casing that held some form of protection in its outer field. Nothing came to her senses, so she moved around the creature still not showing any signs of life set within some kind of ancient stone that looked a lot like clear solidified rock the closer she examined it. As soon as she got within range, she could see that the Valkyrji was actually encased in the liquid portion of a very large elestialized quartz Crystal, which had the properties of amberlite mixed in with its minerals.

This particular one the Sea Witch had assimilated and used had the properties of one of the older variations that had been integrated millions of years ago with some form of old sea water; which had been enhydronated within the old formations of crystals as it formed and grew in some ancient seabed. Now, looking at its actual existence here in the underwater cavern, Kashha wondered how the creature was able to actually move it to its new location, far away from the mineral nursery that had given birth to it.

The reality of the complex undertaking of moving it made her wonder whether the stone, and its unusual prisoner, was actually real. She looked around and found a small stone among the many that the ground was covered in, and went to toss it at the Valkyrji in her stone encasement, just in case it was an illusion set up for her entertainment. Before she could chuck it towards the creature, she felt a shimmering vibration from her crystal pendant's proximity to the stone she had just reached for, producing a slight brilliance to the unusually focused light it had been emitting, lighting up the area she now stood in.

She pulled it nearer to the stone to examine it closer, holding it up to the pendant around her neck, and realized that it was part of a bigger chunk of amethyst that had been broken off a fairly substantial formation. The moment she had touched it, the wall where it had broken off from, lit up, illuminating the family of crystals where it had once lived. She took the pendent off her neck and held it higher towards the area around where she was currently standing, and discovered the entire room was actually part of a massive illusion that flickered and reset itself as she moved her pendant along the walls.

All around her, on every part of the wall, the inner workings of the room had been made to appear to be a simple cave of common stone. In fact they were far from common, as Kashha now found out. The moment her pendant's light touched the edges, the whole illusion disintegrated right in front of her eyes, providing her with the actual half geoded sphere of it, including several other minerals that had barnacled themselves to it. They came out of the dark, one section at a time, resetting to their proper locations where they had been hidden from view from anyone that accidentally came across the old stone threshold, unexpectedly.

There were termination points in all different directions, in more than one kind of gemstone, which refracted as the light moved over their shadows. How, she had missed it when first she came though the corridor was simply amazing. It was astounding that anyone would go to that length to trick the eyes. For what reason, was still unknown to her. However, the amount of minerals was mind boggling to witness, as each came out of the darkness and settled alongside others not normally compatible with one another. But here, they seemed to live almost symbiotically with each other, and she spotted pairings of at least four others besides the amethyst, including quartz that was maybe three feet in length and sheeted into different occlusions of the same matrix, hidden deep within the outer reaches of the room.

Alongside the quartz was a beautiful and spectacular Agua Aura, in a turquoise blue, amidst this bright red Ruby Aura, which mainly consisted of the remnants of what was falling all over the floor, as if someone had tried to smash it into smithereens. Kashha was enchanted by the energy that was produced, and marveled at the complexity of how something this beautiful had been achieved. Crystals didn't normally form this way; in fact they didn't cross contaminate with others and grow different minerals inside the same mother matrix without another mother being found within the mix. She looked to see if she was hidden among the little ones that might have grown over or through her stone base. But nothing remained of her if she had been there at their inception, and only the first geoded mother remained amongst them, adopting the entire lot of the orphaned ones into her own matrix.

Amazing! She loved the feeling it was giving off, and wondered if she ever was able to get away, how she could incorporate something this beautiful inside the Damonian Woods where she lived. However, the massive brilliance only stayed her mind momentarily, and she was forced to focus her attention on the situation she was actually in and not that which she had been dragged into without her permission. Had she been any other species, she seriously doubted that she would have been able to snap herself out of the illusion it created, with so much energy running about the room trying to confuse her.

It took a few moments but it finally released her mind from the deception, and she shook what remaining molecules lingered, letting them separate in their majikal confusion to the Fey that remained in place. Whereas, the Valkyrji that remained beside her was not so lucky. Kashha released the stone crystal she held inside her grip with as much muster as she could apply. As to why, she still didn't know. The moment it left her fingers, she had no memory of why she had decided to actually follow through with the action. It was simply done, and with as much malice as she could muster, as if hate was sending signals along her fingertips without her own awareness and needed the action to formulate a reaction. So she threw it as hard as she could at the creature that had such a fierce reputation along the killing fields, and felt just a little bit vindicated for her own coven that had been taken without any regret to the memory it created.

The Amethyst bounced off the stone encasement, not even leaving a crack in the stone surface. She watched it ricochet off the crystal and land across the floor on the other-side of the room. Another series of crystal stone prisms lit up on the far side of the chamber, simulating where the shard had been broken away from, trying to reclaim one of its own as it lay along the gutted floor. Before she could examine the reason that had happened, another movement caught her eyes much closer to her.

Snickann-Freymyi's eyes opened the moment the shard had hit the enclosure, while the minerals lit up on the far side of the room momentarily keeping Kashandarhh unaware. But Kashha had been aware, watching both simultaneously inside a Selkie molecular wave variance; her heart pounding with the unknown, in rhythm to the action she had created. She froze, fixed in place, watching the thing happen in slow motion, not even able to formulate a scream she felt should be coming from somewhere deep down on the inside of her throat. Had she seen what had just happened, or imagined it? She couldn't tell. Her inquisitive mind told her to stay, and with new found resilience threading itself through her veins, she held up the pendant to reflect the light that might just show her it was an illusion.

It wasn't. A fierce pair of eyes looked back at her from within the crystallized tomb; whereas before they had definitely been closed, without showing any signs of life. It took several minutes of holding her breath before Kashha felt that she was safe to move, and even though every bone in her body screamed for her to run, she refused to allow it to frighten her further. Instead she found herself moving closer towards the creature, to inspect the encasement, placing her hands on the smooth edges as the Valkyrji followed her movements with her eyes, unable to move anything more than those eyes within the stony enclosure she had been entombed in.

Kashha regained her composure and realized the Valkyrji couldn't harm her while she was locked inside that crystal. She ignored them, allowing her hands to touch the outside of the material with only her fingertips. The mineral in the gems began to shine and flow with her touch as she felt the smoothness of its surface texture as she traced their outlines.

She went around the entire stone, checking for fractures or imperfections along the flawless stone which accompanied all parts of the genetic makeup of the rocks. Nothing caught her hands; all was smooth and unspoiled from the outside. Strange, Elestial shards had a tendency to be very rough, if not extremely sharp with their flatted almost shale like layers sticking out irregularly in every direction. But this one had none of these that she could feel with her bare hands; in fact it seemed uncommonly flat, like it had been melted down within some Alchemist cooking pot, then molded smooth in the shape of a tear drop.

She took a really good look at the creature inside the stone prison, while cruel eyes followed her every movement, giving her the creeps. She ignored the eyes and focused on several things inside the interior area that had suddenly come to life when she had opened her eyes, seemingly set free. There were liquid bubbles all throughout the inner core, moving as if they had been boiling over an open flame. They constantly shifted around the Valkyrji like they were annoyed at being captured in the vast current locked inside the shard's infrastructure.

How they had become sealed inside was very strange. As she watched them dance with a frenzied kind of downward flow, it became even more dramatic as soon as they reached the bottom, where they could be seen turning themselves over, then swimming belly up to the top of the shard like lunatics. Kashha watched them move around like bubbles, rolling around in a hot cauldron; suddenly changing course midstream and couldn't make up their minds which way they wanted to swim. They did this several times flipping back and forth, as she watched somewhat fascinated, before realizing they were Firecript Water Spits that had been caught or impregnated into the fluid of the gemstone. The creatures were not only trying to escape, they seemed to be extremely agitated at sharing the same prison as the creature caught occupying the same space alongside them.

"How in the world did they get you into here?" Kashha half whispered to the tiny creatures. All of them resided within the liquid world of deep caverns far down in the depths of Tantaris's ocean seabed. Is that where she was? Goddess, she hoped not; she would never be able to make her way to the surface before her lungs exploded from the lack of oxygen, let alone the pressure that was procured at these depths. No wonder her body had gone into nitrogen intoxication, and tried to blow out her eardrums! She reached up and touched her ears remembering they had been injured in the decent. They seemed to be fine now...strange, she could have sworn they were bleeding.

She heard a crawling movement in the far reaches of the cave-like room. She froze, straining her hearing to its capacity. Nothing; maybe they were, still injured. She felt for blood; it came back empty. She carried on her inspection, and the sound returned to her left. There it was again. Was there some kind of animal living in this environment, where it sat watching her every move since she had first wandered in here? Was this what she had picked up when she first entered the room? If so, she braced herself for the arrival of its signature, knowing full well its energy would be picked up by her senses long before its identity arrived. But, she was wrong again; this time as it moved within her line of sight, she groaned in recognition of the creature that had snatched her away from the beach.

She backed up slowly, looking for a place to exit away from the creature. But before she had even a chance to move very far, the creature opened her mouth and Kashha could do nothing but stare transfixed at the horrible mess that stood before her.

"Ain't she a pretty sight, all decked out in her finest?" she drawled, pointing to Snickann with a sneer on her face, as several creatures living in her hair ducked back into the matted mess out of Kashha's sight. Apparently she also hated the Valkyrji.

She waddled into the middle of the room on the other-side of Kashha, sliding her tail around back of her as if to hide its existence. Kashha didn't need to see with her eyes that something was horribly wrong with the beast; she sensed it immediately as the creature strolled into the room from the shadows. Though, true be told, it wasn't so much a stroll; it was more of an awkward shuffle with the tangible obstinacy of one that had lost her sense of direction. She moved about the floor on legs that seemed too big for her body, waddling with the shuffle of one that moves better in water than on land.

It was far from pretty, and far from the beautiful creatures that plied these waterways, moving with grace, hunting the shallows and currents along their kind's hunting grounds. And if that wasn't bad enough, as if the creature suddenly noticed her horrific stare, she tried to hide the legs further, without much success, and almost fell forward in an awkward dance to hide her imperfections from the eyes of her prisoner.

Unfortunately she could do nothing more, as Kashha's eyes betrayed her horror. In defiance to her reaction, the creature lifted herself up and stood on the balls of her feet, doing her best to look the part of some form of majestic jailer as she moved about the uneven floor space that pooled with water. In her wake, several tiny pieces of coral shrimp fell to the floor; she ignored them, and continued to make her way towards Kashandarhh, occasionally using a tail still very much attached and part of the malformed figure she produced in front of Kashha's eyes. It was this tail that Kashha watched her use, like a hand, to carry one of the hapless creatures that had fallen into the pool of water upwards and into her mouth before swallowing it whole and ignoring the screams of others just out of her reach.

The water creature she had first thought was a malformed member of the Mermaid clan stopped and moved her head from side to side, smirking as Kashha, now fully grossed out, held her ground. Whatever this creature had turned into, it was no longer any part of that particular group of Fey she had been born into. As a matter of fact, Kashha could have sworn she had what appeared to be Gargoyle blood in her icy veins. How that had come to happen, mustn't have been easy, and by the look of her you could say that whatever spell she had used, it had backfired in a big way and spat her out slightly uglier than she had entered.

Kashha looked on in disgust and stayed just out of range. She nodded at Kashha's newly found stick, and asked her sarcastically with some form of salty spit drooling down her face.

"So, you planning on bashing me with that little girl, or are you in need of such a thing to keep you upright?" Kashandarhh tried to sound diplomatic, but then again it never was her strong suit. Instead the words that came out sounded more like she was about five or six years old, and barely away from her mother.

"Well now, that depends on you, you hideous piece of sea-tripe! From where I'm standing, you're looking a little worn-out and in need of it more than me." Kashha directed her assessment with absolute clarity at the creature as it first frowned at her rudeness, then laughed heartily at some personal joke, moving in some sort of sideways jig, away from the direct area she might actually try and enforce the threat with.

"Pardon me your highness, didn't know you wanted to dance." She moved in a lopsided sort of tango, which made more of the crustaceans fall to the floor, as she shuffled along with both legs and tail colliding within reach of each other. She danced and sang while Kashandarhh looked on, holding her stick between her and the empty air that stood before them. The old hag, immediately finding herself to be the center of attention, quickly reversed both her direction and speed, showing unusual agility for one not seemingly accustomed to such ability. She was just there at one point, and then somewhere else the next.

"Crap!" shouted Kashha, now spying her alongside the frozen Valkyrji, tapping on the outer wall of its crystallized prison.

"Such a creature as you, sweet thing, should never try to outsmart the one that lives on the outside of your new little kingdom. I might take offense to such a challenge, if indeed one was to try." She turned to look at Kashandarhh, tilting her head sideways with a cruel grin forming on her lips. Then, catching sight of her own image in the mineral's surface, she returned to stare at her own reflection, ignoring Kashha altogether.

She stared momentarily at the surface of the crystal shard where it was at its smoothest. Her hands moved lovingly in a sweet caress, as they moved upwards trying to smooth down curls full of various pieces of things that still squiggled and squirmed in the thickest matts of her brine filled hair. But it was for naught; the entire facial circumference of her head remained in a complete state of disarray, not conforming to what she had tried to achieve. She sighed, stamping her foot.

"Stupid hair, always wants to do, what I don't."

She remained quiet in thought for more than a minute, still picking pieces of green stuff out of her matts, seemingly still entranced with the image looking back at her from the reflection off the stone walls of the Valkyrji's prison, as Kashha had been able to lever herself away from her swaying movements.

She turned to Kashha unexpectedly, and smirked with a satisfied smile as she clapped both hands together, until she saw something that needed to be dealt with. She put all her fingers, one at a time into her mouth slowly, ignoring Kashha's attempts to slowly edge down the wall, and licked their salty coating, tasting her finger nails with her tongue and looking at her with an evil smile.

"You'll never be able to leave my home my little Witchery, so try to be a good little thing, and put the Caorunn Board on the ground." She reached out with the speed of a serpent, knocking aside Kashha's arm in the process, and sent the board flying in the direction of the doorway Kashha had first entered through. The creature tried to grab onto Kashha's neck with the claws of a vice, and ended up finding her wrist instead. Then raking her nails down one side of Kashha's face, drawing blood as she went, letting the pressure take her to her knees she smiled with unmitigated glee.

"Remember dear," she spoke with the acid breath of a Banshee, "you will never get free. Now be a good girl and quit fighting the inevitable." She spoke with such fierceness, winding her fingertips around Kashha's wrist and pulling her into her vice-like grip. But Kashha had dug her nails into the board and held onto a splinter that had been yanked out of it with her fingernails when it had gone flying away, and rolled that splinter closer to the inside of her free hand.

The moment she realized that it was Caorunn wood she had in her hand, something clicked inside her brain at the memory. Caorunn was majikally infused with Rowan Berry, and the properties of its poison were something only a Witch would know. And as it turned out, the hag hadn't realized just which Witch, Kashha really was.

That made Kashandarhh smile, forming a plan that could actually work in her favour. As soon as she was able to move it into position, she yelled in mock pain as she leaned forward to throw the old hag off. Then she reversed her trajectory briefly, bringing the sliver of Caorunn wood forward and stabbing the creature in the other hand she didn't have attached to Kashha's wrist, with all the strength that she could force into her body.

The sliver went right through to the other-side of her wrist and wedged just below the exit point on the far side of the skin and stopped, producing an instantaneous bulge in the back of her hand. The old hag let go of Kashha, and screamed in pain, sucking in great gulps of stale air as she hyperventilated, pulling amethyst dust into her lungs, which sent several limpet crabs scurrying out of her nostrils and down her face into the rags around her throat.

But that was all Kashha needed to get free, and the moment she reached the area where the old Sea Hag had entered, the walls held their place, and she was able to flee. She followed them through blindly, back into the other chamber as fast as she was able to get her limbs moving again, while the old monster yelled obscenities at her from the crystallized cave until she was mad with pain and blinded by the blood that poured out of her eyes from the poisonous effects of the old Caorunn branch.

Kashha used that time to run recklessly and without fear into chambers she had not previously seen when first she had entered the geoded cavern. Her sight was limited but her senses were sharp in the darkness. She had spent time in caves much deeper in the old worlds of the Humans when she had been in the midst of her schooling years. This one bore an uncanny resemblance to one of those in its structure and proximity to the ocean, she remembered. So, given time and a lot of headway, she might just be able to find one of the old airshafts that gave them the ability to breathe in this horrible nest that the hag had taken her into.

"Remember, little Witch...you have to sleep sometime, and then all bets are fragging off. I'll cook your skin black, and suck on your old bones until there's nothing left on your old skeleton and you beg me to kill you!" she screamed at Kashha's retreating form, becoming unintelligible as she howled in pain, sending echoes of her cursing to reverberate through the tunnel system of other caves that followed the sound wave, and tucked it-self into their rocks.

The Sea Witch tried to suck the venom out of her very badly swollen wrist, where the Caorunn poison had entered her bloodstream, while a deepening black streak moved up her arm. She howled with rage, and pulled at the limpet crabs still nestled around her throat and threw them across the room. They flattened themselves on the wall when they hit, deflating airbags that had filled as they whistled through the air, and then slid down the sharpened points of gemstones and disappeared into several cracks along the floor, licking their wounds.

Kashha sped through the darkness the best that she could, stumbling as she went like a blind mouse — forcing herself to extinguish the light source around her neck, as she moved along the stone corridors towards other chambers and safety. With her pendant now securely tucked away inside her cloak, she shivered somewhat, still hearing the screams of "Bitch, bitch, freaken little bitch..." over and over again, as they echoed through each of the caverns and beyond, somewhere off in the far distance.

She could use her inner-senses now without fear of detection — literally breathing new life to the surrounding walls, as she moved within the underground cavern of some lost and abandoned cave system, deep inside the ocean from wherever this creature had taken her to.

There were many things that she in another circumstance, would have found very interesting to stop and research further, but she couldn't take the time to explore her surroundings as of yet. She was still trying to put distance between her and the hag who would eventually get over the injury and be on the warpath, putting her life in jeopardy. Instead she could only take note of all that passed, as she scuttled around several obstacles and carried on through the passing cavern walls, listening for any form of pursuit. For the time being she was alone, but that could change at a moment's notice now that she was thoroughly pissed due to the injury Kashha had dealt to her.

Time was of the essence as she carried on in flight, moving deeper into the depths of the nest site she had created out of things others had no use for. But Kashha also knew she was not alone with this creature. No, the Valkyrji was still up there somewhere behind her, and if all else failed she would find the means to let her go, out of spite for the old hag that had almost tried to kill her.

Then she felt something odd, as the skin around the area that had been covered in the odd tattoo on her arm began to get warm. It came on suddenly, without reason. She watched an image form in her head, producing a slightly better view of things than it had previously ever shown her before. Somewhere out there, deep in another part of the bowels of this place, she could just begin to feel the threads of the image she had seen, and if she refused its entry it would surely have forced the issue further.

She watched it form, showing the exact location of where it wanted her to be, and if she hadn't seen it for herself, she would have missed the entrance way easily in the dark and passed it by. Upon arriving, as she headed towards the hidden area shown to her, it proved to be much deeper in the depths down the tunnel off to her right. As she squatted, squeezing her form through the narrow slit in the wall, she realized that she had moved into another cave that was smaller and darker than the others she had just ran through. However, it was big enough to house her and several others if the need arose, showing the trappings of a much earlier time when something else had made its home here.

She held up the crystal she had activated once again and saw the floors had stone tiles with very strange markings on them — which upon following the pattern, soon all joined up in a circle in the center of the tiny room. She wondered how anyone had ever survived down here in a place so far removed from the surface world above. However, it soon became very apparent the further in she walked — this was no place born to Tantaris, as the region explicitly began to look very familiar to another place she had once visited on the planet Earth.

'Ah sweetheart, what in the ancestors have they done to you,' she whispered to the stone walls as they blended into a carved indent that flowed downward under the crest of a bird shaped deity — with the tell-tail symbol of a Mauntrated half-moon crest that lay on her breast. Around the outer-walls the markings looked almost nomadic in origin, with Ruinetic images marked in faded ochre. The markings were definitely from the old city of Crete, but something shadowed their origins that smelled suspiciously of Spice. The only city of Earth she had seen that filled her senses with the smell of spice was Petra, and that was far removed from any of the Fey colonies that resided here on the opposite side of that particular area of space.

Finding new things was something of a specialty for Kashandarhh; at least it was up to the time she fell into it. It never seemed to fail that no matter where she was, or how much danger she was in, things seem to expand out of the woodwork to attract her attention and drag her in. She tried to shake the need to investigate further, choosing instead to keep moving with the sound of the Sea Witch still not fully out of ear shot yet. She made a mental note of the proximity of where she was in relation to her surroundings, and started to back away out of the hidden chamber and carry on down the back passage.

It was here, before she had exited the chamber that a gold piece of metal caught her eye among the dust that had settled in the room. It appeared to be almost cylindrical in shape and had the markings of an old Human King etched on its surface. She held it up to her pendant to see its features, but it was way too dark for her light to be able to make out any more of the distinguishable marks on its surface.

However, it was plain as the nose on her face that it was of Human origins. She had herself spent time off world in the past hundred or so years, and knew its smell fairly well. However, how does an old Human coin reach the oceans of a fairly large Fey planet, thousands of light years away from the Milky Way galaxy? The Fey collected many things in times of need, but most of those things didn't include what would be considered currency. They didn't use Human currency here on the Fey worlds. Instead, she wondered if maybe it had at one time another important use for someone down here in this world of hidden things.

She put it in the leather pouch, deciding to keep it until she could inspect it further, and tucked it around her neck with the other things she carried with her. It held many things that were emotionally viable in the situation that she now found herself to be in. It would not be easy to forget what had happened to her, but there were ways that she knew of to protect her mind, should it become unbearable to sustain her in the coming days.

Her eyes began to feel tired in the semi-dark, and her head had been pounding for the better part of an hour, where the Witch had raked her in the head with her claws. She could not waste any more time staying here. She was already starting to stumble from her ordeal of the capture and further imprisonment. She didn't know how long she had been unconscious when the nitrogen molecules had claimed her before, but her mind told her that she needed to find some sort of shelter that would protect her should she become too tired to stay awake. She wished the old cave was closer to somewhere she could feel safe, for there were many things inside that she could have been able to spend time with.

So, she kept moving and stumbling along in the dark, with a beacon that was beginning to lose its majik, as she moved into another part of the system of caverns that had been made her prison for the time being; not yet aware of what was waiting for her down in the darkened system of tunnels ahead.

Back alongside the Valkyrji's stone enclosure, the Sea Witch groaned, softly licking badly swollen fingers affected by the Caorunn wood Kashha had successfully stuck into the backside of her wrist. She was starting to hate the wicked little creature, and was considering eating her instead of following the much anticipated plans she had for her.

Evidently she had a spy in the works, and someone had deceived her in her battle to gain the upper hand in this world of another Queen's kingdom. She would be having words with the creature that helped her maintain these tunnels, next time she summoned it, regardless of whether it knew anything or not. She smiled wickedly. She liked to make things squirm. She coughed, sending a flurry of activity away from her again.

"Oh for goodness sake, leave me alone, the lot of you," she screamed at the retreating backs of creatures that had found the light, and come forward to bask in its glory. For now, she was too distracted to think, and needed to get this damn thing out of her skin, before she could justify killing the deceptive beast.

She settled down to remove the chunk of wood that was wreaking havoc with her nervous system, which remained stuck inside the back of her wrist. It hung there; thumbing its nose at her while it settled in for a nice long slumber inside her skin. She needed to get it out before it got it in its little head that she was unable to do so. She had about five breaths of a starfish gaggle to find something that could touch it and pull it out, before it became part of her. It had already begun to find the nerve endings which could create a caustic reaction to their running lines, stinging everything around the wound that would start to move its poison out along her upper arm. If that happened she would be dead before she had time to make her next meal.

Something shifted inside her mind, making its way into her brain. That might just work, she thought, moving once again towards the enhydroed crystal; the Valkyrji followed her with her eyes. She ignored the stare, concentrating on balancing herself so she could place her hand within the gateway entrance point to the crystal's mainframe. She knew the place well, and had used it for other things; there was a chance that it would do the same for her.

It was an area that had appeared when she first brought the creature down here. Without knowing the reason why, it had just suddenly broke free of the solid formation. Crystal bridges had healing powers if you used them right, and she had no time to discover the true agenda to its arrival. Instead, she had played cat and mouse with its shadow, and tortured those smaller inconsequential creatures that she cared little for, with its opening maw. She had watched them squirm, as the crystal's powers had either made them whole, or killed them outright.

She hadn't known that the healing properties the crystal used were directly linked to this particular opening, and she had no time to adjust the strength she would require to help her with its properties. Instead she used the edges for another reason and one never intended for the purpose. Nonetheless, for now it would have to do, as she picked around the loose edges of a particularly sharper variety — with a protruding edge and used the surface of the crystal like an extension of her fingers to touch the edge of the sliver of Caorunn — trying to use the whetted minerals to pick the annoyance from her skin. Unfortunately, she misjudged the curvature of the opening, and found herself actually placing the skin of her wrist against its sides, which resulted in another condition she had not first considered. The searing pain that resulted in neutralizing the Caorunn core seemed to dull the pain for the time being, making her look up. She found herself directly in front of Snickann's face, which seemed to have changed.

That had never happened before. How was it even possible, when she was completely imbedded inside the formation? Whatever the reason, she had no time to think about it, as the Water Spits began to move frantically around the inner chamber, causing her to quicken her pace. Instead, she focused on the sides of the sliver, trying desperately to pull it free. She had little time to accomplish that process; if it was not removed by nightfall, she would not be able to stand its poison infecting her body.

She shifted sideways, trying to engage over stretched legs that would not always do as instructed. Each time she moved forward, to lever herself into position to yank the damn sliver out, she forced it further inside her skin.

"Dammit," she cursed, bloody land creatures were a strange lot, and one that she had not grown overly used to even with these damn useless legs she had received from birth. Back when she was still a squidling, you would have thought someone would have found a way to fix her appearance, while there had still been time. But no, they had simply ignored it and thrown her young body out into the tidal rift, hoping some Sea Worm would have eaten her for a meal and they wouldn't have to. She had survived by the skin of her tail and they all had been horrified when she had appeared some years later, challenging the sovereign for rights to her throne.

They had all laughed at her and she had been banished from their feeding grounds instead of administering the disciplinary Whenshi for allowing their Queen to produce such a monstrosity. She should have killed the matriarch of the Mermaid clan outright when she had been old enough, for allowing her to survive with such pain. She laughed in her lunacy. 'Oh right, she already had. Silly me, I'd forgotten that lovely bit of nostalgia, with all this freaking mess, didn't I?' she mused. Then...

"Does anyone hear that insistent clanging?" she screamed at the walls. "Whoever you are, could you shut it awhile and let me concentrate." She continued to mutter away to herself.

She continued to drone on as the poison unrelentingly ignored her, choosing instead to invade her body. There would come a day very soon, when she would seriously give some thought to having the current ruling Sea Queen remove these ridiculous appendages; at least the ones that proved to be of no use. But she needed something to steal to sweeten up the deal; as of yet the derelict old beast had declined all her recent offers.

With that drifting through her mind; she looked at the Valkyrji and noticed that her eyes once again had moved. An odd sense of hatred seemed to fill her senses to the core. It had been more than a century that she had been able to keep the Valkyrji hidden from prying eyes in the depths of this watery world of hers, and Snickann had remained closely guarded and completely as she was from the moment she had been captured. Whatever had changed, she didn't have the time to ponder its execution. The pain tore her away from the solution, and began to pull itself into the deeper depths of her despair.

For so long now, she had been the keeper of the hidden things that others dreamed and paid a high price to be eliminated from their lives. Had she waited too long in wondering why she had been chosen? She never asked questions as to the morbidity of their choices made in the dead of night. But she was always able to manifest their desires within a fortnight of the dream arriving and becoming energy that passed into her line of senses. It never mattered if they changed the dream, it was all the same thought pattern to her. All that needed to be executed was the hatching of a veritable plan that would get her the inevitable prize that she was always able to achieve in the end.

Something started to drift into her mind. But it quickly left without leaving a thread for her to pick up; the pain continued to go uncontrolled.

This time it came back without leaving as the crystal minerals touched her skin. It made perfect sense. Now all she needed was the Witch within her grasp, to execute another silence for the voice that shouted loudly in her head. She needed to concentrate harder, if the plan was to work. She reached towards another of the ruby auras that remained within the geode's

matrix, and ripped its roots off the wall, crumbling part of another structure that followed as the shard came loose. She held it up to the Valkyrji
prison and shoved it into its apex to protect herself from the violence that
would occur once the ritual began.

She had need of the Valkyrji aggression; it was one of the special things
about this particular find that had been gloriously unexpected. When the
thought process of that wandering dream came across her in the dead of
night all those long arns ago, she had almost lost her mind. To have had
such luck that someone wanted this particular Valkyrji gone, and that she
proved to be available for the hunt, was a perfect marriage for her not kill
the creature, as she had done to others in the past.

With pleasure comes pain, and that was accomplished by finding the
multitude of caverns that were down here, far from where others of her
kind would search for the creature when it disappeared off their radar. For
this she brought in a Selmathen that she had found wounded in the old
city of Kashhahaeer, close to the Selkie Island on which she had located
Kashandarhh. Upon healing its wounds, she had forced its energy vibrations to knock the Valkyrji to her knees, and at that time she was able to
capture her prey. She then removed the Selmathen to its natural demise.

She worked hard in the next few months to devise the perfect plan; one
that would find a way to bring Snickann here unconscious in the depths
of her little nest, while her kind continued their search of her old haunts.
Moving her at the time of her capture would have proved to be a mistake,
one that she daren't think of trying with so many creatures seeking her
signature link. Even with the Selmathen majik, a molecular tracing of her
particulates would have eventually been found. Instead, she linked her own
signature with that of the Valkyrji and used it to stack one on top of the
other to mask her whereabouts.

When the search had been scaled down, she dragged her backwards
into the water, sinking her inside one of her other finds she had received
as payment which had stood full of bones from another hapless creature:
That one had taken only a moment to rip from its interior walls and fling
aside, as she took the drugged Valkyrji from its world, and replaced the
seal with Snickann inside. What she hadn't seen was the rail made out of
Caorunn wood that had been wrapped around the bones from something

the thing had carried with it. When she had removed the bones from the interior cell, the damn wood had been exposed, causing her appendages to be rendered useless when she moved between land and sea. This unnatural occurrence had been her payment for taking the creature without considering the repercussions. Unfortunately, it was a side-effect that couldn't be reversed, and the karma had been dealt to her with the harshest of payments one could have expected from such a deed.

She had tripped on it accidentally, when it first appeared on that day long ago; payment probably received for something she had done and hadn't remembered. Much to her annoyance, it was a mystery that hadn't as of yet been solved, and she had done her best to smash it into smithereens to destroy the majik that still had a determined effect on making her horribly sick.

When that didn't work, she tried to lug it out, and only found herself even more angry, as the wood became almost volatile and tried to haul off and kill her outright. She finally conceded, by dragging a very strange creature into the mix that had inexplicably arrived in the caverns on the day of the move. It had taken more time to control its mind than she had liked, to the point of getting it to pull the wood to the far side of the room, to be as far away from her movements around the natural cave as she could and simply left it there. However, for some damn reason the creature remained and continued to harass her day, after day, until she was able to come up with a ritual to control its movements.

Mind you, at that time she had no control over how far the creature she had summoned had thrown the rail of Caorunn, but it was out there along the edge of the cave far removed from where her tail would come into contact with it, and had been for going on a thousand turns of the Mauntra that burned brightly high up on the surface world above. It coming back and metaphorically biting her in the so called ass, brought these memories to the forefront and she was not necessarily happy to once again relive them.

She concentrated on trying to get that damn sliver out of her body now, pressing it firmly against the sides of the crystal prism her death-dealer now called home. Why now, of all the centuries she had lived and collected her menagerie, had it come back to annoy her? She should have done something about it years ago, but she had done to it, as she had done to so many other things inside this cavern — she simply ignored it. That was proving to be a pain in the ass.

Damn land Witch, she couldn't even enjoy her newest acquisition. She hadn't even taken the time to find out what she was, and whether her unusual breeding was a new found species or a one off. In the days to come, she had decided, she had time to find that out. But if this was any example of what she was going to be presented with, in future she had better take precautions. It had been far easier when the Valkyrji had arrived. She had even upped the meanest in her everyday hunting practices, now that she was able to acquire her permanently inside the caverns with her, so she could use Snickann's energy at will to make her wicked and morbid fascinations into reality. She wondered what would be the new found acquisition the Witch would bring with her. Maybe this time luck would shine on her and things would turn around.

She licked her lips, cursing away, trying to get the poison off her tongue where she had tried to pull the sliver out with her teeth. Obviously things had not begun to change quite yet. How had this gone so wrong? Her mouth had begun to go numb. It should have been nothing more than a simple task to kidnap the creature off the Selkie beach. But no; she started to stumble with her words, sounding almost like she had a lisp; something always went wrong of late. She banged her head up against the elestial crystal walls, ignoring the evil inside, wondered how long the Karmatic repercussions had left to play out.

She was starting to make mistakes on even the simplest of things. She was, after all, everything her kind taught her to be. Except for one thing, she had... ah right, these freaking appendages called...legs, which had suddenly decided not to move the way the others used theirs. No wonder she wasn't allowed to stay in the old city of her birth and swim the waters that their kind ruled in that vicinity. It made her angry to think that she had been ostracized because of this.

Frustrated at waiting for the Aura crystal to do its work, she decided to give it a little push. She turned quickly, tripped on her tail, and screamed. Something higher pitched and much more unintelligible came out of her lips than she had anticipated; the scream carried on echoing through the chambers, throughout the cave system down the corridors.

It broke through walls and flowed across ceiling as it reached another of the caves where Kashandarhh had just arrived, and echoed through its interior like a Banshee. Kashha covered her ears and hurried; she still wasn't far enough away by the sounds of it. She worried that nothing within the caves would be far enough to find refuge for the night. Kashha knew she needed to move faster. She moved without much thought to her surroundings, ignoring several glyphs that were carved along the passageway walls; doing her best to get as far away as she could from the original cavern and that horrendous screech, still hunting her every move.

Back in the original underwater cave, something floated inward from the ocean floor, moving upward out of the sea bed into the cavern where the old Sea Witch was now squatting on her tail. She had started the summoning without clearing a pathway from that which was slowly beginning to hunt. With no direction in its request to arrive, the forgotten summoning rite to protect those that had started the ritual calling was immediately noted.

It slithered and folded its huge long leathery body into the form it suited for what was needed to make it into the structure it was pulled towards. Underwater slime oozed from its body, coating the floor as it moved towards the room that had called it into being. Its entrance formally begun was met with a clapping of appendages that looked more like the arms of a tree trunk than a Sea Witch and her deformity, as the Mermaid was still in the process of removing the offending sliver. She greeted the thing with a sideways smile, and dismissed it towards the area it would be able to rest in, while she completed the last of the preparations to the cause of its arrival.

She forgot that she had originally called it forth, and had begun the preparations for another entirely different situation; one that required the sliver to be underneath the heels of a rock, smashed into the stone floor. The beast continued on by and slithered sideways towards its nest box, stopping for just a moment at the energy signatures that were swimming alongside the imprisoned Valkyrji. The Water Spits moved towards the outer-edges of their containment field, pressing little faces up to the mineral walls. The creature simply stared at the Spits unblinking, before moving off as instructed, leaving them to move about madly trying to find any area that would allow them to follow. Their search would be in vain, for nothing remained of the original structure where they had first been tricked inside. Tiny little cries of sorrow wouldn't be heard by its ears. They never had, in all these long years.

It turned quickly away as emotions came to the edges of its mind, and it was careful of exposing the truth of what she felt. It had always been this way, and true to form she was able to keep things in check before she betrayed evidence of its arrival. But something had changed, there could be no doubt, and she had felt its arrival the moment she rematerialized inside these briny corridors, where another of much more strength than what she was given to believe, stared back at her. She followed the stare and briefly paused, finding what she wanted among the spits imprisoned alongside her; the nest box forgotten.

This time she had heard them echo through the chamber sending out tiny pitiful cries along the air currents of the cave, as the creature was beginning to make her way to the area she was always safe in, away from the Mermaid's rituals on the far side of the protection field. It was the first time since the Water Spits had been taken and the Valkyrji had been imprisoned that those voices had come across as clear as rain. She turned and stared at the one who had called her briefly, acknowledging this gift, and then advanced towards the shard, ignoring Shalimar Ridiculous's frantic humming to encourage her elsewhere.

The creature known as an Octtipede would not be fooled twice; the Mermaid could not control her any longer, the Valkyrji had called her home. It brought on a fiercer determination and another side previously unknown to the Mermaid. Her species were hermaphrodites, or chameleonatonic in nature. This meant she was able to change from one sex to another immediately, at will, without warning. Her male side turned, and then started to curl around the stone escarpment, disobeying Shalimar's commands. This was something the creature had not shown to the Mermaid in all these years, and her body found the appropriate colour that was associated with her male counterpart. She became the he. The male version of this creature, which the Mermaid had not known about, finalized what was needed with a single touch of the stone and arrived in all its glory.

It was here the whispers of the Valkyrji had been at their strongest, and where he received the direction with the final transference of the transformational core offerings that Snickann would give to it, breaking the ritual that had called him forth. Their Spits had directed him to that opening; the moment Snickann had been able to give them their voices back.

His true form, the Pyriticle Scapolite Octtipede, twisted and curled around the center piece, bending the sponginess of his outer lining inward and through several layers of doorway crystals that Shalimar had not previously seen. His soft larva skin split into the husk of his outer shell's density and, emerging from the inside, he slid into this species that belonged to none other than Snickann herself.

Shalimar had forgotten to extinguish the mantle that formed the outer casing on the gateway crystal. In doing so, she had unleashed the very creature that could not only harm the Witch who ran, but could very well harm her as well. Quickly she threw up a half circle with a flat edge that wound itself around the wall that she had crawled towards, and placed her back up against it, trying to repair what he had weakened. The Octtipede stopped, and hissed; sniffing the air he simply just stood there swaying back and forth in the room looking at her.

Shalimar reached into her pockets and retrieved a light stick lighting its flux. She began to flick Sulphur and sea salt around the perimeter as she moved to protect herself in fire. It exploded into flame, as the Octtipede shied away briefly from the flare up, and then seemed to be transfixed by its fiery dance, bobbing up and down as the intensity flowed through the air.

She began the ritual of intent she had demanded the beast to attend to in this realm before it had tried to defy her. The creature stayed transfixed waiting, unable to move more than a few inches from his original position. Time might be slowed, but the Mermaid would only be able to hold him for a short time. He waited while the words came quickly; slightly unattached out of her mouth. He grinned with their hollow meaning, pausing only briefly while his powers recharged.

"The wind will shift and the bane shall howl, give unto us thy Selkie fowl.

Half of Witch and half of moon, rendered clean by ancient rune.
Water wet upon the sea, stop her movement away from me.
Bring the surge and bring it fast, lock her down and make it last.
Send the eight and cross the floor, up the wall and guard the door.
Nothing passes, nothing moves, so mote the reason and the mood.

Find her quickly, find her now, before she escapes," she looked at the Octtipede and made one last unexplained mistake, *"you sodden COW!"*

She reacted to the Octtipede continuing to stand in the same place, without moving off as instructed. "NOW GO, YOU STUPID CREATURE!" She waved him off, her last word stuck on her lips in disgust. It had been thrown in as a last resort, she being unable to fathom the emotions of anything not related to her. She held her fingertips up to her mouth, looking at the blackened tips absolutely in denial of anything that could go wrong in her assumption that what she said was what would happen.

Instead she continued to fuss with her fingers, trying to get the swelling down to a more realistic tolerance. She wasn't watching the creature as he rose up, forming something out of nightmares as he grew behind her and stood fully erect, brushing the Stalactites of Flame Aura Crystallites with the top of his head. They briefly ignited.

She had never completed any of her ritual compressions; having done small lower caliber spells that never quite had the punch that this one had twisted itself into. Her past conjuring's had always manifested nothing that would create dangerous amplifications for herself, so it never occurred to her that this would be anything different than her usual weirdness. She continued to be unaware and picked at her nails, turning her back on what should have been gone from the room.

She had at one time a single small Imp she had tricked into helping her with her spells in the past, and didn't really do anything for herself, as a rule. This was a new thing to have to function bodily, all on her own, and she hadn't the knowledge that she could admit to herself, of how things were supposed to be done.

When the Imp had been killed; after she misplaced another ritual step and threw him through the heart of a Starfire energy burst; it made her laugh when it blew up like exploding glass. She now hiccupped, sending a few shrimp shells out her nose, hastening its birth of inception inside her brain, and giggled, picking several other crustaceans that had been crawling across the floor with the memory. Having others do her bidding was far easier than dragging her deformed body through the whole process to accomplish the deeds alone.

She had to admit she was perfectly normal; everyone else who had been anyone within the employ of the sea Queen's court was expected to have someone do their bidding, and she was no different than them. No, she was far better; she giggled thinking what the Valkyrji would do with that information, as soon as her realm realized it was she that had caught their most prized felon.

Something behind her flickered along the ground and caught her attention when she took her fingers and brushed them off along slimy skirts made of barnacles. She changed the filters on her eyelids briefly to see why things seemed to be starting to wallow. This time something had changed; she saw it again as it moved around her and to the left. The moment it occurred to her that something was not as it should be, the circle below that she was now standing on sputtered: She had forgotten to release its image. She stepped away from the inner-rings and waved her hand, releasing its structure, satisfied that was all it had been.

She couldn't have been more wrong. And, as she gazed up from the outside of her protection rings, she was met face to face with an image that could turn your blood cold. She looked up meeting it, and froze. The Octtipede had not left. As a matter of fact, it had been rather silent in its final hunt. Now, with the circle that had protected her halfway gone, she could hear the small rumble beneath its breast bone vibrate into the outside hissing growl that these creatures emitted before they strike.

Then, with their outer legs they surround you in a vice-like grip and squeeze the life out of every inch of your lungs, and rip you limb from limb. She didn't have time to gulp in the stagnant air that remained in the room after the ritual fires became extinguished, and the rings fizzled into nothing at her feet. It moved with lightning speed that moved the air in the room; striking down her face from tip to tail, and putting her visual cortex into the next world of the now very, very, dead.

Kashha heard the deathly scream from the very air that shifted inside the rock strewn cavern which she had just entered to find some protection. The blood curdling scream bounced off several walls inside, and had only just started to follow its way around a second time when it was suddenly, inexplicably, cut short.

Sensing now the sheer volume of the slaughter that lay bare in all its intensity within the stone sarcophagi room that held a very alive but trapped living form of Snickann, sent shivers down her spine. Her senses told her to find somewhere small to hide, as an energy field flowed from one chamber to another like a pyroclastic flow with parts of the Sea Witch spewing forth like puss all through the air.

It moved quickly from one chamber to another, as she held her breath until it passed, spewing pieces of the old hag along the edges of the ceiling and walls. They stuck and wedged themselves along the sharpened edges until there was nothing of her left.

Inside the stone sarcophagus, if one had looked they would have seen a smile of satisfaction form within the liquid environment; one that housed the still but breathing silhouette of a killer. Even trapped, she had been able to call into being those that still followed her thought patterns. She had seen to that by other means not understood by that fool of a Mermaid. Their instructions would come via through sources other than her own voice. But either way her voice would come through in the end across the void, defeating anything that tried to prevent her from seeing to the demise of one that thought she could hold her within the stone for as long as she had, and live. Silly creature; vanity had its risks. It had been only a matter of time before she would have found a way to get her back. How could she not have known that? Well it was done; now, for her release.

That might require a bit of time to expedite. Needless to say, someway with the time-shift resistance, there would be allowances for that crack in time she would need, and a hungrier creature than what she had would be required in its formulation.

Pyriticle Scapolite Octtipede proceeded towards the crystal host; winding around his central portion and making its warm surface the resting place of his head. With tail tucked around the Valkyrji and all of his many legs folded around the stone's termination points, he rested to digest the spinney bone matter that he had just consumed. With a meal like this, it was going to be a bit of a wait before he could move once again. He transformed again and became the female of his kind, protecting those it cherished inside the stone.

Kashha on the other-hand, continued to move until she found a cave not filled with any of the scent of the Sea Witch's destruction. When she found sleep, she did so with knowledge she would be safe for the time being. Before she actually lost consciousness, she placed a circle around her body and sealed it with two salt lines she had scraped off a wall from the tops of the stones she was currently resting on, and then laid down against the salty floor that still reeked of the briny mineral the cave consisted of.

CHAPTER THIRTY-SEVEN

The Gift

The chances of her father following her into her dream had a probability factor of zero. Yet here he was walking through the interior of the room that Sibrey believed she had awoken in. There could only be one reason for his arrival, she thought quickly, still wiping the sleep away from her eyes. She supposed she must still be in that half-sleep world where lucid dreams lay; taking the previous wish and transposing it onto her current thoughts. She had, after all, wished he would come to find her and take her back home again in the previous summons. So when she spotted the image from the bed, when first she opened her eyes after a very long and productive sleep — that is what she had envisioned.

"Go away, you're not here; let me be," she yawned, moving to wake herself up fully, only to find the image remained as she wiped the sleep from her eyes. His silhouette stayed unchanged and wavered very little. In fact, the image of her father only got clearer as he advanced into the room, presenting itself as not a dream at all, where a dream would have grown foggier and disappeared altogether.

"Father, is that really you?" she asked wistfully, reaching out and hoping he wouldn't disappear in a cloud of dream dust.

"I think you will find that this indeed is who I am," he said, smiling with the pronunciation on the word 'indeed.' Sibrey immediately sat straight up in bed, now wide awake, letting the molecules of sleep instantly dissolve into that wakefulness. This was not the first time she had dreamed someone was talking to her, only to discover that her own self was passing through her and the two would leave her in her room alone again.

But this time it felt different. This father was from the Sombreia village, and that was her reality, not the one that kept repeating itself in shadows throughout the rooms that she walked in daylight. That one had royal blood in its veins, and looked very different than the Sombreia Togernaut, father of now.

She quickly moved out to follow through with her reach and touched his arm, finding it to be warm and solid. He moved to allow her the time to feel that his presence was not part of the dream she was having prior to his arrival, and gave her the assurance that it was indeed him.

"See, all Shapeshifter me, with a little extra to boot." He pointed to his whiskers, which had started to find their way into the final stages of a beard. "We've been looking for you for a while, and it seems that you as well have been moving around much faster than even your old da can keep up."

"Papa, is it really you?" she yelled before leaping into his arms. He smoothed down her hair and kissed her forehead, letting her feel the whiskers in all their gruffness. He laughed at her exploratory searching; listening to her babble on as she tried to tell him all that had happened since last they saw each other, back in Sombreia village.

"I dinna think that this here beard is good for the face that stares back at me inside the walls of this here dream. Do you think maybe you might want to shave it before Mother sees it?" she asked. He laughed heartily and nodded at the tiny tears starting to well up in her big dark eyes. He got up and moved towards the window that remained in the room before its next shift.

"Have you seen the water that moves like silver lace?" he asked her, trying to change the subject when she let him go by the window ledge and pointed to the ocean waves below.

"Where, Papa? The water is crashing onto the rocks below, as if a storm is brewing." She moved towards its shadow and wedged her toes to the every edges of the sill. "That's not what I see when I look out into the water." She moved out further, straining to look out the window in the direction he was pointing.

"There," he said, "look at the outer-edge of the sea. Can you see it now?" he asked, pointing to an area where Sibrey watched a huge wave that she had seen earlier, but try as she might it still didn't look like lace.

"It's just a wave, father."

"Really; are you sure that is what you see? To me it's as smooth as glass," he said. He moved to retrieve his spectacles from his pocket, placing them on his eyes and around his ears. The Sea might be stormy and wild to her, but he saw something entirely different with his Shapeshifter vision. Sibrey was still partly in the world of the Goddesses, as several large systems seemed to be building into one bigger offshore wave.

"Must be an illusion to my field of vision," he told her, cleaning his spectacles then placing them on again, trying to visualize what she was talking about. But try as he may, he couldn't see what his foundling was seeing, and the beginning inkling of a feeling emerged that she was looking at a very different world than the one that was currently portraying itself to him.

"What does the room we are in look like to you? He asked, starting a different line of thought.

"Father?" she looked puzzled.

"Just answer the question Ree, and play the game before it changes again."

"Well it's a castle with stone walls that are done with beautiful carvings, all put together by a stonemason's hand. But, truth be told father, it's done with such suburb craftsmanship, that I've never seen the likes of it before. Sort of like what you told me the old ancient city of the Earth Elementals lived in," she smiled, looking up at her father.

"Really," he thought about it for a few seconds then continued speaking with a little more excitement in his voice this time. "Did the sea, when it was wild with its storms, sometime earlier in the day perhaps, have the streaks of darkened valleys in its tips?" he asked, speaking quickly and with a bit of understanding to her window that she was able to see through. Sibrey nodded.

"They are there right now father, and by the looks of it very angry indeed." she replied, pointing to their cresting motion, which he could not see.

"Ah, so it is there even though the sea is full of emotion. Well, that's a first," he whispered mostly to himself. "Hum, does the sea give you other colours that I do not see?" he asked her, trying to lessen the frustration he was beginning to see in his child's eyes.

"You do not see as I do, do you?" she asked warily, as he continued.

"No child, but that does not mean that you are seeing things that aren't there. It's just that what you are seeing at the moment was presented over a thousand years ago, and has long been gone from this world since the year of your birth."

Sibrey's intake of breath could barely be registered at the moment, as she took what he said internally. Things that she saw in her dream world, with the male that answered to the name of father, were starting to make sense. In the beginning, she thought they had seen her, but it was the other little one that they had reached for, that was actually part of their world. She initially thought that they were voices from her own imagination, that had been playing tricks on her, and later that she must have been dreaming when she had seen them the first day.

"Papa, how did you get past the warriors in the old castle battlements?" she inquired, feeling unsure of what she was seeing now. He didn't answer her, instead chose to explore the inner workings of the room. As he paced he picked up several pieces of stone that had fallen to the floor, examining them.

"It was their fault that I was dragged into this place in the first place, you know?" She tried further prompting him. He continued to ignore her questions, prompting her to wonder if this wasn't part of an elaborate dreamscape. 'Crap, not again,' she whispered. 'It seemed so real this time.'

Daniel started to fade from view slowly, as Sibrey began to get really tired and her limbs had become almost impossible to move, as he grew further and further away from her line of sight.

"Papa, don't go; I need you here with me." She started to whimper slightly, as the majik began to fill the room and started the process of slowly knocking her out.

"I can't see you anymore Papa, are you still there?" She yawned, not realizing she was still on the bed. Another yawn escaped her mouth and she went out like a light. She hit the pillow with her head, and slowly sank into the feather quilts that had been provided for her since the moment the Goddesses had appointed themselves as her guardian.

With Sibrey out once again, Daniel waited, not moving until she was completely unaware of him again. He watched her eyes grow tired and his image fade from view moving to the outside portal, before he called Nina into the room to reset the dream world towards nicer things than what she had been currently tossing and turning with. She escorted Daniel back to another of the many terrace gardens that ran upwards towards the roof top, finding Horae moving about the plants watering their little stems with Star Anise cream.

Horae looked up as they entered, smiling at them, and welcomed Daniel the moment he got within range. They moved towards the Time Goddesses giving them an update as to what Daniel thought would be a little more comforting than the usual dreamscape that was previously set for her. Each mused quietly about the setting then continued on with other things.

"Are you settling in ok?" Horae said looking at him, getting to know the movements that accompanied a Shapeshifter male of the Fey realm.

"I think so, but it still takes a bit of getting used to, this world." He pointed to all that was around him. "One that fits inside another," he added, smiling at the Goddess, before Horae turned away towards another sound that had not been within the gardens a moment ago.

"Ah," she pointed to one of the falcons that had just landed on one of the large falconry branches that had been set out for just this kind of a visitor. "I wondered when you planned to show up."

She reached into her pocket and extracted one of the smaller rodents she had tucked away, passing it to the bird she handled on one of her outstretched arms.

"Anapher is one of my favourites. He likes to hang out in the gardens, watching for the smaller birds that arrive to enjoy the shade and come to feed on the seeds we put out. It never really occurs to him that the gardens are protected from hunting of any sort, yet he never fails to try and do his best to get through their protection wards. It is with great humor that we all watch his antics at trying to undermine the system which is put in place to guard the smaller birds from the birds of prey that are raised here. He can sit for hours at a time, watching the inner workings of the energy field. Then, without reason he will disappear into the barrier and come out the other-side with feathers all askew and standing outward like a duck in heat." She laughed when Daniel seemed somewhat shocked at her bluntness, and then carried on as if she had need of his approval of the yarn she was recalibrating.

"He is an exceptional beast, and has the mentality of a bull Cathor folding himself into the most unusual of circumstances, all for the slightest chance of making it through to hunt at will. But that will never happen. So, from time to time I will bring him one of the rodents we find that has slipped under the cavern's entrance in the process of destroying some part of the garden's inner growth."

Daniel was still looking at her pocket, where the rodent had come from. It still had that majikal illumination marker that was created to bind something in place to keep it from escaping. Small bits of the electrically charged dust fell to the ground in a scattering of silver and crystal amethyst sparkles. It began to move outward along the grounds when it hit the soil, becoming absorbed by the protection spell that grounded everything in place within the garden's atmosphere.

Horae looked up from the falcon to see Daniel's eyes on the energy that fell from her pocket to the ground. Pointing to the disbursement of energy dust on the ground, she said with a bit of cautious hesitation.

"We live in a majikal world, you and I, and this surprises you Daniel?"

"Actually, surprise is not the word I would use in this situation. More like I'd hate to be the mouse," he said with great passion. Horae laughed with enthusiasm, letting it tumble from her mouth until it fed her soul and fell outwards, spreading like a majikal particle as it met its maker.

Unfortunately the falcon found it not so amusing; taking the offer to wing and disappearing upwards into the canopy of trees that lined the gardens down below, choosing instead to forgo the hilarity they seemed to be having at its expense.

"Yes you little bugger. And stay away from my peas," she added with laughter, while Daniel roared his approval exuberantly. She turned her attention to Daniel once again, and spoke, smiling warmly. "So, it is good to finally meet you after so many long years of hiding in the open arena of Shapeshifter feathers."

Kneeling, she wiped her hands clean using the small gurgling waterfall that meandered about the garden by their feet, and moved to seek his essence from the field of Shapeshifter quantum's still running down his body, as it grounded itself into the soil at his feet.

Daniel had never met a Goddess. Especially one that worked with the Earth Elementals that grew the things that he and his family needed to eat to survive. It was here that literally everything that grew in the Fey realm stopped in transition, and then came into being with one quiet whispered movement of a Time Goddess's hands. He had truly never thought of them as anything but ethereal. So imagine his surprise to find that they looked and lived pretty much like all the rest of the Fey residents, that resided within this part of the realm. Only difference was that they were the ones that created virtually everything that came into being. He now had a few questions about other strange cravings he had of late; wondering whether those things could be incorporated into the scheme of things down on the planet. He was, after all, in the presence of one that could actually make that happen.

Horae brushed the loose dirt from her clothes and proceeded to ground all the extra energy particles that still clung to her outer clothing, giving them back to the earth that she had borrowed them from in the first place. Her response was simple and to the point.

"Always return what is no longer needed, even if you think you may have need of it at a later date." She smiled. "It makes us happier to lend it in the future," she said as they both grew silent for a moment, her blinking at the rate of the cycle of her time dilation.

"If you are of need, first think what you will give up in return for the gift." She looked directly in his face, as she moved to get up.

"Ah then, I must decline with admiration." Daniel watched her with quiet fascination, as the last of the dusting of pieces made their way back down into the soil, returning to the energy life-force that sustained the planet's entire building blocks of quantum particles. She smiled with his response.

"A wee one for the road then, in case you think we are just being greedy." She leaned forward and whispered something in the wind in his direction that he didn't hear, giving him an instant memory that had been lost in his youth so very many years ago from the time that was no longer part of his visitation. Then, as if by majik, there was a lost memory that rose up to his surface world and caught him by surprise, as it resurfaced from the fallen reaches of his younger mind.

Every child within their lifetime has that small window of opportunity to experience the sights and sounds of the world of the Goddesses in their youth. But somewhere, as time presents itself and we seem to grow mentally in other directions, the need for that belief vanishes in the wind and we become fascinated with other voyages that take us away from the true reality of their initial creation. It is with this thought that comes to mind, he suddenly remembered a time that they visited his home in the wee hours of the night, one snowy winter's eve. It was a time Daniel remembered vividly, that what should never have been real, had found its way into the world of dreams he had had when he was just a child, anyways.

It was around the time of Yule; there had been jasmine floating in the air, and he had thought that that in itself seemed to be a peculiar aroma for a winter's solstice. Even with him as young as he was, he could honestly say that he knew that this smell was unusual in all shape and form of the winter's ritual that lay just around the morning hours of a new day ahead. It should have been more conducive to the aroma of a lovely fresh snowfall, as had been falling on the ground for most of a fortnight, and not the smell of summer flowers long since finished their bloom from a past summer month, now lying dead and gone.

He had opened his eyes for only a fraction of a moment, in the second that it took for one such ethereal creature to pass through his small window of sight into the stone casement, and allow his vision to adjust to her signature of translucent light shadows, as she floated toward his small cot. She then reached through a gateway to the outside world and brought the falling snow from outside to him. She brought it shimmering into the room, and blew ever so softly the feather light dusting of icicle crystals along his eyelashes, making him blink and sneeze with the falling cascade of ice crystals that fell about his face.

When he had recalibrate his mind to accept the image that appeared before him, and opened his eyes again in the next millisecond of time, she had been gone. The only thing left to mark her passing from her world to his, was the snow on his face that drifted downwards onto the pillow upon which he laid his head, not one second before.

There had been no time correlation of her entrance to his space in time and that of her own shift into this realm of the Fey. Had anyone within his father's cottage believed the child that had sworn on his life to have seen one of the ancients that was said to have deposited the snow that was now melting on a pillow of feathers, no one said. But, having had that particular event occur in a room that had only shadows adhere to the walls from the one remaining window that still hung in its placement, without it having ever been opened, was still much discussed within his childhood memories, and continued far into his adult dreams.

Furthermore, it had started another set of occurrences inside other hovels of shippels of similar ages, claiming they too had similar visits within their dreams. But the authenticity of their claims was speculated on, as was the real nature of their identities, and not simply the factor that any child born of his clan from that moment of time onward, tried to duplicate its arrival without actually having success. Although many tried to regale them with stories of similar occurrences of other visits real or made-up, Daniel had not known its truth. But he had liked to think that someone out there really had come into play with the snow on the window sills, while he dreamed of their eventual return in future times when he would be able to tell his own shippels about their arrival, and the stories that were true, on his part anyway.

The memory was still fresh in is mind as he watched Horae in real time, breathe the same molecules as his own, and take a small bit of feathers that had fallen from one of the birds which flew past among the tree tops, and gently return them back to the wind. Her direction was true and her aim was complete. Now flying inside the wind she created to take them upwards into the air, then changing their direction towards Daniel, they continued to move about his face and smiling eyes. He blinked as each one touched the outer-edges of his forehead and floated, spiraling downwards as his lashes caught their tips and made him sneeze. Instantly upon leaving his skin they turned in to new birds, compliments of the Goddess that had turned the new hatchings into something alive and very real. They could be seen adjusting their molecules, along freshly made wingtips, then flying away through the underbrush to places unknown.

She looked at him with amusement. "How did you think they were made, Daniel?" as she continued to be unfazed by his reaction, while he continued to be dumbfounded by snowflakes and birds with just the slight dusting of Jasmine in the air.

His face grew wide and his mouth began to say something but the words could not find form amongst his newly released thoughts. She nodded slowly and smiled, letting him know that a little bit of snow landing on the face of a child almost a lifetime ago still had precedence in today's place of the ever present world, of the real Faery Realm of the Goddesses.

CHAPTER THIRTY-EIGHT

The Underground World of the Dark-Faeries

Markus was frustrated now; no that wasn't it, he was downright mad. He circled around the exit and still couldn't find a way around the obstacle that he and Theiry were trapped beneath. It hadn't been more than a few minutes since they discovered the Ferrishyn moss hanging inside the main tunnel that led somewhere down below, and they had returned the way they came to retrieve Dyareius and the others from above, to explore its properties.

But now, all they could do was stare, grunting in exasperation at the lovely sky above them from inside of the old stone walls of the well where they remained at the bottom, with apparently no bloody way out. Oh, they had tried, believe me, but to no avail. Now they looked at each other in stunned silence, before one of them hurled another boulder at its crux.

Both Aelves had returned to the old entranceway near the surface light where they had jumped down from the outside world, into whatever presented itself beneath the old stone well. Their curiosity as to what the tunnels had to offer the riders had been too much to ignore, and with the upside down world of their village having shown a sign of something being slightly off, they needed to get to the bottom of whatever it was that had shown its teeth to the outside air.

They surmised that maybe down below something would reveal itself to the riders, and even at that, something that was going on up on the surface seemed to be creeping into their memory and squatting its hind legs preventing them from seeing it; even down here. Dyareius was known to try and placate Assha, knowing fair-well that if something had been up Theiry would have instantly picked it up had he been close by. So, was the command they had been instructed to follow been implanted by Dyareius to waylay Theiry from realizing what Assha was up to, or had it been simple command strategy that he had wanted them to follow?

Damn Aelf, always messing with your brain screwing it sideways, and pushing it through some nasal cavity. However, had it been a ploy, there must be a good reason for having done so. Had they stayed, they could have messed up the airways further with them running interference. So instead they swore, grunted, and yelled their heads off in true Dragonlord fashion; unbecoming of the creatures they had been up above on solid ground.

So, now that you're totally confused, let's take you back to when all this started.

Upon discovering that the well was dry, when they first peered over into the darkness, they had discovered not only that it contained no water where a once prolific well had always had an abundance of crystal clear water, but now the space it occupied was only a few feet deep. This well always had one of the deeper holes dug into the mountainside to feed its artesian springs, which ran for miles along the Capourian Mountain Range and fed many outlying villages of old cropper families. For the life of them, nothing seemed to make any sense as to how it had changed its composition.

It wasn't until both of them actually jumped down into the narrow corridor and landed on the bottom, that the true nature of the thing was revealed. And the hidden passages below the old wellhead off to the side came into view, and its full potential was exposed, along with the dusty walls of more bloody unanswered questions.

But, like everything else, it seemed like a memory no longer meant for them, and it quickly faded from view, only maybe a few micro-seconds before the Sidhe moss had been detected along the outer-edges of another deeper tunnel system just ahead. Now it seemed to pull them towards other mysteries they no longer felt were part of their own interests and part of a greater puppeteer orchestrating their movements towards whatever lay in wait, much further down and around the corner.

That one, which seemed to move at a steeper incline than the one they were moving inside, and whatever secrets it held, was something neither Markus nor Theiry wanted to entertain on their own. For Sidhe tunnels were often created with strong off world majiks and, with the possibility of something majikally induced and created by Sidhe humour inside these tunnels they were not familiar with, they were taking no chances of finding themselves involved in an all-out war in these close quarters on unfamiliar turf.

They both knew when the Sidhe were involved; no matter what the course of it proved to be, it always turned out rather bad for anyone else within a hundred mile radius. And with only two of them down here they didn't stand a chance. Without the others having their backs, they dared not advance any further on alone when the majik came on to its natural beginnings.

So they had tried to go back. But, as you all know, that was not to be. For, as they made their way back to the entranceway above the ground, where the others awaited, things began to appear all around them with renewed vigor, materializing with some kind of harried execution set into the stage that they unwillingly had been participating in from the start.

The tunnel walls seemed to continue changing their shape as they transformed, twisting and turning into many obstacles that had not been there when they had first passed by. One such pattern that appeared to their left seemed to be reminiscent of the old staircase of the coven house that belonged to the Paracleese Witches. They heard stories about that faction from the sorceress Kamera on one of their many jaunts into her turf. But, as they moved past its structure, it instantly dissolved the illusion into the stone façade with a majikally induced hiss, while they could only quicken their pace to get the heck out of there.

Markus put his abilities into play, and watched the particles attach themselves momentarily to their cloaks, as they moved towards the light at the end of the tunnel; then detach themselves as they were almost within range of the main shaft, and bounce along the floor like mad hens. He watched the particles move away, and go through the solid stone that opened its mouth with an almost humorous amusement of gestures, and then disappear into what looked like the remnants of a shade; now long gone from the soil it had once lived within.

"I know that look," Theiry said, as Markus watched it shift and swirl, invisible within his inner-sight line, outward and through Theiry's vision. He nodded and pointed to the vacant space that held no molecules inside the darkness of their eyesight, revealing its location, as it moved with non-sentient life around the rocks up above and watched them with slitted vacant eyes. Both Aelves slide their bodies around its substance as it blinked before it turned into dust, dispersing the memory from the walls with Markus's guidance, and moved off away from its strangeness.

"What was it?" Theiry asked when Markus didn't speak. It was only then that Markus realized he was still holding his breath. Theiry shoved him lightly and brought him back to the present, repeating the question a little louder, while his lungs finally conceded to gulp in air, while Theiry returned to glare at the older Aelf.

"Really, holding your breath is considered rectifying the problem? Seriously old man, how is that going to get us out of here?"

Before he could respond with something witty, something new started to form in the darkness, and settle along the bottom edges of the stones they were walking on. He signaled Theiry to stay quiet, as they watched it form and push its way out of the rocks. It came forth in a swirling soft mist, pouring along the area they were walking in, filling the chamber part of the floor and floating along towards them.

Both Aelves watched the cavern's heavier molecules, drenched in this strangle-hold of fog, as it seeped in around their feet. They sidestepped through the lighter tendrils as it opened other entrances from little cracks and fissures that had been laid bear with every footstep they made along the floor. When they could no longer move around it they plowed through it, leaving swirling clouds of disjointed mist that circled their bodies, and continued to rise around their knee joints, squatting like some form of Vampiric Tree Morrigan waiting on newly sighted prey.

The texture was warm, and had an almost melancholy feel to it; Markus pushed them both to the end of the tunnel before it came on stronger and prevented them from continuing along their path. The Paracleese staircase made another appearance directly in front of them and they had to reverse direction before they plunged down into the inky darkness.

This time it was in reverse, heading into the bowels of the soil instead of climbing up through the ceiling like the last one. As they moved around its opening maw, it beckoned them with the smells of warm bread left to cool on a windowsill, back from some far off lost summer day with bakers and ploughers swatting at young ones that got in the way.

The well entrance they first came through loomed dimly to their right, and had Markus even blinked he would have missed the turn-off, while the mist continued to envelope the area trying to obscure it from view. He signaled Theiry to follow, but the Aelf ignored him and continued to walk down the corridor ahead of him, stumbling away. Markus grabbed him by the shoulders, and shoved him through the hole, turning him around and pointing him in the direction he wanted Theiry to follow.

As soon as they both stepped over the threshold, Theiry stopped moving. He stood there like a fool that had lost his mind, with his mouth drooling and his mind on what warm bread tasted like, as he bit into the tasty texture of freshly baked molecules of Sidhe dust.

"It's not real you fool; take that out of your mouth before something takes your head off," Markus said as he pried a piece of rock out of Theiry's fingers which was on its way to being swallowed whole. Theiry looked at him with a dumb look on his face, putting one foot in front of the other, and ran straight into the wall. Markus directed him forward, pushing him along as he tried to reverse the majik that had successfully infiltrated his brain.

He had felt its arrival the moment they had decided to head back up and away from the moss they had come across down below. Whatever it was, it was moving far quicker than he could find the correct calculations to hold it back. They needed to keep moving forward and away from what was now obviously tracking them. They made their way away from the strange corridors that continued to appear alongside others that would undoubtedly have similar occurrences for both of them.

They didn't get far before he could feel its threads start to unwind, reaching into their isolated mainframes and pulling away the aura that ran topside of their heads to begin feeding on their brains. It was creepy, and full of sick

Sidhe majikal dustings still not showing their full potential or their true nature. Whatever it was, it was too late to avoid it altogether; it already knew they were here and fumbling around in the darkness and it was hel-bent on whatever mission of proclivity it had intended to do with them.

What they needed was Assha; he would understand this far better than they. His unusual ability to see things that weren't always apparent to the naked eye was something as a group they had been able to rely on. Down here, away from him, it was going to be challenging to find the nucleus and give them an advantage, especially if Theiry kept eating bloody rocks. Case in point, another such stone had found its way into his hand.

"Listen you idiot, put that down before it decides to grow legs and really give you something to chew on." He was starting to sound like his damn mother. Only he had another remedy in mind; one not particularly health conscious, that would supersede those of a nurturing aspect.

Theiry instantly dropped the rock, but went no further than that, as Markus tried to steer him clear. He simply stopped moving, as Markus cuffed him across the sides of his head to get his attention, one for good measure and one for just because it was starting to piss him off. It worked for a second, and then stronger measures were needed to restrain the idiot.

Theiry turned his head in the direction of the stairs one last time, to fill his lungs with its sweet scent, as Markus yanked him harder and almost took all his strength to redirect his mind into the actuality of where it was they really needed to go. The cuff had brought his attention back to the present, but Theiry was hearing none of it as he ducked from Markus's second attempt at bringing him around, and moved backwards towards the smell of hot freshly made bread that he could now see sitting on the top of a beautiful stone table.

Markus picked him up physically and threw him over his shoulders, getting Theiry out of the line of molecules that seemed to have him fully in their control, removing him from whatever it was that wanted them to go down the bloody stairs. The image dissolved behind them without another thought.

He had only taken a few steps to the side, when both sight and smell instantly dissolved, bringing Theiry around to full awareness of his sur-roundings. That allowed Markus to unceremoniously dump his delusional ass on the ground. He shook his head doing his best to clear the cobwebs and started to come back to the land of the living.

"What the freaking hel was that?" Theiry said, coughing his head off. Markus looked at him and started to laugh.

"Seriously dude, you need to stay off this stone diet down here, it does things to your mind."

"My mind; crap, I thought I was back at the encampment on bloody Leberone, eating a banquet with Lugh," he spoke with his hands flailing.

"Seriously, I really thought we'd gotten out of here, and he was feeding us bread pudding." Markus looked at him and grinned.

"That should have been your first clue. What the heck is bread pudding?"

"I have no idea, but whatever it is, it tasted delicious." Theiry giggled. Both started laughing and tried to move down the corridor.

"So, you like eating rocks?" Markus clapped his hands on his shoulders.

"Apparently," Theiry shrugged back, "they taste just like chicken."

"You, my friend, are one bent dude. First this bread pudding, and now chicken. The things you come up with." Markus shook his head at his friend.

"Next you're going to tell me foxes can fly. Come on my little freak, we need to get topside to bring Assha down here to help locate what's living in this damn air, and hiding in plain sight."

They continued on without another incident for a while, until they rounded a bend in the main tunnel system and ran smack into another problem much larger and far more deadly than the one that had found them around the last one. Ok, deadlier might not be the word, but it definitely wasn't how they left the damn well-head when they last passed through. They were so preoccupied with getting Theiry back on his feet that, when it passed overhead of them, they at first didn't see it.

It began bringing in little whiffs of fresh air, placating their senses with the illusion of freedom that was still up for grabs. The closer they got to the entranceway, the cleaner the air became. Wisps of wind from a small breeze pushed down from above, moving past them; seemingly replacing the stagnant air they had been breathing and giving it new life. Markus started to hurry; he was feeling uneasy, even though they were within reaching distance of the outside world. He had an uncomfortable feeling that something big was about to explode outwards and try to waylay them again. He was right.

By the time Theiry felt it, it was too late; time had only been able to hold things off for so long. Already things had changed since the last time they had passed through this corridor; things were simply not as they had left them, and the smell of Sage ran thickly in the air. Majik was all around them now, and both watched the walls shift in and out of their line of sight, like a simple mirage forming on a hot summer day out in the dunes. It was here the forward momentum changed, filling the chamber with majikal vibrations and knocking them briefly to their knees before both keeled over, landing flat out on their backs. It was an odd position to be lying in, but both felt better the moment they hit the ground.

They watched in quiet fascination, from their vantage point, as whatever had failed to stop them from advancing towards this chamber, finally found the correct sequence of threads to incapacitate them from finding a way out and breaking free. It was only a short time later that they began to lose consciousness, the wellhead they had first entered looming over them, looking to the entire world like it was beginning to spin downwards, forcing the daylight to find its way into the world of the shadows of the cave; any more time that was left inside their conscious memory as they slid into darkness and lost their battle to remain alert, was only further complicated by the realization that they had been outsmarted by something much meaner than they understood. Then, as all else seemed bleak...it faded from grey to black.

How long they were out was anyone's guess, but what met their eyes as they struggled to open them sometime later, only further revealed what they both had suspected the moment they were knocked to their knees, and they lost sight of their conscious souls. Up above, the tunnel that opened up to the outside world was now gone. Not missing in the virtual sense, but it was definitely, not anytime soon, going to be able to move them back freely into the outside world at this particular juncture.

They started to rise from the floor and dust off their breeks, as boot tops to buckles were covered in long fingers of Ferrishyn fronds, where the moss had dripped down onto their fallen forms and tried to claim them as one of its own. Markus ripped through several layers of the stuff, and finally resorted to kicking the substance away with his feet where it tried to hold onto the leather of his soles with fingers darkened by age. It was sticky and had barbs that ran in an anti-clockwork direction. He tore through the remaining tethers, and wiped his hands from any remaining particles while he moved away from it doing its best to reattach itself to any body part that was within reach.

Meanwhile, within touching range and not further than a few finger spaces away, Theiry was not having any more luck dealing with his confinement, but after he made several attempts at unsticking them, the tendrils of moss finally fell away from his body, and reattached themselves to the outer-edges of the walls as they climbed upwards to join the others hanging there grinning at the Aelfs.

It remained there clicking away, full of sentient life, watching them advance, as other large cracking noises from the sides of the wall brought them to its arrival. They stopped to watch another creature make its way into the room. The moss slid sideways, letting the creature through, as it literally poured from several different sections on different sides at the same time. This one was both fascinating and eerie all at the same time, and although they were still a bit groggy and couldn't be absolutely sure that what they saw was entirely real, it would prove to be more dangerous than anything they had seen so far.

They watched as the entity, which really had no substance that linked each of them together, come forward, squeezing through cracks and fissures that had lain almost invisible to the Dragon-riders. Theiry could feel no life inside its soul, but something was moving its dead mind, as the ethereal fingers suddenly reached out, merging its bits and pieces of thick gaseous material and punching through the seamless rock into the surface world above to drag any remaining rocks and soil downwards, firmly closing the last of the opening off to them that had lain bare and free.

"What the hel is this?" Markus asked, looking between the creature and Theiry, who stood there watching with his mouth wide-open. Nothing could be put into words, as their exasperated faces took in the last remaining daylight streaming down upon their faces through several slits in the branches that had replaced the narrow opening above them, and watched helplessly as the creature from the land of the dead firmly sealed their escape route off, finalizing their fate.

A simple mocking brought forward to further frustrate their little hides, as they looked on in horror. It turned, looked directly at them, turning blank eyes in their direction, and hissed. Markus turned as Theiry swore a blue streak, while the creature moved closer to them, dangling downward and swaying methodically between the two like some advance guard sent to stay their hands.

While the standoff continued, several tap-roots of some large tree that was living somewhere outside in the vast forest above, started to systematically punch through the walls, destroying the structure of the last remaining sections that were dangling around the overhead opening. They moved independent of each other, winding themselves into a web of undergrowth that was several feet thick, leaving both Aelfs to duck and cover as the roots tried to incorporate whatever was in reach into the mixture.

Any flora that had made it down safely, when the creature pulled the soil from above, began to grow in the new matting; finding new life among that which had only seen darkness. If the Aelves had any remaining thoughts that they could simply tear away any part of the new growth, they was quickly dashed, as the flora pushed their way into the last remaining hand-holds the Aelves could have used to get to the surface world above, sealing them into what lay in wait, just around the corner and around the bend.

Both Aelves watched as they literally forced themselves from the bedrock, sending dirt from the walls to fall and skitter along the floor as they interlaced themselves into the web formation. They wove and spun themselves right out of the solid rock, creating a finely decorated web, unlike those of the Bagorin spiders of Kepet Minor; the recently occupied planet of the Bagorin race of Aelves.

They had no time to admire the unique craftsmanship that was made out of shimmering threads and razor sharp tendrils of some foreign material neither Markus nor Theiry had ever seen before, because the creature was on the move again. This time it turned back towards the newly formed material, touched it lightly with its tail and began to transform, literally stripping the skin right off its body, as both Aelves backed away slowly from the carnage that followed.

When it was all said and done, what was left had nothing to do with the creature it had once been when it was alive. Whoever was controlling its limbs from the land of the dead, now presented itself to the two riders below as a silver set of metallic bones. Then, as the Aelves looked on in horror, it started to disassemble its appendages right in front of their eyes. They immediately came apart, as something unseen seemed to have it completely in its control. It manipulated each of the limbs as they came off with a solid snap, floating without form high up in the air above the Aelves. Then, without fanfare of any kind, while the thing continued to hiss and spit at anything in its pathway, the body reassembled itself among the razor sharp tendrils of the web, and transformed its main torso into several spinning rings. Having completely changed its appearance into the vast network of those silver colored rings, the final piece of the puzzle came outwards from deep inside the madness of the floor beneath their feet, and landed smack-dab in the middle of its still spinning skull.

Several large electrical bursts surged forward towards the eyes, singeing the hair along one of Markus's arms as it passed them by, as both Aelves did their best to stay out of damn its way. It then took the hissing skull and wove itself into the underlying fabric of the rings' metallic background, charging the entire system with its molecules, as it settled into place with a sizzling snap, while red orbs glared wildly back at them, firmly set in their new habitation.

The beastly rings reset themselves and whirled into life with the recently charged skull. They spun and rotated high above the puny creatures down below, locking themselves in place. Whatever it was, it covered the area above them completely, preventing anything from escaping its lair as it vibrated and swiveled in a spinning motion, inviting the resident flora to take up residence as they firmly wound themselves around the threads of the net's main arteries, anchoring it to the edges of the wall and holding it in place.

"Bloody hel," whispered Theiry. "Now freaken what? Have you any more bright ideas? Because, from where I'm standing, I think eating rocks might just have been kinder." He started to back away, moving behind Markus.

Markus reacted by throwing his sword into the electrical charging mechanism, but all it did was hiss, flinging a few rocks to the ground, as the sword was flung back towards them and they both had to duck as it came straight at them, almost taking their heads off.

"Oh bloody brilliant! That's something Soren would have done. Thank the Goddesses he's not here or we'd all be dead by now." Theiry hissed at Markus, just as he stepped back and pointed to the falling rock.

"I'm not trying to physically do damage," he replied, "I'm trying to hit that lever along the bottom of the charging mechanism that for some reason had been hidden from us. Theiry looked at him puzzled, then squinted to see what he was talking about, spying something small and metallic showing through the rock.

"How in the world did you know it was there?" he asked, finally seeing what Markus had tried to open.

"Well, while you were yakking your jaw off, I went in and had a little peek between the rocks. No sense both of us losing our minds, because that would just be unproductive and get us nowhere," he replied simply, returning to retrieve his sword from behind them and getting ready to have another go at it.

They took turns for the next few minutes until the rocks slid loose, and a small pile of tree roots began to vibrate along the edge. When they got it almost free, they tried to move it with their bare hands along the edges of the locking lever and away from the charging mechanism that seemed to flow in and out of their line of sight. But, it was never for more than a few milliseconds before it would then disappear, only to reappear down further in another section of the wall, and they would have to start all over again, as it taunted them by dragging them from place to place.

"If I didn't know any better, I'd say this damn cave is freaking haunted," Markus said to no one in particular. They continued on doing whatever they could to reach it, however it was always just as they managed to reach a certain area of the lock, that it would reverse itself and come into full view further along in another part of the revolving circle, then dissolve once more into thin air the moment they moved to touch the particles in the center, which surrounded its molecular transference.

"Something tells me it's trying its best to stall us from seeing something else. What are we missing here?" Markus mused. Theiry looked around them, from one side of the cave to the other. "Because it seems like it has a life of its own. Do you think maybe the Sidhe moss is having a go at our perception of this whole thing? Because, from where I'm standing, at times it seemed to have a puppeteer elsewhere in some far off part of another tunnel system we can't bloody see." Theiry frowned, and then got stung by an electrical charge as he looked away for a moment at Markus to respond to what he had said.

"Damn it, stop that, you stupid thing," he yelped, trying to flick the sting away.

"Here, let me give it a go," Markus said, pushing him aside as he continued to nurse his burned fingers. But that too, had the same results. After getting stung several times with their bare hands exposed to the charging mechanism, they realized that they had another line of attack they had not thought of before. With their swords placed perfectly balanced in just the right position, on either side of its charging mechanism, they could very well interfere with the direct surge of the main charging ring.

They retrieved their swords and placed the metal blades on either side of the rotating mass of vines that continued to circulate in a clockwise direction, and watched as it started to intermittently interrupt the electrical flow of energy that filled the web with its power. It took only a short amount of time as the process slowed the current down to a trickle, before another grand idea entered their little Dragonlord brains, which comprised mostly of requiring further direct action, of stronger majik to further their cause.

From here, they considered a different line of approach that was somewhat barbaric in nature, but proved, in times of past complications, to be just the right amount of simplicity without the majik of their elders coming into play and kicking their asses when it required payment for its use. So, with that kind of stupidity, they simply reverted to trying their best at beating the hel out of it, then attempting to tear the bloody rings apart with their bare hands.

That went on without much success, for the better part of a micro-arn. They hollered like a bunch of foundlings on an outing at the fair, until they felt like the skin on their knuckles would simply rip off down past the muscles and right on to the bone beneath; then to complicate things further, something ripped their swords right out of the wall and flung them as hard as they could, in their direction. They spun in a semi-circle, end over end, and then came back at them locking themselves once again into the same fragment.

Perhaps the retribution part might have worked better, as they dove for cover. But Aelven males are not known for their brains, when brawn is easier to use. Simply ripping something apart was secondary to their endorsements of male Aelven pride and the increasing need to destroy something, when frustration was added into the mixture.

It was as this was happening, with such lunkheadedness and a lot of grunting topped off with the occasional obscenity thrown in to boot that they realized that the rings above had stopped rotating and had opened the well head momentarily to the outside world. It wasn't a means of escape mind you; it was disbelief at the open sky and the multitude of stars starting to appear one by one up above.

Something was toying with them, and wanted them to attempt to climb up the vast netting put in place, where they would once again become trapped in the underworld of this stupid cavern, while whatever was orchestrating the chamber from below ate them for bloody lunch. It finally dawned on them that this wasn't going to work, no matter how much they tore it apart.

Both stopped almost simultaneously short of bleeding out, and looked at each other with mud and debris all over their hands and faces, finally realizing they would have to find another route through the tunnels below. Smiles emerged on their faces, replacing the snarls still on their lips, at the bits of dusty mud and moss that hung from their arms and shoulder blades. They gave in to laughter. The hilarity finally overtook their little brains with the realization of what they had been doing, and the stars disappeared slowly from up above while they continued to hoot their heads off in a form of quiet consecution.

Still they moved no further than what was necessary to retrieve their swords from the locking mechanism, as they continued to recover from being bested by bloody vines and one nasty looking piece of silver fauna. They looked at each other fully caked and full of scratches that were lightly bleeding Aelven blood all over their hands and faces, and moved a couple of steps backwards to reassess their situation.

Absolutely this wasn't going to bloody work; they knew that now, without a shadow of a doubt. As they came to the realization that brute force would simply not get the job done, they turned back towards the Sidhe tunnels and settled into the fact that they simply had to go back inside to find another way around this situation that now had them firmly trapped below ground, without any help from above.

Meanwhile, as Markus and Theiry moved off towards the main tunnel they had previously been in, someone else arrived underground in virtually the same area of this underground world. It was to this world, which had never previously been mapped by those that now found themselves to be part of its strange hidden interior, that two more members of that family of Dragon-riders were introduced, resulting in some unforeseen injuries.

They emerged suddenly, as light opened another worm hole in one of the smaller caves, and pushed through two more brethren Aelves from the strange mirage above, into the dimness down below. They landed with a soft thud and became another statistic below ground; joining the others just a few tunnels away.

Up on the surface, they had been running as fast as they could go, as Dyareius called them back between the stone walls of the fortress they thought they had lived in for most of the last twenty or so years of their lives. But before the truth of the situation could be revealed to them, as they came running around the south wall of the castle's false façade, both Bynffore and Elyizeam had unexpectedly joined the unknown world below ground, just south of the tunnel that Markus and Theiry had first encountered the Ferrishyn moss in.

Up above ground, near where Dyareius and the others were converging on the area around the east wall of the castle, something sounded like a sizzle just before a single burst of electrons ran lengthwise through their bodies, lifting them weightlessly for a fraction in time, as both Aelves yelped in surprise and disappeared. Dyareius watched helplessly as the pair was caught by something unseen, lying in wait; while all they could do was pull back before the rest of the group became caught in the crosshairs of its threads.

From the standpoint of the riders on the surface, something seemed to pull the pair of them backwards with incredible force, leaving not a trace of them or their signatures and they simply disappeared through a solid rock wall in a puff of mystical smoke.

As soon as they disappeared, the riders moved through a short tunnel that resembled a rather large hole of scattered light, and then everything turned sideways as they were pulled by some unseen force through its center. It swallowed them whole and dragged them through feet first to the other-side. They landed without incident with all of their body molecules whole — but slightly askew, strewn on the edge of a mountain of stuff piled high on the floor and deep underground in an old filthy cave. They didn't even have time to grab onto the edges of the abyss and hold their breath, as their weightless bodies seem to betray their intentions of staying put, letting something simply push them forwards at an odd angle before they had time to actually stabilize themselves.

As soon as they came through, the momentum simply stopped and ejected them headfirst, spitting them out to tumble downward through several layers of small hilly mounds as they lost their footing on the uneven ground below. Both continued to roll, until they came to an abrupt stop for no other reason than their bodies simply ran out of steam. Then something had other ideas and the hill of material they found themselves on, simply gave way.

Each gasped for air in the new environment, unable to right themselves before a second slide sent them further along. They lost their footing and began to slide ass over teakettle towards another rocky ledge about fifty feet from the first, until they landed unceremoniously on a shaky outcropping of calcified layers of some kind of alien stone. From there they would join other creatures that had met a similar fate, in an unknown underground tunnel that had been literally torn apart by some past catastrophe of another age that they now seemed to have been mysteriously deposited in, far from the world of the village of Tameron.

Elyizeam pitched forward again taking Bynffore with him, just as their bodies had come to an abrupt stop as something else gave way underneath him. They began rolling towards one of the fallen stones that lay across part of the tunnel system they had been set inside. Then, suddenly just as fast as it started, they stopped. Elyi was lucky, stopping short of hitting his head by millitrons if not quadrapitions. Bynffore was only lucky for about a breath of that time, before catastrophe took over and he found himself in much graver danger than was initially apparent during their original fall.

That dangerous situation produced itself only after he had crashed through whatever it was that took them downwards, like ten oars in a boat that had suddenly fallen over the edge of a waterfall. It seemed innocent enough at first, to laugh slightly at the hilarity of Elyizeam rolling around on the ground in front of him, swearing his head off like a duck.

Then luck seemed to run out and take a holiday, as Bynffore had one of the stones that had come through the barrier with him crash down from the air above them. It followed him into a pile of something shiny, and landed full on the edge of whatever it was, as something else from that pile of old rags came upwards like a spear and impaled his right ankle and pierced his shin from one side of his ankle straight on through to the other!

That was when the screaming started in earnest, and all hel broke loose; the awful sound of bones snapping followed by the cascading of more falling glass, and him hollering his head off, sent the smaller stones scattering across the cavern floor in all directions, as he finally came to a sudden and rather abrupt stop and went no further.

Pain became the main focus of his shattered bones, as the cascading rock continued to slither forward. The sound continued echoing through the cave and bouncing off several of the walls; it then slowed to a dull roar, as a few stones simply rolled out of place, skidding further down the center of the cave and stopped alongside him; without causing further injury to both the cave itself, or his injured ankle.

But that was enough. The damage had been done.

One good thing had come out of it though, if you were counting cockles to handshakes; as far as luck would have it, and it was something desperately needed at the time, as part of this story would have had tragic results allowing for an entirely different tale to have developed — and one non-too-pretty either, if you were to ask Elyizeam regarding his opinion on the matter. But then again, I'm jumping ahead of the real truth of the matter....

You see, Bynffore had a gift like all the Dragonlords, and with that gift came the uncanny ability to change some things, into other things. One of his most prized possessions that he carried with him was a Seer Stone, which had been on his person as he fell, wrapped tightly around his wrist to enhance those powers of which I had just spoken; to a much higher level.

He was after all a Dragonlord, specifically chosen for his unique abilities, so, as he fell through the ceiling behind Elyizeam, holding onto this precious cargo that had come along for the ride, something atmospheric had tried unsuccessfully to rip it from his wrist when they got pulled through the middle. He had managed to hang on to it, creating enough energy within his own protection barrier to protect him from having it ripped out of his hands by the tremendous winds that were inside the hole, and landed with its majik intact, despite the preparations of those that had hijacked his body here in the first place.

Obviously, whoever was responsible for the original majik that yanked them backwards into this realm didn't know the difference between illusion and reality, nor what a Dragonlord was capable of in times of danger. For the only thing that saved it from tumbling away into the abyss, as they were sucked into the void, was quick thinking; for whatever it was that pulled them through, had scanned them as soon as they went backwards through the void, and having no success at ripping it out of his custody, left it alone as they continued to fall.

As he disguised its nature as nothing more than simple leather strapping wrapped tightly around his wrist, he felt the line of energy come towards them and move from one side of their falling bodies to the other. However, the majik couldn't stop the sensations he was feeling, as both Aelves continued falling through the downward spiral that moved them through solid rock at a dizzying speed. Only Assha had that kind of majik, and he was nowhere near where they had fallen through, to protect them. As they fell, Bynffore felt like his brains were being sucked out of his head, and by Elyizeam's reaction, as they momentarily locked minds when the drift point crossed pathways, he was having a similar reaction with his own vital organs as they moved in a downward spiral.

As they picked up in velocity, and tumbled into the rift point, he called the Seer Stone's powers into being, and its hidden properties became activated as they moved through the void and it smoothed down the transition of their fall. As soon as that was initiated, the energy threads immediately pulled a protective barrier around his body, as he held onto to the crystal's fully charged energy pattern while his eye sockets tried to pluck out his eyeballs and fling them to whatever birds might have been lingering in the dark. He hollered several rather strongly worded oaths which echoed through the tunnels, bouncing off the walls inside the main cavern they entered, as he held on for dear life and screamed his head off to the Goddesses that be.

He didn't have time to be sure whether it was able to activate around Elyizeam as well, or the sky crowd had heard him, but the power gave him just enough time to veer out of the way as another much larger stone came careening down behind him, almost killing him in the process as it passed them by, then landed just out of reach slightly below him. It moved towards the energy field in its final rotational pass and skidded over the surface of the protection field of the Seer Stone. The activation molecules reversed their condensing phase, sputtered and died. He picked up speed once again, crashing downward at an angle unbecoming of a meteorite on a collision course through the Nebula, and ended up being dumped head first unceremoniously about halfway down the pile of debris where said birds had there been any, might have been able to finish off the job.

He rolled as the rock crashed down alongside him and skidded through several larger pieces of stalactites and crushed wall fragments, where it landed on top of a mound of something else that had been smashed to smithereens, piled high along the ridge of sheet rock beside him. He had made it down alive, and by the sounds of Elyizeam groaning off in the distance, he too had found his footing on whatever it was they landed on, as the rock could be heard skittering off onto the floor and away from smashing his thin Aelven head in.

He closed his eyes momentarily, covering his head as his breath came out in short pants, trying to gain his momentum from the pain while the room spun around him and his night vision started to find its course. He was able to finally open his eyes amid the remnants of the falling debris that had come down with them, and try to find what was left of his balance.

The floor was nothing short of a disaster zone from whatever vantage point one took; the sight that met their eyes was not quite ready to firmly settle down. Instead it continued to rain particles of lightly colored molecules all around them, leaving both Aelves to dodge several pieces of ceiling stone that came dangerously close to caving their heads in, as well as several other precious body parts they had grown mighty fond of owning in the past years since their birth.

Everywhere you looked the place was turned upside down; the dust continued to hang thickly about the room, colliding with the occasional piece of crystallized shard that had come loose from somewhere underneath the pile of loose fabric that seemed to be strewn all over the floor. It brushed the tops of their faces, sticking to their eyelashes while they wiped several layers of black soot from their clothing and spitting the remnants out on the ground that had found their teeth.

Glass seemed to be everywhere; scattered about in piles all over the place where they had landed. When their eyes adjusted to the view they could see in whatever direction they looked, things were in the same condition. All around them looked like some kind of apocalyptic event; evidence of something that had at one time crash landed from great heights, much further than from where they had come in from, and definitely not belonging to anything that had just arrived alongside them.

From their vantage point down on the floor, the remnants of its contents looked like they hadn't been changed in centuries. It lay strewn across the floor in exactly the same place as it might have been had they been able to go back in time to precisely the moment it had occurred. The only thing truly giving away its age was the layers upon layers of cave silt that had descended down upon its surface, from many years of it going untouched by anything since it had been deposited there.

To Elyizeam, what he saw within visual range, must have come through the ceiling at an accelerated rate of speed in the departed past of a different era. Further inspection revealed it to have been literally blown outwards in every direction when it had arrived, destroying whatever this place previously had been, as the blast sealed it off from the outside world above and things moved inward repairing the rift.

He used his unique gift to watch the aftershock as it plummeted from out of nowhere, arriving in much the same way they had. The only thing they had going for them was the simple fact that it could have been so much worse. That was if, indeed, they had come down in some cave, and not been suddenly transported to another world whose very existence was life below ground. Crap, he hadn't thought of that. What then were both of them going to do, if they had moved beyond the molecules of trace that Assha would have been able to track them with?

While his brain struggled with the reality of this new train of thought, it was interrupted by the realism of a scream inside the room. He quickly came back down to actuality, as Bynffore's shattered thoughts began to infiltrate his mind and he could see in the darkened space that he was not moving the way he should have been, once things had settled. As a matter of fact, the lack of movement should have shown him that something was wrong the moment he had arrived at his final destination inside the cavern. It was a little hard, being mostly in dense shadow, but something else almost alien was infiltrating his senses, and when he went to use his inner-sight, it momentarily closed off his outward senses making him blind.

Shortly after that realization, it appeared as though something was reading his mind, and some form of crystallized light seemed to radiate along the far wall as his eyes struggled to see Bynffore and the room. It continued to grow slightly brighter, taking away the shadows into its center dais, then circling around the two of them as it lit up the area, leaving the rest in shadow.

He moved to stand, but only got partway to his knees before the tiny little pieces of fossilized glass embedded in some form of strange stone started to hum as the light moved slightly up the cave walls. Their activation seemed to be directly connected with his present thoughts, and the higher they resonated with the energy inside the chamber, the brighter the crystals became. So, whatever was lying about in pieces now appeared to have woken up, then quickly recalibrated before aligning itself to the awareness of Fey patterns. He wondered how something with such an alien design could track the thought configurations of another race that at the time of the crash might not have been aware of their arrival on this planet.

What had triggered them to self-activate was anyone's guess. Whatever it was, he was just happy to be able to concentrate on his friend's silhouette, as the room revealed its true treasures. Unfortunately for them, it seemed that, upon seeing some of them, they may have been better left in the dark.

Treasure was just a word of convenience. What really was found to occupy the cave was nothing short of breath taking. It literally took his breath away when he retrieved his hand from below several layers of dust that had accumulated along the floor. The dust fell along his skin just like droplets from a river of silt. He dug himself up out of the muck to find some form of footing he could actually stand on and not fall over whatever still lay buried beneath its bottom layers.

His body came up on command, no worse for the wear, and appeared rather small and effervescent in nature, as the stark colour of his skin seemed to be the colour of Leberone in the cave's shadows and not his normal hue. All around them it joined other bland and nondescript things where colour seemed to be non-existent, as he discovered this dirty room absolutely full of shredded pieces of blackened fabric with melted chunks of metal and charred bone throughout.

It smelled strangely like sautéed boar; a curious thought that brought his mind back to memories of pleasure, while he felt like he had just been dragged through the backside of the Starshaper Meteor, making its rounds across the farthest known Nebulae and back. Nonetheless, it was a memory, and strangely one that helped him acclimatize himself to the eventuality that he might not be ascending to the surface light again anytime soon. And, should that actually transpire, he wanted to remember that they used to eat that delectable meat on the festivals of the Bale Fires.

What a strange thought to have come to the surface of his brain. Especially when he was neither hungry nor really thinking about food here in this Goddess forsaken world of the dark. Now, of course, mused his mind, it would be oddly layered with helpings of several layers of falling stalactites, all mixed in with a healthy helping of filthy dirt, and you would have the final feast that fed the creatures that lived in this underground barrow.

None of which had accompanied the actual roast pig during those meals. But one now wondered how both senses seemed to be drifting along his nasal passages while they were essentially buried below several layers of solid rock. But stranger things had affected his brain before, so he tried to shrug it off as nothing more than improvised settlement, confined to the restrictions of the interior walls of the room that now held them in its confinement, all mixed in with a healthy dose of majikal stew.

However, that was not true for Bynffore, who was desperately trying to find his center, but found that that particular mode of movement was not going to be happening anytime soon without help, as something seemed to have him pinned firmly in place. It didn't hurt much at first, considering he had screamed his head off after the initial shock of it piercing his skin as it wrenched his body around something that held him still very much trapped within that pile of rubble. He had felt it move upwards and pierce his ankle, but strangely he had felt only numbness as it happened. Thinking it was in direct response to the fall and what they had passed through on their way down; it had surprised him when he moved to touch it and his skin began to get warm with a prickling sensation — returning all senses to him, as the pain manifested and he screamed out in agony.

The pain, although still very much a part of him, was quickly dulled from the sharpness of only a few moments ago and settled down to a disseminating throb. In comparison to what it should have been, this was a relief; Elyizeam, on the other hand, had found his footing after holding himself in place with the rumbling of the interior walls finally slowing their forward motion then coming to a full stop. He advanced in Bynffore's direction to see what was keeping him from standing, just as another set of earthquakes sent him flying again. It rumbled through the strange cave system and he had to stop his advancement and wait it out while Bynffore continued to fight with his emotions.

The rolling sensation of the small quake didn't last as long as the others and quickly disappeared, with Elyizeam making it the last few feet he needed to go in order to get to his friend. He arrived just in time to see Bynffore sprawled out in front of him with something sticking out of his ankle bone that shone with an odd metallic colour, alongside the now broken bone protruding at an awful angle.

Whatever the material was, Bynffore had landed right in the middle of the pile, and Elyizeam had to actually climb through several layers of it to reach him, when he was greeted by one of those ghastly pieces of bone sticking out of his friend's ankle just under the surface skin. The protrusion glared back at him, bringing on a host of other illustrations of the white and bony matter set before him, making him want to pluck his eyes clean out of their sockets with the sight they presented.

He didn't, much to his relief, considering the amount of work he had ahead of him to actually drag his friend from the remains of whatever it was that had waylaid the two of them in this ghastly place. He didn't have time to actually be sick, and with his friend sitting there yelling his head off it would have been rather in poor taste. It wasn't so much that he would have been embarrassed to let Bynffore see him respond to his pain in such a manner, but more that he would have had to drag him threw the bloody crap when he tried to get him out of the situation they now found themselves in.

Once Elyizeam was finally able to get to him, Bynffore's face began to take on an even stranger pallor — compliments of the impalement coming outwards and finally settling into the actuality faze. The shock of the injury was in the process of making him delirious and he groaned in pain. Though his mind was probably shouting its damn head off, he reacted with not a single intelligible word. The words instead sounded raw, with a slight connotation of the sublime. Not the inspiring sublime, but a newer version that instead might not have found its way to the ears of those that understood its meaning. He continued to bluster through the pain, until he was quieted down by a voice that seemed to soothe him.

He felt something move towards him ahead of Elyizeam. He thought it was there to comfort him in his delirium, and he sunk down onto the dirty mound, letting his back rest along whatever it was that seemed to reach out and curl itself around his body, as Elyizeam reached for it around the tentacles and flung it away.

It landed and reformed itself into plain old rags with nothing sentient about it, as Elyi shuttered at the thought that something was watching them and had played a big part in their arrival. Bynffore was oddly calm instead of displaying what should have been a totally ear splitting reaction to this new arrival. But, he seemed to not be fazed by what had just transpired; in fact he looked rather stoned and laid back as he relaxed into the mounds of fabric and continued to rock back and forth not seeing anything at all — including himself. His pupils looked dilated and were wide-open with hardly any colour to the iris and as Elyizeam got closer, he seemed to be humming lightly the darker they got.

He had heard stories of the ancients claiming that, when the pain had been difficult to handle they had reverted to this kind of rocking sensation, accompanied by the sound of humming to relieve the pain. He wished it could do something for his eyesight, as the thing that had formed out of

nothing but old rags seemed to take precedence over pretty much everything else that breathed in the room.

It seemed the place didn't just have something from another world
living inside its walls; it also seemed to be haunted by whatever it had
pulled across the threshold when it arrived. Other things began to show
themselves, forming and swirling high up in the air, proving to be nothing
more than the vivid imagination of one very drugged up Aelf teleporting
his thoughts into the wide open air.

On the other-side of things forming inside Bynffore's mind, another
scenario was playing out in front of him. Something was in control of
his senses, and he was actually finding the rest of his body quiet well and
intact, aside from the injury. The pain of his mangled ankle was bad; that
he had been able to feel, although at times it would drift in and out of his
sensation. However, the rest of what was happening around him felt more
like a dream, which was why it wasn't given a timely reaction for the scream
to actually begin to form when the thing had tried to worm its way around
his body. He couldn't have moved even had he wanted to, considering the
sliver of alien bone he encountered was actually stuck and impaled within
his ankle, up to the first set of bones in his lower leg.

In fact the pain seemed to find its purpose in other parts of his body
more than in the location of the actual injury he was currently looking
at, and it was further irritated when Elyizeam tried to move up the pile
towards him and the pile shifted and started to change direction. And it
was thanks to this that he finally found speech, as it continued to puncture
the sides of his hands as he tried to get Elyizeam's attention to the danger
he was putting them both into.

Of course his friend could not see the threat that was all around them,
and he himself had only just recently realized that he was in the middle
of a mound of tiny slivers of some kind of volcanic glass; not all of which
had been melted into the mess, but definitely more than just a handful
that were about to participate in this new war that was brewing just under
the surface coil — almost ready to explode outwards with pulsating life.
As Elyizeam started towards him, they hatched into existence and then
extended their angry mouths and branched out in all different directions,

pointing their sharp termination points directly at him — each seeming to be alive with some form of sentient brain activity.

Elyizeam froze in mid-step, catching the sides of his boot-heels with the tops of several of their open-mouths, as he too finally observed their strange behavior and lunged at the closest ones with his sword, literally taking the tops off them and smashing his way towards Bynffore's side until they released him. Whatever this place had been, the energy was still full of life inside the cave and it dripped and crawled through and around the shadows — staying just out of sight, while he moved to his friend's side.

What was this place? And why in the name of several of his ancestors were they taken here against their wills and thrown almost sideways into this heap of sentient insanity? To say it pissed him off, was putting it mildly. But what really rankled him,was nothing short of exasperated anger at being left to handle the bloody mess of something that had decided this was the perfect place for them to arrive into this bloody hel hole in the first place.

Bynffore wished Elyizeam would quit horsing around and pull him to safety, before something else decided to pay them another visit; while Elyizeam did his best to immobilize Bynffore's ankle, to move him across the area where he had used his sword to smash through the different layers of melted glass that had tried to attack them.

No sooner had that begun and he was being dragged downwards, he got jammed up on another piece of the sharp edge of whatever this material was, and it shoved the silver thing further up his ankle joint, causing another heated conversation to explode with some very colourful words to match, as Bynffore reached out and made contact with Elyizeam's jaw and the two of them had a hissy fit, with one of them swinging and the other cursing him out in every language he could think of and the cave inhabitants sat back and enjoyed the fight.

This created a visual effect not unlike something caught in the snare of an old fishing net as a fisherman reeled in his catch and the fish flopped around trying to hit him in the head before they made their escape while he dove in after it and dragged it back into the boat.

Bynffore's ankle was not only broken, it was shattered and starting to bleed as Bynffore tried to put his fist in Elyizeam's face while they wrestled each other around the pile of material it had made contact with in the beginning. The shard of material that impaled his ankle now contained other foreign material not related to the original injury, which wedged itself in tightly against the bone and squatted like a fly waiting for dinner on a plate of gravy.

Ode to the Dragonlord was a tale that was not for the faint of heart, and would be heard for decades in stories one told their offspring when they screamed from something that resulted in nothing more than a little old sliver. Their parents would remind them of Bynffore's ankle while they sniveled in solitude and drifted off to sleep completely immersed in their own misery, and dreamed of days when they too would be able to handle the simple pain of a sliver of wood that might just have been something far more alien in design come morning time than their parents had eluded to.

After the fight, and objection of grievances, and their tempers calmed down to a more manageable level of Aelfan insanity, Elyizeam had to remove two things. However, before he even attempted something so idiotic, he had to first stop moving. He didn't have time to second guess what the pile of creatures might have to say about this, because he knew without a shadow of a doubt the moment he did, they would find another way to sharpen their attacks.

While everything seemed to grow quiet, he quickly got to work and bent to examine the glass before attempting to remove it from his ankle; listening for the rumble he knew would erupt directly beneath them once he began. He had to first remove the silver shiny thing that was resting up along the bone fragments that were pressing into his wound; he yanked it lengthwise through the surface skin, tearing the first section of platelets that had already begun to form over the wound and flung it away from the pile of rags. Once that began, while Bynffore was still numb with the pain that was coursing through his body, he had to somehow get both of them down the pile of crap all around them. Then he had to get both of them to safety, down to the actual floor of the cave; a deed that might be considerably more problematic with Bynffore beginning to come around again and beginning to beg Elyizeam to kill him outright.

He looked around the area they were in and tried to see if anything within sight might be used as some kind of sling; the pile had plenty of things that could be used for this, but did he dare? He reached for a piece of leather strapping and watched it slithered away, moving out of reach underneath another pile of debris, while the pile seemed to slightly shift around them and continue to move.

He needed to get moving before the whole stinking mess started to come alive and swallow them whole. He chose to rip his own shirt and used parts of some kind of slim ornate stone that appeared to not have the properties of what the other crap seemed to be infested with. He dusted it off and the stone stayed dormant; he sensed it was not part of whatever was infested inside this chamber. As he was moving to wrap the wound to transport him, something seemed to catch the edge of the skin, and this resulted in a few drops of blood dripping through the open wound and onto the cave debris they had fallen into.

He watched it disappear through several folds of cloth, which immediately seemed to come alive with Plagasfear molecules and then move sideways — of its own violation; providing the means to wobble on through. What didn't make it in; literally crawled away all on its own, to wherever it could hide, as Elyizeam tried to stop a shiver that threatened to erupt along his spine in absolute revulsion at its strange behavior. It was at this point, watching the oddity of the blood, he knew they needed to not only keep moving, but they needed more help than was available to them.

Elyizeam continued to work, and had just freed the final piece he was wrapping the wound with, when he heard what he thought were voices coming from another part of the underground system; he silently cursed, thinking he had spoken out-loud and the cave had indulged his wish. But, they continued to be getting closer from somewhere outside the area they were in.

He reached up and put his hand over Bynffore's mouth, shushing him to remain still while Bynffore thought he had finally decided to put him out of his misery and was actually was going to kill him. Chaos ensued briefly, with Elyizeam holding on for dear life and Bynffore deciding it was a good time to kick both his shins with his good foot. He stifled a scream, as something started to make its way around his foot. He kicked it away; as he waited for something that would give both of them reason to move. It slithered out of sight, and he continued to drag Bynffore towards the larger mounds across the backside of the pile where they could easily hide should the voices prove to be something that could endanger their lives.

He put his finger up to his lips and gave Bynffore the hand signal to try and breathe quietly. His friend finally got the message that the killing had been delayed, and instantly heard several voices about to arrive on scene amongst the chaos. Elyizeam then got slowly into position to roll his friend closer to his side, holding him in a defensive stance that would give him a better advantage to defend them. He hadn't a clue who could be moving below ground; whoever it was, might prove to be more dangerous than what they were currently dealing with as Bynffore momentarily tried to still the pain. It was difficult, but he maintained as much composure as he could, before remembering he still had enough senses left in his body to change the creatures into something benign should it prove to be needed. The footsteps grew louder and began to enter from the right.

Thankfully it wasn't necessary, as the bones, flesh, and skin of the voices advanced towards them into the room, instantly releasing a flurry of images to return to their infancy, before Bynffore had time to release them into the wild. What arrived gave the tense muscles in both of their bodies' immediate release, allowing reflexes to return to normal, instead of preparing for a fight in this bewitched cavern of strange majiks that neither would win.

It wasn't until the two figures came into the room bearing broad smiles from ear to ear, with the earmarkings belonging to their own kind that Elyizeam relaxed his hold on Bynffore, letting him sink gently to the floor. He groaned, as the pain returned, producing several images that stayed in the room, not fully able to complete the draw-back into his imagination.

They went wide; ricocheting around several strange pieces of material that had gotten stuck on the ceiling — back when the cave blew up and then fell without substance back into the cavity of Bynffore's thoughts — now dissipating back into its proper place, while Elyizeam's heart continued to betray their apprehension of what it could have been. He sunk down, placing his hands on his knees and drawing in breath that had been held in check for too long, looking from one of them to the other shaking his head.

It was Markus who entered first — coming from the right, grinning away oblivious to what they had been going through. He found the familiar pattern in the others who had held their breath waiting and had only just called out to them to give warning that they were coming through, before they appeared around the corner.

"I don't particularly like being thought of as a small toad, but hey if that's what it takes to reach out and bloody touch you, then let it be," he called out, laughing at Bynffore's wild eyes, as the words came into focus in what he had intended to change both of them into; then there was nothing, as blackness didn't require any form of answer to his now unconscious thoughts. The silence that had waited patiently in the wings claimed its first payment, as he slipped into its world and things went still.

Their arrival sent waves of relief through Elyizeam's shoulders, the moment the two of them came around the bend. They moved quickly up the pile to give him a hand with questioning eyes looking at their fallen companion. But it was only momentary relief, when they too realized that Bynffore was really hurt and they moved quickly, to find its reason.

There was a slight groan, as all three looked down at the stricken Aelf who could no longer see them, then nothing. Not only had he not responded to what Markus had said about the toad, all three of them instantly realized something wasn't even close to being right. Elyizeam still trying to maintain some semblance of calm, looked over their shoulders to see if the other riders had come to join them inside the cave, just as he came into contact with Theiry's face. He shook his head and spoke quietly.

"It's only the two of us." Elyizeam swore.

"Damit! I was hoping everyone made it through! We need to stay close together if it's only us. Something's wrong with this place and things just keep moving out of the corners of my eyes and I can't figure it out before the next one strikes." Proving his point; something took the opportunity to go unnoticed while they talked and slithered closer to the unconscious Aelf who had suddenly gone quiet. Apparently, while he lay unconscious he had been lying in something other than just plain old rags that were strewn all over the cave floor.

Three swords claimed its head, as the creature became particles of nothing more than dust spacklings; they dispersed in the air around them, landing to join the rest of the pile of debris.

"What the hel was that?" Markus asked, kicking some of the glass underfoot as he leaned forward to balance himself grunting with Bynffore's weight. The pile started to move and another shard rose up, revealing blackened teeth pointing right at his booted foot. He smashed it with the heel of one foot as the other grazed the points of several others that tried to form behind it.

"Move him, now! The natives are restless and bringing friends." Markus shouted in alarm, just as another bunch of the blackened fabric became lodged underfoot as they struggled down the mound Bynffore had been lying on. He kicked it further along the wall's edge — so it wouldn't get in the way, just before it too snaked to life and climbed back up into the darkened mess to continue the hunt.

"Damn Faery majik," he shouted to the others, as another one changed the playing field and slithered towards the mound around the area where they first came through the ceiling and burst into flames. Theiry shuddered as it momentarily touched his foot when it scuttled past; fully engulfed in purple flame. He stepped over it as it shrieked; screaming at them as they moved past, still trying its best to attach itself to their feet, then without anything holding it together, simply fell apart as the cinders dissolved its majikal body into the pile. Several others could be seen moving slowly towards them, stalking their position. All three Aelves moved as quickly as they could, skirting around obstacles fully twisting to life as the pile seemed to activate all around them, pursuing them with renewed force, the faster they moved away from its mass.

"Oh I have a hunch it's more than just coincidental." Theiry chirped away in the background. "If we don't get him out of here, it will be more than just a little bit of dust trying to bite our ankles." Elyizeam heard the words, and picked up his urgency just as another piece of leather tried to wrap itself around his ankle. He crushed the semi-formed head with the heel of his boot and it exploded into another ball of ethereal dust.

"You'd think they'd get it by now, we're on to them." Markus laughed, as they continued on towards the floor that presented itself along the far wall. They got down just as the entire mound came to life, twisting and turning into a swirling mess of snarling and snapping creatures not belonging to this side of the Fey continuum.

However, they had seemed to have luck on their side; the creatures stayed where they were and didn't follow them across the bare floor, seemingly holding their place along the edge of the debris where they had pulled themselves tightly against the wall. Apparently, something else was present alone the edge of the room that the creatures couldn't get near, and it was here that they seemed to have crossed over to some kind of protection field, as if something had aligned itself to them and was working things on their side of the veil.

The creatures not happy at loosing their prisoners, hovered along its edge constantly testing its strength. They grew in mass creating new bodies, trying to find the right formulation that could cross the barrier put in place. Strange alien shapes followed their movements around the pile constantly changing, while the Aelves progressed along the foot of the wall towards the tunnel Markus and Theiry had emerged from. It was here, as they finally transformed themselves into some kind of alien porcupine, with the strange pieces of melted glass and raw minerals poking haphazardly out of various areas of their rapidly composed bodies that they could go no further. Instead, they resorted to intimidation; hissing away and taunting them.

The Aelves ignored them and moved slowly along the edge of the cave, taking the time to maneuver where the creatures seemed to not be able to follow them. Markus turned briefly to Elyizeam as the creatures skulked away, following them at a distance but advanced no further.

"So how the hel did you get down here in the first place?" he asked. Elyizeam shook his head, looking annoyed.

"It makes no sense," Elyizeam said as he shrugged his shoulders. "Seriously, we were just heading towards Dyareius after he summoned all of us back together in formation, when something strong opened behind us, and literally yanked us through the open vortex, and we found ourselves here underground." Markus whistled, before Elyizeam continued.

"At first when we came through, I wasn't even sure we were underground, or even still on Tantaris. You know how these things work. We were just lucky it didn't pull us through the middle of some damn star, leaving us seriously maimed or full of bloody rocks." Markus looked at Theiry, and started to laugh, leaving Elyizeam to wonder what the joke was about.

"Don't ask, or even encourage him." Theiry said, as Markus tried to contain himself, grinning away.

"What am I missing?" Elyizeam asked, looking between the two of them. But Markus only shook his head.

"Not important; just rather funny. I'll tell you later," he replied, ducking out of range just as Theiry took a swing at him, and they both burst out laughing.

"Promise me you'll tell him when I'm either unconscious or bloody dead, and not before," he said, looking rather silly.

"Really, you're going with that one, hum? Well, I'll be damned. Seems like you're a bit star-bitten to think I'll not use that one when the time suits."

"Oh come on; let's just let that one die a kind death, shall we. Really, had we been on Leberone when it happened, you might have taken a different opinion."

"Yeah you freak, let's go with that one," smirked Markus. Elyizeam was watching the banter back and forth, all the while keeping an eye open from the swirling mass of alien porcupineous that were starting to accumulate within throwing range. He was having a hard time keeping up with the storyline and the situation they were finding themselves to be living amidst.

"We are still on Tantaris, right?" Elyizeam looked a little worried. Both nodded, saying nothing more of the incident.

"We are, at that," Markus said, stepping over another small stone that had been flung their way by the creatures that had resorted to throwing things at them. Several volleys of stones joined the other and the Aelves ducked as each one came closer than the one before it.

"Insistent little buggers, aren't they?" Theiry said before he continued answering part of the question that was still up in the wind about their own whereabouts.

"When both of us got to the well that Dyareius had asked us to move towards, in order to keep me away from seeing what Assha was up to..."

"Oh you knew that, did you?" Markus interrupted, frowning. "Huh, might have to let Dyareius know our covers been blown." Theiry glared at him.

"Seriously, what do you take me for? Of course, I'm not blind. There isn't a thing alive that could hide itself from what I can pick up. I just knew that if Dyareius wanted me out of the way, then there was a damn good reason for him to have sent us to a flipping well. Anyways, when we got there and it seemed to be empty of any form of water, I knew we had to go down there to see what might be hidden underneath the structure that had put up such an elaborate ruse to hide itself." Markus nodded in agreement, as Theiry paused, trying to adjust his hold on Bynffore, who had begun to slide sideways as they moved down the corridor and took up the story from where Theiry had left off.

"It was upon going down into the damn hole — out where the old well head had been brimming with water when we last left it, when we found this system of tunnels that led us to several more behind us. To be honest, I don't think we landed much further away than a hundred or so strides from your own arrival, or we wouldn't have actually picked you up. I'm not sure when you came through, but the moment your faunt became aware of us and moved underground towards us, Theiry felt something cross our path and we both moved to intercept it's movements before they disappeared altogether." Markus spoke quickly, ducking the last of the projectiles coming his way, while the other two moved past what they thought was the last of them.

"Are we near the wellhead then?" Elyi asked him. Markus nodded. "Great, lets head there and get the hel out of here. I think we're going to need some help." Elyizeam yelled as another volley of stones hit the wall and ricocheted, hitting him in the arm and causing him to almost drop Bynffore as he began to slide. Markus shook his head in disagreement, struggling with the weight of Bynffore as well, as Elyizeam went off balance and Markus had to shift his own weight to accommodate the difference.

"Not going to happen anytime soon, unless we have something to blow it up," Markus yelled back at them, deflecting several of the smaller stones that had found their target.

"What do you mean blow it up?" Elyizeam yelled back. "Can we get out of here or not?"

"Well that depends. The well's not far, but that's the least of our problems," he shouted back to Elyizeam. "We're in Sidhe territory now and that makes for a whole host of other unforeseen problems. You see we found some very interesting things along the way after we went down here, before discovering that the bloody thing we had called a well, wouldn't let us back up." He bent down to place his hands back in the right position and looked behind him to judge the distance they were heading, along the wall ahead.

"Who wouldn't let you back up?" Elyizeam looked at them both with the question raised, half expecting them both to disappear right in front of him. Another violent shaking from above made them stop and center themselves between Bynffore, keeping their grip on his shoulders while the ground continued to move.

"I'm beginning to think someone doesn't really want us down here," Markus yelled at the other two. It was as Markus was wiping the dust from the quake out of his eyes and off his brow, which brought Elyizeam's attention to the open wounds for the first time.

"What happened to your hands?" he asked as they repositioned their hold on Bynffore.

"Oh, we'll get to that in a minute; for now let us get him to safety before something else prevents us from finding some form of bloody sanctuary," Marcus replied sarcastically while Theiry nodded in agreement as several cuts on his hands also started to bleed once again.

Huge chunks of stone fell to the floor from above, landing in clouds of dust that rose up from both their passage through the corridor and the recent shower of boulders that had come loose from the volley of stones behind them. The noise roused their comatose patient and Bynffore came too briefly, squirming in the makeshift sling between strides, sending the other three careening into each other as they juggled the now semi-consciousness Aelf, who suddenly realized he was being transferred in mid-air by three sets of hands.

"In case any of you are wondering as you plan our great escape, we are no longer near the grounds of our castle." Bynffore responded between trying to breathe and the rising discomfort he was experiencing. He was trying to stay focused on his movements and not the pain that radiated through his lower spine, when he heard the others of his clan yelling their heads off as he was swung back and forth, creating several new tears in his skin.

"Hold up, just give me a moment to catch my damn breath, you bunch of lunatics," he said, drawing in big gulps of air through his teeth. "My back is killing me," he whispered with the movement, visibly starting to shake from the pain.

"I thought you said it was his ankle?" Theiry said, moving him through the last leg of the doorway they came through, getting ready to put him down. Elyizeam shifted his weight towards the floor of the corridor as soon as they rounded the corner, away from the missiles that had continued to assault the trio until they were out of sight.

Bynffore groaned as his back came into contact with the hard surface. Elyizeam helped him into a seated position, grabbing onto his arms and lifted him without trying to cause any further discomfort. Theiry moved his cloak under his knees before he could elevate his ankle above the other, and handed it over to Markus to continue the examination.

"Seriously, get me the hel off the floor. I'm trying to tell you something is wrong with my damn back."

"Stop fussing, you moron, and let me look the ankle over first. You seem to have a radiating fracture along the area where the damn bone is sticking out of your skin. Seriously Bynny, can't you feel that?" he asked, poking the area around the bone where the skin was beginning to heal over the opening.

"What the hel?" Markus looked at the wound, which shouldn't have been anywhere near the healing stage. "The bloody skin is trying to fuse itself right over top of the bone. What a freaking mess. Have anyone of you seen this?" He turned to Elyizeam who had suddenly grown quite pale.

"Listen, you bunch of idiots, my ankle is fine. Check out my damn back, will ya? I know something is starting to crawl up and plant its bloody teeth into my spine," Bynffore continued to rave. But Elyizeam was a little preoccupied with what they were seeing.

"That wasn't there when I first looked it over, honest. Oh freaken hel, I'm almost afraid to see what might be hiding when we turn him over." Markus frowned.

"Maybe we should take a look at his back, before I try anything more." he mused, moving Bynffore's shirt up to have a look at where he was trying to show him the pain had been coming from, and was startled to see several severe black and blue markings come into view. Theiry whistled.

"No way, where did that come from?" Elyizeam asked Bynffore as Markus sucked in his breath.

"I pulled a piece of glass out of your ankle the size of a small squash, and you said there was no pain involved. Why didn't you tell me that something had pierced your bloody back?" Elyizeam yelled at him.

"I didn't know that then, only that my ankle was broken and pain was coming from somewhere. I thought it was from that," Bynffore screamed back and then yelped as Markus found another small glass shard embedded inside his lower back down by where his tailbone started.

"Ouch, you bunch of freaks. What the hel is it?" he exclaimed, trying to level his position to get a better look at the object that had been lodged deep along the area of his own spine, only to find two more sets of hands holding him back from reaching around to move them out of the way.

"Don't move, you idiot, or you're going to shove it back in further," Theiry yelled at him.

"Take it easy. Here, use my knife, its sharper." He handed Markus the knife he had around his left shin, as Markus continued on with the conversation.

"Can you pull it taut on either side of the injured skin?" Someone grunted, and Markus had to put the knife sideways in his own mouth to hold the skin tight and show them where he wanted them to put their fingers. "No, more like this. Perfect, that way I can shift the position of the knife sideways, and pop it out without causing damage to his spine.

"Oh no you don't!" screamed Bynffore, trying to find a way to roll away from all of them. "You're not going to cut me up, down here in this hole!" he ranted further, trying his best to fight his way out. He didn't get very far as Markus transferred the knife to his hands, and quickly moved to put blade to skin. He almost got there, but before the blade actually entered the skin, the shard of glass moved, and Markus watched as several claws seemed to take flight and try and dig themselves in deeper, wrapping themselves around the outer-edges of his lower vertebrae.

"Something tells me we are not in Kansas anymore, Dorothy. Come on boys, let's find some spunk and remove damn Toto from out of his back," smirked Markus still smiling away at the analogy. Both Aelves beside him looked at him with absolute confusion.

"Who the heck is Dorothy and what does it have to do with a something that is damned that you called a Toto?" Elyizeam sniffed, looking between Markus and Theiry.

"Ok, you boys need to get out more and travel." Markus smirked, still doing his best to balance the knife and move ahead of the critter. "It's an old Earth story that is required reading on your down time next time we are stranded between jobs. And by the by, Toto is her dog and there is really nothing damned about it, just using the words for fun." He nodded when both looked rather puzzled back at him.

"Really, I'm kidding you idiots, bloody pay attention." He whistled loudly, bringing them back around to reality. "Now, hold him down before this damn blade slips and cuts an artery."

"Toto and some chick called Dorothy. Oh my God, is it really necessary to confuse the shit out of the only extra pairs of hands that are needed to take this damn thing out of my freaking back? What is wrong with you? Can't you at least shut the hel up until its bloody done, and then go into some Earth tale that happened to some Human and not us living in the here and bloody now?" Bynffore squirmed, trying to smack Markus's legs away from him. Two extra pairs of hands came to Markus's rescue, and he efficiently cut the area where the glass had punctured the skin and lodged itself inside. With quick fingers, and precise positioning of his hand, Markus moved faster than Bynffore could fully produce a functioning scream.

The impalement proved to be a little challenging, inherently stuck near his spinal column, while they repositioned themselves for the final removal. Markus couldn't just flick the damn thing out with it being in the position it was in, and wait until he was sure Bynffore wouldn't bleed out when they did. However, it didn't stop Bynffore from sarcastically adding his own disapproval of their heavy handed tactics into the mix.

"There was a time when whiskey would have been offered to the sick and injured, before cutting off a bloody limb. Whatever happened to that kind of damn protocol, instead of some unheard of nursery rhyme that has nothing to do with what is currently pissing me off?" Bynffore screamed and tried to fight them off further, but this time he was even less successful with his attempt than the last time.

"Well now, at least he has his voice to humor us, along with his lack of Aelven pride." Markus snickered. "Seriously my friend, you sound like a little shippel. And by the by, it's not a nursery rhyme at all, it's a book that was made into a film; get it straight." Markus grunted, pursing his lips and looking down at what he was doing. Then, with one final pull, and with those words, the thing was finally dislodged.

"Voila, my little angry one," Markus spoke, looking at the foreign piece of junk that had been yanked free without any further struggle, straight out of the ridge-bone of his back. Without waiting for Bynffore to respond, it was carried up into the open air with triumph for all to admire.

"Now Bynny, what have you to say for yourself, after all that whining?"

"What's a film?" Theiry whispered to Elyizeam, who was in the middle of laughing at Markus when the words came out. He shrugged.

"I have no idea. To be fair, I don't understand half of the crap that comes out of his mouth; you just need to smile back at him while he carries on about one tale after another, until he's done." Elyizeam said shaking his head unable to comprehend what Markus was babbling about in the middle of him grinning widely, and nodding with the triumph of releasing the little bugger from its hold.

However, Bynffore had not heard the sarcasm. In fact, shortly after calling them all out, he had passed out from the blood that now poured openly out of the wound where Markus had removed the living shard. The question now lost, went to the wayside.

"Damn it!" Markus yelled, finally noticing his condition. He moved quickly out of Elyizeam's way, while he tried to staunch the flow of blood with hands still firmly attached to the open wound. Markus needed to get out of Elyizeam's way; he was without a doubt, in the most dangerous of all three of their positions with regards to Bynffore's safety. You see, Markus was still carrying the sharp knife with the piece of shard balanced precariously on the end of it, which, if he moved the wrong way, could theoretically shove the whole thing out of sync, threatening all their hard work as it balanced over the precipice of the open wound like a dangling participial.

The little shard had all the makings of a horror show gone horribly wrong. If it decided to come to life and make a leap for it, returning back into the open wound, there was nothing they could do to prevent it. So, as he watched Bynny begin to slump over, all he could do as he moved in slow motion alongside him was get out of the way, while Theiry reached over and positioned his own body between that and the floor and helped his unconscious form to the ground. Theiry couldn't help himself. He looked at Markus and smirked.

"It's a good thing he passed out before hearing that lovely bit of advice, or he would have reached up and punched you in your pretty little head, and that knife would have slit your bloody throat, jamming that piece of space junk right back in to your own body." Markus smirked.

"Probably; I would have done the same." The other two Aelves nodded at the remark, knowing perfectly well indeed that would have been the correct response by one of their own, who felt he had been insulted. Dragonlord oaths were specific in their nature and the conversation quickly would stop before its inception. Though, to put it into context, that was not the reason for their hesitation. For, down below, as the blood had slid along the ground and filled up several cracks that made up the surface of the floor, they had watched the blood get up, wobble in its coagulation and expand outwards, producing several well defined legs.

Now to be kind, strange things have always happened in the Fey worlds and none so much, as in a bloody Sidhe stronghold that one was currently visiting uninvited. However, if that wasn't enough to make them feel out of sorts, what happened next would test them to their limits. For no sooner had the legs appeared, it further freaked them out by finding the means to rise up about a foot or so from the floor; where it could be seen staring back at them with these oddly shaped almond eyes that pushed their way to the outside of the gelatinous mass, and then blankly blinked those red corpuscles cells, right down its proverbial cheeks.

"FLIPPING HEL IN SOPDETIFIED TARNATION; are my eyes playing tricks, or is that thing looking like it's about to chow down on our flipping skulls?" yelled Markus, dropping the shard that was still precariously balanced in his hands, as they watched in horror at the eyes moving fluidly about the substance that held no shape; moving from one spot then off to another without formally pairing up. Then, to make matters worse, the blood returned to its original ooze, got up and literally skittered away on those damn legs, finding a similar crack in the floor and squeezing below the stones, as the legs snapped up back into its body and filtrated its way to places unknown.

"May the Goddesses protect us all," Theiry spoke aloud for all of them, while all three of them felt the shivers that ran down their backs take a turn and bite them square in the ass. The sight had come from out of nowhere, and had no visible explanation that one could put into words. However, *'BLOODY HEL'* repeated several times after, accompanied by some off-handed vulgar oaths, turned out to be more than sufficient, leaving Markus and Theiry both simultaneously looking for answers to questions that were directed at Elyizeam.

"THAT," he said with exaggerated emphasis and a lot of hand waving, "is what is wrong with this damn freaking hole, and concludes our foray into the underground world of the extremely messed up. Now move." With that put into context, it was enough to quicken an already accelerated pace, sending each of them to realize just what they had gotten themselves involved in.

"Damned talking Dragons. If Soren doesn't kill them, I'm going to have a whack at them myself when we get out of this," Markus muttered under his breath. "Nothing bad ever happened to us, until Quist starting yacking up a storm. You would have thought they would have kept that little tidbit to themselves a little longer; at least until I was bloody dead and buried. Damn freaking Sidhe crap, why...." He would have continued on with several other well placed oaths, but Elyizeam moved to quell the swearing and bring him back to reality.

Once setting that precedence, they instantly busied themselves with various things that needed doing to cauterize and clean the now actively bleeding wound. While the occasional sudden outburst of swearing by Markus in the background could still be heard as he huffed and puffed, until he no longer felt the urge to vent above the clatter. But it wasn't enough to impede their efforts to get Bynffore mobile enough for them to move further along, and away from this strange cavern and any further blood incidences, they were sure would arise if they decided to stay. They all knew if they were to linger any longer than was necessary, it was a fair bet they would lose that battle; it was something none of them wanted to gamble on, including a very pissed off Aelf.

Needlessly, the blood coming out of Bynffore's veins seemed to have other plans, taking on a more sinister life of its own. It was doing its best to ignore their valiant efforts to stay ahead of its continued arrival, as even stronger sentient life-forces were unrelenting in ambushing them, as it tried to move along Bynffore's unconscious soul and feed itself right out of the living essence of his veins.

They worked for almost a full micro-arn, doing whatever they could to prevent it from causing any further damage, thereby blowing out anything else that lay just under the surface of his spine. Putting the laughter aside, sounds dwindled to hushed silence and they realized just what they had pulled out of his back. Markus retrieved it from the floor, and held it up to the torch that Theiry had just been able to light. He had been relieved long enough from the blood situation to do just that, combining several things together that consisted of leaves that floated down from above, wrapped in parts of the old cloth that he had found lying nearby.

Not far from that, something else had proved to be useful. He soaked the material he had ripped into strips with some form of oily substance and majikally lit the whole mess into a raging flame. They had had enough of tiptoeing around trying not to set off what might happen to them; whatever was down here knew by now that they had arrived. They figured if it took life it could damn well return it, so they used what had been in reach to help them achieve that goal.

As it turned out, the glass shard was not unusual in size, nor was it unusual in its colouring. But that was as far as the piece of what appeared to be glass, went. It was in fact, a clear piece of mineralized quartz that had formed from anything but normal conditions, and had come from one of the purest forms it could have been brought into being, as it slid into this side of the crack it had crawled out of.

It would appear that the cave had a different agenda than their own, and was quickly becoming more of an enigma than they had first believed. Whatever had lived in these caves at one time had nothing to do with the Sidhe horde they believed had taken it over. What was unusual was that the shard they had removed came from one of the rarest crystals ever to be heard from on this side of the known Fey worlds. It was even rarer on this side of the great divide that separated them from the Human realms.

Elyizeam well knew of the tale it foretold in times of ancient majik. Its very existence was an oxymoronic notion unto itself and it shouldn't even be in existence in any of these worlds anymore; as far as he knew it was still an urban myth holding court in fabled words of an old story book: This, I might add, had been greatly embellished and spoken aloud in tales at night beneath the balefires in the gathering of clans.

Yet here it was, all alive and pulsing, pushing warmth and energy directly straight from the heart of an ancient piece of an old exploded star that had died long before the primordial soup of their own world had come into being, and ran smack into the spine of one of their own. How was that even possible? They must have passed that thing around between them at least ten different times, each folding it over and over in their hands, showing off the light in different angles, and positioning it to watch the light dance amid the rocks and cave dust they were sitting in.

Markus finally took possession of it, while the other two began to work on Bynffore, cleaning out the wounds and surface area now that he was no longer in danger. Majikal light infused the tunnel and drifted along Bynffore's skin. Markus used it to find something he could lay the stricken Aelf on, giving him relief from the cold floor. He found a bundle of discarded clothing lying in the corridor, pushed up against the far wall, and bent to drag it into the light. It was in an odd spot, but proved to be free of any debris that they had just walked through from the original chamber. How it had arrived here, was still a mystery; one that Markus cared not for exploring at this time, and one that he cared little to understand, considering the circumstances. As long as it was clean and didn't contain the stench of the previous cave, it was good to go. He would soon found out that the assumption was inherently wrong; for he did have feelings, just not the ones he thought he would.

The fabric he had picked up turned out to be not black, as first assumed, but silver. That silver caught the light from the torch just as he moved to cover Bynffore's limp body with it; then discovered it wasn't just a piece of ordinary fabric, either. He bent to examine its texture, as something shimmered within its weave and caught his attention and the fabric presented itself to them as a finely woven cloak. As he reached out towards it, he saw several metallic threads sticking out of the intricate weave that flowed within the fabric's interior cells. Markus reached towards them, fingers touching their molecules and felt the strange sensation of warmth held in its weave. This was good, but puzzling to him. He wondered if maybe it was part of the cave's uniqueness lulling him into a false sense of security.

Either way, Bynffore's old cloak was covered in blood and no longer a contender in warming the shivering Aelf from the dampness of the cave's floor; it would have to do. He bent down to wrap Bynffore in its warmth and had almost reached him, when the threads seem to lift themselves away from the weave, releasing their hold on the ornately spun fabric and shape-shifted into a round metallic disk.

Theiry gasped over his shoulder, watching it unfold from a distance, as the threads began to form themselves into the cylindrical shape that Markus now held in his hands. He slipped it into the middle of his palm, feeling the smooth metal on its surface, as whatever it was settled back into the warmth of his own skin. He tucked a section of his own cloak under his arm, to get a better look at it, removing the obstacle that prevented him from moving quickly should the need arise, and moved towards the torch as it flickered in the flames.

The disk changed its appearance as it came into focus, and he realized it was a perfect match for the broken section of the crystal shard that had been lodged in Bynffore's spine. He instantly dropped it and moved away, hoping it too, wouldn't come to life and begin the cycle all over again. It landed quietly on the stone floor and rolled slightly to the left. But what-ever might have been inside it, was either dead, or long gone, because it neither pulsated, nor produced any activity and before long his curiosity got the better of him and he went over to investigate it further.

He poked it with his foot, but the crystal shard had returned to its former shape and the metallic threads remained dormant, almost lifeless, where it lay. In fact, whatever it was appeared to not have any energy at all inside it silken edges. When he bent over to pick it up, to see if it would again change shape, he spied several other pieces of shiny metal that had been more or less in the same area and bent towards them to dig them out.

Whatever the lumps of metal were, they were far enough away from the main doorway that the light had hidden them from sight; where they remained in several layers of broken rocks. He reached down and picked one of them up, turning it over in the palm of his hand, finding it just as warm to the touch, as the strange shard of metal thread lying at his feet.

It turned out to be an old melted coin and a rather rare one at that. Had it been intact, it would have produced some pretty lucrative barter for them when brought forward into the light of day at any of the currency markets out on the planet Tifas. The metals that had been used to mint them — when the occasional one had resurfaced, hadn't been seen in a very long time and judging by the state they were in, they had been involved in the mess behind them as well.

Elyizeam moved towards Markus, intrigued as he watched him picked up several others lying in the same vicinity and passed one of the pieces over to him. He held it up to the light, brushing off the black soot that seemed to fill almost every inch of the coin's surface as they inspected them further, while their efforts revealed nothing more than melted faces.

How Markus had even spotted them in all that muck was a miracle. Unfortunately, their viability was long gone with the heat that had turned them into simple hunks of nothing more than melted lumps of metal. Nonetheless, they had arrived and it was to these impurities that particles from their surface slowly moved flowing softly over Markus's hands. From there they attached themselves to his energy pattern, systematically taking time to taste each of the bone ridges along his fingers and flowed fluidly off their tips to the edges of the precipice of his hands and drifted downwards towards the shapeshifting thread.

It was here on the ground, that it found what it had been searching for and tasted their signature on Markus's fingertips, where the identical pattern of the ones that had been woven into the fabric of the cloak had been held. It wasn't long before they began to merge together, forming some kind of ancient bond that had been programmed into its matrix and the broken pieces melded together. Theiry had joined the two from the sidelines, enthralled at the commotion it had caused, while the energy from the silver threads and the melted coins reunited before their eyes to form a perfect metallic cylinder.

This time it was able to maintain its flux and the cylinder wobbled slightly, as it moved towards Markus and rested up against his boot. There it stayed for the time being, shining away in the dim light of the cave, while they held their breath waiting for its next incarnation. But it never came; instead it lay dormant and smooth, waiting for the Aelves to either kick it away or pick it up, and neither Markus nor the others, were having any of it until something told them otherwise.

So, it stayed, as they left it lying on the ground; what it was, wasn't known at the time, but whatever it was, it was important enough to show the Aelves they belonged together as a whole unit. Markus went off to inspect the fabric of the cloak and the others had Bynffore to attend to.

The cloak had been beautiful and someone had dropped it on purpose, as they moved into the corridor away from whatever had sealed the other chamber off from above. It would appear that the cloak had indeed, been in the other room and someone or something had either dragged it, or peeled it off where the shadows were at their thickest; theoretically hiding it in plain view, from whoever had closed off the corridor in the other room. Obviously, it had worked or they would have found it. But why hide it? Was there something inside its fabrication of the cylinder or was the cloak itself the prize?

He sucked in his breath, thinking that someone had actually lived, through that mess and had either been dragged into this corridor, or had miraculously been able to move on his own accord, to where he had disen-tangled himself from the beautiful material as the injured creature had made its way to who knows where. He wondered if it still contained the molecules from the original creature that had owned it. If so, was it friend, or foe; bring-ing with it the unusual ability to warm itself as a way to protect it? And more importantly, did they have something in their grasp that could cause them harm, or had the cloak come forth out of the darkness to help them?

If the old coins had been part of that majik, and the hastily formed ritual after all these years had hidden both things from the sight of the one it had been intended for, then it might have made sense. The cloak might have made it through, but the crystal tucked inside its inner layers surely didn't come through unscathed; having been split in two with the violence of the entrance. It had remained there where it lay undetected until Bynffore and Elyizeam had been yanked through and literally fell on the other much larger half, which had been hidden inside several layers of mangled fibres that were strewn about the bigger cave. That was beginning to feel slightly orchestrated with their untimely arrival here below ground. Who knew they were here, besides the obvious?

The cloak's owner, now having been long gone from the cave they now found themselves to be in, brought a new thought into Markus's whirling mind. How was it suddenly, without any provocation on the Aelves' side, incidentally discovered by them, without having formally been given the riddle that seemingly would have lead the riders to its location. Something else had its hand in this; it was just too much of a coincidence for Markus to swallow and its smell was all around, silently waiting just out of their limited reach. It had the telltale stink of the Sidhe written all over it, as it now appeared to be infiltrating the underground tunnels, stalking their every move inside these walls.

Markus needed answers as they waited for Bynffore to find his conscious self once again. He sensed that had the cloak been dangerous, either he or one of the others would have felt it by now. With that being said, surely something would have remained from the old ritual that would have begun to cause them some form of grief long before now. After all, when the blast had blackened these walls, surely something had survived, no matter how little, in order to mark its passing. He knew he would be the one to stay and look, leaving him to take care of Bynffore, while Elyizeam could be better utilized by going back to the wellhead tunnel with Theiry, to decipher several of the glyphs he had seen as they made their way towards this location. Maybe he could pick up something they had missed that would give them a clue as to the owner of what was left behind.

The tunnel system had been intertwined with many sub-ground cisterns, each having a dramatic effect on one of the main thoroughfares that had brought them together in the chamber he now waited in — alongside his wounded friend. Theiry would be able to direct Elyizeam to the wellhead's original entrance, but Elyizeam might be able to have the eyes to read things they had not seen before, back when they had first become trapped.

The main problem that he could see was written along the glyphs on some of the walls that they had encountered along the way, long before they reached the others here in this room. They had been examining them at the time he had felt the others' presence, when his ears had picked up the arrival of someone else's signature in the caverns besides their own. It had definitely not been an Aelf, and they had no time to examine its presence. It had been left behind shortly after they realized just who was below ground with them, and both of them had missed vital clues as to its nature in search of their own kind.

As soon as Bynffore had stabilized enough, that was what he needed to do. Both Aelves agreed and had not even waited for his orders before they disappeared from the chamber in search of its contents, hoping that there might be something they could use that would explain what this place was and give them an idea where all the tunnels were in conjunction with each other; just in case they needed to make that hasty dash in the other direction.

As soon as they left, Markus had been planning something of his own; he paced from one side of the narrow corridor to the other, trying to figure out how to accomplish leaving Bynffore and exploring on his own. He accomplished just that by stumbling accidentally on another piece of crushed glyph that seemed to have received a similar fate — on the far side of the room, laying in pieces on the ground. It should not have been here on this side of the barrier and they had not spotted it, when they had first arrived in all the chaos. But he also knew they had stepped over a lot of things, as they moved Bynffore through the mess that was strewn all over the chamber floor on the other-side of the tunnel's walls. How it had gotten outside the original room and so far away from where the others had landed, was a mystery that he intended to explore. He hoped he wasn't wrong in doing so; if it was; he was on his own.

He took the time now to execute that excursion from this side of the cave, while he waited for the others to return. He was hoping it wouldn't take long, as Bynffore continued to snore after receiving a higher dose of willow bark salve than what he considered to be adequate for the job. Mind you, he had not been exposed to that kind of injury himself and the ones he had found himself to be involved in, had not taken a piece of alien shard right through a damn tendon, so he guessed it might be warranted.

If he was going to go through the wall, he was taking the cylinder with him. He didn't need something latching onto his own signature, preventing his inability to return; the only thing that didn't need a touchstone to bring him back through the void, would be nothing short of simple vapour. It was a simple procedure, as he went through the wall with it tucked firmly inside his cloak, knowing full well the creatures didn't need more than a few small movements to bring themselves out of the ether, to join his vaporous soul. That is, if they were actually creatures belonging to simple Fey, and not those made up with a majikal intent brought into being by the Sidhe Fey that claimed their souls as their own.

The stone that the wall was made out of opened up and he glided through between the molecules, stepping lightly into the other room without disturbing more than a few fragments of air inside the room. The room was vacant of life and showed no trace of them or their soulless accomplices; however, they could simply be lying in wait, just out of eyesight and in the direct line of fire just under the surface of the pile. For his protection, he created a simple vortex that allowed him visual clarity to where Bynffore continued to sleep, allowing him direct contact with the other room while he was here, in case things went south.

As soon as he got situated and the energy wave settled down, he noticed the area he had arrived in, appeared to have also been part of the entry point to what had obviously come through the ceiling stones. By the look of the damage, it had descended down into the chamber's underground world without anything put in place to slow down its re-entry into this realm, taking part of the upper roof with it and literally blowing it apart as the velocity it had reached, hadn't been able to contain its structure.

It must have been some blast; whatever it was, was long since gone and its final resting place had been quickly filled in by the cave-in it created, so there was no chance that they could escape and get out of here to the surface world above. He moved on.

He sifted through the large amounts of debris all over the cave's middle section, pushing aside several layers of crumbling stone that had been destroyed alongside several layers of well-placed dust. Calculating by the pieces of crystallized star dust lying about his feet, he would say that this very spot seemed to be one of the harder hit regions of the entire corridor; receiving more burn marks than the surrounding areas. This undoubtedly was the point of entry.

He brought some of the burnt fabric up to his nose and smelled its distinctive odour, taking time to study its texture and color, still finding nothing he had ever seen that could account for its intricate weave and fine craftsmanship. He looked around for a moment to watch Bynffore's breathing to make sure he was ok. He seemed fine. Nothing appeared out of the ordinary, and nothing dangerous that could be taken to be life-threatening from his sleeping form on the other-side of the wall was evident. He returned his attention to the debris field.

When they first entered the cave and had been helping Bynffore's unconscious form, they had been lucky he had more or less landed to the side of this pile by the time he had finished rolling. They had pretty much stayed out of range of wading into the depths of whatever this was, not having the time to sift through the wreckage, with Bynffore's injury taking precedence and the creatures waking up and moving them along.

Now he needed to keep his movements from disturbing things that could be caught underneath the heap of debris, which could prove to be dangerous. The last thing that they all needed was for him to phase on something else, causing more bodily damage underfoot and another injury with unnecessary grief for the others when they returned.

He used his majik to ignite the tail of one of the closest molecules as it passed by — to light the way and then held it aloft as it smoked and swirled into a brilliant yellow glow. He brought it over to the blackened material on the floor and moved his hands into the depths of the mess, finding several pieces of strange coin resting within the shredded material's inside layers. He raised them up towards the torch to see what they could be and maybe give him an idea where they might have come from. But, they were far too melted and twisted for him to make them out.

He listened again, trying to pick up anything that might still be lurking in the room hidden from view. He got nothing, not even a whisper of Sidhe smoke, so he continued his search and moved in deeper.

The outer-rim of the floor seemed to confirm his findings as he continued to find a fairly large scorch mark from something that had been exposed to extremely high temperatures from underneath the cloth he pulled away. No wonder nothing had been found in one piece; this whole area had been involved in some kind of bloody inferno. He wondered now if he had been mistaken in the assumption of someone making it out alive. The odds were definitely not in its favour, and it simply would have been presumptuous to think whoever he was, had.

He scoured the floor, continuing his search, and saw the markings that seem to prove otherwise. It was here he located several pieces of broken glyph, fallen about the floor of the room that should not have been here. In fact, they weren't even from this planet. He didn't touch the pieces, instead noted their existence with his photographic memory and placed it on the list for Elyizeam and Theiry's eventual return.

Not having the ability to re-instate that archive to its fullest purpose or intent could cost them all valuable time in the pursuit of finding the means to get back up to the surface world. As soon as Elyizeam returned, Markus would endeavor to send him to take in as much of the information as possible, then try and decipher what should be done with its remains and possible recovery of its true meaning. Maybe bringing Elyizeam along with him through the twist — would give them a better chance at not being detected and with Bynffore hopefully on the mend by then, they could spend more time figuring it out.

As he moved about the chamber, Markus listened for Bynffore's breathing to worsen as he made his way along the outer-edges of the room, and away from his actual line of sight. He found other pieces of another seriously huge stone column that had been pulled in from Goddess only knew where, lying upside down amongst the rocks and burnt debris. He turned part of the smaller bits that had broken off over, and noticed this one had highlighted pieces that had been etched in what had one time been silver outlines, leaving him to think it had been part of an ancient Standing Stone at one time. It had carvings, now burnt beyond repair unless you were some Uber-Elemental that worked in repairing these kinds of lost works of art; it was now useless. He brushed some of the dusty remnants off the edges and saw what had one time been planet shaped etchings, covered in some kind of celestial star chart around it. He moved on, cursing the lost pieces of antiquity. Someone had truly screwed up, caring little for the artifacts.

He continued his search of the area and gave it another reasonable tick in his brain for later retrieval, one he had not the knowledge to piece together without Elyizeam's eyes. Nothing of these things made any sense to his uneducated eyes, but Elyizeam would find things that he and the others would not think to look for — his knowledge being much farther advanced than any of them. He would like this one; it appeared to record some form of language that he had never seen before. Its very nature had been carved out of the solid stone within the rock wall and was noteworthy enough to take another look at. Besides, at the very least it would be proper to pay homage to the ancients of whatever land that had once thought to record its history within these very rocks, without bringing the wrath of the Gods down on their heads and causing them further damage while they were visiting their realm.

He turned and brought one of the coins with him, tucking it into his jacket, and went back to see how Bynffore was doing, fazing back into the wall and closing it off behind him.

CHAPTER THIRTY-NINE

Trying to find a way out, without getting
one-self killed in the process

It didn't take more than a few minutes to reach the area where Markus and Theiry had first entered the well cap from above. It was exactly where it should be, and exactly where they had left it. The chambers for once, had remained intact and had not tried to trick them with another illusion that took them accidentally off course and over some damn cliff. Ferrishyn moss had a tendency to make you see things that weren't really there and the corridors were literally covered in this lovely Bryophyte, which seemed to fill parts of the low ceilings as they crossed between tunnels, with its lacy webbing. For all they knew, they could have been heading in the total opposite direction and straight into a trap, which was exactly what happened when last they had been in its vicinity

The stairs however were absent, to which Theiry breathed a sigh of relief and didn't reappear as they had when they had last walked these tunnels; he was grateful and a wee bit embarrassed in his silliness and didn't need a repeat of his run in with the illusion — also he hadn't the inclination nor the time to explain the consequences they had faced with their last journey through this chamber. However, just to show him he had no control over its arrival, they did have the reminiscent smell of warm bread as they followed the tunnel back up to the bottom of the well. Elyizeam simply nodded and pointed for them to keep moving.

"Damn Faeries," was all that was said, as they continued on unimpeded by the smell. This time it had left them alone, without adding new stupidity into the mixture. Obviously, he had known what to expect in an old Sidhe mound, for other than closely watching the air, it had gone pretty much without a single hitch.

Once in the chamber, Theiry noticed that the energy rings that had been brimming with a full electrical charge were no longer there. In their place was a simple set of metal rings. He frowned, not quite able to explain their disappearance to Elyizeam, who looked up to see that they seemed to be the only thing holding them back from getting out.

"Hum, I wonder," he said as he moved forward to feel the cold metal that had moved down about four feet, giving him access to a small lever that had not been there before for the others. He didn't actually touch it, as the metal began to almost vibrate with anticipation of his actual skin making contact. He backed away pursing his lips.

"Well now, that is different."

"That was not there when we were here last," Theiry explained, pointing to the lever. "And that bloody thing was full of arching madness that was a bit grumpier than the benign appearance that it is trying to portray now." Elyizeam scratched his head, thinking as he took it all in, walking around the mechanism above them.

"Well," Elyi sighed. "It seems to be a bit of an enigma in its actual design and if I didn't know better, I would say it's showing us what it wants us to see and not what it actually does" — he said slightly frowning. Then thinking out-loud with the veracity of a scholar, he drew Theiry back into the conversation as if he hadn't paused, startling a few cave bats as they took to wing hollering their heads off to places unknown — leaving him blinking in annoyance at the disruption. He shook his head at the offending duo — waved them off and continued.

"Now look here, see how it looks like it's actually set into a patterned back-flushed reversed locking lever, when in fact that system is outdated and never worked efficiently back when it was in style. That leads me to believe that the switch is in reach and belongs to something else it wants us to touch that is far more deadly than a simple lock. Hum, I wonder what else is hidden out of sight," he said, mostly to himself; stepping cautiously around the chamber to feel it out.

He hated the Sidhe; they made him nervous. Actually to be fair, Elyizeam knew they probably made most Fey nervous and he wasn't alone in this matter — even on a good day. They were pretty well-known on most parts of the Fey planets and even when you thought you knew their next move — they would try to trip you up, no matter how well prepared you came to the fight. When it came to dealing with these creatures, they simply had their own agendas. In most cases it would turn rather nasty in the blink of an eye. That is, if they left you with an eye to actually see out of, after they took anything else that wasn't nailed down on your skeletal remains.

Theiry had time only to tell Elyizeam of their experiences once they had actually entered the room. Before that, silence had been called for; so he could listen to what lay ahead in case of ambush. Seeing the truth, and watching Theiry describe what he and Markus had seen when it had first punched itself into what it was today, was all he needed to get a view of what happened.

Elyizeam moved to try something else that wouldn't hurt him, as the lever suggested. He began instead, to attempt to pry the center rings away from the edge of the well from another angle below, out where the others had not been able to reach. It proved to be more of a lesson in futility; each time he pulled, another ring of equal size and shape would set itself into place around it, then close the gap. It was aggravating to say the least, but nothing either of them could do would release the lock that was set before them. The lever tried to beckon them once again, but neither of them was having anything to do with it.

Both stood back to rethink their next move.

The locks were well crafted, and for the life of them they could not break the unusual mechanism without the help of Symin's strange and extremely volatile energy wave. Locks were never a problem for him, and they had always used his ability to blast through them with ease. This one would have been no match for Symin, given the antiquity of its creation that they now faced. In fact, it probably would have been more of a curiosity than anything challenging and its construction nothing more than a play thing, given his unusual abilities. But he, was no longer with the group in this area of Tameron, and without him, it was useless to even try.

He now was beginning to wonder if that had not been planned. The energy Symin carried always traveled throughout and around the riders in their movements, for as long as they had been together; in situations far more dangerous than what presented itself underground right now. It had always been there for them to rely on, even when the Dragons had been away; whether it was on their own island, or down in another somewhere in the mountainous terrain of another world. It had even been there when that Sorcerer had tricked them and turned them into bloody leaves. But then again he knew Symin was hiding from the Sorcerer, so who knows what might have happened.

The group had felt the loss immediately after they watched Dyareius go, knowing his energy signature was by far the strongest felt, within the group's own single core structure; why they had taken him and not Symin was still up for debate, but if he were a betting Aelf he would think that Symin had his hands full of something else far more lethal than he was letting on. He wondered now what that might be?

Anyway, it had made no never mind and they at first had been horrified after the fight that Soren had started with Quist. It knocked everything sideways in the war of words with a Dragon that began to unexpectedly speak. For who would have imagined that a speaking Dragon could have such an effect on the war-hardened troop that had been through far worse, on even a good day? And in doing so, he had taken their only lead of Symin away from them, in that one swift final blow.

But, it did catch them by surprise; that was an unquestionable truth. And everyone that witnessed its arrival into their world that day would have been equally astonished with the fact of a Dragonlord not knowing his own mount had a tongue for speech, never mind one for foul language. Right now it seemed pretty funny, considering all of them except for maybe Assha, could swear up a blue streak, but then again nobody really knew Assha's uniqueness, and what would transpire in the days and weeks to come.

Elyizeam yawned, moving his head in the direction of Theiry suddenly calling for his attention with his thoughts, before he began to get caught up with the strange mixture of air pressure he could feel that had entered the room while he had been preoccupied with a past memory. Crap, he needed to pay attention to what he was doing. Their air supply had definitely changed since they first set foot in the chamber and was becoming thicker with every minute. It wouldn't take long at this speed before both of them would be no good to anyone, anything, or even each other; for however it took to acclimatize this into their bodies' bloodstream.

"We need to go." Theiry said again, when he didn't respond. With the thinning atmosphere starting to severely hamper their movements at this moment, neither really wanted to go back and explain to Markus that they weren't getting out this way any time soon. They needed to keep moving, at least to be able to stay awake long enough to get out of this area, as thicker air moved into the room at an even greater pace and heated up just enough to create the perfect atmosphere for sleep.

"Ok, let's head back; anything's better than beating our heads on this bloody locking system." Elyizeam agreed then looked away, following the rings upwards as he wandered slowly, advancing around the downward junction point, calculating their mass one last time. He could still see daylight outside as he looked up. The clouds continued to roll by overhead without too much variation in their drift, then pick up speed doing its best to roar through each of the tunnel systems they had arrived in, echoing through and among other chambers somewhere far down below. He needed to move faster if he was going to finish his calculations, allowing him to compare them to the setting of the Mauntra's cycle, as the clouds began to cloud over the outside viewing port once again.

The wind had quietened somewhat between gusts and whatever had disturbed the air molecules, was no longer there. He cocked his head to the side to get another angle on what still seemed to be near them, but much further away this time. He heard it again just before the wind picked up its next big gust and started to howl in earnest once more. Whatever it was, it wasn't trying to hide itself, as both heard the unmistakable sound of laughter ringing through the tunnels that were running in parallel, to this one somewhere below.

He stopped and listened. A full ten seconds between each system had traveled past the opening outside and the movement of the clouds seems to be drifting with even greater speed with each passing tick of the clock.

Something inside his brain didn't register that the opening was an illusion set to keep him here.

Then he heard something, quietly at first, and hushed Elyizeam to silence somewhere off to the left. Both felt the shiver of the unknown start to find its way into the room, as the night began to pull more shadows into the room from above. They moved their cloaks closer to their bodies as the leaves floated down from the canopy of trees high above; Elyizeam looked with face upwards, watching them rain down dropping into the well water that lay in the center of the chamber. They floated ever so gently into the space that had conspired to trap the four of them, as they now moved in perfect harmony with the sound of the laughter. They could wait no longer; they needed to get back to the others.

Theiry's knuckles were still sore from trying to force the rings on the pieces he had been trying to pry apart, when he and Markus had first come through. They had begun to bleed sometime back, but he had forgotten about them in the rush that followed when the other riders came through. It was time to stop and take into account the fact that they would not be using this juncture point. He put them up to his mouth to lick the blood away when a small amount of water rose up from somewhere beneath his feet and pooled in the deeper part of what looked like an old catch basin.

Elyizeam stopped and they both stared at the liquid shinning in the cistern. The illusion was thorough in its visual reference. Why had it suddenly decided to show itself now that they were already trapped and in its grasp? There was no water when Markus and Theiry had first entered the system, and yet here it was in all its liquid perfection, pooling up in the center of the room. He had not only heard the sound of water, but both Elyizeam and Theiry now watched as several leaves entered the system and fell into the liquid that ran underneath the area they were standing in; now coupled off to the side of the room, where the shadow of something dark seem to appear that had not been there before.

The cave-in was not noticeable at first, as it squatted like a fat turtle out along the darkened fringes of the room. But, as each took his turn watching the upper-rings resetting themselves and growing smaller and smaller the farther they moved away from them, they could see small filtered light drifting slowly within the chamber from the opening of some far off crack in the side wall.

The chamber they found themselves in currently housed nothing more than falling rock from the wall that had collapsed, with the exception of a few pieces of coin that had bounced from the upper wall-edges that someone at some time had thrown in for good luck. They stared at the dripping walls inside the space, listening to an echo that seemed to get louder and punch its way into the chamber. It seemed to be more active by the locked rings, which still seemed to be moving in and out of some kind of flux begging them to touch it.

Several different species of moss and fern began to push through the undergrowth, as mushrooms and fungi of all shapes and colours, could be seen majikally growing throughout the various shadows now filling every recess of the stone that made up the cave's walls. The room changed its appearance quickly, becoming alive with plant life that grew and shifted into the most central area of the new room, and wound itself around the two that now stood at its center.

Neither Aelf thought to move. Instead they watched, fascinated at the spectacle playing out in front of them, providing a floor show of wondrous grandeur, as it grew all around them filled with life. It was beautiful, almost reminiscent of the hanging gardens of Kaliea they had once seen on a previous trip through the realm of the planet worlds. The moss seemed to be alive with a form of animated mobility, stretching outwards and migrating across the stone floor, looking for the correct volume of its productivity. Reaching that potential, it quickly began to change the environment inside the cave, morphing the entire area it was in with a new coat of some kind of floraidised moss.

The sudden change in atmosphere immediately provided enough oxygen in the room to produce new life, and soon several buds popped out of the leafy texture with an audible surge as they began to bloom. It produced several different species of white flower, which quickly opened and sent out an intoxicating perfume upwards towards their nostrils.

They should have run as fast as they could down the other tunnel that had begun to close off behind them. Instead, unable to comprehend what was happening, they began to inhale the perfume. *Right move, for the wrong reason.* And now, unable to flee, they smelled the beautiful flowers set in front of them without wondering why they had done so. The only thing that made any sense was that each flower was more magnificent than the previous one, until the entire cave was draped in these unusual blooms, leaving the old cave to be indistinguishable from the creation of this new habitat.

Emotions ran high, as each of the Aelves began to hallucinate individually, away from each other. Elyizeam heard the distinctive sound of water gurgling in the background; while Theiry heard what appeared to be more like the waves of a lake lapping at the shore. But as the seconds turned into minutes, it was quickly agreed upon that they both heard the familiar sound of Faery bells moving about overhead. And that was the sound that both heard loud and clear, as it rang out into the air — alongside a very uniquely shaped vine that was moving in their direction and stretching itself along the ceiling as it made its way down the wall.

It was time to move, this they knew without a shadow of a doubt, as good old Aelven fear set itself finally into the marrow of their bones. But neither did; nor did they find the muscles in their legs to be cooperating with the fleeting feelings each of them needed to use in order to remove themselves from the chamber, as it continued to creep across the floor to their current position and work its way towards their feet.

The air around them was starting to become denser in its structure, and was now filling the room with the tincture of majikal sparks along the atoms of what had just left the cave previous to their arrival; while the vine slowly hunted them and moved in silently without causing them any further alarm. Particles of majikal dust were unmistakably all around the area, and their own bodies soon became part of the ignition source, as they met with the exposed molecules of an older majik that still existed in the chamber from before. Both collided and produced severe hallucinations, as the dead arrived and shadows pulled themselves out of the rocks. They flowed and slipped past them, passing through whatever lay within the sounds that called them and filled the room with past recordings of what had at one time been a very active room full of life and love.

By now both Aelves were back to back, as they watched the parade of souls creep through the walls and move through each of them, before exiting into another part of the tunnels where the rooms of things that used to belong to them were housed in their individual life-lines. Neither the dead nor the living touched one another at first, but simply passed each other as they acknowledged their spirit, and disappeared without further interference.

It didn't appear to be dangerous, and the room seemed to be giving off some unusual fluctuations within their own bodies, as the course of its arrival shifted into their air space and moved inside their lungs. Feelings began to be created that weren't their own, as each drifted and sought other interferences within their breath. It slowly changed, continuing to move around their brain stem and allowing their faculties to remain intact while the dead from time to time seemed to follow a different path. It was here, at this time, that they began to move into and around each of them during their visit from wherever they had been summoned from, as they whirled and swam along the rings' energy field and down into the cave's chamber in a maddening rush.

But soon, another thing arrived to join the parade, bringing hot flashes of warmth and light, as they began to infiltrate their own blood stream, moving inside them into the very heart of their veins. It was at this time that they started to feel its tiny fingers beginning to fill every single void of space that encircled the very air around lungs not used to its form or structure; while its birth grew inside their blood, and filled their lungs with its memory.

It would only be temporary, they would soon find out. But then again, a necessary transference; or if you like, an exchangement of sorts — from the above ground air, to a thinner and lighter medium which floated within the cavern's interior walls. This was something that wasn't just necessary if they were going to be staying for a while, it was simply vital if they wanted to continue to live.

Both Theiry and Elyizeam felt almost stoned from the sudden drop in temperature that the illusion produced inside their memories. But, just as they started to feel like they were going to fall to their knees, they felt something begin to wrap around their legs and find its teeth along the backs of their necks as the pressure of the vine tightened its grip and bit them deeply along the edges of their spine.

It held them for no more than a millisecond, as it brought them up off the floor then loosened its grip and released them from its hold after they had regained their balance. Their toes made contact with the stone floor and the vine moved off and disappeared from view, taking with it some of the headiness of the room's atmosphere. From there, their senses became sharper, as they watched the dead dissolve in front of their eyes, while the atoms swirled and moved upwards towards the spinning rings above them. Then, as the last of them departed and their ethereal beings became part of the genetic makeup of those rings, the Aelves could see that they were not metal at all, but comprised mostly of compressed dust and crystallized stars.

Yet they didn't try to leave to the surface world; it would have been a simple procedure to find their way upwards and leave the world of the Sidhe behind. Instead they stayed, unwilling to leave their friends behind for something as simple as freedom. Nothing made sense to the Dragonriders, as they continued to take in the tunnel's strange atmosphere and things inside their brains began to reposition themselves. The world began to blur and the chamber's air supply misted up in front of them, causing some form of eerie fog that started to move through the chamber, circling around their knees.

They moved closer together, keeping contact with each other as things started to become difficult to see. Certain features of the cave were beginning to swim in and out of their line of sight; then mysteriously it would clear and disappear into the solid rocks around them. Strange air-roots began to press through the fractures around the spinning rings and squeeze themselves into the room, forming into symbols and letters. They drifted through the chamber and attached themselves to the plants and vines that had just begun life in their new home. From there, these symbols were pulled through the plants' inner molecular cells and brought out into the open, illuminating the photosynthesis that was in the air from the protein that they exuded.

When they reached their fill, they drifted downwards towards the Aelves, moving through the protective barriers of their bodies and landing on their skin. From here they seemed to be recording all the information of their lives through the root filaments, passing through their molecular signatures and finding the outdated Aelven programing no longer needed below ground and releasing it outwards into the open air.

As fast as it has been written it was absorbed by the skin and then what was left, detached itself to hang in the air — right in front of their faces and transformed themselves into the dialect of an ancient formula of Runenitic Symboltry. There they hung, drifting on the warm air currents that slowly filled the room, as they watched them shimmering in and out of sync with the room's strange vibrations and auditory proclivity.

Elyizeam stretched out his fingers and touched each of the markings, listening to this new orchestra of imagery and sounds that the letters had allowed him to hear in their meaning, and felt the old language move through him with its gift. Theiry simply stood there with his mouth open, watching the display move around him, as it shimmered with a reddish glow, making him stoned. The particles floated through his fingertips, and reset themselves to his sight, giving him what he needed then withdrew the rest, taking his high away from him with their passing.

"Hey, come back," he whispered to them as they passed on by. But they continued moving away without a backwards glance. Elyizeam used touch, ignoring Theiry as he tried to chase something around the room that wasn't there. Eventually he would figure it out on his own. He moved on to the next symbol that entered and merged with his mind until he was done with each of them. The language was old and one that he was not familiar with in all his years of learning. Yet, he knew every nuance of its vocabulary as if he was born into the language from birth. Then leaving nothing lost in translation, he absorbed every gradation of the meanings it was translating, until he understood the content.

Theiry, on the other hand was given something entirely different, letting him see the thoughts of others more openly, adding clarity to its signature. Either way they both absorbed the content completely, each processing it in the way it would benefit them to amplify their own individual gifts and bring them to a new level not previously seen. Nothing was given that was not needed, and each that was given was directly created and designed for them alone.

Whatever the vine had done to them when it bit them, they found that their language skills were considerably more adept than before; giving a new awareness into their minds than any previous knowledge that had been taught before by their clan's linguistic masters. Then, without warning, everything retreated and they were left in the room, wondering why they had not continued on finding another way out.

Theiry had no doubt that Markus would be feeling the same effects of lightheadedness and similar emotions that each of them had begun to experience. With the volume of fresh air moving off through the tunnels, it only made sense it would follow the path downwards to where he was waiting on them to come back.

Bynffore should be already coming to and fighting consciousness by now. If he wasn't, the air would find a way to heal him, and give him that option as it taught all of them to cope in this underground world. How, he had no clue. Nevertheless, it was there whether they wanted it or not. As it was, the moment he regained that consciousness, he would be hard pressed to stay put, and they would have to have cause to get him to remain resting before he tried to get up and tear the bandages that Markus would have replaced by now, around his ankle and lower back. Theiry smiled, knowing Bynffore's mind; a mind that was constantly moving and one that even though his body had been dropped to the ground, would have continued to function. If it had its way, he was probably already on the surface, bringing reinforcements.

Markus would have dealt with that by now, being able to make anyone do what he wanted them to. That was why he took lead with the riders when Dyareius was not with them, if they got separated. So, with that in mind, Bynffore's over-functioning mind would have to be curtailed to remain quiet, and for that they would need all three of them present should he decide to disobey Markus's obvious authority over the situation.

His ability to change things into something else mentally would prove to be very handy when he was able to find his way back to his fighting strength, but it was brutal when his unconscious mind turned things loose into the outside air that were not actually happening to everyone else, from something that was very real inside his brain. They should have thought of that when Markus had asked them to check out the well-head. It was too late to worry about that now, whatever was about to happen had already begun its arrival.

Markus would have had to put a leash on his abilities, to utilize those gifts for everyone involved, as the unconscious mind struggled to distinguish fact from fiction. It wouldn't be until he was fully conscious that Markus's umbilicus would tear itself away, and his mind would once again be able to produce those abilities outwards towards an unsuspecting host. His ability was strong, and to be able to put things into people's minds that aren't really there was a gift that they had used on many occasions. This was something they were going to need down here in these tunnels, should they come across the Sidhe horde that had been living within chambers going on as long as the Aelves themselves had been here on this planet.

Theiry tried again one last time, as a parting gift to himself — without knowing the reason he did, nor having success in its conclusion. He should have known better than to think the Sidhe would have let him discover the hidden lever the others had not been able to find, all for the hunt of that elusive backup system that he was pretty sure would be used in case of a system failure. But the room had its secrets well hidden from anything that could readily be found. Nothing extra seemed to fall away or mislead his hands or, for that matter, create an illusion to his search. The deception of the builders to hide a part of it was not within this room. They needed to move on and make their way back to the others and hopefully not enter into someone else's domain, in one of the other tunnels they would have to pass through, to get out of the underground world of the Ferrishyn mosses.

The Fey worlds had some of the most unusual residents in their piece of fallen real-estate. This could prove to be one of those strange and elusive kingdoms that had slipped within the cracks of both worlds that occupied this space in time. They still would have to be diligent in their travels, to find a way out of here. And the question remained as to who could have possibly armed these triggers of almost alien design, as the pattern on the markings he was beginning to see curving silently around the stonework, were a mystery he was beginning to understand and one he was not too happy to know.

The sparks that filtered down their bodies from earlier, had begun to fester inside his skin, making him itch. They gave him an almost unrealistic view of everything around him. It appeared to change the barrier into something even more deadly, most likely to prevent those who dared to find themselves within the rings' inner most sanctuary, uninvited. But he would bet they were nothing more than a warning system, set so someone would be prevented from hunting on their turf, without knowledge of their arrival. The rest had definitely been tweaked; that left them unable to leave, knowing they had.

They would have to report back to Markus that they were now officially barred from the creatures below ground, letting them escape. The cave-in the dead creature had produced with some elaborate effect, was a non-functioning entrance way within the rubble to this subterranean world, but the wave of energy needed to produce this effect was not part of the cave's original function. It would appear that their friends both Aelf and Dragon alike would no longer be able to trace their movements, within this strange and cavernistic environment.

Something was definitely underfoot and had theoretically shut them off from all outside help for whatever it had in store for them, and until it played out or they could find their way out by other means, the hard work was about to begin and they were on their own. Markus would be both pissed and concerned by what appeared to be more than a simple locking mechanism malfunction. He had his doubts that this was something done without intent; he could feel it deep inside his bones. Its forward mechanical motion, which brought on an activication line of sight along the simplified function of energy fields, was no longer functioning, but something else was also at work. They were being stalked by something that had strong telepathic abilities and was feeding them sights and sounds that were unrealistic and fanciful. His new eyesight had proven that easily. It had all the makings of someone with immense power playing games with them. He could feel it drift down his back and try and feed from his soul.

Sidhe Queens had that kind of power, and he had no doubt they had stumbled on an entire nest of them. Unfortunately for them, if indeed that is what this was, she was not up to full speed yet. Had she been, they would already be dead and buried. He started to snicker, almost snorting with the realization of the play on words. Too late for that little insightful recognition of where they were; they were already buried, so that left dead to come. He settled down, getting back to the point, knowing full well it had already begun.

This one, for what it was, must still be in waiting and gathering her horde. That was more dangerous for all of them. In order to accomplish a takeover they used extraordinary measures to undertake that goal. If this indeed was what it was, all four of them were in imminent danger.

He told Theiry to cover up with ritual markers for protection, and started the motion of moving back towards the others, just in-case something decided to make a meal out of them. They hadn't gone very far, only around the corner, when some kind of marking in one of the tunnels caught his attention. They had been carved right in the wall in front of them. He bent down to examine the eroded runenitic design, running his fingers along the etchings that crumbled the moment he touched them. He stopped, letting the stone settle, while they pushed a pale powdery substance that looked similar to miner's dust out into the air and down the rock.

He rubbed it between his forefinger and thumb, and watched it change to several shades darker, with the oil from his skin. He cocked his neck upwards and saw similar etchings that seemed to follow a direct line in the cracks that filtered through deeper sediments of harder stone behind it. They seemed to come to life, growing into the corridor and coming out of the bedrock where they had been sitting, carved in the stone, for centuries.

How had they not noticed the carved symbols that seemed to be all over the walls, everywhere they looked? The entire cave system began to shift and move with their new sight, as if it was alive with life and living in the branches of some majikal vine. The stones seemed to rumble and fight for position along the tunnels walls, each finding their place and settling into some form of codex written in stone. It floated in the language it had been written in, and their meanings were simple and decisive, as the highlighted carvings took on a more densely shaped texture. It was carved within different styles of numeric designs, each one allowing them to see what had been hidden in the text when they had first passed by.

There had only been a small amount of carved markings at the tip of the entrance way earlier, and they were so faint and nondescript, that Theiry had passed them by without a second glance. But now those carvings seemed to take on a life of their own, as if they had been annoyed by his initial decision, and cabrofariously decided to get his attention by covering the entire walls and ceiling of the tunnels they had passed through, ignoring their warning.

The sight that was given, opened up and began to work, as Elyizeam placed his hands on the stones' surface and followed their flow along the borders of each of the letters. Several hundred years of sand and dirt started to fall away, as he moved his fingers into each of the carved surfaces and brushed their markings clean of dirt and grit, releasing what had been chiseled by hand so very long ago. Even then the letters had not been done in glyph beforehand; now they were pushed outwards, coming straight out of the wall and carved in the language of the Witch with such intent that even a whelp would understand their meaning.

They read simply, in letters of stone carved glyphs planted along the wall:
DANGER AHEAD, STAY AWAY!

They had come to an impasse. Obviously there was nothing more to be done but bite the bullet and move forwards in the only way that presented itself to them, despite whatever held them firmly in their grasp, waiting with anticipation on their impending doom. Both Aelves turned to face each other, looking for answers that simply weren't there. If they went forward they risked the warning the Witches had given them with such prominent emphasis. If they went back, they would be stuck in the old chamber of the well, which had no exit. Their choices had been simply eradicated and disposed of, presenting them with only one option, one that offered no hope of their coming through this unscathed and in one piece.

With that, they moved towards the tunnels presented to them, even though the warning had been crystal clear. The protection symbols they had wrapped around them were pulled in tighter against their skin, leaving little to be desired of the road ahead. They moved cautiously, closely monitoring the walls, and deeper into the depths of someone else's territory. With each step they made towards whatever was stalking them and holding them firmly within its grip, the chambers below began to come alive with activity.

"Stay vigilant; Markus will require answers from both of us. If something happens, stay together no matter how hard they make it." Theiry nodded quietly at Elyizeam, as they both proceeded onwards towards the very thing they had tried to stay clear of.

They hadn't gone far, when the older etchings they had spotted stopped, and were replaced by a newer dialect; one that was in use by several of the Faery clans of today's world. Those writings were all around them now, and filled the room to capacity. Every available space seemed to have been put to use, and some of them seemed to have migrated from the walls and were now occupying space along the sides of the floor.

The tunnel they were walking in became narrow, as the words seemed to find the Aelves' movements inside these walls as an affront to their years of peace and quiet. But they didn't give them a chance to find another route, spinning all around them like angry bees, out of control and at dizzying height, as the Aelves fought their way through to move through the hornet's nest. They came on en-masse, drifting off the walls and out of places that had kept their secrets for thousands of lifetimes. The Aelves, undeterred, scampered up the walls and skittered where they could to avoid the attack, as the writings moved underneath their feet and snapped at their ankles.

A set of steps opened up from the right and drifted down the corridor in front of them, leaving them no option but to descend down the casement or fight the beasts of insanity behind them. They seemed to be the focal point of a room that now found them moving downwards and forwards, opening up into another chamber that dwarfed the others from above. They had also not seen this chamber when they first walked to the room with the well. The letters and messages gave them no relief, squeezing all around them, touching their skin. They physically pushed the Aelves from behind, sending them scurrying downward in that direction, prodding them along when they tried to move away and return up the stairs to safety.

The chamber, in all its decadence was beautiful, whatever it was, providing them with ceilings that were vaulted and had carvings of ancient Shadowland imagery carved into the façade. Strange Gothic imagery found its way along the walls, bringing an almost mystical feeling into the chamber, as the smell of heady incense filled the air around them.

The chamber was covered throughout with beautiful, elaborately carved engravings of cartouched symbolry. Each of them seemed to be much more elaborate than the next, and each was drawn in the old Aelven dialects that were spoken fluently about 100,000 years ago. However, for some reason that was simply out of place, a recently activated Faery circle was drawn up in the sandy soil, smack dab in the middle of the room. Theiry could see the soil markings of soft soled footprints all over the place, and deep drag marks along the sand where someone had taken a large piece of sheeted quartz crystal, then lined the inner sanctum of that circle with its huge mass.

There was only one reason a mineral of such huge proportions was ever used in this manner, and that was only as a precautionary measure if someone wasn't able to finish getting the ritualistic scrying rings set up in the correct sequence. It was used as a buffer to equalize the pressure of an enormous mass that was suddenly called forward without the proper protocols set in place to guide it in, and the mass it constituted was a vortex of such monumental proportions that it was not easily contained.

Someone was playing with Sopdet's Goddess particles, and trying to overrule her authority. Someone was not only playing with fire, they were taking over and starting a coup. Whoever it was had recently been in the room, and to prove their point both Elyizeam and Theiry could see they had left tiny footprints outlined along the sand on the outside of what appeared to be a very much operational protection ring, around a circle that had been set up and was in full activation.

The footprints disappeared once they crossed the line, and were no longer visible once the creature had stepped inside its protected space. Theiry moved towards the edges of the circle that had been roughly drawn into the loose sand along the floor, and gazed around the room to see what looked to be an elaborately carved staff propped up against the far wall. It was clean and had been used recently. He followed the signature finger-prints along its handle, which was still not covered in dust like everything else that lie inside these underground corridors, and saw the markings of one of the old Faery Queens that used to visit this realm in the distant past.

That particular coven — the Synatarrae, had been mysteriously absent from any of the formal meetings the Ka`afrey Coven Members had called to order. No one had heard a word of where they had gone to, and why suddenly they seemed to have just dropped off the face of Tantaris. Not a single Faery from that fairly large coven had been heard from or seen in almost 100 years, and to see the staff of one of the more organized coven houses simply leaning against the wall and out of sight of the Queen, meant something was drastically wrong, and the coven was either dead or in danger.

They needed to get back to Markus and see if he could follow the scent, but first they went towards the sealed circle and did a controlled opening to its bursting particles that still were active and fighting like mad to contain themselves along the inner-rings. Elyizeam gently sent them back to where the four Guardians would be able to release them back into the Elemental void, and both Aelves watched them dissolve into the walls and the space in-between.

The circle held no power now and all inside was instantly revealed. It had been active for only about a day, but already one could see the destruction of the inner structure along the bottom of the sands, where the sheet of perfectly clear Quartz was translucently thin; providing an unobstructed view of the floor through to another room far below.

Nothing written among the carvings they had read coming into this cave had any reference to what they were about to encounter below. But, as they turned around to leave the space, they noticed that on this side of the doorway, the way back through was ornately carved with Selmathen protection symbols. Why would someone only carve on the one side and not the other? This room was beginning to stink of ritualistic activities and it became evident that they needed to remove themselves from this particular area, as soon as possible.

To the left they peered into yet another smaller cave-like room. This one had another kind of design on its walls, covered in tapestry and lit by tallow candles. This one they actually made it through, staying away from the other chamber and coming closer to the middle of the room. Once inside, it began to make it very evident as to what this room was intended to be.

This was a room they could use. Its function had been set up and illustrated completely without an opinion or illusional diagram set to confuse them or trip them up. In fact, it was a simple cave with a rather large carving on the wall; one that provided a map of the entire underground caverns of the Tameron area that they were currently in. And although it was Elyi's specialty this speaking of dialects, it was this and not some Sidhe Queen that finally brought his focus away from the world above and finding Markus, into the stone walls beneath.

Once that had transpired, nothing could break his concentration away from the letters and symbols currently being pored over by his hands, roughened by years of turning pages and reading texts covered with dust and dampness. Faery majik might have been at work, but here, he ruled the roost. All over the walls he was up to his ears, and eyeballs, in beautiful languages written in different dialects all over the paintings on the map that was set before him. It was here that all things Feyly written had been recorded for those who studied these things to see. Somewhere back in time, someone had gone to a lot of trouble to see that all was put to stone, with a record of things that had happened to this planet and any other planet in the vicinity. It was a gold mine and one that Elyizeam understood well.

There were over fifty-one languages which Elyizeam understood and spoke fluently, during the course of his lifetime as a student. Those were now among the others all carved within these walls. He had been trained in sounds and dialects all his young life in the teaching of the old masters of linguistics. This was like a whelp in a waterfall finding the Bowl of Kalmayta.

In the beginning years of his Tutelage, it had been a major undertaking to get a feel for what he had always known his calling would be. Having this gift brought to the attention of the Tuatha, he had become an instructor later in all things linguistic, and then asked to join the private hunters as a Dragonlord — which would gain him notoriety and warranted his rank in their private association with Tamerk and the Tuatha De' Danann.

It was this kind of Tutelage that often came in handy when situations such as these presented themselves to him. But nothing could compare to the sight that both of them had received above. This gift greatly enhanced his ability and sent him off in a totally new direction within his mind, allowing him to instantly receive others that he hadn't learned previously and opened up the possibility of even more in the coming years.

His knowledge of dialects that were spoken — even up to the coming in of the Resquenance period of survival during the Selmathen's birthing period, encompassed rare and highly regarded nuances in the Tuatha De' Danann's level of expertise. The consequences of his very survival in those early years had ramifications with the understanding of vast knowledge as an expert in his chosen field. He had always been shadowed by the military ranks of the Tuatha in order to protect him from harm in almost everything that he was sent to do, before the coming of the Black Dragons.

It could be the difference between life and death in any species' survival, having Elyizeam brought in to understand what they could not. He had done just that, when tribes were hunting near the badlands out along the Sadllenay borders, where majikal symbolism suddenly without provocation would show up without rhyme or reason.

The Sidhe owned that turf, albeit stolen from others, but they claimed it nonetheless. Sometimes he would find it right away, other times it would take some time before it showed up carved on the side of their bows when they moved along an unknown Leyline, drawn up in the sand near one of their hunts. But always he would find its texture and give them the intent before it killed someone.

It was more in the likelihood that it meant survival to the species that requested his gift, if he could learn to read their written or spoken languages ahead of someone creating an all-out war. It was what he did for the riders wherever they came into contact with other races during their movements between the doorways. Especially since some had only recently been opened, with the constantly shifting Fey coming and going all over the place; especially now that one of the main thoroughfares of the Selmathen race had been given permission to travel thorough their space.

During the beginning of their arrival as Dragonlords, they worked as a team and all would feel some part of the effect, which melded the group into Dyareius's mind. It was a specialty that was needed within any of the Dragon-riders' epochs that had come and gone, and he was one of the best that Sopdet had to offer. His training had brought him through many of the different worlds — both of the old and a few of the new and to date, his system was flawless by far and one of the most elaborate that had existed since their bringing the doorways on-line. That was, until today.

Without that part of the symmetry, they would be blinded by the darkness that was starting to set itself within the chamber from above. Not having Dyareius here would definitely cost them time, which was something they could ill afford at the moment; they needed to get back to Markus to make him understand that what was now deeply locked inside their minds, might just be able to bring his system back on line with Dyareius's link.

Elyi's hands could feel the raw-edges, and although the light was considerably dimmer, the reliefs had a special Quartzite rising around their edges, marking their reading as Wulushian in design. In the center of the chamber was a strange wooden desk that scholars had at one time used as they pored over their charts, mapping and correcting any inconsistencies in the long dim hours of many a winter's night. Theiry flashed up the oil globe sitting in the middle of the chamber on that desk, bringing light and warmth to its interior.

The instant illumination brought the beautiful paint they had used into focus, showing long years of disuse, indicative, of the age of the walls deep inside this cave. If Elyizeam had to give them a number, he would guess that they were in the hundreds of thousands of year's old, back in the Ereton Age of this growing rift of volcanic traveling. That in itself, brought new speculation as to what they had got themselves into.

"Ok that's odd. These items," he pointed to the old desk and fresh lamp oil — "should not be here." He pushed the desk to see if it was actually real, or just an illusion put there to trick them. But it held, leaving him somewhat perplexed.

"Something is wrong with them being part of this room; they have no dust on them," Elyizeam frowned, narrowing his eyes as he scanned the chamber motioning for Theiry to use a simple majik trick to illuminate the lamp.

"See it's here, just out of sight. Watch....there! Can you feel it now?" he whispered softly to Theiry, nodding towards the flickering light.

"Now it's even more apparent. Look closely and watch the flame as it moves," he said with a strange awe. Both Aelves watched the telltale formation of a Fire Elemental making its way around the glass globe, swirling away in the fire Theiry had lit.

"It's beautiful." Theiry blinked, watching the tiny creature come to life.

"Hello little one, where did you come from?" Elyizeam spoke with kindness to the Fey who stared wildly back and forth between the two of them as it continued to light the way. Elyizeam opened the globe that had it trapped; giving it its freedom. It stopped swirling and stood there for a moment, vibrating away, looking at the features of the two creatures that had freed it from captivity. Then it was off and moving through the tunnels, flying freely at last as it shimmered with happiness.

"Well that is odd," Theiry said, looking between it and the globe that Elyizeam still held in his hands. "How does one capture a Fire Elemental and trap its essence inside a globe and make it stay virtually a prisoner while they aren't using the lamp?"

"Sidhe!" they both said at the same time.

"Damn Faeries, never did have any scruples." Elyizeam shook his head watching the retreating light vanish down the tunnel then disappear from sight. "Who does that without having one of the larger varieties looking for the missing hatchling? Probably had just hatched when it was caught and couldn't find its way through the underground Brand holes." Elyizeam continued with disgust, as Theiry turned to go.

"Dammit, we really need to get the hel out of here, before the freaking entire horde comes after us, and does something to us like it did to that poor hatchling. I'm going for Markus; I can feel his energy just over about four or five tunnels through this wall. I think his energy would be more helpful in getting this done." Theiry spoke to Elyizeam, as he was examining the wall.

"I cannot do much more than make the light expand to help your eyesight, but he can extend the energy in your mind to work faster in this fast approaching stink." Elyizeam carried on looking at the relief, without making eye contact with Theiry.

"I would prefer that you stay; it is easier to read with light than to expand my mind without the means to actually see." He looked up, smiling, only to find himself staring at nothing but an empty wall. Theiry was already gone from the chamber; after making his decision, without waiting for an answer.

He realized Markus could provide something he could not and gone ahead anyways, already deciding what was best for both of them in the long run. He bent to retrieve another of the smoking torch lamps that was burning brightly against the wall, compliments of Theiry's majikal offering on his way out the door. He began to explore, knowing it had been the right choice even if he hadn't admitted it at the time. This time as he scoured the surface on a certain part of the map's relief, he found something just a little more interesting than before; reaching for that torch, he held it high in his hands and quickly returned to work scraping the dust off the stone with his bare hands and fingertips — out along the edges of what appeared to be a circle. He had never been very good at keeping another's company ahead of his work, so it wasn't much of a surprise to find Theiry gone.

There had not been many mapping sites that were left intact on this side of the Hydrous Secular partnership of planetary space. Mostly they were found near the Crystal Horse Nebula and much more concealed in the depths of their notorious and highly documented cave systems. That was where he had been born; living in deep space following the rifts through different time barriers towards edges of galaxies that brought him closer to the Tuatha De' Danann and the edges of what now lay before him.

Now these here, at least the ones he was working on, seemed out of place in this tunnel of rock and Faery dust. They were markedly different than the ones that had originally been carved in these old rocks. The latter having settled among the cracks and crevices that filtered through the caves walls, while these particular ones had only just recently been placed not more than a few cycles since the last rotation of the full moon.

It was so very strange to see them carved only on the surface walls, instead of deep in the matrix of the crystallized rock that held their birthing. There they would have been literally linked with the arrival of the rock's nucleus, and not just simple un-hosted carving made by some crude chisel that had hastily been smashed into the bedrock. In the Crystal Horse Nebula, down on the far side of ancient forest floors on that one area of seeded planets that hosted these glyphs, they had been covered in a thermal layer of super-heated water. This was not only a rare find; it had never been recorded to have been able to sustain itself so far away from the main crystalline matrix. And as far as he knew, nothing had been documented to have lived outside the matrices field of energy vibrations. He was beginning to wonder if there was another shift-point doorway in one of the other caves they had not entered — down somewhere below where they were currently standing that linked the two systems together. It made more sense as to the reason it had arrived here, and was still functioning in its survival mode.

The mineral content of the areas that hosted these reliefs had high concentrations of silver and copper flash-lines nearby. It was one of the tell-tale signs that hosted the Ferrishyn cities of the old worlds. They were known to have their doorways buried deep below their own cities, within the burrows that they lived and bred in, beneath the planet's inner crust.

These flash-lines should be no different here than on Esoyat Island on the planet Naunas, except they were a little more brilliant in colour. They should prove to be, he would think — just as ancient in age by their carving alone. That is, unless it was an illusion set to confuse them.

Then there was the moss that covered the tunnels from ceiling to floor, and when both Aelves had to move it sideways to finish reading some of the text that had been carved along its lace-like edges, it had grown with such speed as to bring to thought that something with a more ritualistic edge must be giving it the power to seed itself.

The Faery had always encouraged this particular species to grow within all of their burrows along the ley lines of their homes. The very essence of its nature discouraged anything from disturbing its root system, but the flash-lines they now found amongst its silken threads were usually not amongst their lacy veils. It was everywhere, Elyizeam noticed, slightly confused, knowing full well that the copper mineral was almost at toxic levels compared to their delicate living organism. Instead it preferred to grow along much damper surfaces than those conduits of copper mixed with silver, which had now begun to show their colour along the roots of its lovely stems. So why was it here in such an unlikely area with nothing to feed itself but the stones wedged in between and nothing else?

The walls also had other minerals that would be useful deeper down in the cave system below, and these were what he concentrated on now. He moved methodically, taking samples of the flash he would need to continue deciphering the markings in the other chambers at the stairs he was starting to descend along. He picked out a perfect specimen, leaning forward to inspect its qualities. He reached for his knife to extract a single sliver of the mineral Magnetite, which was set near the Pliminary Octahedron of the main tunnel's rock face. Between the two of them it would be more than useful; he dropped it into his pocket.

The former specimen had grown into one of the biggest Spinel Law-Twin formations he had seen in a good long while, giving it the unique visual effect of falling water. Its colouring was normally deep black or dark grey, but this one seemed to scream with indigo blue all around the inner vein, bubbling up with flashings of silver cobbled throughout its exterior housing.

"We might need it, to find our way back, won't we girl?" he said, more on the thought that they might suddenly find that the tunnels came into a solid conclusion heeding their progress, and need to get out in a hurry.

He didn't say the last bit, as he had turned to speak to Theiry, and realized he was no longer within hearing range. It had not occurred to him that he was alone by the stairs. Nor did he hesitate, as he moved along the map's edges, which took him in that general direction, bending to feel one of the last bits of wax he had managed to keep in his pouch, just in case the lamp decided to sputter and die. He found the lump rolling around the bottom and moved to examine the map, knowing it would be there should he need it.

He was so preoccupied that he didn't even notice he had systematically decided to actually move on ahead, alone. He progressed onto the first set without thinking too much of the danger, almost oblivious to the extraneous noise around him, talking away to himself as he always did. It alleviated the hollowness of his steps on the stairs, thereby preventing him from remembering that he was alone and without help should the need arise. He chatted to the walls as he had always done in the past, not always listening to his words, so caught up in the fascination of what lay bare before his fingers.

However, talking to himself came with the territory, and he was one of the worst culprits he knew of among the subterranean diggers he had come into contact with in his lifetime. Each downward step he took, brought him deeper and deeper into the catatonic stage of his thoughts, while he continued to whisper to himself recording the sight to photographic memory. It was nothing new, and all of the masters had at times been found to be actively holding long winded conversations with nothing but the wind, and going over great detail as if they needed to record the memory by whatever means was available to them, presenting no other way to find its true course.

As Elyi traveled with his fingers along the reliefs, he saw new changes along the wall patterns as it began to shift him deeper, moving him downward and more angled into the bowels of the earth than ever before. He sensed a presence; looking up he realized Markus had joined him and was sitting on the stairs, quietly waiting for him to acknowledge his arrival. Elyizeam half nodded, saying nothing more, and carried on briefly pointing towards the wall, examining yet another one of the reliefs. He pursed his lips, biting them in the process, and then scratched his cheek thinking.

"Ah, here is where we were at the point of entrance," he stamped his fingers repeatedly. Then he pointed to another sight off to the left, a long way from where they currently stood. "This is where the first juncture is located. And this," he moved his finger along the rough edge — "is another cave system that may be able to give us an exit-point, right alongside this lovely ring they have for some reason inscribed with a key symbol." He smiled, finding what he had come for and stood smirking, not even thinking that he should have said hello first.

Markus grinned wildly, having not been addressed with any formal greeting; he was more than used to Elyizeam and his unusual ways of communication.

"Shall we then?" Markus nodded with the affirmation already accredited to Elyizeam's mind, which suggested they would find much more in the way of other tunnels throughout the area — further along the deepest parts of the presented corridors he had spoken about, without Markus having to add in on the search. The Aelf had always done this, and neither Dyareius nor himself, had any reason to find fault with his unusual way of communication. It was just the way his mind worked.

He was a theoretical genius, and had always found it unnecessary to include formal greetings for any of his companions. He would simply start talking with the understanding that they understood his particular mind set equally, although, rather bordering on rudeness, he did not care; when he was done, he would simply quit talking and walk away. Simple, to the point; with no fuss or explanation.

His father had been the same way, and up to now it had probably never occurred to him that it could be done any other way. Markus grinned, and patted the Aelf on the back with the news that he had been able to find a possible way out, including what appeared to be an operating shift-point doorway that could very well release them from these tunnels.

They moved towards the area that the map had showed them, only to be cut short a few steps away from the top of the stairs. Sometime between when Markus had come down and they had been talking, a wall was silently replaced behind them, cutting them off from advancing in that direction and they came abruptly to a full stop.

"Damn it to tarnational fortitude and two whispers of a Cathor's tail!" yelled Markus, now seriously pissed off. "What, you have nothing better to do than follow us around and fatten up a couple of skinny Aelfs for whatever your preference might be?" Elyizeam started to grin at his words.

"Well," he said, "at least they left us the damn light." Immediately, to the ringing of laughter and to further their frustration and complicate things, the oil lamp sputtered and faded into nothing and everything went dark.

"Perfect, thanks a lot; why don't you just ask them to slit my wrists and be done with it?" Markus said sarcastically.

"That would be inconclusive for them having fulfilled their end game." Elyizeam said simply without emotion. Markus stuck his tongue out at Elyi and they both retraced their steps back down the stairs while Elyizeam sought out the lump of wax.

"Don't even think about lighting it, or we won't have it later when we might really need it." Markus grumbled, taking himself down the steps by feel alone, to reach the part of the relief of the map that Elyizeam had pointed to before. But that too was now completely missing, as his fingers slid along a section of very smooth walls, where the raised relief of the map had been located.

"I'm beginning to think it just likes to play with its food." Markus snorted, using his inner-sight to see that the maps had been completely removed from the walls. In their place were the beginning tendrils of Ferrishyn moss creeping their way along the upper recesses of the ceiling cracks, as it made its way down the stairs.

Markus swore as Elyizeam placed his fingers on the bare walls to see if he could pick up the energy particles of the missing etchings before the moss reached his knuckles. He could feel it slightly flicker and then slowly lose its calibration, vibrating away from his senses like it had been stung by a bee. The reliefs may have appeared to be missing and simply gone, but they still held the energy inside the stone stairwell and Elyizeam picked its threads as easily as if he had seen it with his own eyes. Then they simply left the vicinity like a shiver of a curtain in the wind, and took with them anything that had originally been housed around the stairs. He snorted, ignoring Markus, and concentrated on his search; almost tumbling down the stairs.

"Got yah," he said, feeling the last of them dissolve around his touch between the air space of the rocky facade. "You can run but you can't hide my pretty little ones." He felt the energy leave and with it several other caves and their adjoining tunnels with it.

Markus pulled Elyizeam off the wall where his fingers had remained intact, and shoved them through another doorway that shifted as they moved through it, while everything started to change around them. Each archway they passed in Markus's twist flickered with the remaining energy of what had been there, then quickly dissolved into something else, moving them up at first then down at the next turn. He pulled Elyizeam closer to him and used the particles of his energy to protect them as things began to bleed into one another. Things were morphing and melting the very interior of each of the chambers they came to, as they moved in and out of their rooms ahead of the superficial wave. Yet it kept on coming.

"Try to keep your head still," Elyi said searching Markus's hair with his hands, brushing the fine long strands with fingertips already raw from working them over the walls.

"Stop that, what are you doing? Can't you see I'm a little busy right now?" Markus asked trying to stay ahead of the flow that now seemed to have been replaced by something else that had not been there a millisecond ago. But Elyizeam didn't answer; instead he moved his fingers rapidly through his hair, looking for something that Markus hadn't seen.

"Got yah, you freak!" he yelled while Markus continued to move them through the walls.

"What is it?" Markus asked him, using the pulse points of his temples to stay focused when everything around them was coming and going and trying to attach itself to the twist.

"It's a scrying beetle," he said simply, feeling each set of molecules that whacked them as they went through another set of walls. "It's used as a tracking beacon, and it's the only thing that it could have been."

"Bloody hel, how did I pick that up?" yelled Markus as he moved them through a very dense section that contained more than simple rock.

"You must have picked it up on your way back, after you traded places with Theiry. Someone must have known you had this ability, and since it continued to track us even after we disappeared in your twist, I knew they must have planted it on you and not me. Had it been on me, your protection field would have spun it out and left it behind us. When that didn't happen, it only made sense that you were the one it was hiding in," Elyizeam said, spitting out several pieces of stalactite particles that had passed through his lips, as they moved through another layer between levels.

He turfed the beetle out into the ether; it landed on its back and quickly righted itself, flicking its antennas in their direction and recalibrating where their destination would take them. It began to record their movements, recalculating the trajectory and taking stock of the area they were moving towards. They, on the other hand, left it behind just as the recalibrations were complete and they careened into the lower cavern without it. It shook its head, retrieved its balance, and took off after them just as they came out of flux and into proper faze.

"I think we need to keep moving, before they decide to throw us another curve," Markus said, putting his hands on Elyizeam's back and moving him in the other direction, hoping it would give them another lead further down the corridor towards the room that Bynffore and Theiry were waiting within. The beetle had only just made it to the entrance of the tunnel they had moved into, when suddenly, without warning, it dissolved into dust, letting them go. It screamed in frustration, at whatever had attacked it, virtually stopping his hunt before it had started.

Both Aelves turned, hearing the scream, but nothing of the creature, or what had happened to cause it to squeal, was revealed to them. Instead they ran, as Markus yelled to move, and they both ran as fast as their legs could carry them, while whatever had stopped it vanished into the wind with it. By then they had traveled some distance, and the air became much thicker than up near the old well.

The path they took in their haste to get away from the creature they had thought was hot on their heels, lead them around several harrowing corners and then began to take them once again in an upwards incline. They wondered how far off track they had gone as they ran. Nothing of this new tunnel system had been recorded on the cave walls in the mapping room. They passed a steep embankment that spiraled downwards at a dizzying height, while they balanced themselves on the path, hearing the sound of water thundering away in the background.

Somewhere over there was an enormous waterfall, and even from here it was sending beautiful plumes of mist up the narrow corridor where it dripped and streamed down the cave walls. Beautiful white ferns were growing alongside the wall's edges; completely deprived of any light, yet still they seemed to thrive in the darkness, giving off the heady aroma of gardenia.

It brought their senses around, after spending so long inhaling cave-dust and spiders-dropping in these old nasty corridors and giving them a reprieve from the subterranean life. It was a relief to Markus; he had always hated darkened corridors — even on the surface world in the warmth of their own castle walls, where they were billeted. He had been less than excited when they appeared below the castle armaments and even further annoyed, when the moss had appeared.

The path proceeded to narrow even further and they now needed to follow each other very closely, with the ceiling above starting to disappear amongst stone-work that was definitely no longer part of the cave's natural walls. As they felt their way around the tunnel, they came across an older section of a wall, which belonged to something that had at one time been the outside foundation of some ancient building.

The tunnel began to blend itself into this older building, camouflaging itself into the natural stonework of the cave's interior that ran perpendicular to the old stone fortress. Whatever it was, the rocks were as solid as the steel on their blades, and not built by creatures that lived today on this world. In fact they belonged not even along Sopdet's constellations. Elyizeam had heard of an old city of the Earth Elementals, out along the fringes of a far off world that had suddenly and unexpectedly taken to flight and left the Earth Elementals without their city. Could this be where it had landed?

He highly doubted it, but the memory was brought forward out of the recesses of his mind and made him wonder. In order for that to happen there would have to have been massive energy readings coming off the walls, but he smelled only flowers and rocks. Hum too bad, it could have been the find of a century. He heard laughter again.

"Markus, did you hear that," he asked? But Markus wasn't listening. He was still finding fault with another web that they had just crossed through.

"Freaking spiders! Can't we find a damn tunnel that doesn't consist of every freaking arachnoid on this damn planet?" He was flailing his arms, moving around in circles and trying to get the sticky web off his cloak.

"I heard that laugh again," Elyizeam repeated.

"Well tell it to take the damn spiders with it, and go bother someone else," Markus roared back, fighting an invisible army of black hairy beasts' hel-bent on his annihilation. They continued on, after Elyi cuffed him once for being a brat, and then once again for good measure.

"Right," Markus said. "Onwards and bloody forward, without the heebie jebbies; I get it. It's not like something similar has ever happen to you on one of our other hunts. And quit bloody smacking me or I'm going to shove you into the damn wall," Markus said in retaliation as they continued stepping through and along several large rocks that the pathway was littered with.

"That is true, but its way more fun when it happens to you, oh so illustrious leader who never does anything wrong when we're looking. Now, get it together, them there be Faeries in the rocks," Elyi growled back at him.

"Oh shut up." Markus growled briefly, then moved forward, slightly disturbed by his outward burst of emotion. Instead, he concentrated on the passageway that opened up in front of them, as it continued moving them along at a snail's pace for what seemed like miles. They were coming into contact with more of it, and it was even older than the wall they had seen once they had finally slowed down from their harrowing ordeal with the beetle. The old stones here were not as covered up as it had first appeared to them and the moss was slowly losing its footing — diminishing considerably the further along they got. Its walls were completely exposed now and no trace of the old musty tunnels was visible from this point on. It was fair to say Markus wasn't too unhappy to see it go, for the moss provided the perfect environment for the spiders.

When they finally got into a more open space with high enough ceilings dangling with several different species of stalactites, it was stunning to say the least. Whoever had built this was a suburb craftsman and they had been incredibly accurate in the placement of the stones; each of which, was in the precise sequence and fitted into position to accommodate the one put into place after it with such proficiency — it was difficult to fathom how it had been achieved so far underground. Once squeezing their bodies past a particular difficult corner, they came into another section of the old fortress and the walls they were seeing here, were even older than the previous ones they had seen by the stairs.

"How in the world, did this place never get found? It's bloody huge." Markus said rather stunned. They had come to a fairly narrow corridor and he needed to move in closer to the wall in order to make it pass the stone outcropping. He put his hands on Elyi's shoulders as they passed a very narrow piece of the cave ceiling and came into contact with one of the Nocturnal Caver Nests, causing the occupant to slide down along its web right out in front of them.

"Bloody hel, tell me this passageway is opening up soon?" Markus swore, sucking in his breath as a few well placed oaths escaped into the air. He steered the creature away, as it slowly made its way towards his fingers and just before it scurried off, it took a short nip of his right knuckle. Finding nothing worth eating, it scampered up the tunnel stonework and into a crack in the wall, waiting for something a little smaller and definitely not a bloody Aelf.

"Ouch, you little stinker. That bloody thing just took a chunk out of me. I hate freaking spiders. Yah I'd run if I were you, you little assassin." He shook his hand, sucking on fingers to make his point. Elyizeam ignored him while he continued on ranting about the little bugs, until he spotted the light up ahead starting to change from the dull grey they had been seeing before, to something quite beautiful.

"I think I see more light up ahead." He pointed to a growing shimmer of green, which seemed to be getting brighter the closer they got to a narrow corridor they were coming through.

"I still think it's odd that nothing about this had been ever put to the table of the covens, since our arrival as caretakers in this sector of Tantaris." Elyizeam spoke, watching Markus who was still fully engaged in looking around to see if the spider was bringing any friends along the narrow corridor behind them. He grinned at the sight, and carried on with his thinking.

"How could this tunnel system have been hidden from the Fey that dwelt within these far reaches of Tantaris? I mean we lived in Tameron for how long, and this was here all along underneath our feet? This is seriously ludicrous." He stopped for a minute to see another specimen of spider crawl away before Markus spotted it, and felt his friend actually bump into the back of him. Markus wasn't paying attention to him. He was still looking to see if they were being followed by the last one and its kin, when he came into contact with Elyizeam's outstretched hand smacking him in the head again.

"Hey watch it," he whispered as he sheepishly looked at Elyi's hand. But it was Elyizeam's words, dripping with sarcasm, which made him turn around fully at attention.

"It would appear that even the village lords had never seen the markings on the wellhead, or we might not be down here worrying about spiders chasing our asses out into the streets above."

"It could happen, you know," Markus yelled back.

"Stranger things have, in these bloody caves, but I highly doubt they have the intelligence to purposefully seek you out." Elyizeam shook his head at his friend, and then gave up when he noticed Markus, sticking his tongue out at him. Elyizeam shook his head in feigned disgust, and then started to smile knowing it was always going to be this way.

His traveling companions at times made him really want to raise his arms up in the air, and walk away from their little superstitious minds. All of them at one time or another, except for maybe Assha, had this uncanny ability to find themselves in the middle of some kind of war with the animals and reptiles of this world. It was like they all were out to get them. And right now this was no different than the last time some spider or lizard had crawled into their line of sight, and tried to drown them in some forest lake that they had flown over, far above.

He looked at Markus one last time and watched the rider still trying to pick off whatever pieces of web had attached themselves to the backside of his cloak, like he really thought they were going to carry him off, drag his body into some underground web, and consume his bones with the other hapless travelers that had been down here before them.

They starred at each other for about ten seconds, barely breathing, then started to smirk, shaking their heads and dissolving into what presumably sounded more like female laughter. They progressed to punching each other in the arm, and carried on into the next chamber, hardly containing themselves from the actual though of the spiders. Elyizeam shushed them to keep their voices from carrying to those that may be waiting; knowing the inevitable was eventually going to bite them in the ass and it wasn't going to be a damn spider when it did.

They settled down needing the hilarity of the moment, as each of their steps seemed to take them a little deeper into another place that seemed to have eyes on them at every turn. At the very least they felt something was watching them with the smell of trouble that was growing older and deadlier with each step. Finally they started to open up through the larger section of the tunnel and move to a new section of older tunnels from the previous cave. This one wasn't as dry and they had to move around several streams that threatened to soak them to the skin, as they dodged a few small waterfalls running through the cracks in the rock face.

The moment they emerged into this new space, their ears began to feel like they were underwater and swimming in a lake. The green light from up above made them feel sort of strange, almost hallucinogenic, as if they were deep in the underwater world of one of the Undines. It created a weird sense of pressure on their inner ear, combined with the humidity that filled the room — now bending their eardrums with its density. Something told them to follow their senses, and move quickly through this chamber to get out as fast as possible. But the faster they traveled the worse the sensation affected them and they felt as if they were gliding along without gaining any ground.

They fought the sensation and did their best to buck the tide, but it was like swimming underwater and they were caught in a downdraft as it pushed them forward along the current with the oddest sensation of darkness shrinking the air molecules inside their brains. It was the strangest sensation they had felt in a long while, and yet it continued to defy explanation, making them feel like they were sitting in wet sticky glue, without any means to move to the corridor they could see on the other-side of the room.

It began ever so slowly setting their minds adrift within the shadow — traveling downwards and then forcing them back up towards the surface, like they were trapped underwater and covered in slippery eels. Everything inside their heads felt like they had been thrown into the drink, filled with blindness and shadows. Things didn't make any sense; first they were on hard rock and their hands could feel the actual texture of the stone, and then they felt like they were swimming in a lake full of warm water.

The cavern had the most unusual of smells. It laced their nostrils with the decayed stink of moldy mushrooms, and sent sensations down their noses, while some kind of water droplets continued to land on their faces. However, hard as they tried, they couldn't see it. Everything was just there all around them, causing alarm bells in their heads to ring like crazy and giving off a sense of imminent danger, as it moved like glue around their predatory senses.

Something snapped inside Elyizeam's protection wards and it was then that he realized they were actually swimming, in the bloody water; it shattered the illusion immediately, hauling what was left of the majikal incantation that had been running all around their bodies — pulling them down and pushed it out into the open. Markus only came to, after Elyi hit him with his foot and sent him into the wall, which broke any lingering effects of the spell immediately — waking him from whatever had continued to have a stranglehold over him, as he sputtered away picking out pieces of sodden cave-spacklings from out of his nostrils and flipping ears.

"Damn caves and their Sidhe conspiratory freaks!" hollered Markus, realizing just how close they had come to disaster. "Why is it that we can never have something benign happen to us in these underground environments of bats and creaky old caves," he said with disgust. The water remained silent in its response while he continued spitting into the growing depths that had now past their shoulder blades.

"Where is that darn Sorcerer when you need him? At least here he could have done some damn Wizarding, instead of trying to zap our asses in their nether regions out in that damn meadow," he further ranted.

Elyizeam tried to ignore him; it was like moving along at high speed on a Sylph hel-bent on flying straight through a rock wall on a windy day. Instead he concentrated on the hard contact particles coming into interaction with his skin. Not being from this world, Elyizeam was able to send several that reside inside his signature — that were not part of this landscape, to keep the spell from returning and bringing the hallucination back.

By the looks of it, it had obviously been flowing in around their ankles from almost the moment they had arrived in this new chamber. But, with their senses full of the hallucinogens, they had not realized that they were actually starting to drift downstream almost waist deep in the stuff. When they had finally gained control over their senses, both of them were covered in several layers of the Ferrishyn Moss that had been clinging to the ceiling as they had floated underneath them, causing further toxicity that further enhanced the illusion.

They continued to hang downwards, hitting them in the face as they moved amongst it. He reached up and pulled it free, to the amusement of Markus who, as of yet, hadn't realized he was just as covered. When he did, he pulled it off with such theatrics, much to the amusement of Elyi who watched him in the middle of the river, almost drowning in the water with hilarity. If it wasn't for an oddly shaped boulder that had come out of nowhere and he had been able to get himself on it, as Markus continued to flail like a pigeon caught with a slice of bread around his neck, trying to balance himself on the surface of the water while removing the damn hitchhikers off his skin, he might have lost it completely.

But the water was too fast, continuing to pour from all sides through fissures in the walls, raising steadily all around them. And the boulder soon had disappeared, as he lost his footing, and was swept away in the current without sounding the alarm that they were up to their necks in the stuff. If it hadn't been for Elyizeam, who shifted his molecules into the particulates of the water, and reversed the wards that had been put in place to allow them to hear, they would still have been drifting, oblivious to what lay ahead.

Somewhere down from the surface world above, they remembered the lake that had suddenly appeared over by the west wall of the castle and that Assha had been sent over there to investigate it. They must have gotten turned around in the tunnels when they first made a run for it, and had slowly been making their way underneath it until the clear bottom had been exposed, resulting in the strange feeling they felt when they had first entered the cave.

It had that wonderful, oddly fermented lake smell, which came with Drake Weed from the cattails that rustled in the wind near all lake edges. Except this one had come into contact with some kind of mineral that lay buried beneath the layers of rock, which gave off hallucinogenic properties.

To further complicate things, it would then have had to come into contact with the Ferrishyn moss they had passed through from somewhere up above, to give it that extra punch.

Markus shook his head to clear the cobwebs out of his brain. These cobwebs had nothing to do with the spider clan, and had everything to do with the water from the lake that was making this funny feeling inside his mind, like a fish swimming in a large whirlpool. His arms begun to ache, treading water in the ever deepening depths, with a mind full of spiders that had turned into stinging crawfish and a host of other nocturnal creatures swimming up and biting him in the ass. All of this and so much more — inside a mind that could no longer process the actuality of what was really going on around him, as the water began to grow in depth filling the natural rock causeway they had been pushed towards.

The dam broke and with more water coming in from all sides, it rushed faster down the walls and into the natural incline that had been carved out of the bare rock, taking them with it. They instantly got pulled into the passageway and carried downwards at an astonishing rate, as it took hold of their bodies and pushed them spiraling towards the bowels of the earth, where the moving water spun them out of control, twisting and turning them in the tight quarters, firmly trapping them in.

They had gone maybe, about five hundred arm's lengths, with the current tossing them through the natural slide like they were toy puppets, before they really knew they were in trouble. They heard it long before they saw it, and as they were pushed and pulled like feathers in a whirlpool, there would be nothing that could prevent them from falling over the precipice, as it took them over the brink of the huge waterfall to the world below.

The sound alone was deafening, but it was the actual thought of what was about to happen that had them praying to a Goddess that could no longer hear their screams.

They began to holler even louder, the moment they went over the edge of the falls, knowing there was no hope of recovery. The sensation of falling made them sick to their stomachs, but the actual movement of that rush was what broke them free from the hallucinogen of the upper chamber. Had they not become sick they might have still had the full sensation of going over the falls and actually making landfall below. As it stood, they continued to scream, finding that they actually had been so busy feeling the terror that the actual falling had stopped almost as fast as it had started. By the time they actually stopped yelling their heads off, it was all said and done and they realized they had simply stopped moving altogether.

However, that was as far as the falling was concerned. For, when their eyes adjusted to the surroundings with the roar of the falls still ringing in their ears, they found they were actually still high enough to cause immediate death — should they fall, and not low enough to actually jump. You see, the illusion of actually going over the falls had been apparently real; however, while hundreds of millions of gallons of a fast moving river hurtled on past them, they remained suspended in the middle of a free-fall, just about three feet from the sides of the wall, with the water tumbling all around them as it roared on by.

It was almost comical, if one had humor in the situation, as they hung there out from the wall, controlled by nothing more than what appeared to be a hasty erected force field that had majikally reached up and captured their bodies on their way down and saving them for whatever purpose it had intended to inflict on them. So there they stayed, as it continued to keep them momentarily from falling to their deaths with them firmly ensconced inside it, while they were left hanging about twenty feet down from the edge above, with nothing but a hundred feet of river water rushing by them on all sides.

"What in hel is this place?" yelled Markus, still pissed from the spider incident. This was followed shortly after by Elyizeam screaming obscenities at the wind. Then, to make matters worse, the bubble popped, dissolving right in front of them and both instantly closed their eyes with the realization of the upcoming fall, as they began to drop. They heard laughter as they fell almost a full ten meters, and then for some apparent reason only known to whoever had prevented them from further annihilation, something seemed once again to reach out and break their fall and the laughter stopped. Only to be replaced with an even stranger noise while they dangled like a participle high above the rocks below — yes, the Faeries were back and they brought with them the unmistakable sound of skittering feet.

Above the racket of the falls, Markus swore he heard a hiss just behind his left ear. Afraid of what he would see, he clamped his eyes tighter almost giving him the feeling of popping his poor eyeballs right through the back side of their sockets. When nothing further appeared and the hiss echoed out into the mist of the falls, it occurred to him that once again their actual deaths had been spared. Finally, both of them felt safe enough to pry their eyes open enough to witness their impending doom, hoping for whatever reason that those who had a hand in saving their asses from total destruction would be kind enough to put everything right, and get their feet down on solid ground and take the Faeries with them.

However, that was not too be — well, quickly anyways and slowly they came to the realization that something was not only playing with them, they were beginning to wonder if it was also trying to knock them off, before the fall actually killed them. Elyizeam heard the skittering again, but whatever it was, it seemed to disregard the immediate danger they were in, unless it was part of the elaborate ruse to keep them dangling from some unseen tether, without anything actually holding them back. Unfortunately, whoever was in charge, had them completely trapped and stuck in that position, having long since lost their boots, and if it wasn't bad enough the water had gotten significantly colder and was threatening to pull them in by their toes and drag them down.

Shortly after, their skin began to freeze, causing icicles to form on anything that they could; further hampering the situation they had gotten themselves in. It deliberately pulled at their clothes and threatened to tear them off, until the first of the icicles broke free and tumbled on past into the raging water below. It wasn't long after that when anything ice-bearing that had attached to them began to slowly come unbalanced. Then, with one final audible crack, it sent all the ice downwards and away from their bodies and they felt the release bringing warmth back to their extremities.

It seemed something was fighting over laying claim to their bodies and the moment something bad would happen, something equally nice would reset the balance from up above. Whatever creature was causing this, it wasn't visible from their vantage point of the cavern above, or anywhere they were situated in nearby. However, it was definitely on their side, and the game of ownership continued on for the better part of a micro-arn, without any willing participation from either of them.

Whatever creature is was, was obliterated from view from where they had fallen. The falls had simply covered everything from where they were hanging as it thundered on by, leaving nothing but a waiting game for those whose existence hung in the balance, while something played Feytonian Roulette with their lives.

Meanwhile, as they continued to cursed and swear their heads off; down below several huge boulders began to poke their heads out of the receding fog bank, as if they needed to have another visual reminder of what lay beneath them, given the possibility of their slipping from out of whatever held them firmly in its grip. It was here that a thought began to formulate inside Elyizeam's mind, as they dangled over the threshold of what eventually would be smashing them into ribbons should they suddenly become unstuck. If majik was holding them up, eventually majik would fail.

They had no choice it was now or never. If they didn't take charge of this game of puppetry as they danced around like live Marionettes in the air, who would come to their rescue? Given the fact that neither of them had seen any trace of the others, who hopefully had stayed hidden and away from this game of Sidhe insanity, he kind of thought they were on their own. He wondered now if it was even possible to try; I mean if they could actually swing themselves out to find a hand hold behind the falls they might just stand a chance.

On the other hand there wasn't time for the actual planning of that idea within its Aelven host; for, immediately after deciding they were going to reach over and try their luck at swinging over, they were suddenly pulled through by unseen hands into the rushing onslaught of water behind them, and yanked backwards into the wall.

The force of the water knocked them out cold before contact with the actual wall did anything to them. And by the time they woke up, the falls were not even present, nor the thought of how they had actually arrived on the ground among the grass that now waved high above their heads on a fairly warm summer's day out in the fields. Instead, their bodies were dry now, presenting to anyone who had decided to stroll among the barley on this lovely day as nothing out of the norm. Had they come across the Aelves in all their glory, they would have found the riders with their hair sticking out in all directions like something had simply placed them there and forgot to finish the rest of the ruse...

Markus reached over and picked several pieces of sticky plant off the back of Elyizeam's cloak as he brushed down his own clothes, got up and proceeded to move towards the trail head that presented itself to them from the thick of the tall grasses. Their past encounter was suddenly wiped clean from their minds and they whistled and laughed like shippels out on a walk on their day off. It never occurred to them how they had arrived here; they were just all of a sudden walking on solid ground with their boots firmly planted on their feet, talking between themselves as a cottage came into view. They moved towards it, forgetting the field, the falls, and their freaking future....

...TO BE CONTINUED IN BOOK THREE, *TRANSCENDING*...

A brief glimpse, into that first Chapter.

T he cottage looked empty as both of them moved through the trees alongside the edges of a shallow brook. As they passed by, numerous small bubbles broke the surface, revealing several strange looking heads that came out of the water to feed on the insects that buzzed overhead. What they were, Markus couldn't tell. But whatever they were, they apparently had plenty of food in this stream judging by the small rings constantly breaking along the surface, as insects were dragged beneath the waters, not long for this world.

The structure that pushed itself out of the bare earth appeared to have been lifeless for going on some-time. They moved around it as it revealed a ramshackled exterior literally coming apart at the seams and in total disrepair. The forest itself was in the final stages of reclaiming the land and had already moved up the back stairs, in the final process of laying claim to the back door. It wouldn't be too long before it jumped the landing grate, moved with renewed enthusiasm upwards to the roof and dragged it towards the forest behind.

Moving towards the far side of one of the broken boards, they noticed half of an old door that had come away from its hinges, and rested among the weeds that were beginning to make their way inside through a pane-less window. The other half of it was swinging freely against the free-floating upper jam on rusted old hinges no longer able to hold its weight. It was hanging there at an odd angle, waiting for the creeping weeds to fling its timbers into the grass to join its brethren; it didn't have long to wait. As soon as they stepped on the porch it fell, and something in the shape of a vine dragged it backwards into the weeds. They stepped over it, making sure they didn't impede its progress and it left them alone — hauling away its trophy.

Even here, the evidence was overwhelming that this cottage wasn't long for this world; even the garden herbs had re-seeded themselves and had established themselves as a strong competitor to the fast approaching forest floor that had found its way into the cottage's old garden, claiming most of the vegetation there already as its own.

Peering inside the broken bones of the cottage, through the shattered frames, nothing could be seen but fragmented furniture in the final stages of turning to dust. Off to the right a few pieces of silken fibres, resembling the tattered edges of what could have been at one time some lovely tapestry, were simply lying in disarray; a sad ending for such time consuming workmanship. The timber frames of those ragtag pieces lay scattered and broken, about the room; mixed in with several window dressings whose remains were hanging in shreds on their original hooks, on the far side of the wall.

Whoever had occupied the cottage was clearly someone of wealth, and not just any land-plougher that belonged to the village cooperative of the current Baron of this parcel of land. This was someone who may have been part of the Baron's actual family; although now in complete ruin, the pieces were extremely well crafted, and covered in various forms of the cobbled-webbings from the Minerarious Katwalk Fleabanes.

This particular species was known to only the richer landowners of old Tameron, who housed this insect in elaborate nest boxes out back, growing the silken threads for their market. The fibres were a hot commodity in the spice trade, and this particular pricey variety hadn't been seen in almost a thousand years and was thought to have been wiped out in the last planet seeding. Why had they left this rare creature behind, when most Fey would have paid a hefty coin to purchase it for their own family? Even with the planet seeding, things should have reset themselves and provided someone to care for them. To have them here alone made the appearance of the cottage even more of an oddity; for anyone that had moved away would have surely taken them along to their new residence, providing a much safer home in which they could spin their webs.

Markus reached through the door frame, after Elyizeam assured him none of the creatures remained, and removed the last of the broken wood so they wouldn't get snagged on the torn edges. They made their way into the first room, carefully stepping over various things ready to disintegrate with their arrival. Elyizeam followed and gazed around the room knocking the webs out of Markus's way in case something other than Fleabanes was using it as housing. The last thing he needed was Markus starting in again about his spider friends. But he wasn't fast enough; Markus found one of the strays and instantly started to wave his hands in the air, like a little Aelfling.

Elyi shook his head at the lunacy, as Markus twisted around in circles, getting what looked to be copper mine dust all over the room that they had walked through on their way into the house.

"Really, again? How in the blasted did you survive on those excursions we all did in the caves of Almalta? They were covered in webs of the Tacknea Spinder Spider and used to stick to everything we touched." Elyizeam said, looking slightly annoyed. Markus continued to battle with his phobia, as he stomped back again through the rusty colored dust to get away from the spider — too engrossed in what his mind told him he was seeing. Elyizeam ignored him and watched a mouse scuttle across the floor in front of Markus's boots. It made it to safety before Markus noticed him and peered back at them through an old hole in the wall, frightened by the ranting he couldn't understand.

The dust had come from somewhere and had obviously been tracked in by one of the larger animals that had probably wandered in from an old mine-site they had seen in the distance. But, a mouse was not the only creature to have made this cottage its home.

In the not too distant past, something other than a mouse had visited the inside of this ramshackled cottage. Over by the far-side of the room, tiny footprints clustered together at the base of the fire pit showed where the smaller creatures had arrived from above into the interior room when the front door had obviously been still attached to the frame at one time or another. Bigger footprints could be seen amongst them; however what it was, Elyizeam couldn't tell and had yet to determine its origin. They would need to be careful.

Unfortunately, Markus had other ideas and could be seen sidestepping around the place like a Witch moving about the Bale-fires on Samhain with her skirts dancing in the Elemental Breeze. Elyizeam could only watch the insanity unfold, until it played out in full and died a natural death.

"Maybe it would have been wiser for you to have stayed with Bynffore. At least in the cave you might not have looked like a female Praying Mantis about to give birth to her young," Elyizeam mocked. Markus still battling the Shades of the Spider, growled back at him with renewed annoyance.

"Well, at least I would be eating those damn things for dinner instead of trying to pry the little suckers out of my back when they landed out of the thin air to eat my freaking brain," he finished sarcastically. Elyizeam laughed at him as the dance of the spider's continued, while he surveyed the interior of the room.

"One of these days you're going to get hurt in your insanity, and that mind of yours is going to explode from all the crap you keep in there. Really, eat your brain? The things you come up with." He shook his head at Markus and ignored any further responses as Markus grumbled away in the background. Whoever lived here had left in a hurry. Things that would have been taken in a normal migratory move were still lying about all over the place; both of them skirted around the fallen debris to survey their surroundings.

Towards the back wall there were jars still neatly in place, lining pantry shelves covered in a fine layer of dust from years of neglect and disrepair. One came off the shelf and smashed on the floor as Markus bumped into the wooden shelf, not looking where he was going. The contents, marked in black coal, bore the names of some form of herbal supplement and released the odorous smell of rancid decay as it spilled out onto the ground, breaking open.

"Seriously, if you're going to wreck the place maybe you might want to wait outside with the rest of the garbage laying all over the place; at least then you won't bring the house down on our heads the next time you get tangled up in one of these webs you think are out to get you, you idiot!" Elyizeam said, grinning at him.

"Oh shut up and quit bugging me," Markus growled, ignoring the smart-ass remark and continuing through the kitchen area as he moved around the corner of a flat hand-hewn plank that had been placed over a broken board in the floor.

"What are we doing in here anyways? We should be exploring this from the outside. Seems to be a mite presumptuous of us to think there's something here of importance." He poked through a few snippets of stuff on the old side-boards and shivered slightly with the shade of another creepy crawly coming out of thin air and swatted its shadow as it scampered away. Trying to keep occupied, he turned to the staircase off the middle of the fire-pit area and peered into the upper-recesses of what seemed to be the rungs of rotting timbers going up to an attic. The dust made him sneeze as he flicked several pieces of the debris away that had fallen from above on the sleeve of his cloak. Several more sneezes came in quick succession, leaving him with watery eyes and a nasal passage under attack. As soon as he stopped — almost taking the railing with him, they both began to hear rustling noises from up above. Something skittered away from what looked to be a small wooden opening at the top of the staircase and moved out of sight. The opening was hidden from the main entrance of the cottage doorway by another structure of wood that had been part of a beautiful piece of screening at one time.

They were about to move away thinking it was only just animals that had made their way to the upper floors, when they heard it again even louder, and realized it definitely was not something on four legs. They both looked at each other quizzically, as Markus used hand signals to indicate they should go up and investigate further. Elyizeam nodded at him, and Markus kicked the bottom staircase timbers lightly, dispelling any fear that their dilapidated condition would cause them to come crashing down around them due to its rotted timbers. Nothing happened; the stairs remained intact and didn't budge. One foot at a time they made their way up the ten or so stairs — almost afraid to count them out should it jinx their luck in achieving their strength, until they got to the top one.

What they found at the top of the stairs was more than the rustling they heard earlier; this was definitely Fey in origin, but nothing like they had seen before. What showed itself to them was both ugly and gruesome; both stood there and watched it move slowly away towards the wall, trying its best to hide a swollen and disfigured face, obviously distressed at their arrival.

"You should not have come. They will make me do things I have no control over. If I were you, I'd start running now...."

Join us for the conclusion of Stolen Child in the
Third Book of Shadows, called Transcending

So we have completed Two Tales out of the Three that make up this book as a whole. I hope to see you for the final addition of this story that will complete the Tale of the Stolen Child. Until then, I hope you will continue to follow the story as it leads us forward in its unusual tale — out to where the creature the Aelves just discovered, chases them back to the cave of the Sidhe Queen. And our defiant little Shapeshifter goes head to head with the arrival of the Sling called Symbya, as she fights her way into the next world taking several unwilling Fey with her that get caught up in the cross-hairs of her going over the abyss.

FEY DICTIONARY

Aelf... a Fey creature that has some of the characteristics of a Human. Some of the clans have majikal powers and others not so much.

Aelfan... male inflection of the name

Aelfen... female inflection of the name

Aelven... this is the name for the species as a whole

Aelf-fledge... little child

Aelfling... older child, not yet full grown

Ahseekah... to move forward

Alraun... a herb for nightmares

Ambertine Glow... this is the colour of warm browns, infused with bits of yellow light

Anapher... one of the falcons of the Goddesses

Anforian Sugar Maples... one of the larger Maple Trees growing on the land of the Water's Deep continent

Anthrodeans... crystalline Fey from the planet of Anthros, belonging in the Goetutonias Nebula

Arns... a measurement of time; this one specifies it to be on the one year timeline

Astraltarian Waters... waters that keep the in-between worlds from colliding into each other

Attwicks... to stay still

Auick... these Elemental creatures are born in the Trench of Talon, and live among the wide open oceans. They are the protectors in the Selkie energy fields out in the ocean currents around Vaukknea Island. They run with pure Narn molecules during the storm waves, and guide the Selkies to their shedding grounds out around Undinecis Reef.

Axenic Knives... sharpened blades used by the Fey clans

Bairn... a small child of the Fey

Begonin Piglet... a pig that has feathers coming out of its head the colour of its own skin

Blood Fire... the fire that spews out of a Dragon's mouth

Blood-foam... the phlegm of a transforming Quasar Queen just before she turns

Bornlings... pure creatures born into that race of beings

Bowl of Kalmayta... water bowl of the ancients, to see through to other-worlds

Bragna...another word for hell

Branding Times... a time in Fey history that claimed the ownership of those that walked with the spirits and used their council to protect the village from majikal assaults

Bull Cathor... extremely cumbersome animal with bad behaviour

Bull Twicken... an animal that looks something like an old bulldog with fangs

Bumblefied Insects... Tantarian insects that resemble bees

Buttercup Katerpillar Odessa... a plant that grows near any kind of waterfall

Byanadorian Moon... a moon of the August nights

Cabrofairious Tabers... a measurement of hours

Cammond Berry Bush... a bush that has thorns on the end of the fruit

Caorunn Tree... a certain kind of tree; used for making the strongest of wands

Capilictic Period... the time in the beginning of the formation of Tantaris

Capourian Canine Pack Wolves... fierce wild Wolves that are known for their kill ratio

Cartouche... name of a Fey elder carved in stone, with a Celtic circle engraved around it

Caspian Beaverclaw Net Fungus... a type of mushroom

Catacombs of Naunas... a doorway to Leberone used by the Selmathens for travel

Cateferious Disease... this can attach itself to the Fey, when they shift into the in-between realms of Provenance

Cauper Dogs... village dogs of Sombreia

Centaur... Fey creature that is part Aelf and part horse in this rendition, and comes from The False Galaxy of the Crystal Horse Nebula

Clactonian... the age that moves between the Interglacial Era and the Acheulean period of time

Cloud People... Goddesses, Gods, and celestial beings

Cobbledwebs... nesting material from the Minerarious Katwalk Fleas

Cone Bees... stinging insects that store their poison in their duo cone-shaped bodies

Crabiolouses... newly formed pieces of currently dead pieces that are re-animated

Daunt... track or trace of molecules left by a Fey being

Death Monkey Barb... poisonous plant used to kill

Declivous... sloping downward

Deosil... moving in a clockwise direction of flow

Digs... measurement of weight

Doubl`on... currency that is something similar to that of the Doubloon from Earth

Dracore... a Dragon being that moves between both worlds of Dryad and Dragon

Draggert... a sum of money

Drymiais... Fey creatures which resemble mist; they are the nature-spirits of the Fey

Each Uisge... this Fey creature is a member of the Water Elemental family and resembles a wild looking horse, and tries to lure smaller and more docile creatures into the water to drown and consume them. It is extremely vicious and tends to be wilder than its kelpie cousins

Elderkat... older version of matriarchal indifference

Elestial Crystal... a multilayered crystal. This also comes enhydroed, meaning some have fluid inside them

Embryous... the molecules belongings to anything, via the embryotic threads

Energy Bees... a burst of energy in the form of a wave, which is aimed towards someone to calm them down

Energy Sting... a single strand of conjured central contained energy that moves as one being towards an intended target

Enhydronated... to hold some form of water or liquid inside the container

Ereton Ages... an ancient Period of time within the Fey galaxy

Euphoria Issadalfae... a calming drug produced by the Anforian Sugar Maple Tree

Farmian Coir Kat... lives in the caves of the ancestors

Fascuin Centurian Hug... something that knocks you over

Faunt... the energy thread of someone's molecules

Feast of Colours... celebration of light festival found in the cold nights of winter

Feldabob... freaking

Felinical... something that is changed and has the resemblance of a feline creature

Felldakat... creature evoked away from her home-world, by the Sidhe Priestess. She has two tails and looks like the cross between a Dragon, and that of a flying Cat

Ferrishyn... old name for Faeries

Ferrishyn kidlets... children of the Sidhe

Ferrishyn moss... grows near cities of the Sidhe

Ferrishyn Ponds... inhabited by the creatures of the Water Faeries

Fey Lines... similar to Ley Lines of earth, except these ones are shallow cracks within the upper surface layers that hold the energy of the planet's signature core

Feynominal... play on the word phenomenal

Feytonian... the race name of all the Fey

Fickle Tree... member of the Monkey Wart Plant

Finical Spideranthemaous... entity that entered Leonae's atmosphere

Finings... another name for the Selkie race in their Seal form

Firebrands... Elemental fire creature; usually small

Firecript Water Spits... tiny sea creatures that live in the depths of deepest underwater caves, and are the young of the Octtipede

Fires of Falias... a wave of fire

Fires of Osiris... a ritualistic fire festival

Flagnard... three boot lengths long

Flight Monkey... creature that spends its life in the air

Flocculating Forms... coming out of suspension into another formation

Florafied... a sentient creature made up of the chemical structures of plant life

Formediso... highly concentrated metallic coating growing on the skin of the Sirens to prevent the temporal flux from occurring

Fracklesteen... a swear word

Fragged... wrecked

Fragmire... a swear word

Friar Monkeys... cave Monkeys that reach out to travelers in times of illness, giving a boost to depleted energy reserves after being lost or disorientated in the darkness

Fringusha Swallows... cave creature that flies out into the daylight around fields and farms to feed

Fulgurations... to emit major fluctuations of energy, changing it into a form of lightning

Ganmole... Coutinnea's falcon

Garthenon Tree... Earth Elemental city fixture in Gorias

Genesis Planting... planets that are seeded into life by artificial means

Geode... a hollow sphere that contains an inner structure of crystal termination points growing in all different directions within a cave-like appearance

Gillified Bark... this a term for the Rayoola Tree's outer-exterior when it lives beneath the water near the Selkie home-world. This strange tree has the remnants of gills to breathe underwater and uses them to fish in the shallows

Glyph ... highlighted graphics done in carved stone

Glutinous Restaferious... a solid mass, made up quickly by transmorphication and formed into a breathing thing

Gorgon... lives within the Capourian Mountain Range, outside Tameron

Goated Squid...a Squid that grunts like a Goat when caught

Great Boors... live in the caves of the ancestors

Ground... this means to disperse the energy into another object to stabilize it

Gryphon... a mythical beast with the body of a Lion and the wings of a Dragon.

Guttering Shifter... a creature that can take on the forms of things that are not alive, and can form it into a living sentient body as it comes to life. It was thought to be long extinct and no longer part of the Fey worlds

Gwadrafed... feathered bird that belongs to Coutinnea's aunt. His kind is used to protect the Sages of the Fey clans

Gwraqedd Annwn... Water Elementals called Undines; they live in tiny pools near larger sources of fresh water

Hakerling... a swear word

Handfasted... this is a Pagan joining ceremony that is the same as being married

Hel... This is not a misspelling; it is the Fey and pagan spelling of the Christian word hell. Although this manuscript has neither the religious connotation, nor the use of its dogma it is used fluently throughout the story and will not be capitalized

Helical Period... in reference to the age of the planet

Hobbernaut Stones... a swear word

Hot Barbery Sage... leaves of the Sage plant that dissolve circle nasties

Is`lantic homes... water-based fauna that bond together, to make up a living island

Jaboorian Whiskey... Cian's concoction of spirits

Jacobien Camiforean Elm Tree... this species also known as the Rayoola tree. It is also one of the sentient flora species, which can move from place to place

Jadquoius Oysterus... brilliant green and blackened colouring

Jellyfishcals... slimy creature of the sea without any skeletal system

Joie Giun Bear... dangerous mammal living and hunting in the forest

Jump Jaw Crickets... an insect that uses its large legs to sing by rubbing them over its jaw

Kaulfarrier Flare... meteor flares that are part of the Kaulfarrier Asteroids

Kendoffalous Ale... fermented drink brewed on the planet Naunas

Kepet... another word for hel

Kidlet... young Fey are called this just after they pass the infant stage

Kiffersnitt... young Goddesses' name before they come of age

Kip... to sleep

Kiper-fig... a swear-word

Kit... a young Shapeshifter or Selkie

Kitwicks... Island based Homelands of the Selkie clans

Klifferdesh... helish

Kraken Moth... cave insect that has a poisonous stinger not unlike that of a Box Jellyfish from the Planet Earth

Krugs... small warring Pictish Faeries that live among the Tryilamore's landslips. These small Faeries have taken it upon themselves to be the ambassadors of the Island of Vaukknea

Landasticlly... sworn to be land bound

Landfish... animal living on, or within the soil

Liquidine... this term is used when a water source is part of a formula of liquid and brine

LucreousTree... a majikal tree that resides in the village of the Kanoie clan of Witches

Lycanthrope... Werewolf like creature

Mabonistic Gathering... one of the last gathering festivals before the end of the growing season

Malachim Symbols... derived from the Malachim alphabet from the 16th century Earth, consisting of Hebrew and Greek letters maintaining a mystical feel to them

Mathura Tree... this tree is highly sought after for its fire resin that is used in Selmathen Fire Rituals

Mauntra... the hot Star within the Faden Corpeous Galaxy, resembling our Sun

Mercorian Death Blade... swords made within the village of Sombreia's forges

Metalrats... an Aelf that specializes in metalwork in tunnel building

Micro-Arn... a measurement of one hour

Micro-second... a measurement of minutes

Micron... a measurement of inches or feet

Miladram... a molecular measurement in the velocity of placement

Millisecond... a measurement of seconds

Millitrons... a measurement of centimetres

Miraclouscitity... meaning miracle

Moondogs... reflection of light that circles the moon during times of changing weather systems. This occurrence can be simply having an unusually warm day and a cooler night, all clashing away in the atmosphere high-above

Moon Mansions... these are intervals that separate the phases of the moon and Mauntra rotational times, giving them a much more defined working time for a precise spell or ritual

Morgauseine Mylornese... this is a Selkie majikal invisibility spell. It is used to hide things that others cannot see

Muscle Toe Root... allows one to see distances

Mushroom Lichen Stone... this stone accompanies the Ferrishyn Mosses. They are always interwoven, and live symbiotically with each other. It is used as a mapping stone, and can mimic the signatures of the clans that lay claim to a particular tunnel system they are found in

Mycorpian Thread... this runs in the families of the Lemurian line of Fey that lived within this Galaxy, thousands of years ago

Naiads... water creatures that resemble Faeries, but are of a lake environment

Narcan... a reclusive loner

Narn... solitary Selkies that live their lives out at sea and never set foot upon the land

Nest Tree... host tree that houses many different creatures

Newbornling... infant offspring of the clans

Orb Blowers... subterranean Spiders of the Sidhe home-world

Orealis... Elemental sheen

Oxymorpheeis... oxymoronic

Pandora Berries...berries similar to pomegranate and blueberries

Pantherous Succubus... mythical creature of dreams

Penndersnagen Game of Flagernutt Tuttle Cards... a Fey card game

Phantasmagorias... means dreams or the illusion of, including that of hallucinations

Phases... are pertaining to time. Mostly in the hourly quadrants of our clocking systems

Pickle Pop Beets... a vegetable beet that grows in Kamera's garden, and is used in her herbal remedies for pushing things into motion

Pitten Bull... a play on the word Pit Bull; unfortunately this one is the size of an actual Bull, and has three long lavish horns of about five feet long on either side of its head

Pizenean Jellyfish...large looking creatures about three feet across with all the makings of the Earth Jellies. They live out and around the Water Elemental city of Murias.

Plagasfear Majik... this ritual is known on the Earth Worlds as Zombie animation, but here in the Fey Realms it has been practiced only by the Sidhe tribes of the old world of Faeries. Its properties more or less animate simple flora or fauna into an animated creature, which is given a directive to move forward towards its fruition

Polarlithic Flow... movement going in either north or south direction

Potter Pudding... a food that is similar to meat pies

Pyaan... a creature that is similar to the mythical Pan, and has the personality of a trickster

Pyckadyes... cave creature that lives in the bark of the Madder Tree

Pyriticle Scapolite Octtipede... creature that lives deep in the ocean, similar to an Octopus

Quadpoolings of Flux... energy harness; used to fit something into place

Quadra... a measurement

Quadrafed... sent in secret

Quadramass... final resting place after something snaps

Quadrapitions... a measurement of inches

Quadra-second... a measurement of half seconds

Quadriplunket Saberious... a herbal remedy for severe mystical poisonings

Quantum's Body... the minimum amount of any physical entity involved in an interaction that allows one to enter another creature into its core

Quick's Bottom...this is a nature depression in the Dells near the Lypurnen Woods

Radiating Pulse Worm... Earth Creature that lives underground near active volcanoes

Rathskeller Gold... currency trade with higher than average sums to the simple Fey barter

Ratterfellen... a swear word

Red Dragon Salamanders... Salamanders that breathe fire, like a Dragon

Red Tide... a large concentration of algae, blooming within the salted waters of an ocean

Ritual of Shedding... Selkie and Merfolk use the storm seasons for purification rituals of cleansing, to perform this rite. It is also for feeding their energy reserves

Rocklerite... Earth Elemental that lives inside the burrows that it digs. They are usually found near a Witch's homestead

Rokh... means one of the hidden animal colonies of the forests

Runenitic... designs made from the ancient art of runes

Runner... one that fetches things

Salamander Oxenberry Dust... herb used to cleanse one of anything hidden

Salamendrium... tiny Fire Elemental Horse with wings

Sangrinine Butterfluncal Trickells... sea creature living near the reef worlds

Santarian Brandy... a special blend of spirits that Cian and Tamerk endeavored to brew

Santherian Religion... an old world order that was used in helping all the new Quasar Queens to move smoothly into their transition, with the full understanding of their abilities

Sarcophagus... enclosed container to house the dead

Sea Tucker Fish... beautiful and very expensive, well sought after fish

Sea Woraninthias... a large sea creature

Sedmires... land of the protection Goddesses

Seeker... runner

Seer Stone... helps to slow speed or time down, so one can visualize its properties

Seliki... Selkie amphibious state, when they become a water bearing creature of the waves

Selkie... Fey creature that resembles a Seal in the sea, and changes to a creature similar looking to an Aelf on land. However this one is much taller with unusual features

Selkmordian Miracle... Selkie miracle of words

Setti... life beyond living as a Corporeal Fey

Shade... a life force that sits just on the edges of peripheral vision, and can be visualized by those with the sight to see. Also known as a village shade

Shadow Fey... Elemental beings used by the factions of the individual Elemental tribes

Shadowlands... the place where darkness lives among the light worlds and everything is not solid in its touch

Shadow Land Horses... huge Water-Horses that belong to the old world royalty

Shee... The word Sidhe is usually pronounced this way. But here is pertains to the dark Faery or Seelie beings

Shippels... Shapeshifter youngsters

Sidhe... are the nasty dark Faeries; not to be confused with the light Faeries

Sigg... creatures of opportunity living deep within the vastness of deep space

Silvercross-Fillstar Bush... silvery bush that has flowers that resemble small stars

Slips...measurement of time in Fey language. One slip constitutes one hour of their day

Sliverstone... mirror

Sitorer`ay Demon... this creature is part of the venomous Gargoyle family

Slaugh... Wild Boar

Sling... entity called Symbya, originated in the Star of the Sirens

Small Spits... young Fey child

Soft Landers... any Fey creature that lives on land

Sopdet Fly... one of the creatures that live along the spacial fields of the Goddess Sopdet; on Earth she is revered and known as an Egyptian Goddess that lives and resides in the star cluster Sirius. In this novel she is the head of the Goddess race of Fey that controls the constellations around Faden Corpeous

Speleothem... stalactites and stalagmites are a form of this mineral deposit in their caves

Sphere Line Dust... a description of measurement

Spitlet... Shapeshifter child, not yet a fully grown adult

Standing Mirrors... these are creatures of opportunity called the Sigg. They become the Standing Mirrors when they reach maturity, but till then, they live without solid form and breed out in the confines of deep space as a spectral juvenile

Star Point Collision... a collision of spacial molecules spit out by a revolving star

Stingers... dream tendrils that seem to cling to one's mind during the waking stage

Stone of Kaliea... this stone has seeker properties. It searches for what you ask, and shows it to you

Stony Mason Bees... Fey creatures that are conjured by majik

Suter Plank Cat... a ferocious feline that lives within the old city of Jaborria

Sylph... an Elemental creature of the element of air; rides the wind during huge storms

Taber Owl... a pet of Ryyaan's whose species lives in the Lypurnen Woods

Tacknea Spinder Spider... found in the caves of Almalta

Taglow... means simply, a little bugger

Tagmar... name of Sibrey's Wolfen Owlley; her dog

Tambergeen Fickle Fly... one of the fastest insects that lives on Tameron

Tameron the Quick... the village of Tameron's essence; one that the Elementals and Sky Goddesses see

Tameronian Elkhound Rock... a very beautiful and sturdy rock that has veins of minerals in it, that give it the look of fur from an Elkhound dog

Tantarian... language spoken on Tantaris

Tantaris.... Planet where this race of Fey is centrally found

Tantarisian Skin... simple way of saying the creature that belongs to this skin, is from Tantaris

Tantarisian Space... area of space around the planet Tantaris

Tantorian Space... the spacial inflections that the Air Elementals see around Tantaris

Tantry Snakalofous... underground protector of the Dark Faeries, living in the Sidhe tunnels

Taper Deer... one of the wild Deer that roam along the tree-lines, out near the far eastern ridges of the Sydclath Mountain Ranges

Taps... measurement of footprints; equaling one, for about every two of your boot steps

Tayoseian... people of Tayose

Terrand... all seeded land on the planet's surface

Thickals...used as a measurement to judge age; or in place of the word 'years'

Thunderstormation Waves... giant wave action during Selkie energy storms

Tidal barriers... a set area of space that has been limited to another creature's movements

Time Link Crystal... a programed crystal's safety area; always used in the making of ritual spells of protection

Time Star Circle... protection sphere that works in conjunction with the Time Link Crystals

Transdental Factions... beings that belong to a certain race of caretakers

Transmorphication... to change into something different

Transquadrated... shifted from one body, to another

Travelational Point Module... a moving point of transportation

Tree Morrigan... a creature that is one of the forest inhabitants that resembles a tree, and has skin reminiscent of bark

Trenchers... wooden bowls used for food

Trilasecks... a term used like an old Earth exclamation

Trilla-second... a measurement of time one billionth of a micro-second

Trumpet Ivy Vine... a big vine that has leaves the shape of Trumpets

Trysector... a measurement of what ten miles in the Human language, would look like

Tuffa... means something that is instantly happening

Undine... this Elemental creature lives in any source of water. But the creatures of the same species that live primarily in fresh, are also called Gwraqedd Annwn

Valkyrji... a Fey creature that is the chooser of life or death and the dying

Vermodious... a Fey swear word

Vermorbian... this creature from the Carthanthien Nebula has a nasty temperament, and is known for its resistance to dark star matter

Vermorbian Craklenock... a creature of the imagination

Viper Spanger... a creature with paralyzing fangs

Visinean Jars...holds a Fey Queen's inner Elemental rites from the four directional quarters. They are given to her when she comes of age

Volcanic Glowerites... creatures that infiltrate and live in the Tuatha De' Danann's volcanic structures of pumice stone

Wailing... newborn Fey of the Witch clan of Kanoie; or sound sent out in warning

Wards... majikal locks placed on things or places to prevent anyone from getting inside

Watermite Kind... waterfolk

Whenshi Rites... calling of this rite makes something forever

Wick... a name for an area resided by only those of Witch clan; all of which live within this area of the energy field they call the Wick possess majikal molecules needed by those of that race of Fey

Widderschynnes... moving in an anti-clockwise direction to the Sun or celestial objects within the sky; always keep the object to your left while in motion

Willow Wheat... a Fey root staple, used in making bread

Windistic Rhythm... tide of spacial movement

Winged Fire Fox Flies.... Elemental creatures that look like small Flying Foxes

Witchnical Testing... a Witch school that blends all Fey learnings into the highest degree of passages

Wolfen Owlley... a Dog-like creature that the Fey have as Guardians and pets

Wulushian Majik... ritual majik founded within the old cities of Wulusha

Yardlens... measurement of inches

Zedfrens... the Fey name for hours of the day

LIST OF CHARACTERS

Elementals, their Homes and Druid Elders:

The **Earth Elementals** live in the Home city of **Gorias** with a Druid Elder called **Esras**...

The Earth creatures in this novel are: **Aperthan** and **Japonagus**

The **Air Elementals** live in the Home city of **Finias** with their Druid Elder called **Uiscias**...

The Air creatures in this novel are: **Agramon** and **Pipmore**

The **Fire Elementals** live in the Home city of **Falias** with their Druid Elder called **Morfesa**...

The Fire creatures in this novel are: **Nomae** and **Moraig**

The **Water Elementals** live in the Home city of **Murias** with their Druid Elder called **Semias**...

The Water creatures in this novel are: **Azareth** and **Caferish**

Goddesses in The Stolen Child Book:

Danu... Goddess of the Tuatha De`Danann

Hexe...Goddess of Healing

Horae...Goddess of Time

Nina...Goddess of Dreams

Sopdet...Goddess Queen of all the constellations around Faden Corpeous

Nature Spirits:

Arddhu...protector of ancient tree groves

Drymiais...nature spirits of the Fey

Triduana...protector of sacred water sources

Coloured Dragons and their significance:

Black Dragons...these particular Dragons are from the Island of Symarr, and are known as the Dracore

Green Dragons...these are the wild ones

Red Dragons...these belong to another world

White Dragons...these huge Leviathans belong to the outer reaches of space. Sigrith Kithtar is the name of the Dragon that took Symin and Ryyaan to Leberone

Black Dragons:

Aantare... His Dragon-rider is called **Assha:** He is considered a Synotay Aelf; though he is not. He is actually a Llangera Aelf that was found on the Island of Tayose on the planet Naunas. He has strange majik full of mystical powers and his true heritage isn't revealed until the book called Circle of the Fey...

Baelf... His Dragon-rider is called **Dyareius:** He is the commander a joiner of minds and can go in-between realms...

Causeey...His Dragon-rider is called **Theiry:** He is an Earth-Seer from Kanoie; he reads minds and picks up thought patterns...

Fauler...His Dragon-rider is called **Cassmare:** His gift to be determined in the next novel...

Kiptitt...His Dragon-rider is called **Bynffore:** He can change things into other things...

Quist...His Dragon-rider is called **Symin:** He is not an Aelf, though he looks like one. He is extremely dangerous and incredibly powerful...

Reely...His Dragon-rider is called **Phaetum:** He is a Touchstone Aelf, from the Caubertian clan; you can touch him to ground yourself ...

Salmin... His Dragon-rider is called **Kaprey:** His gift is used in the second novel...

Sienn...His Dragon-rider is called **Elyizeam:** He is a language theorist; knowing languages in both written, and spoken formulas. He was born off World...

Tansar...His Dragon-rider is called **Soren:** He is a Tracker from Tameron...

Tayto... His Dragon-rider is called **Markus:** He's a mind Shifter; one that has the ability to make people do things not of their own volition. He can also go between realms, when he calls up a phenomena known as the Twist...

Toomae... His Dragon-rider is called **Feyman:** His gift is yet to be used in another novel...

Toupoe...His Dragon-rider is called **Gantay:** He is a Directional Quantum Phaser; one who has the ability to allow something to shift through anything, without the need of a shift stone or a Dragon...

List of Fey Characters in the first Novel, Stolen Child:

Annagmore... Selkie friend of Vaal's

Balenas... one of Lugh's soldiers

Balor... married to Ceithlenn, father to Eithne; deposed king of the Fomorians

Ballynamullan... Vaal's Selkie best friend that accompanies him to the underworld

Bendamere... one of Lugh's officers

Caberaana... one of the Shapeshifters who traveled with Daniel to Tameron

Carpathious... head Druid of Balor's court

Cian... father of Lugh, lives in Fomor as their Chancellor Regent, married to Eithne

Coutinnea... wife of Stephponias

Daniel... Shapeshifter's father from the village of Sombreia

Eithne... mother of Lugh, daughter to Balor; married to Cian

Eurgerus... first Aelven warrior trying to reach Sibrey in her dream-state, belonging to the Capourian Mountain Wolf pack clan

Freile... Coutinnea's aunt who lives in Kilren

Gabriel... Cian's father

Gelmeg... one of the Tuatha warriors who saw Eithne in the mound when it exploded

Horse... a Centaur that befriends the Shapeshifter clan when they go to Tameron. He is the Gatekeeper to the space In-Between that is on the lower level of the Goddess Realm

Jazmyyn... headmistress and keeper of Cian's estate

Kamera... Witch's mother; she is of the Kanoie clan of Witches from Llavalla and now lives in Kilren; banished for producing a daughter with a Selkie and making the prophecy come true

Kashandarhh... daughter of Kamera and Vaal, she is of Selkie and Witch heritage

Kaber... clan leader of the Llyach Aelfs

Kronn... Selkie healer

Llathieria... Queen of the Aelfs

Llyemyllan... King of the Aelfs

Lugh... leader of the Tuatha De˙Danann; first son of Cian and Eithne

Lunesa... wife of Kaber

Morgan... Shapeshifter; son of Daniel; stepbrother Shifter to Sibrey

Muijalaa... third Aelven warrior of the Capourian Mountain Wolf pack clan

Nymphatious... young Aelven male that befriends Ryyaan at the Tuatha mound

Pharonis... second Aelven warrior of the Capourian Mountain Wolf pack clan

Sibrey.... Shapeshifter from the Village of Sombreia — also known as Ree, single Shapeshifter member of the Panther clan of Shapeshifters

Ryyaan... Human child found in the Lypurnen Woods — also known as Ryy

Selmathens... rod entities that are creatures of both vapour and substance, belonging to the Siren race

Sercovious... married to Jazmyyn; main metalsmith of the Tuatha mound

Siian... previous mate of Kashha's father Vaal; she is the mother of Kashha's brother

Stephponias... Llyach Aelfan medicine elder from Clan Sylmoor

Tamerk... Wood Sprite living in Lypurnen Woods

Thimelteen... mother to Tommarrius

Tommarrius Kuamashe... little Aelflet from Kilren

Tuatha De`Danann... ruling Military Army of Tantaris

Vallmyallyn... Witch's father; he is a Selkie from Vaukknea Island — also known as Vaal

Zheckarria... father to Tommarrius

Sea Creatures and Deities:

Each-Uisge... these creatures are the cousins to the Kelpies. They will be amalgamated with the Kelpies should one of them break their promise of sworn protection, and cast out from the safety of hiding in the space in-between...

Manannan... Sea God

Selkintramblay Capatofic Tryilamores... the true name for the species known as the Selkies

Shalimar Ridiculous... this Sea Witch is one of the strangest you will find in the pages of any of my books, being born into the water world of the Elementals. She has both tail and legs that are twisted and malformed from birth; changing her into a very angry creature...

Snickann-Freymyi... a Venomous Valkyrji that can be a very deadly being; known only for her cruelty and violence within the Sidhe Home-World...

Tailtiu... wife of Manannan, she is a Sea Goddess

Planets, Moons, Nebulae, and Galaxies:

Anthros...wandering planet with no fixed address, living somewhere in the Star Nebula called Anthros Major. It is the planet that is home to the crystal caves, and gave birth to the large pillars of stones that are outside the Tuatha De' Danann's mound and the village of Tameron

Bulgapher... planet in the Crystal Horse Galaxy

Carthanthien Nebula... home of the Vermorbian Race

Centarraura Nebula... home of the race of storm planets that harness and manipulate the weather with unusual energy fluxes

Faden Corpeous... the Galaxy that these planets and moon exist within

False Galaxy of the Crystal Horse... hosts the Rings of Brodgar in a future novel

Goetutonias Nebula... sister galaxy that rotates around Faden Corpeous

Hydrous Secular Nebula... out past the Goetutonias Nebula

Kalieas... second moon of Tantaris, which disappeared into the space in-between

Kepet Minor...this is where the Bagorin race of Aelves live

Leberone... first moon of Tantaris

Leonae... first moon of Hydrous Secular; it hosts the Finical Spideranthemaous — the very thing that can detect the Dragons wherever they are hiding

Mauntra... the sun

Naunas... second planet in Faden Corpeous Galaxy

Northern Rings of Goetutonias... constellational reference point that hangs just south of the main system of shift-point doorways, in this arena of space

Pin Nebula... this nebula has vast energy strands; used for the removal of memory by the Selkie Priestesses

Quinn...Naunas's moon

Star of the Sirens... Selmathen home-world

Star Nebula... home of Anthros the roaming planet

String Nebula... worlds connected by energy strings and threads of light

Suedamorphay... Gargoyle home-world planet

Tantaris Suppramorphis... home planet of this storyline, and first planet in the Faden Corpeous Galaxy

Tuworg Nebula... a drifting Nebula that comes into contact with the Galaxy of the Crystal Horse at a certain time of the year

---

Comets and Meteors:

Angagan... this comet was known for its vast tail debris that could knock a planet out of its rotational path, and cause incredible damage to anything out in the open, as it passes along its way

Lyra... this is a fast moving meteoric comet that occasionally comes into range with some of the planets

Starshaper... this meteor was the center of the largest of all the seed formations and each of the comets or meteors were born from this gigantic field of stardust

Zedrith Mordea Kippsen... this comet is the one that caused the formation of both Naunas and Tantaris

Dark Star Meteor... Balor pulled Symbya through this when he brought him to Tantaris

---

Moons Phases of Water's Deep Continent:

This is a list of Moons and their festival names for both of the Moons during certain times of their year. The months of the year are not used and will be called Moon times, with reference used simply in referring to the names of those Moons, instead of referring to an Earth month. Not all have been used and will continued to be used in the series to give the reader an idea what time they might coincide with — in the human schedule of their Solar-Festivals.

Leberone's festivals:	Coincides with Your Earth Date, of;
Byanadorian Moon... Arthuan Season renewal festival	December 21
Quladah Moon... Oimealg Season purification festival	February 2
Sithka Moon... Earraigh Season beginnings festival	March 21
Fenoria Moon... CalinMai Season fire festival	May 1
Percide Moon... Alban Heruim Season Mauntra festival	June 21
Dynastic Moon... Nasadh Season celebration of Lugh's coming to power	August 1
Fieldmarr Moon... AlbanElued Season remembrance festival	September 21
Twintaea Moon... Samhuinn Season fire festival	November 2

Kaliea's Moon Phases:	Coincides with Your Earth Date of;
Calmystic Moon... Modranicht festival	December 21
Zepheragulous Moon... Lubercalia festival	February 2
Incubus Moon... Caisg festival	March 21
Twiggglemarr Moon... Roodmas festival	May 1

Zahkorbial Moon... Samhraidh festival	*June 21*
Sandnostic Moon... Lughnas festival	*August 1*
Soleus Moon... Fomhair festival	*September 21*
Mantorian Moon... Deadnuaght Festival	*November 2*

Villages and Towns of Water's Deep:

Aggulf Elkcum Mound... Tuatha De᾽Danann stronghold

Fomor... Fomorians clan of Aelfs

Kilren... Sayber Fennone Clan of Aelfs

Llavalla... Kanoie Clan of Witches

Sadllenay...village of the Dryads; overrun by Seelies; used to be the home of the Kyafth clan

Sombreia... Shapeshifter village; Togernaut clan

Sylmoor... Llyach clan of Aelfs

Symarr... home of the Dracore

Tameron... Syann-Clan Aelfs

Tothray... Caubertian Clan of Aelfs; Gypsy offspring of the Sage clan of Fomorian Aelves and ostracized Llavalla Witches

Kashhahaeer... old underwater city near Undinecis Reef

Woods, Forests, Lakes, Islands and the Occasional Rocks:

Beletruxe Island... this island is situated in the North just south of Toraigh Island and is full of sea-caves on its beaches...

Damonian Woods... Kashandarhh's home faunt

Dead Monkey Rocks... place where Kamera met Vallmyallyn for the first time. It is situated on the mainland, northwest of the Island of Vaukknea...

Esoyat Island... is on the Planet of Naunas; there is a shift-point doorway here that was build by the Synotay's and is one of the main doorways used by the Selmathens to move between Galaxies.

Kartouche Island... between Tameron and Sylmoor villages

Killchurn Lake... lake Doorway that leads to the Other Realm of the Cloud People

Loch Na Sul... Balor's lake near Tameron's other realm

Lucidity Lake... water near the Sombreian Village; home of the Naiads

Lypurnen Woods... Tamerk's home

Mangoesa Island... island in the North Sea, above the Tuatha De' Danann Aggulf Elkcum mound

Symarr Island... home of the Dracore

Tayose Island... is situated on the planet Naunas and hosts the largest university of the Fey clans in this galaxy. It is also the home of the ancient race of Synotay Fey...

Toraigh Island... Fomorian's Stronghold

Tryanafie Bay... body of water that is inside the barriers of Vaukknea Island

Vaukknea Island... home of the Selkies

Fields:

Fields of the Cauldron... sacred Fire Elemental grounds

Fields of Odisias... underground within the Symarr Dragon Range

Seas, Rivers, and Oceans:

Morphana River... snakes its way from the north across the Zarconian Falls at the Tuatha De`Danann mound, as it passes on its way south over the Telpphaea Falls at Dragon Claw Drift, then comes out the south-eastern shore of the continent by Kartouche Island...

Ocean of Souls... home of the Merfolk

Saltwater Trench... runs between the continent in the south and the Island of Symarr

Sea of Contentious Souls... body of water that rests above the North-east of the continent around the area of Fomor and the Damonian Woods

The Old Sea of Hioroques... this ocean runs around the Earth Elementals' city of Gorias

Plains or Lowlands:

Plains of Sheymoar... piece of land northwest of the Telpphaea Falls that runs in the area of land where the Morphana River snakes its way around the village of Llavalla and crosses the continent to the outskirts of Sadllenay...

Reefs and Trenches:

Trench of Talon... a deep trench where the mystical waves of gigantic proportions are seeded, from deep beneath the ocean floor; the area is home to the majikal beings called the Auicks. These creatures come to life as sentient beings, to direct the vast contingency of sea creatures to the world of the reefs during the times of the shedding...

Undinecis Reef... underwater reef world just north of the Island of Vaukknea; this is the shedding grounds where they feed on its energy to live and grow strong

Saltwater Trench... this is new land found between the Island of Symarr and the continent

Mountain Ranges, Hills or Canyons:

Capourian Mountain Range... lies to the south and cradles the Stones of Panthor, and mostly circles the village of Tameron

Copper Canyon... situated north of Sylmoor, and rests along the western flank of the Sydclath mountains, south of Kilren

Cydclath Mountain Range... runs from just north of Capourian Mountain's Pickle Canyon; west of Morphana River, and ends at Dragon Claw Drift North of Tothray

Dragonclaw Drift... this piece of land is part of a huge plateau that is near the Morphana River that winds its way through the Cydclath and Sydclath Mountain Ranges. In the middle of both mountains is a huge waterfall that splits the two ranges in half. The drift is part of the Sydclath's northeastern cliff-face and runs sideways through the gulch that forms one of the two sides of these mountains, which come together at this juncture — transforming the surrounding rock into the shape of huge Dragon claws...

Pickle Canyon... deep within the Capourian Mountain Range, bordered on all sides by huge cliffs of red jasper and hematite

Sydclath Mountain Range... starts at the east of Sylmoor village, runs past the tail of Morphana River and ends at Dragon Claw Drift, northwest of Kilren

Symarr Dragon Ranges... situated on the Island of the Dragons and literally surrounds the Island of Symarr

Fault Lines:

Panthorian... this fault line runs from the middle of the two main mountain ranges in the center of the continent and makes its way to the North near the Tuatha's Aggulf Elkcum mound

Waterfalls:

Telpphaea Falls... these falls separate the Sydclath and the Cydclath Mountain Ranges at Dragon Claw Drift

Zarconian Falls... these double falls are part of the head-waters of the Morphana River, as it travels from the north to the Aggulf Elkcum Mound and splits the river in two — just as they go over the edge into the depths of the mound

---

Stone Circles and Leylines:

Ley Lines of Kalmaskis... certain points of energy leading towards the home-worlds of all Fey

Shivonian Ley line... sits high in the north-east of Tantaris's main Aelven Aggulf Elkcum Mound

Standing Stones of Anthros...the stone circle that was a gift from the Selmathen race; it's currently standing guard at the Aggulf Elkcum mound

Stones of Panthor... shift-point stones at the entrance to the village of Tameron

Ley lines of Lemarr... very similar to the Ley Lines of earth, except these ones run deep within the planet's crust near the Standing Stones of Selmathen origins

---

Covens:

**Ka`afrey...** coven of Ka`afrey is an elite group of individuals that look after the well-being of those inside this realm

Kashandarhh's light... Kashha's newest coven of clones

Synatarrae... one of the old Faery Queen covens in the next book

---

Clans and their Destinations:

Bagorin...this is a colony of space faring Aelves that live in the Kepet Minor Star system

Capourian Mountain Pack Wolf... clan of mystery and legend used to protect those of significant importance

Caubertians... clan of Tothray has a mixture of Fey creatures belonging to different parts of Water's Deep and even some from off planet. All species inside the energy rings, have been hunted by various factions and have come here seeking refuge and are protected by the Tuatha De' Danann

Flambosa... Centaur clan

Hebradines... one of the old race of Aelves that lived before and is considered one of the Ancients.

Kyafth... clan of Dryads from Sadllenay

Llavalla... clan of Kanoie is a Witch Clan

Panther... clan of Black Panther felines that have adopted a Shapeshifter from Sombreia called Sibrey

Saber Fennone... clan of Aelves from Kilren

Snapperhead-Knocktaw... Earth-shaper Elemental clan

Syann-Clan... this clan belongs to the village of Tameron. It is the Village where the King and Queen of the Aelves reside when they are on the Planet

Togernaut... clan of Shapeshifters from Sombreia

Trithogeans... coven of warriors primarily used to protect royal patrons along the edges of the rings of space.

Trolladites... clan of Gargoyles from the planet Suedamorphay

---

Cities Belonging to other Worlds:

Finias... Fire Elemental city that is on the planet Naunas. It is deep in the jungles off the main coastline in the southernmost part of its largest continent.

Sairog... this is the home city of the Sidhe elders and their hordes; its location will be included in future novels

Lemuria... city of the ancients

Wastelands of Paramour... gathering place found on the Siren's Home-Star

---

Temples:

Temple of Paracleese... this ethereal temple belongs to the Witch kind of Kanoie

---

Mounds:

Aggulf Elkcum... this is the main Tuatha De ' Danann Mound here on Tantaris. It is situated in the north of Water's Deep, beside a series of hidden Traveler Stones set deep inside its walls — given to them from the Selmathen race of Fey. It also hosts the Standing Stones of Anthros, which are set above the Zarconian Falls up on the surface

---

Caves:

Caves of Almalta... home of the Tacknea Spinder Spider

ABOUT THE AUTHOR

Adele is a Canadian Author who lives on the West-Coast of Vancouver Island. It is here the writer takes her life experiences and merges them into the realm of the Fey, creating these magnificent worlds so her readers can become absorbed into the culture of majikal consequences.

CPSIA information can be obtained at www.ICGtesting.com
Printed in the USA
LVOW06s0446140915

453791LV00002B/24/P

9 781460 265901